"Juilene Osborne-McKnight blends legend, history and mythology into *I Am of Irelaunde*, a powerful and moving first novel about St. Patrick, patron saint of Ireland. It is hard to believe that this is Osborne-McKnight's first novel; it is polished to the brilliance of an emerald. Her characters are well developed and appealing, and the story she tells is engrossing and emotionally satisfying. In true storyteller tradition, Osborne-McKnight takes the old stories and sources and makes them her own. Her view that Padraig's ministry was a gentle, joyful outgrowth of the old ways rather than a brutal replacement is convincing and thought provoking. For a richly written, compelling and utterly triumphant tale, reach for *I Am of Irelaunde*. You'll be glad you did."

—*RAMBLES* (on-line cultural magazine)

Tor Books by Juilene Osborne-McKnight

Daughter of Ireland
I Am of Irelaunde

Daughter of Ireland

JUILENE OSBORNE-MCKNIGHT

TOR®

A TOM DOHERTY ASSOCIATES BOOK
NEW YORK

This is a work of fiction. All the characters and events portrayed in this book are either products of the author's imagination or are used fictitiously.

DAUGHTER OF IRELAND

Copyright © 2002 by Juilene Osborne-McKnight

All rights reserved, including the right to reproduce this book, or portions thereof, in any form.

Edited by Claire Eddy

A Tor Book
Published by Tom Doherty Associates, LLC
175 Fifth Avenue
New York, NY 10010

www.tor.com

Tor® is a registered trademark of Tom Doherty Associates, LLC.

ISBN 0-765-34642-7
Library of Congress Catalog Card Number: 2001054768

First edition: March 2002
First mass market edition: March 2003

Printed in the United States of America

0 9 8 7 6 5 4 3 2 1

For these
With shield, sword, song:

Thomas Glenn,
a ghile mo chroí
Mara Kate,
a ghrá geal
Andrea, Glenn, Mark,
mo clann, mo Fian geal

Bail O Dhia ar an obair.
Bless, O God, the work.

ACKNOWLEDGMENTS

Many thanks to Andrew Pope, artist and formerly agent, who believed in me in moments and on days when I did not believe. This is the work of angels, Andrew. Thank you also to Maureen Walters of Curtis Brown for her indefatigable willingness to give every project a try and for her great good humor. Also to all the staff at Curtis Brown who have been so helpful with foreign editions, subrights, and my endless questions, especially Joanna Durso, Dave Barbor, Doug Stewart, and Ed Wintle.

My editor, Claire Eddy, gave me invaluable and insightful editorial suggestions during the revision process. Thank you, Claire, for helping me to craft a better book. Thank you also to Stephanie Lane and Heather Drucker at Tor for all their help with this book and with my previous novel, *I Am of Irelaunde*.

To Dr. Jean Kelty, mentor and friend, my thanks for her generous gift of time, for the close reading, and for excellent suggestions. You would have been then, and certainly are now, a druidess of great spirit and wisdom.

Thanks also to Dr. Robert Farrell of Cornell University for his informative interview on his crannog research and archaeology.

Gratitude to the members of the Greater Lehigh Valley Writers Group, who have supported my efforts for a number of years, and especially to fellow writers Christine Whittemore Papa and Mitzi Flyte. Appreciation also to my colleagues at CAPE who were so supportive of my first novel.

Above all, thanks must go to fellow historical novelist Eileen Charbonneau, who edited and encouraged on a line-by-line basis and who first gave me the encouragement that it could and should be done. Eileen, your generous friendship continues to be one of the great gifts of my life.

MAJOR CHARACTER NAMES AND PRONUNCIATIONS

All names are pronounced in an approximation of their sound as both spellings and pronunciations in Irish have changed.

Aengus Mac Gabuideach (*aonghus mac ga boo dee*) Father of Eoghan Mac Aidan. Evidently a historical figure, at one time chief of the Deisi.

Aislinn ni Sorar (*ash leen nee sor are*) In Irish, Aislinn means "dream" or "vision." Ni is the feminine patronymic, as in "daughter of Sorar."

Aodhfin (*ee fin*)

Banbh (*ban ev*)

Brighid (*breed*) A goddess of women in pagan times, an Irish saint in Christian times.

Cormac Mac Art (*kor mac*) One of the great kings of early Irish history, he was the high king of all Ireland around 250 A.D. According to legend one of the first three in Ireland to embrace Christianity.

Eibhlain (*i leen*) Mother of Aislinn.

Eoghan Mac Aidan (*ee gan mac ee an*)

Fionn Mac Cumhail (*finn mac cool*) The legendary Irish leader of the Fianna, the standing army of Ireland. In all probability Fionn was an actual historical figure.

Gobinet (*gob nat*)

Macha (*ma ha*)

Maille (*molly*)

O'Domnhnaill (*o don el*)

Oisian (*o sheen*) Son of Fionn Mac Cumhail and legendary poet of the Fianna. Probably a historical figure.

Tomaltagh (*tom el tex*)

Daughter of
Ireland

Daughter of
Iseland

PROLOGUE

The last stone rolled into place with the sound of thunder, cutting off the thin trickle of light that illuminated the chamber at the end of the long passageway.

The woman who crouched beside the low stone platform stretched her hands, felt the body of the man atop the bier.

"Sorar," she cried. "Husband, I am afraid. Will you not come and comfort me?"

She wrapped her arms around her husband. He did not move or stir, gave no comfort. His cold, stiff body was dead these two days. Dead of treachery. And only she to right the wrong. She drew in three deep breaths.

Her eyes adjusted to the gloom, used the fine shaft of light that came from above the lintel of the door. The woman stood, stared around her. The chamber had been furnished with all the things her husband would need in death, goblets and washbasins, a chariot. Even casks of wine and mead were provided.

"They gave you the burial of a king, my husband," she said. "They think to hide their deed with respectful ceremony."

She lifted a goblet from the table, then stopped.

"Nay," she said aloud. "I will do what I must do. I will not prolong this thing by taking fluid."

She hurled the goblet, heard it clang against the cold walls of the tomb.

Fear had been with her since early this morning, since the reality of what was about to befall her set in. Now, in the cold stone of the hewn tomb, the fear became a living thing, clawing up at her throat, stealing her breath. She ran blindly, striking against the wall. She placed her forehead against it, pressed her palms flat against the stone, again forced her breathing to still.

Slowly, she circled her husband's bier, running her hands along the curved stone walls of the chamber. She paced the darkness until some of the fear subsided. At last she sat in one of the two chairs that fronted an intricately designed bronze wall. She gathered her fringed purple tunic close around her, leaned her head against the back of the chair.

"What I am doing will cry injustice," she said aloud. "For is it not the law of Eire that we who fast, even unto death, right a wrong? The people of the Deisi will know what injustice has been done you. My death will cry your righteousness. And perhaps it will save our child."

She stood suddenly, pressed her hands beneath her breasts, cried aloud.

"Oh, my child, my Aislinn! How can I live without you?"

Grim humor seized her and she laughed.

"Why, I will not live. I will die. That is the answer. There will be no reprieve from this fast, no righting of the wrongs. I go with you to your death, Sorar, but your death was swift compared to mine. I will starve here in the darkness of this tomb. My death will be slow."

Again she cried aloud.

"Have I kept you safe, Aislinn? Have I kept you from them? How will I bear this dying without your little face beside me?"

She began to sob then, dropping to her knees, burying her head in her arms.

"O you gods!" she cried. "Will no one comfort me? Will I die thus alone and so afraid?"

The eerie blue light began at her knees, seeped through her fingers where her hands covered her eyes. She raised her head. A woman stood just a few feet from her. She was small, no taller than a child, but her body was a lamp, a candle of incandescence. In her arms, she cradled a lamb of radiant whiteness.

The woman scrambled to her feet, backed away, terrified. This must be one of the sidhe, the ancient, magical people who lived beneath the water and under the hills.

"You are of the Other," she said accusingly to the small woman.

The lighted woman smiled, nodded.

"I know what you have done, Eibhlain, wife of Sorar. You have laid down your life for this man and for the safety of your child. I will not let you be alone in your death-fast."

"You are Brighid, then, she who is protector of women."

"So I have been called. So I shall be called again."

"Tell me of my child, my Aislinn. Is she safe and well?"

"She is safe with those you entrusted her to. Do not question the way you have chosen, Eibhlain. If you had taken your child and tried to flee, they would have hunted you down, killed you both. Your death gives your daughter life. And there will be justice, though not the justice that you envision now. Will you believe what I say?"

Eibhlain tilted her head toward the woman, her chestnut hair cascading forward down her arm.

"Will you be with my daughter when I have gone to Tir Nan Og with him who was my husband? Will you stay with her and protect her?"

"It will be as you ask," said the woman of light.

Eibhlain began to weep again then, at first softly and then in huge wracking sobs.

"Do not think me ungrateful. I wish you here beside me for the death of this body, but it is my heart which will break at this separation from my child. I do not think I can bear to be without her. You cannot understand."

"Seotho a thoil," whispered the woman of light. "Hush, darling. I do understand the weeping of women for their lost children."

She gathered the lamb closer into her arms and allowed her own crystalline tears to fall into his soft coat.

1

Aislinn ni Sorar sat silent at the required place of honor near the fire. She drew her white ceremonial cloak with its spiraling gold embroidery tightly about her, lifted the hood over her head until her youthful features were obscured in shadow.

"You are cold?" The chieftain Brennus Mac Bran shouted at her, though he was seated directly to her right. He was fat and drunken. Grease from the haunch of boar he had devoured was trapped in his red moustache and slathered on his chin. Brennus the Brutal, they called him. Even the people of his own tribe.

Aislinn regarded him silently, said nothing. Beneath the wide sleeves of her robe, she pressed the palms of her hands tight against her forearms. She could feel their sweaty dampness. She breathed slowly and deeply, tried not to let the chieftain hear the ragged sound of her expelled breath.

Surely the child must be here! She had tracked the story of a captive child from village to village for many months. At last, a fortnight ago, she had come to the child's birth village, been given the story that had led her here, to this fireside. Surely, she would find the child here. Now. This was the quest on which her foster-father Aodhfin had sent her, so many turning moons ago. In the way of all important druid teaching, he had given her this quest in a sacred riddle of three.

"Listen to me, daughter!" Aislinn still remembered the urgency in his voice, on his old face, usually so placid and kind. "Much will be woven into this journey you undertake. What is past and what is to come; forces gather around your journey." And then he had begun, his voice a low chant.

"From the place of darkness will come a child to light your journey. To the place of fire will come a man bearing fire for the body and the mind. Between darkness and light, you are the still point."

Still Aislinn had lingered, waited for more than a fortnight, fearing to leave the security of the druid school at Tara, fearing to leave Aodhfin, the only father she had known. Until the night of the Dark One and his vast black wings. The same night on which she first dreamed of a child with copper hair and sea-green eyes, her face upturned, crying, "Máthair! Mother!" The night she had begun this journey, almost two years ago.

Now, by the fire, Aislinn closed her eyes. She could see the sprinkling of freckles across the bridge of the little nose, the fear in the pale green eyes. She would know the child anywhere. Aislinn shivered, opened her eyes.

"Here, you, Corra!" the chieftain bellowed, waving his arm in the air. A thin, sickly looking child of about ten disengaged herself from the women who hovered near the feasting table. She came to Brennus's side, her hands clasped together too tightly. She stood with her head bent, her face obscured in a tangled mat of dirty hair.

"The priestess is cold. Pour another goblet of warm wine to her health and honor!"

The child bent to gather the silver pitcher from beside the chieftain. Her short brown tunic rode up for a moment and Aislinn stared at the back of her legs. They were flayed, bloody, laid open from below the knees to where the welts disappeared beneath the hem of the tunic.

The child moved to the druidess, bent, poured wine into the goblet, her head bowed in polite deference. Aislinn willed the little girl to raise her eyes. Slowly, the child's head lifted. Aislinn gasped in recognition, pressed her palms tight against her arms to quell the wild hammering of her heart. The intense green eyes regarding those of the priestess were those of her dream!

For a moment, the wild green eyes locked with Aislinn's in a silent plea. The druidess gave the barest nod. The child moved away.

"Send this child to her sleeping mat!" Aislinn commanded. "She does not look well!"

From across the fire, one of the other chieftains' wives concurred.

"The druidess speaks true. Who in Eire treats a child in this fashion? Our brehon laws are clear about the rights of children."

"Send her to her night's rest," Aislinn repeated.

Brennus Mac Bran regarded the two women with surprise. The women of his village feared him; none would dare give him a command or they would feel the weight of his anger. He assessed the slight frame of the priestess. It was sacrilege to harm the body of a druid, though such sacrilege might have its pleasures with one as young and ripe as this. Still, it would not do well to argue with one who had the ear of the gods. Brennus acquiesced.

"Go!" He waved his hand at the child, but when she moved toward the south door of the feasting hall, he stopped her.

"Nay. Tonight you will sleep in my chamber."

An awkward silence prevailed among the chieftains around the fire. The child looked desperately in Aislinn's direction. Aislinn turned toward Brennus, regarded him silently for a moment. At last, she nodded at the child, pointed toward the north door. Brennus grunted in satisfaction. The child headed for the chieftain's sleeping lodge, a defeated slump to her shoulders.

The men around the fire shifted position, watched the druidess for a while. One or two made strange signs in the air. Aislinn closed her eyes, waited out the silence.

After a while, a handsome young chieftain stepped into the light at the center of the fire. He dashed his plaid cloak aside, stood clad in only his baggy plaid braichs and soft leather boots. The firelight gleamed from his naked torso.

"Come!" he cried. "Who will meet my challenge for first storytelling rights?"

A second young man leaped laughingly into the ring.

"I am for you!"

They grappled at the shoulders, circled each other, laughing with the delight of the battle. They wrestled each other to kneeling in the ring. The chieftains around the fire shouted and cheered them on. They dropped into the dust, rolling against and over each other until the coals and dirt from the floor clung to their sweat-stained torsos. At last, the first challenger pinned his opponent to the ground, his forearm hard beneath his opponent's throat.

"Yield the right of first boast!" He crammed his arm harder under his companion's chin. "Yield!"

His opponent laughed and sputtered.

"I yield, I yield. Now we will all endure your endless tales of battle."

The two rose, clapped each other on the back, and laughed.

"Drink deep to our champions!" Brennus cried. Whole tankards of mead were downed at one swill. The women hurried to refill them to the brim. Brennus required three refills before he paused in his quaffing.

In the deep darkness of her hood, Aislinn gave a small, satisfied smile. She fingered the leather pouch tied to the belt at her waist, then threw back her hood, lifted the thick length of her black hair free. She smiled at the young champion.

"The druids will salute a man of battle." She raised her wine goblet to him. All the men drank again, Brennus more deeply than the rest. He fixed his eyes on the druidess, on her pale, clear skin, on the curve of breast that lifted beneath the robe when she raised her goblet. He set his tankard beside him in the dirt. He did not notice the small movement of Aislinn's free hand over the surface of the cup.

"Come, warriors!" she cried. "We salute your tales of battle." The men drank deeply again, Brennus among them.

The young champion was swelled with pride that he should be acknowledged by a druidess, and she most beautiful. He signaled to one of his minions, seated in the second circle of the fire. The man rose and left the hall, returning moments later with a braided rope. From the rope hung human heads, shrunken and distorted with age and hard banging against the saddle. The young man held them up.

"Each of these was a prize of war! Shall I tell you their tales?"

"Tell!" cried one of the avid young warriors from the second circle. The long night of storytelling began. One after another, the warriors rose, told tales of battle, stories of love, eerie tales of encountering the little people of the sidhe. Each tale was accompanied by a salute of mead-cups, Aislinn holding her wine goblet forward, passing her free hand above Brennus's cup before he picked it up.

At last Brennus stood among the company, bowed deeply and sloppily in Aislinn's direction. He wiped some spittle from the beard at the base of his chin. His words slurred.

"Nay, brother warriors, such battles are nothing!" He looked at Aislinn, raised his eyebrows, stumbled a little, regained his footing, gave a loud boisterous laugh. "I, Brennus Mac Bran, have sired more than a score of children on as many women. Few were willing, but I made their choices simple. Do as I ask or die. I have seeded strong sons and daughters the length and breadth of Eire. Now these were battles."

A few of the men in the circle laughed uneasily. Others remained silent.

Aislinn turned her full regard on Brennus, her eyes boring into him, unblinking. She said nothing. Aodhfin, her tutor, had taught her that silence was a weapon, that it could unman more powerfully than words. For a while, Brennus stared back at her, leering and smiling, but after a time, he grew sulky. At last he sat down among the company, fortified himself deeply with drink, called for more.

No other chieftain rose to boast at the contest. After some time of uncomfortable silence, the company began to depart for sleep. Aislinn remained seated, her eyes on Brennus Mac Bran. The chieftain drank steadily and unceasingly. At last he simply slumped over in a drunken stupor, drool oozing down the side of his cheek. Still, Aislinn remained motionless in the firelight while the hall emptied, while the sounds of the village settled down for the night.

When at last she sensed the moment of silence all around her, she stood, sweeping like a soft, white snowfall across the feasting hall, through the north door, into the sleeping chamber of Brennus Mac Bran.

She bent over the child, started back. The child was wide awake, her green eyes staring into the penetrating darkness. Aislinn placed her finger on her lips. The little girl nodded, raised her arms.

Aislinn lifted the frail child, thought for a moment how slight she felt, how angular and boned like a bird. The child twined her arms tightly around Aislinn's neck. Cautiously, they moved out into the night circle of the little tuath. Aislinn looked up, blessed the gods for the moonless night. She kept close against the dwellings, skirting their sides, staying deep beneath their thatch overhangs.

It was only when she reached the quiet fields beyond the village that Aislinn began to run.

The child huddled in the shelter of the low stone wall, her head buried beneath her arms. The early morning rain, which swept across the field in gusts, plastered her copper hair against her brown cloak, over the curve of her small body, and onto the arches of her bare feet where it curled in wet red tendrils. She shook continually.

Aislinn stood beside her, breathing hard. They had run hard until well past dawn, Aislinn carrying the child until at last she stumbled. They had exchanged no words. Aislinn knew that she had not yet put enough distance between them and Brennus Mac Bran. She stared back at the way they had come, knelt beside the child.

"Do not be afraid. Corra? Is that what you are called?"

The little girl turned her head in Aislinn's direction, her face a pale, pinched mask. She nodded once. "Corra ni Brith," she said, her voice small and dry.

"Corra, I promise that he will not hurt you anymore."

She made a cradling motion around the shivering body, then unfastened her own thick white cloak and wrapped it around the child's body, tucking it under her feet.

She stood again. The wind caught at her raven-black hair, no longer trapped in the folds of the cloak. It lifted around her like wings. Aislinn peered at the pockets of mist swirling through the trees beyond the wall and absently fingered the intricately carved golden hilt of the dagger that hung at her waist.

"He will not harm you again," she said, almost to herself. "First he will have to go through me. And if he tries, I swear by the Sacred Tree that I will kill him."

Aislinn shivered. Without her cloak, her bare arms were exposed to the wind and rain. The spiraling gold bracelet that wound around her upper arm felt like ice against her skin. Within the range of her vision, nothing moved but the branches of the trees.

But Brennus would not come now. It was too soon for him to shake off last night's drugged stupor. Too, the loss of his slave child to a woman would be too humiliating before the visiting chiefs. He would keep that a secret until they had gone. For a moment, Aislinn wondered how Brennus would explain her disappearance. The thought made her smile. She was a druid. If Brennus told them all that she had lifted away on the night wind, they would believe it. Brennus himself might believe it. Superstitious fools.

Still, she would need that superstition. For Brennus would come for them eventually.

To steal a cumal, the slave of a chieftain, was against the brehon law, even for a druid priestess. Brennus would boast himself within his rights to come after the child. But this was a freeborn child; so the people of her own village had told Aislinn. Still, there was more. Aislinn remembered the way Brennus had looked at her, had delighted in sending the child to his own bedchamber. She remembered the back of the child's legs. Brennus the Brutal would enjoy coming after them.

So much danger! Why had her tutor insisted that she come on this journey, find this child? And why had she begun it only when the Dark One frightened her into flight? *From the place of darkness will come a child to light your journey*. Was this the child? And if so, what journey had begun?

Aislinn looked at the shivering child beside her and her heart moved with pity. No matter the reason, she must find shelter, food, a measure of safety for them both. She rapped the point of her dagger against the rough top of the stone wall. She turned in all four directions. At last, a small smile twitched at the corners of her mouth. Brennus would come after her, but she would choose a place guaranteed to feed his fear. She looked one last time at the rain-swept field, then crouched and put her arm around the child. Corra bolted up, twined her arms fiercely around Aislinn's neck.

"Do not take me back there!"

"Seotho a thoil. Hush, darling." Aislinn lifted tendrils of wet red hair away from Corra's face. "I will care for you now."

"But where will we go?"

"I have remembered the perfect place," said Aislinn. "It is warm and dry and we can build a fire."

She disentangled the child's arms and stooped to gather her up. The little girl shook her head.

"I am too heavy, priestess. I will walk."

"It is almost a full day's walk. Are you sure that you are strong enough?"

The little girl smiled. "You came for me. I will make myself strong for you."

Aislinn turned away rapidly, blinked. She turned back to the child who held out the white cloak.

"Come then," she said. Hand in hand, they tramped across the muddy field to the edge of the forest. Once they were in the shelter of the trees, Aislinn turned back again. The fields were still empty, sluiced with rain.

"Will Brennus follow us?" The child clung tightly to her hand.

"He will follow us, but he will be afraid."

"Good, because I am afraid of him."

"He was cruel to you?"

"He was. And he killed my mother."

Aislinn regarded the child with sympathy. "I too am a motherless child."

"Is that how you knew to come for me?"

"Nay, I knew to come for you because my teacher sent me to find you."

"Your teacher?" The child seemed disappointed, withdrew her hand.

"Aodhfin the Wise. He told me to search for you."

"And how did you know that I was the one?"

"For many weeks now I have seen you in my dreams."

"Ah, that explains it then," the little girl said, nodding. She smiled and slipped her hand back into Aislinn's palm.

"What does it explain?"

"I know that the druii possess great magic. You will use your magic against him, won't you, priestess?"

Aislinn smiled at the child.

"I will make myself strong for you," she said.

Together, they began the long walk through the wet forest.

2

The hollow chamber beneath the roots of the giant oak tree smelled damp, but the hard-packed ground where Corra lay sleeping was dry. Aislinn was grateful to be out of the continuous rain after a long day of trudging through the wet forest. She had put almost twelve hours between the child and Mac Bran. Good distance from a village that had no horses and whose chieftain was fat, drunken, and drugged.

Aislinn lit two tapers of bound pine needles, set them into the sconces in the earthen walls. Smoky light filled the cave and illuminated the thick roots of the tree that formed its sides and ceiling.

The child stirred in her sleep.

"Máthair," she whispered.

Aislinn knelt beside her, stroked the wet hair away from Corra's cheek.

"Seotho a thoil. Hush, darling. I am here."

Corra smiled contentedly in her sleep. Aislinn sat beside her, regarded the pale face with its sprinkling of freckles. She could not be more than ten. Her angular body was all bones, the skin stretched tight across the underfed frame. Aislinn felt the blood-lust for Mac Bran rise in her. Her hand moved to her dagger.

From the corner of her eye, Aislinn thought she saw someone—something—move in the darkness beyond the cave. Something black and gleaming with the rain-wet feathers of a crow. Fear crowded up her throat and she eased along the wall of the cave and peered into the darkness. Beyond, a few branches swayed, rain-wet and gleaming in the night forest. Aislinn whispered into the darkness.

"I feel you, Dark One. Even when you are not here. In each day of these past two years, though I have fled across all of Eire to escape you, I have sensed you watching me."

She turned back and looked at the small sleeping figure of the little girl. She faced the dark woods directly and spoke aloud.

"I will not flee you any longer. Do you hear me, Dark One of my dreams?"

She closed her eyes, let remembrance flood over her. She remembered a crow, larger than a man, its wide black wings outspread, bearing down above her, a crow with the black eyes of Banbh, the vortex of night. She remembered what he had said, that it was not he who wanted her, but his goddess. That his goddess had deemed her a worthy servant of the darkness. Aislinn shivered. There was a darkness in her, a place where no light and no vision could go. Aislinn acknowledged it, had known it since childhood. More than once in this past year of her journey, she wondered if she had fled not just Banbh, but her own darkness. How little Aodhfin's quest seemed to have in common with the journey of the past year. Aislinn had been running not toward the child, but away from Banbh.

Until the night in the child's birth village. Until her people had told Aislinn the story of the mother and child captured into slavery. Until she knew the darkness in Brennus Mac Bran. That night Aislinn had felt kinship with the child, such need to find her and free her. From that night forward, she had traveled unswervingly toward Brennus Mac Bran. And closer, she feared, to something at the core of her own life that she had never acknowledged before.

Aislinn shook off her dark thoughts. The child needed tending as did their dwelling space. She stretched her arms forward and around to ease the tightening behind her shoulders. She gathered pine needles from a recess in the back of the cave and laid them carefully in the small archway that served as altar and oven. She watched as the smoke rose through the chimney hole cut among the roots of the tree. Soon, the damp above the ground would cause the smoke to lie around the tree like a foggy shroud. She intoned over the needles as the smoke rose.

"Hear me, Brighid, you who protect the women and children of Eire. I prepare this fire in your name. Encircle us with your protecting veil that we may rest safe and unseen this night. I am too tired to fight this night. Protect me now that I may protect this child."

She lifted the tapers from the walls, extinguished them in the sandy dirt of the floor.

Before she lay down to sleep, she whispered the prayer of the God above the Gods, whose Name is known to none:

> *"I am the wind which breathes on the water,*
> *I am the swell of the sea,*
> *I am the light of the sun,*
> *I am the point of the battle spear.*
> *I am the God who gives fire to the mind.*
> *Who announces the ages of the moon?*
> *Who speaks to the setting of the sun?*
> *I, only I."*

Putting her trust in the strength of the God, Aislinn stretched out beside the child, entwined both of them beneath her white cloak, and slept.

*   *   *

Aislinn awoke on the damp ground to find the child's arm wrapped around her. The morning was dry and the sky that shade of endless blue that follows rain. It would be a good day to gather berries and edible roots. Aislinn knew that she would also need comfrey for poultices to treat the child's wounds.

She lifted Corra's arm from her shoulders and stood. She brushed a little at the crusted mud on her feet, then abandoned the task. From a recess in the twining roots at the far end of the cave, she took a small bundle of herbs and an iron cauldron. She left the cave silently, moving like a white wraith to the spring below the hill. She laid a few of the dried herbs at the small shrine by the spring. The masklike, laughing face of the goddess of water and of openings into the earth stared at her from her rough-hewn wooden statue in its niche beside the spring. She would understand the meager offering, Aislinn thought. She smiled and touched some of the cool liquid to the goddess's carved lips. Women always understood first necessities.

Aislinn filled the little pot with water and then sat beside the spring and lowered her feet into the icy water. She felt the swelling from yesterday's flight ease from her feet as the water shaped itself around them and restored them to pale whiteness. She lay back on the bank and stared at the overhead leaves, now changing to gold and red above her head.

Aislinn shivered at the thought of the upcoming season of snow and rain. Where should she take the child? A few more weeks would bring the need for a warmer and more secure place to winter. Perhaps, she thought, she should take the child home. Home to Tara. To Aodhfin who would raise her as he had raised Aislinn. The thought filled Aislinn with hope, though Tara was a journey of weeks on foot. She decided to check on the child.

She lifted her feet from the water and had just begun to dry them with the hem of her dress when she heard Corra scream.

Clutching at the small vines on the hillside near the spring, Aislinn tried to drag herself to the top of the hill. Her bare feet skidded against the wet ground and mired in the sucking mud. She had a terrible sensation of moving in a dream until at last her feet came free and she bolted to the top of the little hill.

At the entrance to the cave, she peered in and saw the child, her face transfixed with horror as she stared at the opposite wall.

Aislinn unsheathed her dagger and moved against the wall so that the sunlight would not cast her shadow.

She whirled around the corner and sagged with relief when she saw what had so terrified the child. A row of grinning skulls lined up on a low shelf along the wall of the cave were smiling straight at Corra.

She rushed to the child and enfolded her in her arms. "Hush, now hush," she crooned, rocking Corra against her body. "They are the old ones, the smiling faces of the long-dead."

Corra's screaming became a series of pitiful wracking sobs. "I am in the house of the dead," she gasped out between fits of weeping. "The house of the dead."

"No," said Aislinn, easing the child's face between her hands and bringing it up to look into her eyes. "They protect us and plead for us among the gods. You must not fear them. The house of Mac Bran is the house of the dead. He has lost all that becomes a Gael. Here you are in the house of the spirits and I am a druid, their priestess. Here we are loved and protected by the gods and by our ancestors."

Corra stopped weeping and stared at the skulls. "Are the spirits of my máthair and athair here too?" she asked.

Aislinn again felt the strong kinship with Corra. The mother that Corra called for in sleep was dead. She nodded at the child. "They are here. I sense their love. They will protect you and teach me how to care for you as they did."

A long silence came between them as the child locked the wild green of her eyes with Aislinn's own.

"Tell me of how you came for me, priestess."

"They told me your story in the village of your birth, that your father had been killed in battle, that your mother and you had been taken as cumals by Brennus. The women of your village had heard recently that your mother had died. They feared for you. They told me that Brennus had evil eating at his heart."

She saw the child's body stiffen at the mention of Mac Bran, stopped speaking.

"But you do not know me. You are not of my people. Yet, last night when I saw you, I knew that you had come for me. Why, priestess?"

"I was sent for you by my teacher, my foster-father, Aodhfin the Wise. But I too have been frightened by an evil man, Corra." Aislinn closed her eyes, saw the dark feathers of a crow. She remembered Banbh's hands groping for her like talons, his foul breath, and the oily black sheen of his crow-feather robes. She breathed deeply to continue.

"When I heard your story, I could not let another child be hurt."

"Why did you come alone to my village, priestess? My mother told me that the great druii of Ireland travel in splendor with two dozen retainers at their call. Were you alone because you were running away from the evil one?"

"How did one so young come to be such a seanmhai-thair, little grandmother? I would not have said that I was running away. But perhaps you see more clearly than I at that. I will admit that he is the cause of my aloneness for I have spent nigh upon two years as a wanderer. For many turnings of the moon, I have performed ceremonies and made predictions for whatever chieftain took me in."

"Are you an orphan like I am?" asked Corra.

"I am. I was raised by Aodhfin the Wise. My parents died when I was very small; I do not remember them at all."

Corra seemed lost in thought, then smiled and spoke aloud. "Máthair, athair, thank you for sending me the priestess Aislinn to be my protector. I will serve her with joy."

Aislinn fought back the tears that threatened to overwhelm her.

"No, Corra, there will be no more serving. You are a freeborn child. The people of your village told me that your father was a bo-aire, a freeborn cattleman. Brennus Mac Bran had no rights in law to take you or your mother as slaves. There will be no more serving, Corra. I will be your teacher and your friend."

The shining look on the child's face tore at Aislinn's heart. She stood.

"Come now," she said briskly. "Your stomach must be calling for food and drink and we must make poultices for the wounds on your legs. We cannot give the poison any more time."

She stood to go back to the spring, and the child was instantly at her side, slipping her hand shyly inside Aislinn's. Aislinn felt some long emptiness inside herself begin to fill. She bent and pressed the child's hand to her cheek, then cradled it in her own as they walked to the spring together. At the bank, Corra raised the hem of her tunic and tied it in a knot to wade into the water.

"By the gods!"

The skin on Corra's legs was flayed and open. It curled back in oozing white layers. Blood and infection ran in stripes from just above Corra's knees, disappearing beneath the sagging edge of the robe.

"Come, child, hold my hands. You must wade into the center of the stream and let the cold water bathe your wounds."

Corra held Aislinn's hands, then waded into the center of the stream where the water lapped at the edges of her robe. She gasped as the icy water struck her legs, then grimaced in pain for a few minutes. At last her face relaxed into a smile.

"Now I cannot feel the wounds, priestess. This water has made them numb."

"It will cleanse them as well and later we will put poultices of herbs against the skin. But you should have told me how horrible these wounds were. I would have tended them last night."

"I was afraid that if you knew, you might not take me with you. That you might think that I was a bad child to have deserved such a beating."

"No child ever deserves this, sweeting. I would have taken you and tended you all the faster had I known."

Corra smiled, held both of Aislinn's hands, and swayed a little back and forth in the water. She looked over Aislinn's shoulder and a puzzled look came over her face.

"I do not see the cave that we slept in last night, priestess. Have you hidden it by sorcery?"

Aislinn laughed aloud.

"You mistake my powers, Corra, if you think I could hide so great a thing as that oak tree."

"We slept in the oak tree?" Corra studied it seriously. "It is a great tree, with a huge, wide trunk."

"It is. But we did not sleep in the trunk. We slept below the tree, below the roots. Do you see how the tree stands at the top of this hill?"

Corra nodded.

"There is a cave underneath the hill, beneath the roots of the tree. That is where the druids store herbs and medicaments, tapers for light and our utensils. That is where we slept."

Corra looked around her, wide-eyed.

"What is this place, priestess?"

"It is a fidnemed, a sacred woodland shrine. Druids gather here at the full moon."

"Why?"

"Do you see how the tree stretches its arms toward the sky?"

Corra nodded.

"The tree is a house for spirits, as I told you. When we knock on the wood with our sacred daggers, the spirits awake and soar up. They speak for us to the gods. The mistletoe that winds up the trunk of the tree is sacred as well, for it heals. It must be cut with a golden knife and must never touch the ground."

"Will it heal my legs?"

"The mistletoe heals the wasting disease, that eats the body from the inside. Your legs will heal with comfrey, sweet, and that is what we must do now, before the water freezes you."

Laughing, Aislinn drew Corra from the stream and gently patted her legs dry with her own white robe. Corra glanced around again.

"Will Mac Bran find us here?"

"He will. I think that he will come today. But we will know that he is coming."

"How?"

"Look around you. What do you see circling the base of the hill?"

"Blackthorn!" Corra laughed aloud and clapped her hands. "I know these." She quoted a children's rhyme: " 'Blackthorn gives us flowers white, gives us plums so sweet and ripe, but beware the blackthorn's bite.' There was a boy in our village who fell into them once. His mother was picking thorns from him for many days!"

"So you see that Mac Bran will not come to us that way, for there are three rings of blackthorn around this holy place."

"Then how will he find us?"

"He must come through the dolmen. Come, I will show you."

Aislinn led Corra to the top of the hill where a ring of stones eight inches high encircled a little altar.

"Is that the dolmen?"

"No, child, that is a ceremonial altar. It is a high holy place. When Brennus comes, I will go inside the circle, for he will be afraid to enter."

"Why?"

"Because it is where we druids perform sacrifices to the gods."

Corra shuddered. Aislinn pointed into the green distance of the forest far away at the bottom of the long hill.

"There is the dolmen." Among the dense green trees, a huge pair of upright stones capped with a lintel stone of massive size stood like a doorway. Moss-covered stone steps led from the crest of the hill down into the dark archway of the stones.

Beside Aislinn, Corra shivered. "I do not like that. It has the look of dark magic."

Aislinn looked at her surprised. "You see well, little one. Perhaps you have the second sight, as I do."

"What is the second sight?"

"It is the gift of being able to know, in some times and in some places, what is about to befall. I sense it in you, for you have told me that you knew that I had come for you last night in your village. When I was very small, my teacher, Aodhfin, sensed it in me. He put me into the training to be a druidess and had me practice with it over and over again until I could use it at my will."

"How will it help you with Mac Bran?"

"It is the way that I will know when Mac Bran is coming. You are right about the dolmen, Corra. It is magical. The dolmens were erected by the ancient ones, the god-men who came before the men of now. It is like a doorway between worlds. When you are underneath it, the sense of everything is concentrated. When Mac Bran passes beneath it, I will know that he is coming and I will have time to prepare. But for now, I must prepare the medicines for your legs."

* * *

Toward afternoon, when Aislinn had boiled the water, she made comfrey poultices in the soft boiled linen from the bottom of her undertunic, slicing it into long strips with her knife. She helped Corra to lie down by the fire and lifted the hem of the child's tattered brown robe.

"Don't move, little one. Stay still," Aislinn told Corra as the warm fragrant linen came in contact with the raw wounds.

Corra gasped, clenched her fists, turned her little head from side to side.

"I am sorry that it hurts you, child. The poultices must remain there against your legs so that no sickness can get into the wounds. Rest, and I will make you a shepherd's purse tea. It will strengthen the blood inside your body and help your wounds to heal faster."

Aislinn put fresh strips of linen to boiling again in the iron cauldron. She sifted herbs into an earthenware cup and poured the hot water over them. She lifted the fresh strips of linen from the water and aired them a little to cool. When she pressed the fresh warmth against Corra's legs, the child sighed.

"The warmth feels good now, priestess. I wish I had had these linens for my back."

"Your back?"

Aislinn lifted the child's robe away from her thin shoulders. Again, the blood-lust for Mac Bran rose in her throat as she stared at the child's back. Knotted white ropes of scar tissue crisscrossed the skin, where Corra had been whipped before.

Aislinn leaned closer and ran her finger along the scars. Someone had ministered to these, someone with druii medical training. The skin had been closed carefully against itself and speedwell had been applied to reduce the scarring. In time, she thought, these scars might fade. She wondered who had given the child such tender care. Perhaps, she thought, she should seek out this caregiver. Someone with a village and a warm house to care for this lost child. Aislinn worried at the thought. How would she,

a wanderer, care for the child with winter coming on?
Again she thought that perhaps she should return to Tara
and felt the wash of fear, the dark wings of Banbh above
her. Someone must protect this child.

Still worrying at the thought, Aislinn dipped a large
square of linen in the warm water and laid it against
Corra's back. Gently, she used her fingers to rub the
warmth against the child's skin. Corra's fisted hands
slowly unclenched. She turned her face, which had been
pressed into her robe, until she faced Aislinn.

"Tell me everything," Aislinn said gently, "and I will
help you to bear it. How long have you been with Mac
Bran?"

The little girl sighed. "He took us just after the last
samhain festival. My máthair and me. My athair was a
bo-aire, a cattleman. Mac Bran killed him in the cattle
raid. We were Mac Bran's prize." She turned her head in
shame. "My máthair was very beautiful."

"Almost one year ago," Aislinn said, massaging gently
at her back.

Corra looked at Aislinn again, her face a mask of surprise.

"So little time?" she said. "I thought it was many
years."

"When did he start hurting you like this?"

"At first he left me alone. He took us to his fort, and I
sometimes served his mead or ale, but sometimes the
other children would play with me. When the poet came,
Mac Bran ignored me for days. I could stay with the poet
and he taught me stories and songs.

"Mac Bran hurt my máthair though. At night I would
hear her screaming and she would call out my athair's
name. Later she would come to me weeping, and she
would hold me and tell me to say nothing. 'As long as
he hurts me, he will not hurt you, my little bird,' she
would say. 'I do not mind the hurt.'

"But one night she did not come to me. In the morning
I found her limp on the ground outside the door of the

slaves' dwelling. Some of the women said he had broken her neck. They held me back but I broke loose from them. I ran into his lodge and curled my hand in his hair and stabbed at his eyes and nose. I told him that the gods would punish him, for he was evil, and I screamed until the women pulled me away from him.

"After that he started to hurt me. If I did not serve his food or drink in the way he liked, he would swat me down with his hand. Once I tried to run away and find the poet, but Mac Bran came after me on his horse and caught me up by the hair. That is when he whipped my back."

"Who ministered to your wounds?" Aislinn asked gently.

"The poet. Eoghan Mac Aidan," said Corra. "When he returned to our village, he cut my scars open and laid them flat and placed medicine on them as you have."

"Mac Bran permitted this?"

"He was afraid. They call Mac Aidan the warrior poet. It is said that he is fierce with his enemies. Mac Bran left me alone when he was at our camp."

"And why did Mac Bran whip your legs?"

"The night before you came to our village, Mac Bran came for me in the night. He dragged me to his lodge and he touched me here." She gestured in the direction of her chest. "But he said that I was not ripe enough. I screamed and ran to the women's dwelling. They took me in. He whipped me the next morning. That was the day that you came to the camp. You were sitting with the chieftains, and when I saw your eyes I knew that the god had sent you and that you would take me from Mac Bran." She reached out and stroked Aislinn's arm.

"That is why I lay awake all night. Just before dawn when it was very dark, I felt someone lifting me and I knew it was you and that the god had answered my prayer. You came for me just as I knew you would."

Aislinn let the tears spill from her eyes and she bent and kissed the white cheek. She lifted a length of Corra's copper hair.

"Will you braid it as my máthair did?" the little girl asked shyly.

"I will wash it in the warm water and sweet herbs and braid it," said Aislinn, glad of the opportunity to make the little girl happy. "But first we will bind your legs with fresh bandages." She tore more strips from her tunic and wrapped the little girl's legs, then brought her fragrant kettle of warm water to the ground beside them. She lifted the copper hair, combing through it with her fingers, then lowering it into the sweet herbs. She let Corra rest gently against her arm while she tipped her head into the cauldron and thoroughly washed her hair. When it was gleaming wet, Corra sat cross-legged and Aislinn began to plait the copper braid.

"Will you tell me too, priestess? About the evil one who tried to harm you?"

She turned her head sideways toward Aislinn.

"My máthair said that when I listened, it eased her heart."

Aislinn paused with her hands in the silky hair.

"All right, little seanmhaithair. I will tell you what I can. His name is Banbh. He is a dark druid, one who follows the ways of the evil ones. He began to pursue me when I had thirteen summers, after my first moon-blood came, but I was more fortunate than you. I had a foster-father, old Aodhfin the Wise, who protected me. At least until that night two years ago. And then I knew that he could protect me no longer."

Aislinn closed her eyes, said nothing further. She did not want to frighten the little girl with the black and terrifying memory.

"He is a sorcerer then?"

"Banbh? Yes, a sorcerer and a shape-changer. Some of us follow the gods of the light, others the gods of the darkness. Both have power. But Banbh follows the Morrigu, she of battle and death and war. Her shape is a raven, a dark crow of the forest. She has granted that shape to

Banbh, so well does he do her bidding." Aislinn shook her head.

"I fled that night without even telling Aodhfin, my teacher." She felt a wash of shame at her midnight flight, at the worry she must have caused Aodhfin. She returned her trembling hands to the braid.

"But you said that your teacher had told you to come on this journey. Perhaps it was the Dark One who made you go at last. And I am glad that you came."

Aislinn laughed aloud. "All my training, child, and I never saw it that way. Perhaps the darkness served the light. How strange."

"Do you fear him still, priestess?"

"The Dark One? Until yesterday, I feared him still, child. But you have made me fierce."

Suddenly, the feeling coursed through her like light, like heat, like wind. She closed her eyes and tipped her head back, drinking in the vision, letting the sense of things pervade her being. She felt calm and sure.

"What is it?" Corra asked in a terrified voice, her face transfixed at the look that had come over Aislinn.

"Mac Bran comes," she said. "He has just passed through the dolmen. And he is not alone. He is closely followed by another."

Aislinn stood in a single fluid movement and slid her dagger into the belt at her waist.

"Stay here, child," she said to Corra. "I must go to the sacred circle. Now the battle begins."

3

Aislinn stood in the holy circle of stones with her back to the altar, facing the direction of Mac Bran's approach. She bound her hair into a quick braid, held her hand loose near her dagger. The gold torque at her neck and the spiraling bracelet on her arm gleamed in the sunlight.

Mac Bran reached the crest of the hill, his head bent toward the signs of their passage on the still-muddy ground. He was puffing from the climb, clouds of steam moving around his florid face. He was more than six feet tall with flaming red hair and a thick red moustache. His hair was limed for battle and it stood up from his head like a forest of birches. He held his long wooden shield with his left hand, and his spear, with its vicious iron head, in his right. He was naked but for his sandals, his battle apron, and the golden torque at his neck.

Aislinn, counting on the fact that he had not yet seen her, laughed aloud.

His head snapped up and Aislinn rejoiced in the raw fear that passed across his features. She took a deep breath, spoke in her most sarcastic voice.

"Of course I knew that you were coming, foolish chieftain. Have you forgotten that I am druii? I see that you come garbed as the ancient warriors against this frail woman. I am flattered that you accord me so much respect, Brennus Mac Bran. Or is it fear of my powers?"

Mac Bran snarled. "Thieving witch. I know your powers, but they are no match for those of a warrior. Have I not trailed you all night to take back what is mine? Have I not entered this place? I have the powers of a warrior."

Aislinn inclined her hand toward the heavy weight of his stomach and laughed lightly. "Your power seems to have collected at your midsection," she said. "You will be a poor man soon for the fines your tribe will levy on your girth. Or you will no longer be chieftain, for a leader of the Gaels must perfect his body. Perhaps you rely too much on your ale for strength."

The face of the chieftain flushed with anger.

"You will feel the weight of my strength before this morning is finished."

Aislinn felt a surge of victory that she had found one of his weak spots, pushed her advantage.

"Though I bear but little weight, the weight of the goddess is in my every word. You would do wise to remember that and leave now, while she will permit you to go."

Mac Bran grunted, moved in closer. He faced her outside the circle of stones, pacing back and forth like a lumbering beast, afraid to enter. Aislinn edged toward his spear arm, along the inner perimeter of the circle, remaining within the protective barrier the stones gave her. She kept her eyes on the pulse that beat at the side of his neck, judged its height, hefted her dagger back and forth between her hands. If she should take him there, she would have to reach above her height, with her weak arm. She must force him to expose his heart. She played again on his weight and his masculine pride.

"I fight unshielded, Mac Bran, but it is true that you have a great deal more to shield than I. Your fear for your body is justified."

"I fear nothing," he shouted, throwing the shield aside.

Aislinn threw her head back and stretched out both arms. "I serve the triune goddess, protector of women and children. Fear her, who knows your evil toward women and children. She will protect her priestess and the life of the innocent child."

Mac Bran looked around him as if expecting to see the goddess there in the clearing. He used his free shield hand to make a sign in the air.

Aislinn fed his fear. In her most sonorous priestly voice she began the druii initiation ritual:

> *"Anger of fire*
> *Fire of speech,*
> *Breath of knowledge*
> *Wisdom of wealth*
> *Sword of song*
> *Song of bitter-edge"*

She raised her dagger and turned it deliberately so that the light glinted off the blade and slivered against the trees in the sacred clearing. It was druii knowledge, this judgment of the placement of sunlight, and it stood her in good stead now.

Mac Bran involuntarily lifted his hand to shield his face from the flash of light. Aislinn read the fear of the power of words and women on his face and in his stance. She took her first step toward the unshielded left side of his body, grasped her dagger tight in her palm. Her heart struggled like a pinioned hawk beneath her ribs. Now!

At that instant, Corra dashed from the cave into the sunlight. Aislinn was distracted, turned in Corra's direction. Mac Bran followed Aislinn's gaze toward Corra.

. "Go back," Aislinn commanded. "Go inside."

But Corra raised her hands from behind her back. In each hand was a burning taper of pine needles.

"If you harm the priestess Aislinn," Corra said defiantly to Mac Bran, "I will light your hair on fire."

Mac Bran let out a roar of anger.

"Brat," he shouted. "You are my cumal, my property. You will pay for this attempt to steal from me."

He moved away from Aislinn, striding toward Corra. His bearlike hand twisted in her copper hair, holding it aloft. He dropped his spear and snatched with his now free hand at one of the lighted tapers she held. Corra screamed again and again, waved the tapers around the sides of his head and face. He leaned back and around them in a strange dance.

"Mother goddess," Aislinn prayed in the hollows of her head. "Mother goddess, you sent me to this child. Help me now."

She felt white calm descend around her. In the center of that stillness, Aislinn remembered the crow man, the look of his eyes, the way he bore down above her. She nodded, understood the source of Mac Bran's second weakness. Quickly, she cut through the shoulders of her white gown and let it drop to her waist. Her white breasts gleamed in the sunlight.

"Brennus Mac Bran," she called in her most commanding druid voice. Mac Bran turned his shaggy head in her direction. He stopped groping for the tapers that Corra was swinging to and fro.

Aislinn slit the rope at her waist and the dress dropped to the ground. She lifted her head, forced her concentration to remain on Mac Bran.

She raised both arms out by her sides, letting the dagger rest in the open palm of her right hand and letting Mac Bran stare at her nakedness. Her skin was milky white, her waist and thighs slender, her breasts so pale that the tiny blue veins were visible at their surface. The wind picked up her hair and it undulated at the same time that her nipples grew hard. Mac Bran made a strangled sound halfway between lust and superstitious fear.

"Will you spare the child?" she asked softly, seductively.

"I will have you and the child," he shouted, but he

released his hold on Corra ni Brith's hair. She crumpled to the ground, sobbing. Mac Bran lumbered toward Aislinn like a bear, lunged out at the last minute, sweeping her against his chest with his empty spear arm. Aislinn quickly closed her palm around her dagger to keep it from slipping to the ground.

Her breasts were crushed so hard against the sweaty red hairs of his chest that Aislinn could feel her heart beat against his skin. She smelled the foul ale smell of his breath and felt the swelling of his manhood beneath his leather battle apron.

She tried to bring her dagger hand up to stab him, but her arm was locked between Mac Bran's chest and his huge left arm and she could not raise it above the elbow. She drew back, stabbed at his thigh.

Mac Bran released her body, slapping his left hand against her right, knocking the dagger to the ground. Before Aislinn could leap aside to pick it up, a second man appeared at the top of the hill to her right. Aislinn saw the blue-green flash of his cloak, smelled the scent of the wolfhound that accompanied him. Mac Bran turned his head in the direction of the newcomer, made a grunting sound. Recognition. The blue-cloaked one stopped abruptly.

Aislinn made a lunge for the dagger, but Mac Bran caught her by the hair, twining his left hand in her braid as he had done with Corra. He bent her head back so that she looked up into his red and sweating face leering above her. His free right hand moved up and clasped her breast, pinching the nipple between his thumb and forefinger and pulling it upward.

"Now we will see if the breasts of a priestess bleed like the breasts of any other woman," he said. He bared his teeth and lowered his head.

Aislinn saw the rushing blur of Corra streaming across the clearing behind Mac Bran's back, the burning torch held in front of her like a spear.

"No!" she cried, but she felt the flame rush between

them, smelled the acrid smell of Mac Bran's hair as it caught fire. Now the one in the blue cloak moved in swiftly. Aislinn expected him to extinguish Mac Bran's burning hair, but instead he grabbed Corra by the waist, carried her backward to a safe distance. His wolfhound growled low in its throat.

Mac Bran released Aislinn, lifted his free hand to his hair, and began to beat against it at the same time that he turned in the direction of the dog. Aislinn followed his glance, seeing the blue-cloaked man clearly for the first time. He stood with his left arm around Corra. He made a forward motion with his right hand, spoke a single word.

"Sheary!"

The huge dog was on them instantly, throwing its body between them, scratching, biting, its teeth bared. Aislinn was knocked to the ground, scrabbled on her knees for her dagger, came to her feet holding it.

Mac Bran dove for his shield, raised it with both hands against the onslaught of the dog. The wolfhound threw its body against the shield, knocking it from Mac Bran's hands into the dust outside the circle.

Mac Bran raised both arms to his face. Two of the twisted licks of his hair were fully aflame now and fire spewed in two red torches from the top of his head.

Aislinn clenched the dagger hard with both hands, ran straight for the exposed spot beneath Mac Bran's raised left arm.

The dagger found its soft target and drove home. Mac Bran made a grunting sound and straightened. His right hand rose toward the dagger, closed around the hilt. He looked as though he might draw the hilt from his bleeding side, but he stopped and regarded Aislinn with a look of pure surprise. He swayed there in the dappled clearing, fire spitting from his head, then toppled like a tree into the dirt outside the circle of stones. The fire sputtered out against the damp ground.

The blue-cloaked one spoke his word again.

"Sheary."

The dog moved away, sat by his side.

Aislinn began to shake. She felt her stomach roil and turned toward the altar, leaning her bloodstained hands against it. She brought up the weak tea of her breakfast, gasped for breath, and retched again.

She turned toward the one in the blue cloak and brought her arms up in a protective gesture over her breasts, wincing in pain when her forearm brushed against the breast that Mac Bran had been mauling.

"Will you fight me naked and unarmed?" she asked him, aware of the desperation in her voice.

A flicker of what seemed to be sorrow crossed his face, replaced at once by something else, something exceedingly gentle. Then Corra was at Aislinn's side, closing her little arms around Aislinn's waist.

"Don't be afraid, priestess," she said calmly. "He is my friend. Eoghan Mac Aidan. The warrior poet."

His eyes were blue, deep water, drowning. He took his blue and green plaid cloak from his shoulders and wrapped it gently around Aislinn, then lifted her bloodstained hand between his two and pressed it against his lips.

"Bring water for the priestess Aislinn," he said softly to Corra. The little girl ran to the cave for the linen towels, returning with them soaked in the cold spring water. He pressed them first to Aislinn's lips, then washed her hands of the blood, sponging gently, never releasing her eyes. Aislinn felt a strange sense of recognition.

Suddenly, the air around Aislinn felt viscous and slow, as though she were moving beneath water. She clung around little Corra. There in the sacred circle, they composed a triangle, the perfect Celtic holy number three. Aislinn tipped her head back into the light and cried out in victory and terror. She felt presences gathering just above her head, waiting.

"What begins here?" she cried aloud. "What begins at last?"

She felt her spirit rise out of her body, watched the

empty body collapse into Mac Aidan's arms, saw the bloodstained corpse of Mac Bran. The look on Corra's face shifted from puzzlement to terror.

"Do not leave me," she cried.

But the water of the vision carried Aislinn away from them and she could no more stop it than she could stop the wind. Like a leaf falling, Aislinn's spirit spiraled into the vision that had eluded her since childhood.

4

The tunnel stretched in front of her, the light a distant pinpoint. Aislinn stretched her arms out to her sides and felt along the walls. A tomb. Had she left the land of the living? Had her battle wounds placed her among the ancestors? What would happen to Corra if she was now among the dead? Would the poet care for her? He had not taken her from Mac Bran before. A wash of fear and sorrow came over Aislinn at the thought of the little girl all alone. She tried to steady her breathing, pressed her hands against the wall. Beneath her palms she felt the whirling pattern that told her that all life spiraled into itself again. Above and below the spirals she felt the ancient vertical stick words, the secret ogham language so named for Ogma, the "honey-mouthed" god of tales.

The stones whispered the names of gods, of generations of chieftains too ancient to remember. In Aislinn's childhood, in the lush green valley that surrounded the river-goddess Boann, there had been hundreds of such passage graves cut into the sides of hills or built into artificial hills. Generation after generation of chieftains used the tombs for the burial of their dead.

Aislinn remembered the central chamber of the tomb,

concentrated her attention on the light at the far side of the tunnel. In a sudden acceleration of vision, she was in the chamber. Light streamed down upon a couple seated together at the center of the room.

The woman stood when she saw Aislinn, gave a glad cry. At his wife's movement the man beside her also rose. His black hair and thick moustache receded behind the piercing all-seeing blue of his eyes. He wore the seven Celtic colors of kingship. His blue and green plaid cloak parted to reveal a short wool tunic of brilliant red embroidered with spiraling designs in green, blue, purple, gold, and silver. Over the tunic, he wore a soft leather battle apron worked almost to white. The hilt of the intricately etched sword that hung by his side boasted a design of a human head, repository of the Celtic soul.

The woman tipped her head toward Aislinn. Her chestnut hair cascaded down the arm of her fringed purple cloak. The little bells that were woven into the end of each braid tinkled softly. Aislinn cried aloud at the memory of the sound.

"I remember you!" she cried. "Máthair, athair. You have returned for me." She started toward them across the crowded chamber.

The floor around her parents was scattered with objects—goblets with scenes of hounds and hares, a wood and bronze shield almost as large as her father's body, and behind her parents an entire bronze wall carved with spiraling designs and the entwined heads of humans and animals. Nearby, a two-man chariot with intricately carved side panels stood ready to return them to the country of the soul, Tir Nan Og.

The chariot reminded Aislinn that she was in a tomb—a visionary tomb. The sense of despair and loss that had haunted her since childhood pressed in on her. She let out a sob.

"Why did you abandon me?"

The woman's eyes grew wide. She pressed her hands to her lips, made a small, anguished sound.

"What do you feel for the child Corra ni Brith?" asked Aislinn's father in a sharp tone.

Aislinn straightened her back and drew breath. She blinked back tears. It was the way of the Gaels to answer a question with a question.

"I have defended the child with my life," she answered her father quietly.

"So your mother and I did with you," her father replied. "Your mother gave her life that you would have yours. There is much that you do not know."

Aislinn's mother spoke for the first time.

"Would it cause you great pain to be separated from Corra ni Brith, now?"

"It would."

"Yet, if Mac Bran had killed you, the pain would have belonged to Corra ni Brith."

"As the pain has belonged to me for these fifteen years," said Aislinn. She regarded her mother thoughtfully. Something that had been lodged against her heart since childhood shifted its weight.

"I understand," she said. "You did not wish to leave me."

"My heart never left you, daughter," said the woman.

"Máthair," Aislinn whispered, stretching out her arms.

"My beautiful daughter. I have missed you so terribly. How I wish that I could hold you now, but you are flesh and I am spirit. We cannot mingle between the worlds."

"Then why have you come back to me now?"

Her father reached his arm around his wife.

"Your mother and I have come to give you this warning. You began a quest when you saved the child ni Brith. There is a prophecy, daughter, more ancient than any the druii have taught you. These events are foredestined. You must return to the druid Aodhfin at the feis at Tara Hill. You must discover how you came to be his foster-child. What you learn will endanger you, but it will also free you. You must be wise, daughter. You must use the gifts the druids have given you, the love you are learning to feel for the child. Above all, you must beware of the shape-changer, of the druid called Banbh. He is your enemy. As there is light in this chamber, there is full darkness in the corridor before it. You are the point between."

Her mother leaned forward, looked at her urgently. "Daughter, this Mac Aidan who has come here today. He is a bringer of fire."

"I am a druid priestess, máthair. I have chosen my path," Aislinn replied.

"You are first woman, now mother to Corra. You are protected by the triune goddess. You must learn to hear her wisdom in your thoughts and in your body. Hear what I say. Hear the voice in the heart."

Aislinn felt the strange acceleration of vision begin again. Her parents began to recede from her, the objects around them growing smaller, blurring in her vision. She stretched out her arms.

"No! Do not leave me again."

"Husband," cried Aislinn's mother, clutching at his arm as if he could somehow stop the flow of the vision. "Husband, Sorar, not again." But he shook his head in sorrow.

"In both worlds have we always loved and protected you," cried her mother, stretching her arms toward Aislinn.

"Then do not leave me," Aislinn cried again. She saw a spasm of terrible pain cross her mother's face. "Druii speak the truth in suffering," she whispered from her training.

"Always I have loved you both," she cried out from some wellspring. "Always have I known your love for me." The pain on her mother's face was replaced by a look of infinite gentleness.

There was the rushing darkness of the tunnel, then daylight. Aislinn looked down from some height on her body, propped against Mac Aidan on the ground. A sudden spiraling feeling swirled behind her eyes. Then Aislinn could feel her naked body itching inside the blue and green of

Mac Aidan's cloak, feel the cool cloth that Corra ni Brith held against her forehead, and hear her own wracking sobs as she reached for the child's hand.

The firelight played quietly against the walls of the cave. Outside an owl called softly and Aislinn heard Mac Aidan's approaching steps and that of the wolfhound. She sat up and began braiding her hair, concentrating her shaking fingers on the black streams.

Beside her, she felt Corra look up, felt the warmth that flowed from the child to Eoghan Mac Aidan. She forced herself to look up as well. The fire cast his features in gold as he stood in the cave entrance. He was tall, taller even than most of the men of the Celts. His thick dark hair swept back from his forehead in waves and was braided down the center of his back. Though he must have had at least thirty summers, as yet, he showed no trace of gray.

Aislinn released her hands from the half-finished braid and stood. "So, fili," she began, addressing him with the title befitting only the most learned and respected of the bards. He stepped toward her and she saw the blood that began at his shoulder and was dried in rivulets down the front of his cloak. "You have returned him to his tribe?"

"I have," Mac Aidan said, in a tone so sorrowful that Aislinn felt her anger rise again.

"What would you have had me do? Let him kill the child? Rape me? Kill us both? He was hurting me and you did nothing, warrior bard! You stood there like a great silent tree."

Mac Aidan laughed, throwing back his head and shouting aloud with mirth until he stopped to brush the tears from his eyes. Little Corra took his laughter as a sign that all was well. She ran to him and he bent to half his height and enfolded her.

Aislinn locked her hands before her. A part of her wanted to run to him as Corra had and be comforted by the laughter and the size of him. Something deeper knew that if she came close to him, she would strike out, slashing at him with hands and fists, slapping the laughter from him. Men like Mac Bran and Banbh were to be hated and feared, men like her teacher Aodhfin to be respected and loved. Why did she feel both things toward this man?

She chose as her weapon words.

"Laugh then, ox. You are not he who will pay the penalty for this murder. I who have long been an outcast will be cast further away while you tell your tales by the warmest lodge fires."

Immediately he was silent. The look that recaptured his face was at once remorseful and strangely guilty.

"I know that you have been cast away," he began. He stopped, turned his face away from the light, drew breath. "I do not laugh at your plight, nor do I sorrow for the death of Mac Bran. He was a beast; brehon law decrees that a chieftain must die when he no longer acts in accord with the laws of Eire. I will see to it that you pay no penalty."

"And how will you do that, teller-of-tales?"

He smiled. "We who rely on words are not without influence," he said. He was mocking her. Again she felt the urge to laugh struggle against the urge to strike at him.

She looked pointedly at his dagger. "The power of your words, or of anything else you might possess, did nothing to help me yesterday." Immediately she regretted having said it; Mac Aidan had carried her to the cave when the vision left her limp as water, made strong tea and held her gentle as a mother. He had built the fire and wrapped her beside it until her trembling had ceased. Later, he had hoisted the body of Mac Bran across his shoulders and disappeared silently into the forest. Hoofbeats followed his disappearance, telling Aislinn that his horse had been tethered nearby all along. She expected never to see him again. Yet, now, he had returned when no law required him to do so.

"No, what I said is not true. I am glad that you were here yesterday."

Outside, the cry of a wolf keened in the night air and the large gray dog beside Mac Aidan turned, made growling, whimpering noises toward the darkness. Mac Aidan made a motion with his hand, sweeping it in a long gesture parallel to the ground. He spoke a single word. "Sheary!" The hound lay down beside him.

Aislinn watched in surprise.

"You told him to attack Mac Bran. Why did you do this thing? You had no obligations in law in my battle with Mac Bran."

Mac Aidan stepped forward, took both of her hands in his, and then let them drop. A pained look crossed his face and disappeared. He crouched and put his arm around Corra ni Brith.

"You are strong and well gifted, priestess," he said softly. "I hoped that Mac Bran would fall before your need to protect Corra. But I would not have let him hurt this child again. Or you. I will never let a child be hurt again!" He looked up at her with a terrible intensity, then stood and placed both hands on her shoulders. "You must believe that, Aislinn ni Sorar."

"How is it that you know my name? You spoke it even after my battle with Mac Bran."

She tipped her head back, looked straight into the blue of his eyes. She felt a vision begin to gather at the back of her head. She saw herself at five years old, screaming as she stretched her arms toward her own mother. Her mother was weeping. Someone was standing behind her in the vision. She closed her eyes, stepped into the body of the child, began to turn her head to see the faces of those who were holding her.

"No!" Mac Aidan said harshly. He dropped his hands from her shoulders.

She opened her eyes. His face was ugly, terrified. He composed it, gentled the features.

"You are too tired for more visions this night. I knew your name because I asked in the village of Mac Bran. I came after he left, followed him here."

Aislinn nodded.

"Come," he said, "I will sing for you and you must sleep. Tomorrow, I must find you a quiet haven where you and the child will be safe."

Aislinn acquiesced, strewing rushes for herself and Corra ni Brith, spreading out her cloak, banking the fire.

Mac Aidan unstrapped his harp from his back and removed it from the finely tooled leather case. It was a small six-stringed instrument and its ornate golden frame gleamed in the light from the fire. Aislinn watched him curiously, ventured a question.

"Why do you carry the clarsach? You wear the six colors of a master poet, an ollamh. Your speech is respected by kings. Warriors have been known to cease battle at the words of an ollamh. You need not earn your keep with bardic tales."

Mac Aidan smiled at her, plucked gently at the strings. A haunting discordant music filled the little cave.

"I carry the harp for myself, priestess. It speaks best to my soul when I am troubled. Tonight I will let it speak to you."

Mac Aidan sang songs of the Western Isles, of the seas that moved against the side of Eire like a lover. Aislinn cradled Corra in her arms and Mac Aidan sang the suantraighe, sleeping music of the ancient gods of Eire. When she was nearly asleep, Aislinn felt Mac Aidhan's cloak descend upon them, warm with the smell of peat fire. She allowed her senses to drift into the scent.

She remembered her mother's voice saying, "Daughter, this Mac Aidan. He is a bringer of fire." Old Aodhfin's druid chant slipped into her mind. *To the place of fire will come a man bearing fire for the body and the mind.* Was this that man? She nearly smiled, but something pushed at the edges of her consciousness. Mac Aidan had called her Aislinn ni Sorar! They had not known her father's name in the village of Mac Bran. Her father's name had been one known only to herself and old Aodhfin.

But before she could ask, sleep overtook her, gently erasing the question from her mind.

5

"You need not take us with you, poet. We can make our way on our own."

"Do not go with me if you do not choose to, priestess. But I will take the child. I should have taken her from Mac Bran sooner, cumal or none. My hesitation has cost her dearly."

"If you think to take her from me, you will have to fight me as Mac Bran did. I did not hesitate to steal her from him."

He stopped the saddling and bridling of his horse, turned to look at her directly.

"You love the little girl, then?"

"I do. I would have her as my own fosterling." Surprise gave way to delight as Aislinn spoke the words aloud.

His smile seemed sad.

"I understand then. I learned early the love of women for their children. My foster-father is a chieftain, priestess. His stronghold is a crannog. He and my foster-mother would keep both of you safe." He spread his palms and shrugged. "The choice is yours."

Mac Aidan lifted Corra gently onto the back of his huge black stallion.

Corra laughed aloud, wrapped her arms around the horse's neck.

"What do you call him, Mac Aidan?"

"Becan."

"Little One?" Aislinn laughed aloud. "He is full the largest horse I have ever seen. But you employ, I suppose, the sardonic wit for which our poets are noted."

Eoghan glared in her direction. From high on her perch, Corra broke in again.

"How long is our journey to your father's crannog?"

"He is my foster-father, little one. I was sent to live with him when I was younger still than you. His name is O'Domnhnaill. And the journey will take us all of today."

"Then we had best be about it," Aislinn said.

For several hours, Aislinn and Eoghan walked in total silence on either side of the great horse. The early autumn sun was warm against Aislinn's hair and the leaves that formed the ceiling of the forest cast red and gold light against the path where they walked.

From the height of the horse's back, Corra hummed snatches of old songs, occasionally laughing aloud at the antics of a swooping thrush or of two squirrels playing a game of run-and-catch.

The huge wolf-dog Sheary, himself as big as a pony, loped along beside them, occasionally dashing away through the forest, then returning wet and shaggy to shake off his gray fur for their benefit or to rub against his master's cloak. After one of his forays, the dog thrust its head beneath Aislinn's arm and nuzzled her cheek. Aislinn laughed aloud.

"He seems but little fierce now for a dog who must hunt the wolves of the Irish forest."

"Like his master," said Mac Aidan, laughing, "he can be most fierce when a great need arises. And he recognizes those who are like-minded." He looked directly at her and inclined his head. Aislinn knew that he was once again referring to her bravery against Mac Bran and the compliment made the color rise in her cheeks.

From far off came the thrashing sounds of a wild boar. Becan skittered sideways, snorting. Mac Aidan gripped the reins tighter, looped his arm about the horse's neck. "Hush, Bec," he whispered soothingly. His stroking hand brushed the horse's neck, then stopped atop Aislinn's resting hand. She felt a strange giddy pleasure at the warmth of his hand over hers. Her breathing became uneven and she closed her eyes, trying to will away the blush that came up in her cheeks. At that instant, Mac Aidan withdrew his hand. Aislinn glanced over to see him staring at her with a mixture of suspicion and guilt.

"The priestess Aislinn is the vessel for too many visions," he said.

"I also close my eyes when I sleep and dream," she snapped, embarrassed at the unfamiliar longing the touch of his hand had produced.

They continued walking in strained silence. Aislinn felt awkward. Mac Aidan had more than ten summers on her twenty years; perhaps he thought of her as a foolish child. She set her chin in a stubborn line, determined that she would not be the first to speak. At last he broke the silence.

"Tell me how it is that the foster-daughter and student of Aodhfin, revered among druids, wanders far from Tara, court of the High King, Cormac Mac Art. Tell me why you do not wish me to return you there," Mac Aidan said finally. From over the neck of Becan, he fixed her with his unyielding blue stare.

Aislinn challenged him with her unanswered question of the night before.

"What do you know of me and of my past?"

"A poet knows many things about the people of Eire. We are aes dana. Like the druii, we also have the freedom of Eire's roads. Let us say that I know who you are, and I wish to know why you are here. The question is simple, priestess."

Aislinn sighed and leaned her head against Becan's warm neck.

"The answer is not," she replied. "More than two years ago, Aodhfin, my foster-father, asked me to go on a questing journey. It was a journey to find a child. I now believe it to be this child," she said, squeezing the calf of Corra ni Brith where she rested atop Becan. The child smiled down at her.

"I did not go when my teacher asked. You spoke before of hesitation, poet. I am learning that hesitation can be worse than reckless action. My hesitation probably cost the child her wounds. It nearly cost me my life."

"Your life?" he asked, his voice a mixture of surprise and concern.

"Yes, my life. Tell me, Poet-Who-Must-Know-Many-Things, do you know of the druid called Banbh?"

Mac Aidan's face darkened.

"I know this Banbh," he said. "Were he not druii, I would have killed him long ago. Perhaps one day, I will."

"But you would die! The law forbids us to harm the person of a druid."

"The part of me that is dead already will kill him," he said. "The part of me that he had a hand in killing."

"That is how I know him too, poet. As a killer of souls. He is why I cannot return now to Tara with the child."

He stopped Bec in his tracks by thrusting his shoulder against the horse's neck and stepped around to face Aislinn. He grasped her by both shoulders, gripping until it hurt.

"What did he do to you?" he demanded, his eyes darting over her face. "What did he do?"

"He . . . he . . ." Aislinn lifted her hands to her breasts, unable to speak in the face of his fury or in front of little Corra who was watching with wary curiosity.

Mac Aidan watched the gesture, his face shifting from fury to horror. "Did he force you, green girl? Did he hurt you?"

Aislinn shook her head. "He tried. More than once.

When I was fourteen, he pushed me to the floor and stood over me, but Aodhfin found him and threatened him. Each time I ran away or cried for Aodhfin, but on that last night, Banbh poured his foul mead down my throat. Before my eyes I watched him change shape. Blacker and blacker he grew. His wingspread was wider than the fire and he became the goddess Badb, the carrion crow.

" 'Do you see this form?' he screamed. 'This form will sweep down upon old Aodhfin and he will die. When he is dead, this form will pluck out his eyes. If you wish him to live, then you must submit to the power of my goddess.'

"I could not submit, Mac Aidan, I could not, for there is something more that Banbh wants of me, something deeper than the body. I have always known. So I ran away. I became a wanderer. Do you understand? I could not let him kill my Aodhfin but I could not give to Badb that part of me which would protect Aodhfin. Was the loss of my place at Tara so great a price to pay? I will never let Banbh kill him! I have no máthair and athair. They died when I was a child."

Mac Aidan threw back his head and let out a howl. It echoed against the trees and trembled the leaves at the ceiling of the forest. When he looked at her, his face was twisted with agony.

"I am sorry," he whispered. "I am so sorry." Slowly, he closed his arms around her, a gesture filled with such sorrow and tenderness that Aislinn let her arms rise up around his shoulders, felt herself lift up, let her mouth press against his mouth. He returned the kiss with a fervor that seemed born of sorrow and longing in equal measures. In that moment, there was no Corra, no Becan, no Sheary, no forest.

Mac Aidan pressed his hands against Aislinn's upper arms. He lifted her away from him, broke the kiss by placing his hands on either side of her face. His eyes were sad.

"I will not let him hurt you anymore," he said with an

intensity that was as terrifying as his howl. "Understand that now you are under the protection of Mac Aidan, warrior-bard of the Ard-Ri, the High King, Cormac Mac Art. I will not let him hurt you, child."

Aislinn snapped her head from his hands, pushed hard against his chest. She felt hurt and confused, embarrassed by the remnants of the kiss she had initiated still wet against her lips.

"Child!" she cried. "Child! I am no child, nor have been for many years. You do not see what is before you, poet."

"I see," said Mac Aidan, sadly, "but also I know what you do not yet know."

"What do I not know?" she questioned, her tone heavy with sarcasm. "I do not know how it is that you are a fili of the Ard-Ri, Cormac Mac Art. As poet, your status is ollamh, master. When you travel, you are entitled to a retinue of twenty-four." She gestured at the empty forest around them, continued.

"If what you say is true, you are equal in nobility to the king, entitled to sit beside him at his table. Yet Cormac holds his court at the hill of Tara. For much of my life I have lived at Tara. There I studied at the druii school. As priestess, I have sat on occasion at the high king's table. How is it that I have not known you?"

But Eoghan Mac Aidan shook his head and would not answer.

The long walk to the crannog passed awkwardly now, the contentment of the early morning gone with the kiss, with Aislinn's feeling of childish embarrassment, with Eoghan's sorrowful intensity.

Periodically, Aislinn regarded him over the neck of the horse. Once she tried to speak.

"You are not responsible for me, poet. Nor for mine. Is that how you see it? It is not so. Have I not lived all of my life without your protection?"

Behind the horse's neck he murmured something. *Too tall? Not at all? Not all?* Whatever it was, he would not repeat it, nor even meet her regard.

Was this what Aodhfin had meant with his riddle? *A man to bring fire for the body and the mind.* She placed her fingers surreptitiously against her lips. They burned where she had pressed them on his. But her face also burned at the thought. And her mind. This was a fire they could keep, her tutor and her parents. This was a fire that left scars. Surely this poet was a strange and troubled man, not at all the one they would choose for her. Not at all.

Her fingers strayed again to her lips. Still, they burned. Aislinn dipped her head beneath the great neck of Becan, maintained a deliberate silence for the duration of the walk.

Viewed from the edge of the forest, the crannog of O'Domnhnaill, foster-father of Mac Aidan, shimmered like a crown on the water.

"How many dwell here?" Aislinn asked, breaking their long silence.

"Nearly a hundred."

"It is the largest crannog I have ever seen."

From far across the field came the ringing of a blacksmith's hammer. Smoke curled from the communal bakehouse. The circular wooden palisades that surrounded the man-made island gleamed like rough-hewn gold and the guard tower that surmounted the gate looked much as a jewel in that crown.

The wide field that stretched from the tree line to the edge of the lake was filled with contented cattle grazing on the low autumn pasturage. Two guards dressed in the ornamental plaids of a Celtic chieftain's army and bristling with longswords, daggers, spears, and huge wooden shields decorated with elaborate bronze designs guarded the causeway that led to the crannog.

"What is this place?" From high atop Becan, Corra stared out at the shimmering island with wide-eyed admiration.

Mac Aidan smiled up at her.

"It is an island, little one. An island made by men which sits upon the water."

"And people live upon it?"

"The remnants of my tribe live here," he said softly.

Aislinn broke in, watching him quietly.

"Is this where you spent your fosterage?"

"No," Mac Aidan replied tersely. "In my youth, my foster-father commanded a rath and hundreds of cattle and villagers."

"Why did he come to this island?"

"The most important duty of a chieftain is to keep his people safe. Treachery drove my foster-father to construct this island."

"But how is this done?" Corra broke in. "How can this island stay on the water and not sink below it? I fear that they will drown."

Mac Aidan laughed. He turned and pointed toward the water.

"Look below the water, Corra. What do you see?"

Corra squinted against the afternoon sunlight, stared hard at the surface of the water.

"I see logs! Side by side like soldiers. Standing upright below the water."

"That is how it is done. First we stand the logs upright in the shallows in the pattern of a spoked wheel. Have you ever seen a chariot?"

Corra nodded.

"Then imagine the wheel of a chariot turned on its side, being held up by logs."

"I understand!" She clapped her hands delightedly. "But the wheel of this chariot is larger than the size of Mac Bran's whole village."

"So it is."

"And what of the ground? How does the ground lie still

upon the water? Why does it not float away?"

"The spokes are filled in with stones and gravel all the way to the tops of the logs until a solid base is established."

"Then you lay the dirt upon the stones!"

"Very good." Mac Aidan squeezed her hand in praise. "Layers and layers of dirt until it is thick enough to support this little town and all of the people in it."

"I must see this wonder!" Corra said.

"So you must," said Aislinn, reaching for Becan's bridle. She was impatient to cross the causeway and started for the edge of the field when Mac Aidan's arm stopped her.

"We will wait until dark."

"Corra ni Brith is hungry and thirsty, as am I. It is two hours until dark."

Mac Aidan lifted Corra from his horse and gave her a long drink from his water skin.

"Have you forgotten your recent battle with Mac Bran? We cannot cross the open field to the crannog in full light. We may be in view of your enemies. And I too have enemies that I would not bring upon my foster family. We wait."

The crannog was transformed by darkness. Torches appeared upon the palisade and along the causeway. Their light shimmered in the water and shapes seemed to appear and disappear below the surface. At last, a mist arose off the lake, making the torches look smoky, obscuring the bottom half of the crannog and spinning itself like rivers across the field that ran to the trees. Mac Aidan stood.

"Now we may go."

"No! Not now!" Little Corra stood rooted, one hand clasping the trunk of a young sapling. "The water is the home of the sidhe and this fog is their breath. It will ensnare us in the darkness and we will be trapped with them in the place between the worlds."

Mac Aidan made an impatient sound and reached for Becan's bridle that was loosely secured to a branch. Aislinn stayed his hand.

"Do you not remember the terror of your childhood?" she asked softly, indicating the pinched pale face of Corra in the starlight.

Aislinn knelt before Corra and stretched her hands out before her, seeking the little light that made them gleam. She drew Corra's hands into the light with her.

"You need not be afraid, child, for you and I are like the sidhe."

Corra gasped. "How can this be? They are the Others."

"Long ago and longer, the Others lived like we do upon the land of Eire. They were called the De Danaan, the people of the goddess Dana and they were people of light and song. Then came the sons of Mil, the Milesians, with thirty ships to battle the De Danaan. The De Danaan were afraid. They cast a fog upon the sea and hoped that the Milesians would lose their way, but they sailed around Eire three times, then came to land."

"And they killed the people—the De Danaan?"

"Nay, child, for the old ones were wise. They sent the sons of Mil back to the sea and they raised a storm of magic power. Many of the ships disappeared. At last the survivors came to shore and the De Danaan were defeated."

"Did they die?"

"Not all of them. Those who lived disappeared into the mounds and the hills, beneath the waters where they still remain. Still others sailed away to Tir Nan Og, the land of youth where they live among the gods. Do you see why we need not fear them? We are like the De Danaan, you and I. We are cast away in Eire and those we love have gone to Tir Nan Og."

Corra nodded solemnly.

"I do see now. Can you speak to them, priestess? Can you tell them not to fear us?"

Aislinn smiled.

"We will do this together, child."

Corra reached up for Eoghan's hand. He knelt beside them. Aislinn looked up in surprise at the watery silver tracks that lay along his cheeks. She gathered their hands together in the gleam of the moonlight, intoned her plea to the people of the sidhe.

> "We who are mortal must pass.
> Sing for us the song of the sidhe,
> Light the dancing ring.
> We will return at last, at last.
> Now we who are mortal must pass."

She released their hands, stood, silent, holding her hands still in the light. Then she tipped back her head and issued out a sound, high like wind, half the cry of an animal, half the song of a human. She sustained her keening on a long breath against the darkness, down the field toward the crannog.

Mac Aidan swore beneath his breath. The hackles on Sheary's neck stood up and he began to howl in his peculiar wolfhound way. A small contingent of warriors still strapping on their arms and lighting their torches came streaming across the causeway and into the field at the edge of the water.

Thus, borne upon a druid chant and the howl of a wolfhound, the little party entered the crannog of O'Domnhnaill.

6

The fire at the center of the large chieftain's hall was warm, as was the mulled wine that Aislinn and Corra drank. Already, bread with honey, sweet white butter, and cheese were spread before Aislinn and Corra. Though it was past the hour for supper, a haunch of venison roasted over the fire. Fresh fish steamed between hot stones on the floor of the fire pit, for a feast in honor of the returning poet-son and the druidess he had brought with him.

Aislinn smiled ruefully. The truth was that they were all assiduously avoiding the druidess he had brought with him, all that is except Gobinet, wife of O'Domnhnaill, who was kind and solicitous as her role as hostess required. The rest, even the foster-father of Mac Aidan, glanced her way often, then just as quickly turned away. Probably a result of the chant against the sidhe, she mused. She settled her arm around Corra and stared into the flames.

Mac Aidan was the center of attention at the other side of the fire. His foster-father had let out a whoop upon seeing him and they had clasped arms, then shoulders, then embraced with unabashed joy, O'Domnhnaill shouting to his wife to call the women for a feast and shouting to his oldest son to gather all of the warriors in the hall.

Gobinet too was the recipient of Mac Aidan's joy. He lifted her from her feet and swung her in a circle until she laughingly protested. Then, he kissed both cheeks and wound his hands in her hair crying, "Máthair, beautiful máthair."

O'Domnhaill had acknowledged Aislinn with a sidelong glance at his son. "The singer of the chant, I assume?"

When Mac Aidan simply nodded, O'Domnhaill faced her with the formal ritual greeting.

"Welcome, druidess. Here, among my people, you shall be respected. Here, among my people, you shall be treated with honor."

It was Gobinet who had stared quietly at Aislinn, standing silently with her arm around Corra, Gobinet who gently touched Corra's pale cheek, then gathered both of them into her arms and whispered, "Come sit by my fire where you can rest and be warm."

Now it was Gobinet who faced Aislinn directly with a womanly question.

"How have you come to be in the company of my foster-son?"

"It is a very long tale, honored mother," Aislinn began, drawing herself up for the courteous response, but Gobinet held up her hand and shook her head.

"My question was born of curiosity and was inhospitable. Forgive me, child. You are tired. For tonight, tell me your name and that will suffice. We can talk of longer things tomorrow."

Aislinn smiled in relief. Here in the family enclave she felt safe enough to speak her own name. "I thank you. My name is Aislinn ni Sorar."

Gobinet drew in her breath, riveted her head in Mac Aidan's direction. From across the room he watched them with a fixed stare. The hall grew hushed. Gobinet inclined her head in the direction of her foster-son, as if she asked a question. He shook his head ever so slightly.

Gobinet turned back toward Aislinn with a fixed bright smile.

"This is a name of great honor. Our people are doubly blessed to have you among us."

"More honor to our guest, Aislinn ni Sorar," cried O'Domnhnaill, raising his jewel-encrusted golden goblet into the light.

"Honor to the druidess," cried one of the warriors, and Aislinn noticed that the smiles directed at her warmed and that the fear vanished from many of the faces. But not all.

For above Mac Aidan's raised golden cup, his eyes regarded her with infinite sorrow.

The bench beside the water was just outside one of the water gates in the palisade. Behind her, Aislinn could hear the sounds of the village, the laughter of children skirling about in play. Before her the water sparkled like a sword in the sunlight. She rested her head on the wall behind her, closed her eyes. She thought about Corra ni Brith. How should she winter out with the child? Here among the people of O'Domnhnaill, where everyone was so polite but so distant? Or should she return to Tara? Place Corra under the protective wing of Aodhfin while she herself would have to fight off the dark wings of Banbh.

She sighed. At that very moment, Eoghan sat down beside her.

"This is one of my favorite spots as well, priestess. The water seems so solitary and still, but the sounds of the village behind me are comforting."

"I was thinking that very thought." Aislinn smiled.

"And sadder thoughts too, for I heard your sigh."

"Your foster people are kind to me, Eoghan, but distant. I need to decide where to winter out with Corra."

"That is why I have sought you out. Gobinet, my foster-mother, sends me to invite you to remain here. You and Corra are welcome to winter with my people." He regarded her gently. "Let them keep you safe here, Aislinn. At least for this little while."

"And the distance they keep from me? Have I offended them? Or do they fear me?"

"No! You must not think so. They revere you and your family. It is me they protect, their fosterling. My family . . ."

Aislinn's mind seized on the word.

"Your family? A woman has spoken for you? You are wed?"

"Nay, priestess, nay. I should have said that they protect my name. Among my clan no woman would speak for me." He laughed, a rueful little sound.

"Why not?" Aislinn felt defiant and protective of him. "You are well formed and learned. And I can speak for your courage and your kindness, for I have seen it with Mac Bran and Corra."

He laughed, laid her hand gently inside his, palm up. He traced a circle there.

"If you knew how strange this is, your defending me."

"I cannot know until you tell me. Or until someone tells me."

"We are not blood kin, Aislinn. Under the law, it is the right and duty of blood kin to tell you of your history."

"I have no blood kin, Eoghan."

He made a strangled sound and an expression of pain crossed his face and vanished.

"Then you must ask old Aodhfin. He is your foster-kin. It was he who sent you on this journey."

"Do you say that he meant for us to meet?"

Eoghan shrugged. "I do not know. Only that the child pulled us both to the same place at once. Only that watching the two of you sleeping by the fire, I felt . . . I do not know . . ." He crushed her hand between his, lifted it to the side of his face. He turned the piercing blue of his eyes on her.

"Do you remember me, Aislinn ni Sorar?"

This was not what she had expected him to say. She drew her hand away, regarded him in bafflement.

"Remember you? Have we met before?"

He stood abruptly, seemed angry.

"Ask Aodhfin when you see him. I will be departing on the morrow. You are welcome here among my people. They would be honored if you wintered with them here."

"Departing?" she asked. But she said it to his back, which was already moving away.

Aislinn stepped from the bright morning light into the darkness of the smithy. Eoghan had sent a message for her to meet him here this morning. For a moment, she could see only red sparks rising toward the ceiling. She paused to let her eyes adjust.

On the wall behind Aislinn, iron wagon rims hung in profusion. Horse bridles covered with delicate chasework hung next to a board of delicate women's jewelry. One shelf boasted silver and gold cups and bowls intricately woven with hounds and hinds. Aislinn smiled at the intricate beauty. O'Domnhnaill's smith was one of those considered by the Gaels to be a true artist, a craftsman touched by the gods. She bowed to the blacksmith and made the ritual introduction.

"Son of Gobniu," she shouted above the ringing hammer and the whoosh of the bellows, "I beg permission to enter your forge."

The blacksmith stopped hammering and signaled his bellows boy to cease. The smith regarded Aislinn, wiping the back of his hand across his forehead. His face and arms were black with the soot of the smith, his forearms puckered where they had repeatedly been burned and healed.

Aislinn waited in respectful silence for his response.

He smiled suddenly, his teeth appearing as a surprise below his bushy black moustache.

"The daughter of Sorar is welcome in my smithy and blesses this dwelling with her presence."

He moved to a rack of pegs behind his head. Dozens of bracelets, armlets, and torques gleamed in tones of silver and gold. He removed from the rack an arm bracelet with three flat spirals. The work was delicate, intricate, the three spirals chasing into and out of each other with no beginning or end. He stood before Aislinn and she could feel the reflected heat still lingering on his forge apron. He held the bracelet forward.

"I knew your father, priestess, may the gods be good to him and to your mother. I served him for many a year before I came to the crannog of O'Domnhnaill." His eyes seemed infinitely sad in their regard for her. Aislinn felt again what she had felt last night—the strange sense that everyone here knew something that she did not.

"Did all here know my parents then?"

"All of us who are of an age to remember. We who give allegiance to O'Domnhnaill are of the tribe of the Deisi, as were your parents."

"Tell me of them, smith. I remember little."

"Your mother was beautiful. Surely you know well how she loved you, priestess. Your father was the best horseman among us. He could ride for days and never tire. He was a storyteller and could laugh with even the least of us. He was a good chief." The smith held the armlet forward.

"It would do me honor if the daughter of Sorar would wear my finest work."

Aislinn accepted the bracelet, pushed it high up onto her upper arm, inclined her head graciously.

"I am the one who is honored," she replied. "But speak to me of what you mean when you say how well my mother loved me. I was very small."

A shadow crossed the doorway behind the forge. The smith grew silent. He pointed to the yard behind the smithy.

"He awaits you there in the yard with his horse," he said. He went back to his hammering, signaling to the young boy who held the bellows.

Aislinn walked into the sunlight of the yard behind the forge. The ringing sound of the hammer on iron seemed far away, musical. In the space between the wall of the forge and the encircling wall of the crannog Eoghan Mac Aidan was inspecting Becan's bridle and saddle. He was dressed in his riding cloak, the little harp strapped to Becan.

"Poet, where are you going?"

"I have king's business that I must be about."

Aislinn's anger spoke.

"King's business? You are as much a wandering poet as I am a wandering druid. You do no business for the king. Tell me, fili, who has cast you into exile?"

He whirled back toward Becan then, tightened the saddle girth until the horse sidled away, snorting in protest.

"I have cast myself into exile."

Aislinn stepped close behind him.

"Speak to me, poet. I cannot hear your words from the back of your head."

He turned back angry, then surprised to find her so close to him. He bent his head forward so that his forehead nearly touched hers, whispered.

"I said that I have cast myself into exile."

"Then cease your wandering," she whispered. "Put aside your fear and choose a home." She wondered if she spoke more to herself than to him. The thought surprised her. She tipped her head back, looked wide into his eyes. "We are much alike, are we not, Eoghan, both of us exiles?"

His arms came around her suddenly. This was not the kiss of the forest with its deep sadness. This was deep, hungry, one kiss after another, punctuated by their small moans and sighs. His hands moved down her back, crushed her to him in a viselike grip.

From somewhere behind them, the ringing of the hammers ceased. Eoghan pulled away.

"If you knew me, you would not stay my going, priestess." His voice was anguished, breathless.

"Do you fear what you desire, fili?"

"Sometimes we are wise to fear what we desire."

She pressed her body against his, rested her head against his chest. He lifted one of her hands, entwined it with his. He brought the slender hand to his lips, rested it there. She whispered to him.

"I am a green girl, poet, but I know not to fear this desire. This desire is our beginning. I do know you, Eoghan Mac Aidan. You are the bearer of fire."

He lifted her chin with his hand, regarded her for a moment with great sadness.

"You speak of beginnings, priestess, but you have not followed their long road as I have. The sweetest of beginnings can lead to sorrow's end. Even a child knows what can come of fire."

He released her gently, then mounted Becan and turned away from her. From the far side of the courtyard Sheary rose up and trotted to his master's side.

"Where will you go?" she called after him.

"Anywhere that you are not," he answered.

7

"An, do, tri!" The laughing group of children spun past Aislinn, their breath making clouds of frost on the chill morning air. At the center of the group of heads she could see the copper streams of Corra ni Brith's hair. Corra saw her at the last moment and separated from the group. She ran to Aislinn and hugged her hard around the waist.

"Good morning, máthair!"

Aislinn laughed and closed her arms around the little girl. She kissed the top of her head, then bent and planted kisses on both cheeks. Corra had taken to calling Aislinn mother short days after they arrived at the crannog and Aislinn relished the sound of the word, felt giddy in its sweetness.

"We are having such fun! We play at run-and-catch."

"Go then! Run along. I go to the bakehouse."

Aislinn and Corra had been at the crannog of O'Domnhnaill just a fortnight, but already Aislinn knew that they would stay here forever if they could. Aislinn had come to love the life of the little village. She performed her daily priestly duties with a sense of joy. When she blessed the waters of the lake or the iron of the blacksmith, she found herself thinking, "Our water, our iron."

She dreaded the journey that lay ahead of her, the journey to the samhain feis at the hill of Tara, but she had decided that she must begin it soon. There would be no long wintering out on the crannog of O'Domnhnaill, no safe cocoon against the cold or the dark wings of Banbh. Aodhfin knew her story; he must tell it to her. Yet, each time Aislinn saw Corra's laughing face, each time she felt surrounded by the warmth of the village women, she put off the journey for another day.

The only trouble in her feeling of contentment arose when she thought of Mac Aidan. He had ridden out on that day two weeks ago. Since then, he had not returned, had sent no word. Aislinn glanced at the causeway to the crannog for the first of what would be a hundred times that day, expecting somehow to see his cloaked form astride Becan, waiting for her. The causeway was empty, the field beyond filled with grazing cattle.

She sighed and stepped back into the thatched circular lodge she had been given. She gathered the plaid cloak of the Deisi that Gobinet had given her and made her way to the bakehouse.

The village was circular, with the baking house and food storage areas at the center of the circle near the rectangular feasting hall of the chief. As Aislinn passed the small circular dwellings with their thatched conical roofs, villagers called out to her.

"Good morning, priestess!"

"Health to you, daughter of Sorar!"

From across the causeway, women came into the village with their baking bowls. Aislinn had learned that the hundred people Eoghan had assigned to the crannog did not all live on the man-made island. Many dwellings surrounded the fields at the edge of the lake as did fields for farming and cattle. The crannog was the central meeting place, the safety in time of danger.

Aislinn smiled. She understood the feeling of safety for she too felt surrounded and protected here. She waved to a woman perched under the thatched roof of a platform raised a few feet above the ground.

"Is Gobinet within?" Aislinn called, waving toward the bakehouse.

"There or in the bathhouse," the woman called back. She poured some grain from a storage jar into a large bowl and clambered down from the platform. "Come, we will go in together."

Aislinn stood for a moment in the doorway to allow her eyes to adjust to the darkness. At the center of the bakehouse was a huge spit where a deer roasted slowly over an open fire. Pits lined with stones stood at either end of the fire circle. When the stones were warmed, fish and fowl could be roasted in the pits. Small baking ovens for bread and cakes lined one wall. Gobinet was nowhere to be seen.

Aislinn crossed the room and exited by the far door. From the circular hut nearby she could hear the splashing of water and the laughter of women. She opened the door and stepped inside. Gobinet stood in a huge cauldron, her body dripping with fresh water. She was lathered in soap, so that even her hair seemed white.

"Who comes in with the cold?" she called.

"I was thoughtless," Aislinn replied. "You have my apologies, honored mother."

Gobinet laughed as the women poured pot after pot of hot water down her hair and over her body.

" 'Twas a passing wind only, daughter, and I am warm now as you can see."

Gobinet stepped from the cauldron and the women wrapped her in a soft woolen cloak. She sat before the fire where several cauldrons of water were heating and still more bathing cloaks were laid in warm readiness.

Aislinn lifted Gobinet's comb and drew it gently through the long, thick hair.

"Have you bathed yet, daughter?"

"I slept long, but I will bathe after the baking. I still cannot accustom myself to having warm water each week.

I had forgotten in my wanderings how good it felt to be warm and clean. At Tara, we also bathed often."

"Why are you looking for me?"

"Your foster-son does not return."

"He does not. Does this trouble you, daughter?"

"I believe he remains away because I am here. Is this so?"

The room grew silent. Gobinet turned and regarded Aislinn.

"Nay, priestess. You have committed no offense to him or among us. We honor you for yourself and for your family."

"Will you speak to me of my family then?"

Gobinet sighed. "What has the druid Aodhfin told you?"

"He has told me that my parents were honored members of the tribe of the Deisi, that they died in battle leaving me in his care."

"That is so. I can tell you no more than that. You know the law. It is the duty and the privilege of the foster-parents to bring up the children in their care. What Aodhfin has told you is what he wished you to know."

"What he told me satisfied me well until I met your foster-son, until I came here among you. Now I feel that there is more that I must learn, that some silence surrounds me here. Please, Gobinet."

The older woman sighed, looked down at her hands, looked up at Aislinn. Just then the door burst open. Corra rushed in, rosy-cheeked and out of breath.

"Máthair," she called, running to Aislinn. "I looked for you in the bakehouse. The children ask for your stories. Will you come and tell us one?"

Aislinn looked quietly at Gobinet.

"Go," the older woman said. "I welcome this intrusion, daughter. My heart wishes to speak with you but your druii wisdom is also women's wisdom. Time gathers itself into the proper moment. What harm will I do if I speak when the moment is not right?"

Aislinn took Corra's hand in her own.

"Come then. Gather the children in the garden of Gobinet."

"Tell us of Medb the warrior queen!"

"Nay, we want a tale of the Fomorian monsters. Balor of the One Eye."

"Monsters! No monsters. Tell us of Fionn!"

"Fionn, yes, Fionn. Tell us of Fionn, priestess."

"Fionn it is, then," Aislinn said laughingly, gazing at the circle of upturned faces. "I myself have seen Fionn when he visited the Ard-Ri Cormac Mac Art at the hill of Tara."

A gasp went up from the assembly of children.

Fionn Mac Cumhail was the chief of the Fianna, the standing army of Ireland. His deeds were legend, his prowess as a hunter and warrior fabled. Aislinn thought quietly for a moment to select just one of the many stories that were told of him at the firesides of Eire.

"Who knows what Fionn does when he seeks wisdom?"

"Everyone knows that," said a freckle-faced boy of six years. "He sucks his thumb."

"Very wise," said Aislinn. "But who knows why he sucks his thumb?"

The children glanced at each other, remained silent.

"Long ago and longer," Aislinn began, "when Fionn was just a young boy, there lived on the banks of the Boann a wizard named Finegas."

The children drew closer, their breath suspended, their eyes wide.

"Now Finegas was wise, but he wished to know more, to know the secrets at the center of the world. He had chosen his spot by the river Boann carefully, for beneath the clear waters of the Boann there swam a magical fish— the salmon of knowledge. Each day Finegas sat beside the Boann with his spear in hand watching for the salmon of knowledge to pass by. For it was said that whoever ate of the salmon would know the secrets at the heart of the world.

"At last the day came when the salmon swam by and Finegas threw his spear with all his might. When he drew it out, the salmon, with colors like a rainbow, gleamed from the end of his spear. Finegas immediately set up his spit and set the salmon up for roasting.

"Now as he was watching the salmon cook, a young man of golden hair and great beauty came into the clearing beside the Boann."

"Fionn," whispered the children. "Fionn."

"Fionn indeed. 'Wise Finegas,' he said, 'I have traveled far to seek your knowledge. Will you teach me all that you know?'

" 'Humph,' said Finegas. 'I will teach you only if you promise to take on the most menial tasks.'

" 'I will,' said Fionn. 'Set me now to any task and I will complete it.'

" 'Very well, you may cook this fish. There may be no burn on its skin and no blister. And look that you do not eat it, not any of its flesh! Do you understand?'

" 'I do,' said Fionn, and he set about to watch the fish until it was perfect, being careful that it should not burn. When the fish had roasted a long time, a blister arose on its skin.

" 'What shall I do?' Fionn wondered. 'I have promised my teacher that I will cook his fish to perfection.'

"So he took his own thumb and pressed the blister down against the skin of the fish. Of course his skin was burned and he immediately sucked his thumb to quell the burn. What happened then was beyond understanding. Fionn saw the world as if in a bowl of water, round and clear with all the creatures in it. And he understood the thoughts of the fish and birds, of the deer and hounds and the thoughts of the humans.

"When the fish was perfect, Fionn took it to Finegas.

" 'Have you eaten of the fish?' asked Finegas.

" 'Nay, but I have pressed a blister down and sucked

my thumb and have seen the world most strangely,' said Fionn.

"Finegas nodded, disappointed.

" 'Then you have tasted the salmon of knowledge. Now when you have a question in your life, you must suck your thumb and the answer will come to you.'

"And that is why Fionn sucks his thumb."

The children gathered around her, clamoring.

"Tell us another. Please, priestess, another."

But Aislinn had no time to reply, for the cry came from the guardhouse at the end of the causeway.

"Strangers come to the crannog!"

The children leaped away, running to this new diversion. Aislinn ran behind, her heart filled with thoughts of Eoghan.

Instead, she saw the guards surrounding a young woman. The girl was leading a huge white bull by a leash. Aislinn pressed through the crowd and walked down the causeway until she could hear what the child was saying.

"I must present this gift to the cailleach, the living goddess," the girl was pleading with the guards. "Please call her for me, for my tribe has sent me, who is not yet woman, with this gift for She-Who-Is-Protector-of-Children."

Far behind the girl, near the tree line, Aislinn saw four men in warrior plaid, who had obviously accompanied the girl on her journey, but who were considered unworthy to present the gift.

The guards looked first at each other, then at Aislinn, now standing between them.

"There is no cailleach among us, child. We are the tribe of O'Domhnaill. You have been misled," the older of the two guards offered gently.

"But you are welcome to stay until you do become a woman," said the younger guard, smirking at the beautiful young girl.

She blushed but stood her ground. "This is the white bull, the perfect sacrificial offering. My tribe has sent me to bring it to the one who spirits the children from harm, the one whose magic has slain the evil Mac Bran. It is our gift of thanks. I search for the high priestess, Aislinn."

The guards turned in Aislinn's direction.

She smiled gently at the child. "I am she whom you seek. I am the druidess Aislinn. But I do not know of this goddess."

The child's face shone and she stepped forward dragging on the halter of the bull. "You are the cailleach, for that is what the poet of the High King sings of you. He says that your powers come from the triune goddess and that her light shines forth from you and makes you strong. It is how you are known in all of the villages."

She paused, mindful of the guards, and blushed again. She stepped closer to Aislinn and spoke softly. "In our village, our mothers say that they no longer need fear for themselves or their daughters and our fathers say that it took the druidess to open their eyes to the true state of their chieftain."

Aislinn shook her head and smiled. "I am not these things that you say, but a woman who loves a child."

But inside she felt a lifting of her spirits at the child's words. So it was the poet of the Ard-Ri who was saying these things of her. Surely Eoghan too must feel their connection, to create a poem of such praise.

"You must call your escort and we must bring this bull within the walls of our crannog. Tonight we will sacrifice and feast and share goodwill between our tribes." She took the halter of the bull from the child and watched her race toward the tree line. Even as she turned to lead the bull to the hall of the chieftain, she could hear the warriors murmuring behind her. The tale would be all over the village by nightfall.

Outside the feasting hall of O'Domnhnaill, a roaring bonfire blazed. The white bull was tethered beside the chieftain stone of O'Domnhnaill, a huge monolith bearing

elaborate carvings of bulls and stags interspersed with spiraling designs. The firelight cast the designs into light and
shadow while the surrounding darkness made the huge
stone appear to thrust even farther heavenward. The eyes
of the white bull glowed red in the firelight.

Aislinn stepped into the circle of firelight and a gasp
went up from the crowd. She was dressed all in white,
from the long white silken gown, a gift of Gobinet, that
clung to her slender form to her white druii cloak with its
elaborate gold embroidery, repaired and made shining
white by the women of O'Domnhnaill.

She raised her arms into the light and the fire played
on the underside of the golden bowl she was holding. A
staggering array of bracelets cascaded down her arms—
silver, gold, bronze, many inlaid with beautiful stones and
precious jewels. Some were circlets, some spirals, some
cuffs that hugged her wrists. All but the armlet of the
blacksmith were gifts of the women of the tribe, who
could be heard whispering of the treasures in the circle
beyond the light.

Aislinn's hair was plaited in twenty or more black
braids, wound through with ribbons of white and silver.
Balls of silver clinked at the ends of each braid. Bells had
been sown to the bottom of her cloak throughout the afternoon, and each movement sent a wave of music across
the crowd.

Aislinn turned around and around in the circle of light
and a hush fell over the crowd.

From the belt of her dress, she took a druii wand, cut
from a branch of a rowan tree. She walked forward to the
bull, tapped him hard between the horns three times, then
turned to the crowd. She raised the wand and the bowl
and hit the rowan stick against the bowl three times.

"O you gods! We are the creatures of Tir inna m Beo,
the Land of the Living. Will you hear our speeches and
our songs? Dagda, the Good, father of gods, giver and
taker of life, of you we ask that we may live and prosper
here among our tribes. We ask that our chieftain be gifted

with Truth, Mercy, and the Wisdom of Silence. Lugh of the Long Arm, son of Dagda, we ask that our warriors be strong and their spears fly straight. We ask that our iron-workers be gifted and their metal be without flaw. Dian Cecht, we ask that our healers dwell in the mind and body of the sick. You, Ogma the honey-mouthed, we ask for the gift of story. We ask that our stories make us wise. Protect for us your fili Eoghan Mac Aidan."

Here, a little stir went through the crowd.

Again, Aislinn tapped three times on the golden bowl with the wand of rowan. "You, the triune goddess, Brighid, Anu, Dana, bring to our women fertility. Watch over them in childbirth, make strong the issue of their wombs. Bring plenty to our hearths and homes. Brighid, goddess of poetry, give to our women the gifts of speech and song."

Now, Corra ni Brith and Gobinet stepped forward to serve as Aislinn's honored attendants in the absence of other druids. Corra took the wand and held it across her heart and Gobinet lifted Aislinn's cloak from her shoulders. From the braided golden belt at her waist, Aislinn withdrew her dagger and held it in the light so that the flames cast beams from its golden hilt. Next, they removed the silken dress. The women of the tribe had spent hours that afternoon painting Aislinn's body with blue dye, so that the spirals and braids that linked this life to the next would be evident when Aislinn performed the sacred ceremony.

She stepped to the bull and with a single fluid motion slit his throat, holding the golden bowl beneath the out-rush of blood to catch as much of it as she could. The bull staggered first to his knees and then down into the dust. As he did so, Aislinn circled him three times, crying aloud, "We thank the spirit of this great one for his sac-rifice. We honor his bones; his blood will bring us strength and plenty."

When the bowl was full she turned again to the crowd. Her blue painted body was splashed with blood and her arms were steeped in blood to the elbows. She stepped again into the light.

"O you gods! We are the flesh and blood of Eire, of this the Tir inna m Beo. Hear our prayers we ask you. We give you our lives, our courage, and our care of the holy land of Eire."

She turned the complete circle of the people and intoned the most ancient of Celtic vows.

"We will keep faith unless the sky fall and crush us or the earth open and swallow us or the sea rise and overwhelm us."

Aislinn tipped the bowl back and drank, then handed it to O'Domnhnaill, who drank as the father and protector of his tribe. He handed the bowl back to Aislinn, who dipped her hands in the blood and sprinkled it repeatedly over the crowd. In the circle beyond the fire she could see all hands raising toward the blood in the hopes that some of the holy drops would spill on them.

She took the bowl and walked to the stone of O'Domnhnaill. She poured blood onto the ground and knelt, rubbing the blood together with the dirt, then standing with her hands covered with the paste. This she rubbed against the guardian stone of the tribe.

"Thus do we unite with the gods, the gods with us, and all with the holy land of Eire."

A wild shout went up from the crowd and the warriors designated to butcher the bull and prepare it for the feast came forward to claim the body. Couples began to move away for the ritual lovemaking that might bring a child, particularly to those who had been blessed by the blood.

Later, when the beast was ready, the entire tribe would gather for a feast of eating, drinking, singing, and telling tales, but for now Gobinet and Corra approached Aislinn with a plain brown earthen-colored cloak and led her away for a ritual bath. Aislinn put her arm around Corra and let her head sag for a moment on Gobinet's shoulder.

"This was good," said Gobinet, her arm circling Aislinn. "I could feel the power of the Truth."

"I am not in truth the voice for the goddess," Aislinn protested, but Gobinet shushed her.

"Do not be so sure. My foster-son has written a legend for you, a legend which will protect you on your journey. But I am beginning to believe that the gods are writing for both of you."

"It is a journey unfolding. Only pray, honored mother, that the gods do not write us too much sorrow."

"I do pray it," whispered Gobinet. "For my son. For all of you."

8

"You must leave the child Corra ni Brith with me!"

Gobinet paused in the task of wrapping Aislinn's ornamental jewelry in soft linens and stared intently at the younger woman.

Aislinn shook her head vehemently.

"I cannot, honored mother. I have promised her that I would not abandon her." She continued folding her cloak, tucking the golden embroidery beneath the folds of linen to protect it. The tribe's seamstresses had repaired and rewoven it so that the cloak gleamed white again and the embroidery shone with radiance. Aislinn wedged the cloak at the bottom of the leather carrying bag.

"You will not abandon her. I will care for her as my own child. You may return for her when your journey is done. You must keep her safe, daughter. You journey into danger; my son has told me of the dark one, Banbh, who pursues you. We of the tribe of the Deisi know him well. Will you expose your child with you? This is not what your mother did!"

"Will you speak to me now of my mother? I have been with your tribe for almost one full turning of the moon. I have asked you and others of the Deisi to tell me of my parents, of their death. All have avoided me, with great kindness, with great show of respect for the law. Am I to find, on the day of my departure, that you have kept secrets from me which could endanger me?"

"I do not know your whole story, daughter, only those parts of it which relate"—here Gobinet flushed and shook her head—"which have been related to me by my foster-son. I do know that your mother sacrificed herself for your safety. I know too that you are journeying into danger. There is a kind of safety in knowing nothing. This is how your tutor Aodhfin protected you throughout your childhood. I will not question his wisdom now for I have lived long enough to know that knowledge and truth often require great sacrifices. Will you ask those also of your foster-child?"

Aislinn sighed. "She who speaks wisdom to me tells me that you are right, but my heart does not wish to be separated from the child. And I fear she will not forgive me."

"I will explain to her if you wish," Gobinet offered, but Aislinn shook her head and stood.

"No, I must do this duty myself."

They sat together on the small stone bench in Gobinet's ornamental garden. Though the autumn day was cool, the sun and the combination of the protecting walls made the garden warm and quiet.

For a long time Corra ni Brith was content to sit holding Aislinn's hand, enjoying the quiet moments with the priestess. Finally, Aislinn lifted Corra's little hand to her lips, kissing it gently.

"You are leaving me, aren't you?" the child asked, tipping her face up to regard Aislinn.

Aislinn nodded.

"I am going to the samhain feis at Tara Hill. Gobinet has argued that you will be safer here with her and with the tribe of O'Domnhnaill and I agree with her wisdom."

"I do not care about being safe. I want to be with you. Remember when Mac Bran came after us and I brought out the tapers to light his hair. If we are not safe I will do that again for you. I want to go with you, máthair."

Aislinn stood and began to pace the garden.

"I go into more danger than we faced with Mac Bran, child. He was a mean and stupid enemy. My adversary is of the type of evil that is mixed with cunning. He would not hesitate to harm you if he thought that he would hurt me by doing so."

"Then why must you go there at all? Stay here with me."

Again Aislinn smiled.

"If you knew how many times I have wished for just that. To stay here among the tribe of the Deisi, to be happy in the dailiness of their lives. But I cannot stay. It is the truth which beckons me to Tara Hill. I must know the truth about my máthair and my athair."

Aislinn sat beside Corra again, looked directly into her eyes.

"You know the truth of what happened to your máthair and athair and it is a terrible truth. But what if you did not know?"

"But I fear that you will not return to me."

"I will return within a fortnight's time."

"There is something else that my heart fears, máthair."

Aislinn folded her arms around Corra, rested her head upon the copper hair of the little girl.

"What is that, love?"

"I fear that your truth may also be terrible."

Aislinn stood at the entrance to the causeway in the traveling cloak of the Deisi that Gobinet had given her. Already the two soldiers that O'Domnhaill had assigned to escort her were mounted and holding her horse between them at the water's edge near the far end of the causeway.

Behind her O'Domnhaill, Gobinet, and assembled

members of the tribe were gathered to see her on her journey. Corra ni Brith stood at Gobinet's side, her arms wrapped around the older woman, her head buried against Gobinet's side in soft weeping.

O'Domhnaill spoke first.

"Ride in safety, honored priestess. May the gods protect you. May the truth you seek not prove to be too heavy a burden. Remember always to temper the truth with mercy."

Here, he looked significantly at Gobinet, as if the speech had been prearranged, but Gobinet shook her head as if his words were not enough.

"Believe in my foster-son, Eoghan Mac Aidan," she said in a pleading tone. A murmur of assent rose from the assembled crowd. A look passed between Gobinet and O'Domhnaill. She said nothing more.

"I am most grateful for your kind hospitality," Aislinn said after an uncomfortable moment of silence. "I call down upon your crannog the blessings of all the gods and the protection of the people of the sidhe. Here you have given me a home of the heart."

She walked over to Corra ni Brith and knelt.

"I love you, Corra. I promise that I will return for you. Be safe here with Gobinet and do not doubt my return to you."

But Corra ni Brith kept her head turned into Gobinet's side. She would not look at Aislinn or speak.

The rain drizzled down along the trees, making the trunks appear ebony and weighting the few remaining leaves so that they fell to the forest floor. Overhead, two crows called to each other. One alighted from a tree, spreading its wings wide as it circled above the forest floor. Aislinn saw one of her escorts make the sign against evil while the other searched the surrounding forest for signs of movement.

Aislinn smiled to herself. It was bad luck to escort the

cailleach, the local goddess. She stared up at the circling crow and shook her head. This was not Badb, the carrion crow, goddess of battle, though she knew the soldiers thought so. This was a simple crow, wheeling about in the rain. Still, she understood their fear. The thought of a battle or of the crows feeding on their remains seemed plausible in the wet, gloomy woods.

She lifted a fold of her cloak over her hair, creating a hood, and plodded on silently between the two men, thinking of Corra, her face turned away with weeping. Already, Aislinn missed her; the longing to turn back, to ride away from danger and back to the child, was overwhelming. But to do that would be to also ride away from truth. She had to know! Who was she after all? No longer just the foster-daughter of Aodhfin the Wise. There was more, much more. And she was no longer a child, too young or too vulnerable to know. And what was Eoghan to her past? For surely he was the man to bring fire, the man of her tutor's riddle. She missed him with a longing that was almost visceral.

"I love him." She whispered it aloud, tasted it, and knew that it was true.

She repeated Aodhfin's riddle aloud. *"From the place of darkness will come a child to light your journey. To the place of fire will come a man bearing fire for the body and the mind. Between darkness and light, you are the still point."*

"So I have begun the third part of my journey. I move between the darkness and the light. But how will I recognize which I am going toward? Which I am turning from?"

Aislinn squared her shoulders, settled herself more deeply into the saddle. The day wore on into afternoon. The rain never ceased and darkness pressed against the trunks of the trees and threatened even the patches of gray sky above them.

Once, far away to south, there was the distant sound of a thrashing boar followed by a strange howling. The warriors drew their daggers instantly, stared from side to side. No further sound came.

"Was it a wolf?" one asked the other.

"Perhaps. I am not sure. The sound moves strangely when the forest is wet and shaking off its leaves."

They sat for a while listening, then sheathed their daggers. The little party moved on.

Toward late afternoon, one of the warriors stopped his horse. He turned, speaking over Aislinn's head to his companion.

"We will no longer have enough light to travel safely. We must make camp."

"Done," said the second warrior, swinging down from his horse and approaching Aislinn to help her dismount.

Suddenly, she heard the other warrior curse under his breath. Ahead of them on the path a horse and rider blocked their way. The huge black steed gleamed rain-wet and his master, cloaked and hooded, turned a circle of whitened face in their direction. Beside him a huge wet wolfhound breathed steam into the chill air. Aislinn's guards drew their daggers, but she gave a glad cry and urged her mount to full gallop toward the steaming breath of Becan and the watchful eyes of Eoghan Mac Aidan.

"It was you that we heard. I am so glad you have come!"

Mac Aidan regarded her solemnly. "I do my duty. Your safety rests with me as it has since"—here he paused—"since I followed Mac Bran to the druii shrine."

Aislinn felt rebuffed.

"I am no more than your duty, then?"

Mac Aidan said nothing, raised his hand to the guards, who had reached them.

"You may return to the crannog. I will guide Aislinn ni Sorar to the feis at Tara Hill."

Aislinn's escorts were giddy with relief. They clasped arms with Mac Aidan, laughed aloud as they mounted and rode back the way they had come.

"Am I so terrible a charge that their first smiles are on leaving me?" Aislinn asked.

"They sense the shape of things that form around you and they are afraid. It is no wonder they wish to be gone."

"And is that how you also feel, Mac Aidan?"

He turned to her then, regarding her quietly. He brought Becan next to her and reached out his hand, cupping it between her chin and her hair.

Aislinn leaned her head against his hand, closed her eyes. The crows silenced in the trees overhead. The only sounds were the steady dripping of water from the trees and the blowing breath of the horses.

Mac Aidan removed his hand and turned Becan's head. "There are caves near here where we can be dry. If we are to reach them by darkness, we must begin." He muttered something then and Aislinn strained forward to hear him.

"Or end. For in this journey, the beginning and the end may come as one."

Far above them a crow, larger than the others, its wings almost blue in their blackness, its eyes bright, lifted away from the trees, circled, and flew eastward.

The cave was dry but damp. While Eoghan and Sheary stalked food, Aislinn made a bright warm fire and laid her cloak to dry against the stones. She was seated close to the fire, untangling her hair with a silver comb when he returned.

He stood for a moment in the cave entrance, watching her, then came forward and dumped the carcasses of two rabbits near the fire.

"We will have no pine boughs to sleep on this night, priestess. The forest is too wet for even the lowest branches to be dry."

"No matter. Tomorrow we will reach the great bruidhean on the Slighe Assail. There we can bathe and feast, sleep on linen and wolf skins."

"Nay, there will be no bruidhean on this journey."

"I may not have traveled for as many years or as widely as you have traveled, poet, but even I know that there are five great roads which lead to Tara. Tomorrow we will reach the Slighe Assail which goes from Tara to the west of Meath. There are many bruidhean on that road, poet. True, now that the samhain feis is near, it will be filled with travelers who will welcome the bounty of the bruighaid and his inn and wish to sleep safe in his sleeping chambers, but think you that a good bruighaid will not make room for a poet of the king and a priestess?"

Mac Aidan seemed amused by her tirade. He chuckled to himself as he skinned and skewered the rabbits, setting them to roast above the fire. Occasionally, he shook his head, as if he carried on some internal conversation. At last he spoke to her.

"Do you believe that you ride into danger, priestess?"

"I know that I ride toward Tara and that Banbh is at Tara. Why do you ask me this?"

"The most prudent way to deal with danger is to avoid it. You are correct when you say that all of Eire travels toward Tara and the great samhain feis. If you stay at the crossroads lodgings, feast at their tables, many travelers will see you. Your arrival will be known before you. You give your enemies time to plan. Do you see the logic of this?" He spoke as one would to a student.

The hot blood of embarrassment rose in Aislinn's cheeks.

"So we must spend these days alone?"

Mac Aidan mistook her color for a blush.

"You need not fear me, priestess." He gave her a mocking look. "I would never force my attentions upon you as you forced yours upon me that first day in the forest."

Aislinn's color rose still higher. She felt foolish, young, unsure of what to say or how to behave with this man of all others. She willed herself to look directly at his eyes.

"I did not think my attentions so unwanted."

All the amusement left his face. His eyes locked with hers for a long time.

"Not unwanted, priestess," he said at last. "Just untimely."

They sat in silence, watching the rabbits cook, the only sound the spitting of the hot grease on the coals. When the rabbits were ready, Eoghan speared portions with his dagger and ate from the tip. Aislinn waited quietly. As a druidess, she was accustomed to being served the best portion at every tuath she visited, but Eoghan did nothing. At last she took her own dagger, speared a succulent portion, and ate in silence.

He finished long before she did, wrapped himself in his cloak, spoke to her curtly.

"You will need your sleep, priestess. Two days hard riding lay before us."

He stretched out on the floor and was silent. Sheary came to his left side and stretched out against him.

Aislinn finished her rabbit slowly and deliberately. She lifted her cloak from the rock by the fire and wrapped it around herself. At first it felt warm and comfortable, but when the fire warmth wore off, Aislinn could feel its dampness against her skin. She lay down on the hard floor of the cave and concentrated on trying to sleep, but the damp night, the cold stone, and the wet cloak took their toll. She began to shiver despite herself. She edged closer to the fire, then closer.

Eoghan sat up with a sigh. He spread his cloak on the floor beside him.

"Here," he said. "Come to me."

"Why?"

"We will sleep wrapped together in our cloaks. The heat of our bodies will keep us warm."

She regarded him suspiciously, until he laughed aloud.

"Soldiers do this, priestess. It is either this or spend a wakeful night and a miserable day on horseback tomorrow."

She sat beside him, still wrapped in her cloak. He lifted

the cloak from her shoulders, lay down on his back. He stretched out his arm.

"Come."

She lay down stiffly, placing her head gingerly in the space between his shoulder and his arm. He covered them both with his cloak. She could feel the warmth of his chest, could hear his heartbeat beneath her ear. She lay silent and stiff for a time, but at last her breasts relaxed against the side of his warm body and his steady heartbeat lulled her into a gentle sleep.

She did not know that he lay awake for a long time staring into the darkness of the cave. And she was deep in sleep when his hand came up and gently stroked the fire-warmed length of her midnight hair.

Morning dawned cool but sunny. Outside the cave two squirrels chattered at each other as they chased up and down the side of a tree. Birdsong filled the air.

Aislinn awoke and remembered where she was. She bolted upright. Mac Aidan lay awake, his left arm beneath his head. He smiled lazily at her where she sat next to him.

"You slept well. Were you warm?"

"I was. I give you thanks. May we leave?"

He came to his feet in a single fluid motion, bringing their cloaks up with him, tossing hers at her.

"We may."

The warm autumn sun eased the journey and Aislinn's spirits began to lift. Late in the morning, Eoghan stopped his horse and moved away silently into the forest, his spear in hand. He returned with the carcass of a small deer slung over his shoulders.

"We will feast tonight, priestess."

Aislinn regarded his booty with surprise.

"How swiftly you moved away and found this prize. Did I not know you I would believe that you are Fionn Mac Cumhail, and that you can hear and see as the beasts of the forest do."

"Nay, Áislinn. Fionn is the forest, I am the shadow in it. There is the difference."

"You speak of the legendary Fionn as if you know him."

"Do I?"

He threw the deer across Becan's flanks, then tied its legs together below the horse's belly. He mounted in a single movement. Something about the hunting had made him jovial and he hummed a little snatch of song.

Behind him Aislinn took it up in her clear, sweet voice. He turned back to her and smiled gently. The rest of the day's journey passed in a mix of songs and sweet silences.

Toward nightfall Eoghan built a bothy, a rough hut of pine boughs and branches in the forest at the edge of a wide field. Aislinn tethered and groomed the horses and arranged the little dwelling, while Eoghan prepared the deer and roasted the haunch of venison. They ate their meal after darkness fell, then sat in the shelter of the bothy before the warmth of the fire. Thousands of stars were visible in the sky above the wide field. Mac Aidan drew out his harp and played the geantraighe, the laughing music of Eire.

Afterward, they sat for a long time in companionable silence. Aislinn removed a comb from her traveling bag and began to pull through her tangled black hair. Eoghan watched her, then took the comb from her.

"Let me do this for you."

Aislinn sat before him cross-legged on the ground and he drew the comb gently through her hair again and again until it was tame and shone in the reflected firelight. She felt him lift the hair with his hands, hold it aloft, and let it spill down his arms. She shivered with delight, turned to face him.

Softly he lowered his lips to hers, took her hands in his, kissed her gently. She knelt before him. His hands came up against her sides, pushing gently on the soft flesh of her breasts. Suddenly his arms closed around her and she was lying beside him on the pine-covered floor of the bothy.

He kissed her again, unfastened her cloak, lowered the shoulder of her gown, began to move his lips across the yielding top flesh of her breasts.

"Mo ghra," she whispered. "Beloved."

It was as if her words jolted him awake from some trance.

"No! What do I do? My apology, priestess."

Aislinn sat up confused.

"What have we done? How have we offended any that you must apologize?" Her face took on a questioning look.

"You have said that there is no other woman who has claims upon you. I claim no other man."

"Of all women, only you have claims upon me, priestess, but they are not the claims of the marriage bed."

She shook her head impatiently.

"Speak without the riddles of poetry, fili. What claims do I have upon you? We spoke at the crannog of O'Domhnaill about desire. I feel it for you. I sense that you feel it for me. I am a green girl and untried, but not so green that I cannot sense what moves between us. Tell me now! Is there some shame in this that we have begun?"

"In the body there is no shame, love. But there is a shame in the spirit that dwells inside my body, a shame that makes me unworthy of the love you offer."

"Tell me that I may choose."

Eoghan gestured toward the night sky.

"Do you see these stars?"

Aislinn looked up at the thousands of stars, at their clear pinpoint light. She turned back to Eoghan impatiently.

"What of these?"

"Does each star stand alone in the firmament?"

This was druii teaching and Aislin knew the answer.

"Each star stands alone in the firmament but the stars work also in harmony. Together they tell us of the turnings of the year, of the seasons of planting and harvesting. And in their clusters, they make for us pictures of the gods. What of this for us?"

Eoghan pointed toward the Dagda, with his hunting belt and club.

"We are these stars, love. We are alone but we have always been together. Our story is connected like the pictures formed by these stars. Yes, I desire you." A spasm of something crossed his face. He looked away, looked back at her. "So much that I forget myself, that I forget that I cannot be the one to have you. When all is finished we will remain apart in our firmament, you and I."

"Have I no say in my life? Among the Gaels it is we women who choose the lifemate. Is the choice not mine to make?"

"It is your life which most concerns me, priestess."

He stepped out of the bothy, removed the rest of the deer to the forest so that the wolves would not be drawn to their campsite, tamped the fire so that it settled to glowing embers. He sat, silently staring out at the darkness.

Aislinn stretched out on the pine boughs at the back of the bothy, turned her face to the wall. She did not sleep.

Eoghan sat for a long time watching the stars in the night sky.

"Aislinn?" he whispered at last.

When she did not respond, he took her silence for sleep.

"I love you, Aislinn ni Sorar."

Aislinn's heart leaped and began to pound within her. She felt a rush of joy so pure that she thought she might weep. Then Eoghan continued.

"I loved you even when you were a child. And I will continue to love you when you can no longer abide the sight of me."

Long after Eoghan Mac Aidan had stretched out beside her, long after Aislinn could hear the even rhythms of his breathing, she lay awake, staring into the darkness. For the first time in her life she understood the wall that Aodh-fin had erected around her, the safety of knowing nothing. Just before dawn, she prayed to the goddess that she might never learn the meaning of Eoghan's words.

They crossed the wide river Boann where it meanders south past the hill of Tara on the evening of the third day, stopping at the sacred druid ceremonial grove with its adjacent lodge. The long rectangular lodge stood back from the river. Near it was the grove with its parallel oak trees and its stone altar. Aislinn leaped from her horse and raced to the lodge. She threw open the door only to find it empty.

"They have all gone to Tara," she said to Eoghan. "I had hoped to find Aodhfin here. Oh, Eoghan, I'm home! Here in this lodge I learned the history of Eire, the stories of all the gods." She turned in a circle, her face shining, stopped suddenly.

"What more will I learn, Eoghan? I fear it now. Will you come with me to find Aodhfin?"

He turned away from her, pointed toward Tara.

"See how many hundreds of fires burn at the sides of Tara's hill. Many chieftains and their tuaths have come for this year's festival. Too many," Mac Aidan grumbled. "Let us stay in the druii lodge here tonight, then go to the hall of Cormac Mac Art in the morning."

He dismounted from Becan, helped her down, and began to lift off their belongings.

"The druii lodge will remain empty this night," Aislinn protested. "All of the priests and judges will be in the great hall preparing for the ceremonies of samhain."

"Good," said Eoghan. There was an edgy desperation in his voice now that mirrored the irritable silence that had possessed him during this last day of the ride. He took a deep breath, spoke in a reasonable tone.

"That is well. We can rest and spend our last night together away from the prying eyes of the assembled tribes. We can bathe in the stream in the morning and go to the assembly in our full ceremonial robes."

"Ah, but in the hall of the Ard-Ri we can feast on bread and honey and haunch of wild boar. We can bathe in hot water sweet with herbs and sleep on the softest of skins," Aislinn said, remembering the comforts of Tara.

Mac Aidan turned on her angrily. "Go, then, if you wish, soft woman! We must play out these next days. We have no choice for fate will tell the tale. But tonight could be ours to decree. Will you let cold fate keep us from each other?"

He pulled her up against him and kissed her mouth in a way that he had not before. She could feel the roughness of his unshaven cheeks scraping against the soft skin of her mouth, feel the urgent hardness of him against her thigh. This was not the gentle thinker of the forest, but a warrior, demanding, fearsome, angry. She feared him like this, pushed away in panic.

"I must go to the grove to pray. That is the first duty of a priestess."

"And we must all do our duty, priestess." His voice was rough-edged, angry.

Aislinn turned and nearly ran down the leaf-strewn path toward the rectangular grove of oak trees. As soon as she stepped into the sanctuary, she felt the pervading peace of the grove. The wind moved the top branches of the trees and the remaining leaves seemed to whisper her name. From the trees hung the ceremonial skulls, their candles out now, dark. She walked to the stone altar at the far end of the grove and placed her palms against the stone on either side of the circular basin that caught the blood of sacrificial animals. She felt the trembling of her hands ease against the solid stone. She closed her eyes.

"Triune goddess," she said aloud to the whispering trees. "You who protect the women of Eire, be with me now. Stay with me through these next days. Help me to be strong. Help me to learn the truth and not to fear it. Speak to me now and tell me the way that I must go. You who are the goddess of fire, tell me now. Is this one the bearer of fire? Is this the one I choose?"

She closed her eyes and tipped her head back. Nothing came. No light, no vision, no sound of internal wind. Aislinn fought back a rising sense of panic. Would her vision abandon her now, before the central moment of her life? She opened her eyes. The wind rose around her. A sudden gust made the traveling cloak spread out. Stray wisps of her hair that were not tucked in drifted across her face.

Then, out of the wind or above it, there came a voice. It was around Aislinn and within her instantly. It was neither male nor female, higher than wind, sweeter than song. It sounded for a moment like Mac Aidan's harp.

"Daughter, I will not abandon you," the voice said inside her head and outside her in the grove. "Remember these words: those who forgive are free to love."

The wind died down. Aislinn's cloak went still at her sides. The leaves no longer whispered. She turned to see the shadow of Mac Aidan waiting for her at the entrance to the grove. *To the place of fire will come a man bearing fire for the body and the mind.* She ran to him.

"Did you hear it?"

"I heard the wind and I heard the wind grow still."

"Did you hear the voice?"

"I heard no voice."

She tipped her head back and looked long into Mac Aidan's eyes, then reached up and undid the brooch holding the shoulder of her traveling cloak. She let the cloak fall to the ground and pressed herself against Mac Aidan, twining her arms around his neck and whispering close to his ear.

"I do not know what will come tomorrow. Tonight, I choose you."

Eoghan's arms drew around her gently. He drew in a long, deep sigh that ended on a gasp.

"What is it?"

"Look, mo ghra, look."

In the skulls that hung from the trees, tiny fires began

to blossom one after another until the whole grove was lighted by faces of dancing fire.

"Ah then," said Aislinn. "The goddess brings us fire."

"You are the fire," Eoghan whispered in a choked voice. "And this time with you all the light that my life will ever need."

9

He undressed her by the lodge fire. When she was naked before him he drew in his breath as he had on the hill that day with Mac Bran and closed his eyes. Gently, he drew her against him and enfolded her in the circle of his arms, stroking his hands down the length of her back.

He stepped away from her momentarily, threw off his tunic, stood clad before her in his braichs and boots. Aislinn opened her palm, laid her hand flat against his heart. He pressed his own huge hand over hers.

Aislinn stepped in against him. She tilted her head back and Mac Aidan kissed her cheeks, her neck, and her lips until she thought that the gentle rain would go on forever and that she would die surfeited of Mac Aidan's kisses.

He moved his hands up her sides, then cupped her breasts gently, as if they were the smallest of birds. He rained tiny kisses against them with his lips and tongue until Aislinn's trembling ceased and she cried out from wanting him.

Eoghan sat among the wolf skins on the sleeping platform and reached for his boots, but Aislinn knelt before him on the wolf skins. She let her hair fall around them like a curtain. Sweetly, she buried the soft curls of his head between her breasts while she caressed his back and shoulders.

"I love you," Mac Aidan whispered hoarsely. "May the gods forgive me for how desperately I love you."

Mac Aidan drew his hands down the length of her back and across the soft curve of her hips. Gently, he drew his arms around her and lowered her to the wolf skins, kneeling above her. He removed his braichs and boots, then lowered himself to her, kissing her face and shoulders. Aislinn stroked his chest and the sides of his arms. Her hips began to arch toward him of their own volition and she trembled. Mac Aidan drew away, but Aislinn placed her hands on either side of his face.

"Nay, love," she whispered. "I tremble not with fear but with desire. Come to me and I will not be afraid."

At last Mac Aidan moved within her so gently that the briefest moment of pain tumbled into a river of warmth. Aislinn felt that she was drifting in the goddess-river Boann, warm in the summer of her childhood. When she closed her eyes, she could see the explosions of sunlight on the water. She wrapped her arms around Mac Aidan's shoulders and cried out her love for him.

Later they slept by the lodge fire, warm under the wolf skins. Aislinn's hand was twined in Mac Aidan's and her hair was spread across his chest. She drifted through dreams of warmth and sunlight, of the laughter of children.

The vision began as a dream in the darkness. There were two infants, a boy and a girl, sleeping before the door of a lodge, their dark curly heads bent together in slumber. In the dream Aislinn saw herself come to the door of the lodge. From the sunlight outside the door Corra ni Brith's voice called out, "They are well, máthair." Mac Aidan was nowhere in the dream.

Aislinn sat up suddenly in bed. The lodge fire had dwindled to a few red embers and her shoulders grew cold where the wolf skins slipped from them, but she sat perfectly still and closed her eyes. Gently she placed her hand against the firm white hardness of her belly and listened. Within her, she felt distinctly the presence of two other spirits.

"Mac Aidan," she whispered, pressing at his shoulder in the darkness.

He awoke and smiled sleepily at her, reaching for the wolf pelt to cover her shoulders and draw her down to him.

She bent her head above his and stroked the side of his face.

"From this night something wonderful has happened. From this night, I carry . . ."

The door to the lodge slammed open sending a shower of sparks up toward the smoke hole in the ceiling.

In the doorway was the silhouette of a huge black bird.

"By the gods," Mac Aidan cried, throwing off the wolf skins and diving for his sword on the floor beside him.

"By the gods, indeed," said a voice, thin, nasal, cold.

The bird seemed to stretch forth a talon and powder cascaded onto the fire, so that the room was bathed in an eerie blue glow.

"Banbh," said Mac Aidan, brandishing his sword. Banbh disregarded him, turning instead toward Aislinn.

"I was told that you had returned."

"Who told you this?" Mac Aidan asked menacingly, stepping closer to the druid. The druid laughed harshly.

"Do you think I need to discover things in the same way that you do, poet?"

He stepped closer to the bed. In the blue light, his face looked bloodless, his eyes bright. His tall, thin frame in its black cloak loomed like a shadow beside the bed. Aislinn stood deliberately on the sleeping platform, towering over him, her hair swinging back and forth over her naked frame.

"Not the green girl who left us now, are you?" Banbh said, but he licked his lips as he watched her. "But never mind; my dark goddess still purposes you to her service."

"I have given myself to this man," Aislinn said, throwing back her head and squaring her shoulders.

Banbh turned toward Mac Aidan. "Your father and stepmother will be interested to hear of this development. They are here at the court of Cormac for the samhain festivities, you know."

Mac Aidan made a strangled sound and spat on the floor.

"Go from here, evil one. This woman is under my protection, poet and warrior of the Ard-Ri. None of your evil is to be used against her. Harm her and you will die."

"Harm her? It is you who have harmed her by bedding her before the truth was told. That curse will fall upon you. As for the priestess Aislinn, when you are gone you can be sure that I will not harm her." He faced Aislinn again, his eyes glittering in the blue light.

"In fact, I will deal with her in much the same fashion as you have done this night." From his hand, Banbh threw something that looked like a ball of cobwebs.

"Remember nothing," he hissed.

Mac Aidan rushed at the druid then, but the room seemed to fill suddenly with a fog, the air to grow viscous and thick. Mac Aidan turned in confusion. There was a sudden wind, then total darkness.

When the morning light edged in through the door of the druii lodge only moments later, it found the lovers entwined in heavy sleep, untroubled, as though the visitation had never occurred.

10

In the pearly morning light Aislinn tipped her head back and let the sights and sounds of the Hill of the Kings wash over her.

"Rath na Riogh!" she cried aloud, throwing her arms wide. "I had forgotten how huge it was," she said, turning her face to Mac Aidan. He laughed gently, catching the radiant face between his hands.

"Through your eyes I will see it again new." He kissed her and she leaned forward to receive his lips and to encourage his hands to lift and catch in her hair. For a moment, she leaned in against him, caught her breath as his arms closed around her. Then she pulled away.

"None of that now! I must find Aodhfin!"

Eoghan laughed again.

"Do you think that Rath na Riogh will vanish before your eyes if you do not cross the causeway before the sun is full up?" But he allowed her to pull him toward the hill. He seemed younger in the morning light, the shadows of his face erased.

Rath na Riogh, the Hill of the Kings, seat of the High Kings of Eire, rose in a gentle curve from the surrounding plains like the back of one of the huge whales that traversed the seas of Eire's coast. At its crest, the flat plain of the hill was three hundred yards long and nearly again that wide. It was on that flat circular plain that Cormac Mac Art had established his stronghold.

Three parallel trenches surrounded the hill. Each was ten feet wide. The trench closest to the flat surface of the hill was filled with dangerous sharp rocks and upright wooden palisades with sharply pointed spearlike tips. Earthen causeways, which descended from the crest of the hill, were few and heavily guarded. Encircling the base of the hill were the wide grassy plains used for cattle pasturage.

Today, those plains were filled with the temporary dwellings of dozens of chieftains from all over Eire, for it was the great feis of samhain, most sacred of the ceremonial days and the occasion for the reading of the laws of Eire.

Women of the tribes were already busy at cooking fires, while men were tending horses, decorating them with ornate bits and bridles, or grooming fine teams for the chariot races that would take place later in the morning.

Even in these early dawn hours, the fair had begun.

"Look, Eoghan. They play at hurley!" A loud group of young boys hurtled past, batting the flat-ladled sticks at a ball on the ground. "Perhaps Fionn Mac Cumhail is among them!"

"Fionn is no longer a boy. He played at hurley long ago."

"But here at Tara, anything is possible."

Eoghan shook his head.

"Too much is possible. Samhain is too heavy with the weight of possibilities."

"You sound like an old man, poet. Will you spoil the pleasure of my homecoming with your seriousness?"

"Nay, I will not." Eoghan leaned down and planted a kiss on her forehead. "I will go to look at the hounds and horses. Look you here at the rich jewelry this fellow displays." He pointed toward a booth where brooches and armlets spilled in rich profusion across a deep blue cloth, then headed off toward the pens where the racing dogs were yapping. Aislinn started toward the booth.

The hawker, noting Aislinn's druid robe and the rich fund of gold she wore, reached below the table and brought up an enameled brooch. He gave her a gap-toothed smile.

"For you, druidess, I bring forth the finest piece in my collection."

He placed an intricately enameled brooch in her hand. It was twisted back on itself in the shape of a bird biting its tail. The eye was a deep red ruby, the chased design dark with scrolled heads of animals and entwined spirals. Aislinn stared at it. A crow. Why did the brooch look like a crow? It seemed to grow cold in her hand, to press against her flesh. She had a sudden strange feeling that she should cover her nakedness, that there was something or someone she needed to protect. She threw the brooch on the table, turned away quickly.

She leaned against the wall of the next stall where an embroideress wove red, blue, and gold onto the green cloak of a lady. The woman looked up at her with concern.

"Are you well, priestess?"

Aislinn straightened, smiled.

"I am well now, I thank you. Your work is beautiful."

The woman smiled. A little girl of eight or nine dashed into the little booth.

"Maither, we play at run-and-seek!"

"Stay a good distance from the river."

The child dashed away again. Aislinn thought of Corra ni Brith. She blinked back the sudden tears behind her eyes, pressed her eyelids to shake off the strange sense that there was something she should remember. For a moment, the feeling seemed to coalesce into a memory of blue firelight. Aislinn swayed a little, clutched against the upright of the booth. The woman dropped her embroidery, reached out for Aislinn.

"Priestess, you are not well."

Aislinn patted her hand.

"I think that I am hungry. I have not eaten since yestereven."

The woman smiled and pointed a little down the way.

"There you will find warm stirabout with honey, and fresh cakes and loaves."

Aislinn used one of her gold bracelets to buy a huge bowl of the simmering cereal and tore at a loaf of bread. She could not eat the whole loaf, but by the brehon laws of hospitality, the maker of the bread could offer her no less than a full loaf. She decided to look for Eoghan and share the bounty.

She found him kneeling at the pen where the yapping race dogs were being groomed and examined.

She came up behind him laughing, closed her arms around his shoulders, and wafted the loaf of warm bread beneath his nose. He kissed both hands, then bit off a giant chunk of the bread. He stood beside her.

"We will see each other seldom over the next few days. I will have many duties."

"Too many to add one more to your day?" Aislinn ducked her head and blushed at what she proposed, but Eoghan remained serious, took her face between his palms. "I would die to protect you, Aislinn. Remember that I love you."

"Of course I will remember," she replied. "Was I not the one who chose for us?"

Eoghan sighed, looked up at the hill of Tara with its palisaded walls. He shrugged.

"Let us go in, then," he said, but he shook his head even as he spoke.

They started up the hill. Flanking the main causeway, jugglers vied for attention with harpists singing ballads of the great heroes. Genealogists stood on boxes spaced along the causeway, reciting the heritage and deeds of the clans of Ireland. Each performer boasted his little cluster of listeners.

Aislinn stopped for a moment at the step of the gene-alogist who wore the clan plaid of the Deisi, but Eoghan placed his arm firmly around her waist and led her farther up the hill toward the main gate.

"Brother!" Aislinn looked up at the call, surprised when one of the braided, moustached, and bristling warriors of the Fianna stepped forward.

"Darragh!" Mac Aidan released her and the two men clasped arms from the elbows, then embraced, clapping each other on the back.

Aislinn stared. The Fianna were the standing army of Cormac Mac Art, legendary for their ability to fight, to live from the land, to work outside the strict brehon laws. From May to September, they lived wild in the forests of Eire, but in the winter months they were billeted among the villages, more than nine thousand of them, and that number only in peacetime.

This Fenian had long brown hair braided and woven with deer hide. He wore plaid braichs held up with a wide leather belt and soft leather shoes. His moustache drooped down past the corners of his mouth. His wooden shield was carved with patterns of trumpets and wild fowl, in-terspersed with spirals, and he carried a longsword in an intricately carved bronze scabbard along with a dagger and a spear. He looked every inch the dangerous fighting man of the forests of Eire and Aislinn wondered how it was that Mac Aidan knew him well.

"How goes our leader, Fionn Mac Cumhail?" Mac Ai-dan asked.

"He is well!" Darragh raised his spear above his head in a gesture of jubilance. "For this we thank the gods who gave him life. May he live long among us." Again the two men clasped arms.

Darragh seemed to see Aislinn then and turned in her direction.

"Priestess," he said, inclining his head in her direction. "Plead well for me, a man of the fringes."

But he grinned at Mac Aidan in a way that made the

fringes sound positively alluring. Aislinn made the ritual
sign of blessing, but she was glad when they turned again
up the causeway so that she could satisfy her curiosity.

"How have you come to know this man of the Fianna
so well?"

"I am myself Fianna." A small smile flickered over Mac
Aidan's face and he turned toward Aislinn awaiting her
reaction.

"You are Fianna? This explains why I have never seen
you at Tara! But how have you come to be a man of the
fringes? You do know Fionn, then. Why did you not tell
me this when you hunted for our food? Is this how you
came by the name the 'warrior-bard'? How is it that a
Fenian warrior is also the poet of the High King, Cormac
Mac Art?"

Mac Aidan threw back his head and laughed until the
water ran down the sides of his face. He wiped at his
eyes.

"Even the men of the Fianna can answer only one question at a time!"

But any explanation Mac Aidan might have offered was
swallowed in the wild surge of activity and color that
greeted them at the crest of the hill of the Ard-Ri. Horses
and chariots surged past them, circling the road at the
perimeter of the hill, preparing for the upcoming races.
Tall men in multitudes of clan plaids hurried among the
horses while a few regal women garbed in colored gowns
and weighted down with elaborate golden jewelry clus-
tered together near the hilltop well.

Aislinn stared at the hill of Tara as though seeing it for
the first time.

"Eoghan," she cried. "It is all still the same."

"So it should remain, may our good Cormac rule for
forty years more. You have been gone two years. Did you
think it would have changed so much?"

"Perhaps the change is in me." She smiled and leaned
up to kiss his cheek.

"Look, Eoghan!" She pointed toward the center of the

circle. Two identical circular dwellings stood side by side at the center of the great hill, the Teach Cormac, the house of Cormac Mac Art, the High King of Eire, and the Forradh, the finest school in all of Ireland. Both the Forradh and the Teach Cormac were a hundred yards in circumference, built of wood with roofs of thatched straw.

Behind and beyond these dwellings, still farther back on the hill of Tara, were the great rectangular banqueting hall of Tara, the Grianan, or sun house of the women, and the various smaller dwellings that housed the kings of the four provinces of Eire during all festivals and conferences.

Aislinn broke free from Mac Aidan's arm.

"I must go! I know I will find Aodhfin in the Forradh."

He nodded in her direction and she raced off like a coltish girl toward the Forradh and her tutor.

Although some light filtered in through the chinks in the walls and the spaces in the roof cut for the smoke of fires, the Forradh was dark, and Aislinn paused in the doorway to let her eyes adjust to the dimness. To her right, in one of the large war chambers of the Forradh, she could hear the clink of metal on metal and wood as warriors practiced their fighting skills. She crept forward to the doorway of that great chamber and stared at the warriors who fought naked but for their battle aprons, shield to shield, spears parrying. They stopped when they saw her, bowing respectfully in her direction. She blushed with embarrassment at having interrupted their practice. She stepped back and began to wander through the circular hallways.

As her eyes adjusted to the light, she could make out the wickerwork dividing rooms that circled the Forradh in two concentric rings. She began a slow progression past the doorway openings looking for Aodhfin.

In one room, a group of physicians bent over the carcass of a dog, studying its internal organs by the flickering light of four torches at the corners of their table. In a room that had been darkened with blankets, an aspiring poet lay in the dark, memorizing the sagas of the people or perhaps composing his own poems to recite at tonight's feast.

Aislinn moved quietly past all of the rooms, looking and listening for the sounds of her tutor. When she heard his voice drifting into the hallway, she leaned back against the wall and listened, fighting to control her breathing. She peered around the corner. The class was composed of children, perhaps the children of the visiting chieftains who were to be honored with a story told by Aodhfin, a master seanchai, or storyteller of the people. Aodhfin sat on his little stool of ash, leaning his arms on his elbows to get his face closer to the circle of upraised faces.

Had he aged since she saw him last? His head was bald and the light from the smoke hole shone a beam on its shiny surface. His fringe of white hair hung down over the collar of his druid robe and the torque at his neck seemed almost too large for the slender column within it.

He was gesturing with his long-fingered hands. He laced them together, winging them skyward like birds. Aislinn realized that he was telling the children the story of the children of Lir. She listened to his rhythmic voice, remembered the story from her own childhood.

"High above the world, you can hear them crying even now." He made a sound like a bird of the air, a sad, keening sound. "Do you hear them?"

"I do!" cried a little girl with hair the color of Corra's.

"Why do they cry?" demanded a small boy.

"Because they are trapped in the bodies of swans, boys and girls like yourselves, but trapped, forever."

Gasps went up from the little circle.

"Shall I tell you the story?"

"Aye! Tell, please tell."

"Long ago and longer, there lived a good and wise king named Lir. Lir was the luckiest of men for his wife was his beloved and he was the proud father of two pairs of twins, two boys and one boy and girl. Lir doted upon his little family, but tragedy befell. The wife of Lir, the mother of the children, died.

"Lir was lonely and wept for his sorrow. His father-in-law, father of the wife that had died, took pity on his son-in-law.

" 'It is not good for a man to be alone,' he said. 'I will give you another of my daughters.'

"And so he gave to Lir his daughter Aoife. Now Aoife was beautiful to behold but her heart was jealous of the love that Lir gave to his children. One day in the warmth of summer, she took the children riding beside the shores of a beautiful lake.

" 'Swim!' she bade the children and they took off their clothes and dived into the water.

"But when Aoife had them in the water, she cast a terrible spell upon them.

" 'Swans you shall be,' she cried. 'Winging above the world for three times three hundred years.'

"But Aoife forgot to take from them their human voices. Toward nightfall Lir rode out to find his children and heard them crying. When he saw what Aoife had done he wept, then cast a spell upon her as punishment, hurling her into an evil wind, where she remains trapped even today. Have you heard her when the wind howls?"

The wide-eyed circle of children nodded.

"But what of the children?" cried the copper-haired girl.

"Lir remained beside them there on the shores of that lake for three hundred years, but then the curse sent them away to another lake of Eire, far away where their father could not go. Still of an evening, you can hear them weeping as they fly above the world."

He stopped suddenly and slowly raised his head. Aislinn knew that he had sensed her. She smiled into Aodhfin's soft gray eyes.

Aislinn felt the tears start unbidden from her own eyes and run down her cheeks unstopped.

"You have returned, little one," he said, holding out his arms and Aislinn ran heedless of the gaping students into the outstretched arms.

"Master," she sobbed. "Oh, my athair." And the children in the circle believed that one of the swans, the white daughter of Lir, had descended among them.

They sat on a bench in the formal gardens surrounding the house of Cormac Mac Art. The sun poured down upon them and in the trees of the garden birds still trilled though the day was samhain cool.

"I could not let him hurt you, father," Aislinn said brokenly, "so I left."

Aodhfin shook his head. "He could not have hurt me, foster-daughter. I am a devotee of Lugh, the son of the Sun. Banbh is the student of Badb, the carrion crow, goddess of war. Remember that the power of the light is stronger than the power of dark, even when it does not seem so. I could only be hurt by Banbh if I permitted such a hurt for a higher purpose. I am only sorry that he hurt you and that he frightened you, my little one."

"How is it that he transforms himself as the crow?"

"He does not, daughter. He transforms your mind to believe that he is the crow. All those who follow evil wish to control the bodies and the minds of others. But we will talk of happier things. You are here now and you are safe and though we have been separated, the gods have seen fit to reunite us. This is the way of all things. Trust the gods to guide your course."

"As you trusted them to guide you home after your long captivity in Alba."

"Just so. And it is true, as I told you, that good things come of all life's troubles, for it was during that captivity that I learned the Roman skill of writing."

Aislinn looked around quickly. Aodhfin laughed.

"Daughter, you are too fearful."

"But the druid way forbids this skill, father."

"What we compose and pass down to our children in the sacred skull of our memory, the Romans pass on to theirs by their hand. I am an old enough man to see the advantage in their way. But I do not speak of myself. I speak of you, for I perceive that great good has come to you in your travels."

Aodhfin moved his hand and placed it over Aislinn's belly, then closed his eyes and tipped his head back. When he opened his eyes he smiled at her in delight.

"They are strong, this pair, formed of a strong union. Have you told him?"

Aislinn looked down at her belly in surprise, remembering for the first time today the child spirits who slept within her belly. She searched her memory, trying to recall why she had not yet told Eoghan, why she did not remember the babes upon waking this morning. She shook her head, feeling that she needed to clear it somehow.

"I have not told him, but I will. I love him."

"So you have found the man who is the bearer of fire. Did you also find the child?" Aodhfin smiled, taking Aislinn's hand in the palm of his worn hand.

"I did. She is called Corra ni Brith. She was captive of a bloated chieftain named Mac Bran. I took her from him, but it was necessary to kill him to do so. I left her with Gobinet and the people of the Deisi that she would be safe from Banbh. But she is how I met my beloved one as well, athair. He was my companion and her defender before he was my lover. They call him the warrior-bard. His name is Eoghan Mac Aidan."

Aodhfin stared at her, then stood in the sunshine and turned his back to her. For a moment Aislinn sensed something like fear or disapproval from the set of his shoulders. Then suddenly the shoulders began to shake and Aodhfin began to laugh aloud. He threw his arms high in the air, spreading his hands wide so that the sunlight streamed through his fingers.

"O you gods!" He turned to face Aislinn and she saw that tears were streaming down his face. "Now I understand. Now I see that you conspire always to encircle us."

He made a huge circle of his hands and at the base of the circle brought them to rest against Aislinn's belly.

"Protect these returning souls, the children of Eoghan Mac Aidan and Aislinn ni Sorar."

Aislinn placed her hands over Aodhfin's. "Father, I have returned that you may tell me of my past, that I may know my parents' story."

"Oh, yes, child, it it time for you to know the great blessing the gods have placed upon you." He stood, walked for a moment in a gentle circle, nodded. "I am told that your father was Sorar, chief of the Deisi. By treachery, he was overthrown and defeated, his body entombed. Your mother Eibhlain joined his body in honor fast, that his betrayal would come to justice. But she knew that you would be in danger. Great danger."

"Why? Was I not a child?"

"Yes, a child of five years. But, do you not see, daughter? You are the rightful chief of the Deisi."

"No," Aislinn gasped. "That, then, is what they were all afraid to tell me. Why they treated me with so much respect and honor. The people of O'Domnhnaill knew, knew from the moment I said my name."

"It must be so though I do not know the people of the Deisi."

"Then, how did you come by me?"

"Your mother chose to spirit you away. She found a messenger, one who would bring you to Tara, told that messenger to give you to the oldest and wisest druid who was a servant of the light. That messenger was a boy of seventeen years. His name was Eoghan Mac Aidan."

"O you gods. Then my beloved was he who took me from my mother, who brought me to you!"

"It was."

"Did you know my mother and my father?"

"No, child. Only Eoghan, when he came to me. And then you."

"Why does he feel such shame for this, athair? Was this not a gift, that he saved my life?"

"It was certainly that. But he was of the Deisi. Perhaps

the shame over the death of your mother and father haunt him, though he was but a boy."

"Then we must ease his heart. We must tell him that I know and that I forgive him."

"Ah, my wise Aislinn, my little dream. Come, we will go to the chariot races and find this man of yours. This is a day that the gods have won."

The pre-samhain festivities always began with the chariot races. Later in the day there would be men's and women's foot races, hurling games, initiations of new members of the Fianna, and more, but the spectacle of the chariot races always drew the largest and most vocal crowds.

Three chariots stood side by side in the dust of the racetrack. Their drivers were dressed in breeches and soft leather shoes. Their chests were bare, oiled with fragrant potions, and they gleamed like their brushed and curried horses. The races would be run, three chariots at a time, until the elimination brought the races down to the final three chariots.

Aislinn glanced from one driver to another, then stopped, speechless with surprise. In the chariot behind the gleaming black pair of horses stood Mac Aidan. His hair had been pulled back into a tight black braid in the manner of the Fianna and he held the reins of a pair of huge black horses whose sides heaved with the desire to run.

The first and second charioteers called the names of the kings of Munster and Connaught, two of Ireland's provinces. Each chieftain stood to the cheers of his tribesmen.

Then Mac Aidan climbed upon the wooden bar that stretched between his horses. He held the reins high in his hands and called aloud. "I ride for the Fianna, army of the High King Cormac Mac Art and for our leader Fionn Mac Cumhail." The people screamed and cheered. Mac Aidan remained where he was standing.

"Get down," Aislinn hissed beneath her breath. "Get down, fool!"

She had seen enough chariot races where the daring ones who rode the rigging were knocked beneath their horses' hooves and crushed beneath their own and other chariots. But Mac Aidan remained where he was, a challenge to the other riders, who one by one climbed up between their horses.

A horn sounded. They were off! Mac Aidan swept past her in the dust of the ring, running up and down the bar between the heads of the horses, surefooted and strong. Aislinn realized that he was not afraid, that he knew his power there between the horses. When he came sweeping back around the turn of the track in the lead she felt no surprise. She turned to Aodhfin beside her.

"This is the man I have chosen, honored teacher," she said, a little dryly.

Aodhfin beside her was chuckling like a man well pleased with himself.

"I know, daughter," he said, patting her hand and laughing. "I know everything now. The gods have told me the end of this tale."

11

The steady drizzle had begun late in the afternoon. Outside the Teach Mi-Cuarta the crowd shifted restlessly, waiting for the Day of Laws to begin. Aislinn lifted the hem of her white robe, rising on tiptoe to get a glimpse of Eoghan. She placed her hand on Aodhfin's arm.

"Do you see him yet?"

Aodhfin patted her hand and chuckled.

"I remember well the impatience of my youth. I am glad those days are gone."

"But I have not seen him at all since the chariot races. The Grianan has been filled with chattering women and Eoghan has been with the king or with Fionn Mac Cumhail." She leaned in close and whispered to Aodhfin. "I have had no chance to tell him of the babes."

"It is the day before samhain, daughter. The law must be chanted and cases heard. And then we must all survive the Time Between the Times. Learn patience. Ah. See now where they come."

The crowd parted and three men walked down the pathway toward the main door of the hall. The first, a trumpeter, stopped before the door and turned to face the crowd. He blew three short blasts on the wide-mouthed horn. The crowd fell silent.

Eoghan stepped forward next. He was dressed in the six colors of an ollamh, his red robe interwoven with gold and silver, green, purple, and blue. Birds rose from the hem and stags leaped among the forests embroidered on the rich robe, for the poet commanded all the elements of earth with his words. A silver brooch as large as a fist held the side of his cloak fast. As poet and ollamh of the Ard-Ri he would chant the genealogies and the history of the claimants at law while the brehons or lawyers would interpret their cases.

"Here we meet at Tea-Mur, Tara of the Kings, once every three years. Here can the kings of the provinces come together in peace. Here can the laws of Eire be changed for the betterment of all. Here can all claimants plead their case before the brehons of Cormac Mac Art, wise king of Eire."

It was the ritual beginning but Eoghan turned at his own mention of the brehons and looked directly at Aislinn. She shivered slightly and a cold wave of fear washed over her. She tilted her head toward him in question, but he looked away.

Fionn Mac Cumhail, the leader of the Fianna, stepped forward. He was golden-haired, though now the gold was shot through with gray, for he had ruled the Fianna from the time of Cormac's grandfather, Conn of the Hundred Battles. His cloak was the green of the forests and he bristled with weaponry from a finely enameled sword and a shield wrought with silver and precious stones to a dagger whose golden hilt gleamed from his elaborate girdle. His voice was strong.

"I Fionn, leader of the Fianna, proclaim the king's peace. Here no chieftains may quarrel over land. Here no man may take arms against another. For the duration of this feis all creditors must forgive their debtors. For the duration of this fair all fugitives may walk free among free men. Any man of Eire who violates the samhain peace will pay forfeit of his life."

The three turned and entered the great hall. Behind them the five provincial kings of Ireland filed in with their shield-bearers.

Next came the procession of the aes dana, the learned of Ireland. Druids, brehons, physicians, poets, storytellers, musicians, and teachers filed down the long hall toward the raised platforms at the far end. Aislin and Aodhfin fell into line. Aislinn whispered to Aodhfin again.

"I am nervous, father. I was a student when I fled Tara. I was not entitled to sit at the Great Parliament. What will I see?"

"You will see the finest legal system and the fairest justice in all of the known world. Enter the great hall of Cormac Mac Art and be proud." He took her arm and led her through the wide doors.

Aislinn gasped aloud.

Torches made a smoky haze near the ceiling some forty-five feet above her head. The hall was built of red yew. The cedar pillars that held up the ceiling were decorated with platings of bronze. Each plate was covered with spirals and tendrils, with the secret ogham writing or with the harts and hounds of the great hunts.

The long sides of the hall were partitioned into compartments for the chiefs of tuaths and their families. Each compartment was fronted by another elaborately decorated bronze plate and filled with rich furnishings of yew and oak.

Far away at the end of the hall, the dais that would seat the king was raised high above all others so that he might be seen by the whole assembly. His huge chair was worked in bronze, silver, and gold. The inlaid rubies and emeralds blinked red and green fire.

Below him would sit the five provincial kings and all about him the ollamhs, brehons, druids, and physicians who formed the aes dana, the intellectual class of Eire.

Aislinn seated herself beside Aodhfin. She felt a quick
jostling at her left side and turned. The thin, smiling face
of Banbh moved close to hers.

"Ah, priestess, you will make a long day seem shorter
by the pleasure of your presence next to me."

Aislinn felt a tide of panic rise up her throat.

"I will not sit by you through this long day!"

"Then kneel before me or lay on the ground below me."
He shrugged. "Before long, my goddess and I will see
that you do both."

Aislinn started to rise. From her right side, Aodhfin's
warm hand closed over hers. He leaned around her and
stared at Banbh. Aodhfin's white robe draped before him
like a wing and the torque at his neck caught a flash of
light.

"What say you to my foster-daughter, Dark One?"

Fear flashed briefly in Banbh's eyes.

"I wish her good day for her pleasant company. That
is all."

"Ah, then that is well."

Banbh sat back, pressed his thin lips together, said
nothing more.

A quick blast of the trumpet sounded. Cormac Mac Art,
High King of all Ireland, entered the hall. Aislinn deliberately turned her thoughts away from Banbh.

"Before you comes the wise ruler of all Eire," Eoghan
cried out from his place standing at the right of Cormac's
chair. "Under his wisdom, Eire has prospered. Our fields
are full, our harvests yield plenty, our cattle are too numerous to number. He has fought the just wars, he has
made the wise rulings. Stand, o Eire, for your king."

The assemblage stood as one. Cormac began the procession down the long hall. He was more than six feet
tall, and his golden hair waved softly down to his shoulders. The entire surface of his fringed purple cloak was
covered with elaborate golden embroidery. Golden hooks
and clasps of silver ran the length of the garment that was
lined in rich silver seal fur. At his neck, a braided gold

torque rested on a white silk shirt embroidered with red. The girdle beneath Cormac's cloak flashed gold as he walked. The light from the torches caught the gleaming lights of precious gems. His sandals were threaded with gold and boasted ornamental spiraling gold buckles. Behind him, his champion warrior carried his scarlet shield with its gold engraving and rich blue, green, and red enameling and two spears with gold sockets and red-bronze rivets.

"How beautiful he is," Aislinn whispered to Aodhfin.

"His is the beauty of a life well lived. Cormac is just. I honor him."

On Cormac's right arm was his cet-muintir, his chief wife, Ethne. On his left arm was his concubine, Ciarnat the beautiful, the Pictish woman who had been captured in Alba and brought back to Eire. For her, it was said, Cormac had built the grinding mill that now stood at Tara, that a woman so noble and beautiful should not grind corn at a quern.

Beside Cormac four wolves pranced. There were some who said that Cormac had been raised by a she-wolf, and that these were his litter mates, a legend the wolves themselves seemed to bear out by behaving with the king like beloved family dogs.

As Cormac passed each cubicle, Eoghan's voice called out the name and genealogy of the chieftain and his family. Cormac had a word for each chieftain, a smile, a wave of the hand. Some of the chieftains, Aislinn knew from her travels. Some she had never seen. She was surprised to see the face of O'Domnhnaill halfway down the hall. She noted the tone of pride in Mac Aidan's voice when he announced O'Domnhnaill.

"Enda O'Domnhnaill of the tribe of the Deisi, father of Art and Muirne, foster-father of Eoghan Mac Aidan, ollamh."

Aislinn turned to Aodhfin.

"This is he who sheltered us after I stole the child. But his wife Gobinet is not with him. She remained on the crannog to shelter my Corra." Aislinn felt relief at the thought of Corra safe with Gobinet, delight that now that she knew her past, she could return to her soon.

Aodhfin pointed toward Eoghan who continued his recitation of genealogies in a toneless voice.

"Aengus Mac Gabuideach, of the tribe of the Deisi, father of Eoghan Mac Aidan, and Macha, his wife."

Father of Eoghan Mac Aidan? Her Eoghan? Then why did Eoghan not carry this man's name. Aislinn stared at the pair that Eoghan had named. The man was graying, heavy-jowled, but tall. The woman was beautiful, much younger, with coils of thick brown hair. Even as Aislinn watched, Macha bared her teeth in a gleaming feral smile.

She started to turn to Aodhfin to ask him about the mismatched pair when she felt Banbh move against her arm. His lips pressed cold and wet against the edge of her ear as he whispered.

"You will learn, soon enough, pretty one. You will learn all of the answers. And you will suffer for what you know. You should have let yourself be taught by me, priestess. My goddess and I would have given you power to offset your sufferings. But perhaps there is still time."

She felt the tiniest flick of his tongue against her ear, but when she turned in his direction, Banbh was not seated next to her at all. The druid who nodded sagely at her was a stranger.

Samhain morning dawned rainy and cold, the skies a drizzling foreboding gray. Aislinn could sense the fear in the air, on the faces of the people, for tonight would be the time between the times, the time when the forces of the Others, the people of the sidhe, were loosed on the world.

She left the grianan, the sun hall of the women where she had spent the night, and moved across the yard to the Forradh. She was determined, despite the day, to find Mac Aidan and ask him the questions that burned within her. Why did he not bear his father's name? Who was the woman Macha? Why had he been avoiding her through-out the feis?

The yard was rutted with mud, and the tramplings of horses and chariots had not helped the slippery conditions. She felt her feet go out from beneath her, felt herself beginning to slide when a strong arm caught her. She looked up into the face of Aengus Mac Gabuideach.

"My wife says that you are the one my son loves."

Aislinn, surprised by his bluntness, nodded her response, thought briefly that he must have been waiting for her outside the Grianan.

"She tells me also that you are the daughter of Sorar, granddaughter of Art Corb, daughter of Eibhlain, now called the Wise Mother."

"How is it that you have memorized the genealogy of a stranger?"

Mac Gabuideach looked away for a moment, out over the hills of Eire, peering into the mist as if he would find an answer there. When he turned back, Aislinn saw that what weighted his face was sorrow.

"I want you to know, child, that I have paid dearly for what I have done. I have lost the love of my son. I have lost the love of myself. Am I without honor?" He seemed to ask the question of her or of the rainy sky.

"A Gael without honor is a man in whom the spirit has died." He turned and lumbered away across the mud.

"What have you done?" Aislinn cried to his receding back, but he shook his head.

"Take your case to the brehons," he called. "I will accept their justice."

But it was not the day for the brehons, nor could she ask Eoghan Mac Aidan the questions she longed to ask, for she could find him nowhere. As the day wore on toward darkness, Aislinn began to feel the spirits of the Others move against the walls of the world. She made her way down the hill toward the druii lodge and the sanctuary of Aodhfin.

He was praying in the oak grove when she approached,

garbed already in his ceremonial robe of white deer hide and swan feathers. He seemed to gleam at the center of the grove, his hands pressed against the altar. Aislinn stood quietly at the entrance, but he felt her presence and turned.

"Come, child." He motioned her toward him. "I like a few quiet moments with the gods before the powers are unleashed upon us." He smiled gently.

"You are not afraid," Aislinn said wonderingly.

"I have seen more than fifty samhains, thirty of them as a druid. I have survived them all. I fear the dark forces of men before the dark forces of the Others."

Aislinn stroked the soft swan feathers of his cloak.

"All of your shape-changing spirits are spirits of gentleness and light," she said.

"I have flown with the swans at darkness and heard their singing. I have leaped through the forest with the white hind. I have heard the voice at the center of the world."

"Father, there is much that I would ask you."

Aodhfin nodded.

"I know, daughter, but there is much that I do not know. So much of the truth of your story rests with the father of Eoghan Mac Aidan and the woman Macha."

"Why does Eoghan not bear his father's name? He should be called Eoghan Mac Aengus."

"This you must ask your Eoghan. I do not know the answer. You were brought to me, an orphan from the tribe of the Deisi, when you were five years old. I knew that your parents had died and that it was my duty to keep you safe. It was the greatest gift I have ever been given."

Aislinn smiled at him gently.

"How fortunate I was, then. But why does Eoghan avoid me now? I know what he did; you have told me. There is no shame in this action."

"Perhaps he sees himself responsible for separating a child from her mother. More likely, daughter, he feels shame that he could not stop her death, could not keep her from the honor fast. He was a mere boy entrusted with the responsibility of spiriting a child to safety. I do know this; he was a boy of good heart. From what you have told me, he has become a man of good heart. Trust your love for him, daughter, for I believe it too has been destined."

"Why would he tell me none of this himself?"

"You know the law, daughter. It is the right and duty of the parents or the foster-parents to inform and teach the child."

Aislinn smiled. "I am satisfied, father. But, speak to me of Banbh. Why does he hate me so?"

"That I can answer more thoroughly, daughter, for I have thought on that long. You mistake his emotion if you call it hate, for I think that it is fear. Or some strange, dark desire. He watches you like a bird of prey, like the crow goddess he serves. He sees in you some light that he wishes to extinguish with the force of his own darkness."

"But why?"

"I do not know, daughter. The answer to that remains to be seen. Only keep that light strong within you."

"What light?"

"The light of love. Of belief. They gather strength to themselves like the lightning." He reached his hand to her.

"Come. You will be at my right hand this samhain. You will see that light and darkness dwell in each of us as much as in the world."

The pit at the center of the great field was huge, ten feet deep and that much again wide. At its head, the Lia Fail, the stone of kingship, cast its firelit shadow over the company. Into the hole, the druids poured porridge and stew, placing over them the entire carcass of a roasted boar and the finest haunches of cattle and deer. They cast grain into the pit, corn and wheat scattering over the carcasses in the rain and wind.

Moylann, the high druid of Cormac Mac Art, intoned the plea.

"Dagda, you the good god, you who gives life, you who can take it away, so have we filled your cauldron that you may feast at samhain. Fill the cauldron of the earth below you now. Spill your seed into the river goddess Boann. Make fertile the earth. Make abundant the harvest of our fields."

The druii gathered in a white ring around the bonfire. Those who were ollamh, master druii, wore their shape-changing robes. Aodhfin in his robes of swan wings and white deer was flanked by Moylann in wolf pelts and another druid in a robe of silver sealskins. On the far side of the fire, Aislinn could see Banbh in his robe of carrion crow wings, black against the deeper blackness of the darkness behind him.

The druids watched the moon and stars. They scented the wind. They watched moonlight move across the Lia Fail.

Suddenly, Moylann stepped forward.

"Now the darkness turns to the new day's darkness. Now the old year becomes the new year. Quell the old year's fires!"

The great fire on the hill of Tara was extinguished with dirt and water. On all of the hillsides of Eire, the darkness was echoed as the fires of the old year were put out. The people shifted anxiously in the total darkness, murmured in fear.

"Now is the time between the times," Moylann intoned. "Now do the Other try to work their mischief on the world. Now must our light keep them at bay. For among the Other are spirits of good and spirits of evil."

He lit his torch, a small cluster of pine needles. The flame made a whooshing sound as it jumped to life. The druids followed him in a ragged line as Moylann moved to the huge new pile of wood and straw awaiting the fire of the new year. He lit the straw. Sparks rose toward the starlit sky. With a sound like thunder, the Great New Year

Fire blazed at Tara Hill! Now, runners lit torches from the huge bonfire; holding them aloft, they ran into the darkness. All over the hill of Tara and on to the hills beyond, new fires leaped to life. The fires would be tended through the night to keep the Others away from the habitations of humans.

Swiftly, the druii ringed the fire and turned to face the people, who were assembled in terrified silence on the hill. The master druids took out their wands of yew. On each wand were letters of the ogham language, stick figures that ranged up and down the sides of each wand. With these, the druids would make the predictions for the new year.

Moylann stepped forward and cast his wand away into the darkness of the hill. A runner, a student of the druid school, was sent to fetch the wand. He ran with jerky movements into the darkness outside the circle of fire, returned almost immediately with the wand in hand. The people breathed a sigh of relief. The Others who waited in darkness had not stolen their prophecy. Perhaps this would be a peaceful samhain.

Moylann stared at the stick in silence for a moment, then turned toward Cormac, seated on a high dais next to the Lia Fail.

"My king," he cried. "This will be a year of many changes. I see that one of your eyes is closed. I see a wind of change curling about your sons Cairbry and Cellach."

A gasp went up from the assemblage. It did not bode well that the eye of a king would be closed, for a king who had lost an eye could not rule.

One by one, the druii threw out their wands, one by one predicting good harvests, bountiful fishing, fine spring weather, but the minds of the people lingered on the closed eye of the king. Samhain began the dark half of the year. Did the closed eye of the king increase that darkness? What evil would befall the people of Eire?

At last Aodhfin the Wise came forward and cast his stick. The whistle of it moved far away toward the edge of the hill. The people strained in silence for the sound of its descent. Aodhfin spoke.

"The priestess Aislinn will recover my stick."

Aislinn stared at him, then started obediently for the edge of the crowd. She felt her throat go closed with fear when she passed beyond them into darkness, felt the eyes of the people watching as she moved toward the far edge of the hill. She knew that the stick was here somewhere, felt the wet grass seeping into the leather of her sandals, squeezed her eyes shut and open to close out the feeling that the Others were reaching out to her with their cold, thin hands. Her heart thundered in her ears.

Suddenly, she saw the faint gleam of the polished yew stick below her foot. Before she could bend to retrieve it, it was given to her by the slender gleaming hand of a woman of light.

When Aislinn was to think of her later, she would think always that the woman was like a lamp, for she appeared to be lit from within. Her hair was almost white and it seemed to push the light outward from her scalp. Her face was heart-shaped and pale and she was small, no more than five feet tall, though Aislinn felt that she was gazing directly into her eyes. At her side was a lamb of radiant whiteness. The woman smiled.

"You are of the Other," Aislinn said, sure that this was so.

"I am." Again the woman smiled gently. "This is what you must read from the rowan. You must tell the people that the king will see a great light. You must tell them that in that light he will see all truth. You do not understand this now, but you will. Aislinn ni Sorar, you will wear a new robe, a robe that no druii has worn before you. Your robe will be the soft wool of the lamb and the blood of the lamb. Your robe will be the wings of the dove. Your robe will be the scales of the fish who moves like light in the deepest ocean. This too you do not understand, but we will meet again."

She gathered the lamb up into her arms, holding it against her heart.

"Remember what you were told in the grove of oak. Those who forgive are free to love."

It was Aodhfin who came into the darkness and found Aislinn, Aodhfin who led her back to the fireside, but the people knew that she had been with the Other, for the rowan stick in her hand glowed as if lit from within. When she turned to the king to speak, the voice that came from her was neither male nor female, higher than wind, much like the sound of a harp.

"O my king, you will see a great light. In that light you will see all truth," she cried.

Having spoken, Aislinn placed her hands tightly over her abdomen, knowing that she was going to fall. In the darkness at the other side of the circle, Banbh's eyes narrowed as he watched, but when she crumpled, it was Eoghan who ran from the assembled company to lift her in his arms.

12

For a moment, the gleaming light of the post samhain dawn slipped through the flap of the tent and then was gone, but it was enough for the intruder to see that the woman's long brown hair was undone, hanging below her heavy naked breasts.

"Braid your hair," he snapped. "You know that is how I like it."

She complied immediately, raising her arms behind her head and working the braid with practiced motions. Then she went to a small table, lifted a wine cup, and held it toward him. Her face was avid, hungry.

He shook his head, lifted her robe from the stool where she had folded it, threw it toward her.

"Cover yourself."

Disappointment moved across her face. She allowed the robe to fall to the ground, stepped toward him, her hips moving provocatively. When she spoke, her voice was low and husky.

"I have been four days of this fair without sport," she said, "and many weeks before that with only the tamest of encounters. Will you deny me now?"

He laughed harshly.

"You do enjoy your rough sport, don't you, Macha?"

"Perhaps I could say that rough sport is a taste which you have taught me."

He shook his head, took the wine cup from her hand, set it back on the table. "Then you would be lying to yourself. You are a river of hungers, Macha; you have always been so. I have only fed those hungers."

"Will you tell me that you have not enjoyed such feasting?"

"I will tell you that it has served my purpose. Until now." He pressed his hand against the bony plate between her breasts and shoved. She staggered backward into the chair, anger flashing on her face, but she recovered herself, wound her arms over her head, smiled.

"I would be happy to serve this purpose for you again."

For answer, he lifted the robe from the floor, threw it at her again. She stood and drew the rich embroidered silk over her head and let it slide along her form. She turned away, sulky now. He spoke to her back.

"Where is your fool of a husband?"

"Lost in his mead-cups as usual. Lamenting his lost honor. You would think he could at least enjoy his position as chief of the Deisi, no matter how ill-gotten the gain."

She turned back toward him and gestured at the wealth of jewelry she had laid out on the table.

"I do."

She began the process of layering on the heavy torques and spiraling gold bracelets. They gleamed against the candlelight.

"Ah, yes," her visitor said. "The spoils of war. The jewels of the druidess's mother. Another of your hungers, Macha. And one that I have sated well for you."

"So you have." She raised her arms above her head; the heavy bracelets cascaded down her arms. She made a soft sound of pleasure.

"What do you wish, Dark One, if not the sport that I desire?"

"I want you to kidnap the priestess. Have the warriors in your pay arrange it. And be sure that my name is never mentioned."

"What do you want with her?" The woman turned to him, the golden ornaments clicking.

"You never have understood, have you? You never knew why I wanted you to drug the wine of Sorar so many years ago, never understood why I wanted you to convince foolish Aengus that he should have the chieftainship of the Deisi, never understood any of it. You thought that I wanted it for you, that I wanted you to be the queen of the Deisi."

He laughed his harsh, grating laugh. The woman stood still now, staring at him.

"All along, what I wanted was to prevent what began last night. I had the vision many years ago. I knew that this day would come. She and her vision with the yew stick. And what is still to come. I wanted her to die with her mother and father, but your foolish stepson intervened. Then I thought that I could bring her to me, draw her to my dark goddess when she was still a child. Now this thing has come to pass. But we may be able to stop it yet."

"We?" said the woman. "Why should I help you with this plot? She is no more than a foolish child, worthless to me."

"The druidess is with child. His child. I saw that last night when she fell. Think of that, Macha. The son of the chief of the Deisi, a druidess, and their child. Who do you think the people of the tribe will choose to lead them? Will choose as their queen? You with your hoards of gold? Your drunken husband?"

Dark fear crossed her face and greed. He nodded with satisfaction.

"You must kill the child, Macha."

The woman nodded. "I will kill the priestess too, then. It was an easy enough thing to kill the first wife of Aengus, mother of that brooding boy Eoghan. Once she was gone, it was a simple matter to convince Aengus of his right to chieftainship. So I will kill the priestess." She laughed, delighted.

"No!" He struck her hard at the side of her face. She fell to her knees on the floor, her jewelry clanking.

She scrambled up, angry now. She stepped toward him, pushed her hand against his chest.

"You want her. You want her for yourself, old man. A green and stripling girl."

He dug his nails into the woman's hand, held it away from him, and stared in fascination at the spots of blood his talons drew.

"My goddess wishes her. The girl possesses great power. Think what that power could do in the service of the dark." He smiled a feral smile. "As much or more as I have done with you and the tribe of the Deisi."

"There is more to it, Banbh. I have known you long."

He considered for a moment, nodded.

"There is great pleasure in subverting one so good to evil. With you it was too easy. You already wanted so much; I needed only to feed your hungers." He dipped his finger in the blood at the back of her hand, painted a stripe down the center of her nose, across her lips and chin, down into the neckline of her robe. She shivered, licked her lips. He continued.

"Power, Macha. As we both know, it is the only important thing. You wished to be the queen of the Deisi and I gave you that power. You must do as I ask you now. She and her vision will draw power away from my dark goddess. I cannot let that happen. I must stop her before the vision spreads to your stepson or to that fool Aodhfin, or worse to Cormac. When the people see that she has come to me, they will fear me further. They will respect the powers of my goddess and turn toward her. Humans turn toward power as moths move toward flame."

He lifted the woman's hand, held it over the candle flame. She did not struggle, stood still, eyes wide. He withdrew the hand.

"Very good, Macha. You have learned to respect my power, not to struggle against it. You will do as I ask you now with the druidess so that she may learn to do the same."

"You will fail," the woman said. "I watched her last night in the druid fire circle and beside old Aodhfin at the readings of the law. She is like her mother Eibhlain—so pure of heart. She loves my stepson, he who is *so* noble. And she is protected by Aodhfin the Wise. You fear the light in him. I have seen it in you."

He stepped close, his face almost upon hers. He whispered the words.

"You are wrong if you think I will fail," he said. "Aodhfin has told her that it was Eoghan who brought her to him. That is all he knows, all she knows. They do not know that Eoghan is son to the man who killed her father. But Eoghan knows and has not told her, so great is the weight of his shame. The truth can be twisted subtly, made to look dark in the telling. When she learns these things, her anger will make her vulnerable to me. That and her hatred of you and your Aengus when she learns the truth. Hatred is the open door to darkness. Haven't I taught you that is so?"

He grabbed the braid and pulled hard, yanking her head back.

"You have taught me that, yes," she said through clenched teeth.

"And you will do as I have asked?"

"I will do as you have asked."

He released the braid suddenly.

"Very good," he said. "I believe that I will pleasure you after all, Macha. You have pleased me well."

She moaned and licked her lips. He pointed to the wine cup. She grabbed it up quickly spilling a few drops in her haste to hold it out to him. From the bag at his waist, he drew forth a small vial of powder, emptied it into the wine cup. She drank it in one gulp. For a moment she stood still, then tipped her head back and laughed low in her throat. She swayed a little from side to side.

"Oh, Banbh," she whispered, throaty. "I have been too long without this pleasure you provide."

"Remove the robe," he said, his voice flat.

She slid it from her shoulders and let it drop around her feet.

"Kneel."

She knelt on all fours on the dirt floor. She felt his hand twist hard into her braid. For a moment there was nothing and then she felt the dark gleaming feathers of a crow surround her shoulders and caress her breasts. She was pierced by the sharp talons, impaled, lifted into the darkness, and she moaned over and over again with pleasure and pain.

13

The young man leaped into the waist-high pit eagerly, armed only with his shield and a hazel stick. The nine Fian warriors surrounded him, spears in hand.

From the hill above the testing grounds Aislinn could hear Osian, son of Fionn and poet of the Fianna, counseling the young man.

"First breathe deeply, then let your sight become a circle. No spear must touch you, no pole graze your cheek or lift your hair. This is the first test of Fianna."

She watched the young man nod, watched him lift his shield to readiness and clench the stick in his right hand.

Her heart flew out to him standing alone there in the muddied field. Strike well! she wished across the field to him, for she had so long felt as he felt, her only weapon her position as druidess, her aloneness magnified even more now that she had spoken with one of the Other.

She scanned the field for Mac Aidan for she knew that he would be there, fulfilling his dual role as poet of the Ard-Ri and brother to the Fianna. She shook her head determinedly. The time had come to know.

Last night, after the vision of the woman of the Other, she had awakened in Mac Aidan's arms, opened her eyes to find him rocking her like a child, his head bent close to her.

"Aodhfin has told me," she whispered.

"Told you what?" Eoghan asked, alarmed.

"He has told me that it was you who brought me to him."

"And you bear me no ill will?"

"You saved my life. You were a boy who cared for a child. What ill could I bear you? But Aodhfin cannot tell me why you do not bear your father's name. You must tell me why you have chosen to be ecland—clanless— why you have been Fianna. Tell me everything, Eoghan." And when you do, she thought, I will tell you of the twin souls I carry.

"I carry the name of my mother's people because it is a name of honor. I cannot carry my father's name for he has dishonored it. More than that I cannot tell you now."

"I must know."

"You will know. Tomorrow. I promise you that you will know everything tomorrow. Until then, will you trust me? Will you believe that I am doing what is right? I tell you that I am doing what your mother would wish done. Can you believe that?"

"Amaireach, amaireach. I am tired of tomorrows."

She watched the sorrow shift into his face. For a moment, he looked much like Aengus Mac Gabuideach and suddenly she softened.

"I trust in you, Mac Aidan. But understand that this is my journey, the quest on which my teacher has sent me. I must know the truth." She said nothing about the babes who moved within her.

"Tomorrow. I promise the truth tomorrow."

Below her, she watched as the young man climbed from the pit, untouched. Several men of the Fianna approached him with congratulations. Now, they would braid his long red hair. The next test was the most grueling. The candidate would run in the woods with six men of a Fian chasing him, spears at the ready. He must break no branch beneath his foot. Not a strand of his hair may be pulled free from the braid. His weapon must not tremble in his hand. Should his bare foot encounter a thorn, he must pull it from his foot while running. Should he emerge uncaught and unscathed, he would be accepted for the Fianna, breaking all legal connection with his own clan. He would be ecland—clanless—and dithir—landless.

Why had Mac Aidan made such a choice?

Today, at last, she would know.

Aislinn's mind flew to Corra ni Brith and their own flight from Brennus Mac Bran. What had she begun with her headlong flight with the child, she wondered, watching the young man poised at the edge of the forest. Run swift, she wished him. Run wise. Run as I must run.

She felt the warmth of a presence behind her and turned expecting it to be Eoghan. Instead, she gasped as she recognized Fionn Mac Cumhail of the Fianna. Faced with the man of legend, Aislinn could only stare; no courtesy came to her lips. Fionn spoke first.

He gestured toward the red-haired boy.

"You wish him well, priestess. I can see that in your stance and in the clenching of your hands. This is good. May he run on the strength of your belief in him."

Aislinn had seen Fionn only at a distance and then only two or three times in her life. At this close range she could see what she could not before. The hair that seemed so gold was in fact almost all gray. Deep furrows creased the forehead and radiated out from the eyes that were an odd sea-green color.

In peacetime, Fionn commanded three cathas of Fenians, each with three thousand members. The number swelled to seven cathas in time of war. Aislinn wondered if all of the stories of Fionn were true, for it was said that he could adopt the shape of any creature of the forest and that he had once been married to a woman who was also a deer. It was said too that he conversed openly and often with the Others, the people of the sidhe. Aislinn looked for the signs of these transformations in his face and eyes. He smiled at her searching. Aislinn blushed deeply and lowered her gaze.

"Honored Fenian, my apologies. I am rude to stare in such a manner, but I am a child in the ways of the Fianna and I have heard much of you."

The Fenian sighed.

"They have all heard much of me. Perhaps you have heard too of the mistakes I have made for love."

Aislinn kept her face bent toward the ground, nodded her response. All of Eire knew the tale of Fionn and Grainne, the daughter of Cormac Mac Art, of their betrothal and her escape with Dhiarmuid, another Fenian. Fionn had pursued them relentlessly throughout Eire. Still looking at the ground, Aislinn ventured a question.

"Why do you tell me of your sorrow?"

She felt his hand go under her chin, felt the soothing warmth of the gesture. She looked up, waited. He continued.

"Eoghan Mac Aidan is my Fenian brother and my friend. He came to us just after"—here Mac Cumhail paused—"just after fosterhood in his seventeenth year. Never has another Fenian fended the spears so well, run so well, so desperate was his need to be among us. Even when his eloquence in the great hall caused Cormac to pluck him from our ranks for poetic training, even then he remained a Fenian, landless, clanless, apart from the world of men.

"Until now. Now I see in him that he will return to that world if you are with him."

Aislinn stood still, waiting. From the field below them a huge shout went up. She turned to see the red-haired young man emerge from the forest unscathed. Fionn raised his spear in salute from the crest of the hill.

"See where young Tomaltagh has succeeded. He will

be welcome among us. Perhaps your goodwill sped him through the forest, priestess. Perhaps your love can do the same for Eoghan Mac Aidan."

"Of what forest do we speak, Fenian?"

Mac Cumhail smiled at her gently, answered in an oblique way.

"I have discovered a strange truth in my long life, priestess. We make our greatest mistakes for love and they are the only mistakes we would choose again and yet again."

The feast of the Fianna was a riot of color and noise. The young men who had been accepted as candidates were seated together. Aislinn saw the redheaded boy of this morning among them and her heart gladdened.

At the high dais near the king sat Fionn, leader of the Fianna, Osian his son, and Oscar his grandson. Fionn's beloved dogs Bran and Sceolan lay at his feet.

Spread out across the banqueting hall were hundreds of the Fianna in their blue and green cloaks, many accompanied by their women. For this night, their weaponry had been put aside. Servants came through the door bearing platters of steaming beef and wild boar, loaves of bread and bowls of warm honey, fish roasted in sea grasses and hard white cheeses. Warm mulled wine and mead overflowed in every cup.

Cormac Mac Art stood and the assembly quieted.

"Since the time of my grandfather, Conn of the Hundred Battles, the Fenian warriors have protected our land from invaders and from forces who would destroy us from within. We are in their debt."

He raised his golden cup and the jewels sparkled in the torchlight.

"To the fine young men of Eire who have today completed their test of initiation, we raise our cup."

As one, the two score men stood and raised their meadcups toward the king. He continued.

"At the time of samhain feis, it is our custom to grant the wishes of our warriors. What can we do for any among the Fianna?"

Osian, poet and chronicler of the Fianna, stood.

"My king, we of the Fianna traditionally claim at this feis first choice of the women of Eire for our brides."

A wave of laughter and excitement swept through the room. Young men and women who had declared their love long before the feast looked across the room in anticipation. One or two young girls shifted nervously, looking toward Fenians who had paid them some recent attention. With the exception of this one feast, it was the custom in Eire for young women to choose the lifemate. Occasionally, at this feast, the selections took everyone, including the proposed bride, by surprise.

The entire assembly quieted, waiting to hear which young women would be chosen by the warriors. Osian continued.

"From among our ranks you have chosen your poet, Eoghan, who calls himself Mac Aidan, but we of the Fianna still consider him our brother."

Aislinn's head snapped around to the king's dais. She watched incredulously as Eoghan Mac Aidan rose before the assembled company. A hot blush rose up her face and she felt Aodhfin beside her turn toward her smiling.

"I claim right of the Fianna to first bride choice!" Eoghan shouted before the whole assembly. "I wish the druidess Aislinn ni Sorar as my wife."

Cormac again raised his golden goblet.

"What say you, priestess, to the proposal of my poet?"

Aislinn stood. She felt the room swirl before her eyes. The colors took on a life of their own, spiraling outward to the smoky torches on the walls. Her hand crept over her abdomen and remained there, still. She could feel her fear paralyzing her voice. The great hall buzzed, then grew quiet as Aislinn made no sound. Slowly she lifted her head. From far across the room she met the eyes of Eoghan Mac Aidan. There was much that she did not know, needed to know. What dishonor did his family carry that made him forsake their name? And yet, what had that to do with her? Did she not know his role in her life? Had it not always been that of protector? Was he not the father of the spirits she carried within her? Suddenly, with clarity, Aislinn knew that when she told him, his reaction would be joy, unstinting and true. These thoughts chased across her face. Eoghan smiled gently, made a small gesture in her direction.

The choice was hers alone.

She turned toward Aodhfin. He tipped his palm toward Eoghan. She saw the light spill from his palm, cascade toward her beloved.

Her beloved. The choice was already made, had been made before they met.

She felt the tears start up behind her eyes and she smiled back at Eoghan across the length of the room. She lifted her head to the dais of the king and answered in her proudest voice.

"I say yes."

14

For the second time that week they lay entwined by the fire in the druii lodge. Mac Aidan ran his hands along the length of her hair, bringing it up to his face and breathing in the sweet blossomy scent.

"My wife," he whispered. "My cet-muintir, first woman of my heart."

He stroked the curving length of her back and kissed the hollow at the base of her throat.

"I did not think that you would accept me. I thought that your fears would hold you back." He shook his head wonderingly. "Now we are blood kin. Now I can tell you everything and they will not harm you, now that you are in my protection."

"Who?" Aislinn pushed against his chest a little, lifting her hair over her shoulder, then leaning into the warm muscular center of his chest.

Mac Aidan raised himself to a sitting position, drawing her into the circle of his arms.

"The time has come," he said solemnly. "I must tell you everything, for we must begin with truth."

"I too have something to tell you," said Aislinn, leaning softly into his shoulder.

He kissed her hair, her forehead, her lips. He closed his eyes, composing words, she supposed, in the way poets are taught to do. She waited, to let him speak first.

His voice, when he began the tale, had the tone and pace of a storyteller—removed, lost in the tale.

"I knew your parents, Aislinn ni Sorar. I was a young man of seventeen, just returned from ten years of fosterage with O'Domnhnaill. Your father, Sorar, was chief of all the Deisi."

"This Aodhfin has told me."

Eoghan nodded.

"Your mother, Eibhlain, was the most beautiful woman I had ever seen, until I saw you. How she doted on you. Even as a callow young man of seventeen I could see that the love between her and your father had fire still. I could see the tenderness and passion in their gestures and the way they surrounded you with that passion. I envied them that perfect circle."

He sighed raggedly. "My own mother died while I was in fosterage, a boy of ten, and by the time I returned to my tribe, my father, Aengus Mac Gabuideach, had married the woman, Macha, she whom you have seen here at the feis."

Aislinn shivered. "I do not like her, Eoghan. Her smile is too cunning."

Mac Aidan nodded. "Oh, yes, she is cunning. I had not been back a week when she came to where I was sleeping and offered herself to me. She said that she would take pleasure from sharing herself with the father and the son. I repulsed her.

"Not long after that my father began to talk about being chief of the Deisi. There was no reason for him to even want the position. Your father had been chosen by the tribe; he was a fair ruler. Macha incited my father, I believe that. She wanted to possess your mother's place—her clothes, her jewels, the adoration her husband so obviously gave her."

He shook his head. "I don't know why my father would

do such a thing, would want such a position without honor. There was a feast. My father challenged your father to a boasting combat. Their boasting became a combat of knives.

"The battle between our fathers became a war. All of the people of the Deisi took sides. I sided with O'Domnhnaill against my father, but it was my father who won, who claimed position as chief of the Deisi. I still cannot say how he won. It was as if some dark force assisted him; the Deisi sided with him out of fear. O'Domnhnaill and his followers escaped and built the crannog.

"In shame I took my mother's name, left the tribes, trained for the Fianna. I became ecland and dithir, a man with no name, no clan, no land. I was with the Fianna for four years before my skill at poetic forms caused Cormac to pluck me from their ranks for druii poetic training."

"My father was killed in battle?"

Mac Aidan shook his head, seemed to reach somewhere deep inside him for his voice.

"No, my love. My father killed your father in the hand-to-hand combat of the knives at that last feast of the Deisi."

Aislinn shook her head from side to side, as if trying to clear it.

"Your father killed my father. Why did you not tell me this before? Why did you wait until now? I see no shame in you, for have you not set yourself apart from the name and the deed? Are you not still the one I love?" She looked at him, the last a real question, her eyes uncertain.

He took her hands. "Of course I am. But I am ashamed of what my father has done, of the death of your father, of the division of the Deisi. And I feared for you."

"Why? These deeds are long past."

"As daughter of Sorar, you have a legitimate claim to the land and the chieftainship. You could take it from my father and the cursed Macha. This puts you in terrible danger; Macha is a ruthless woman, that I know. And my father was weak and malleable. That is why Aodhfin has protected you all these years, has raised you in the sacred person of a druidess. And now you are married to me, son of this man who calls himself chief, also with a legitimate claim. Together we are formidable. But do you see that I could not tell you any of this until now? Partly it was my shame. But the other part was the danger to you, the way the knowledge of your position would make you vulnerable. When you were a wandering druidess, ignorant of your name and position, what had Macha and my father to fear? But if you returned to Tara, carrying the knowledge of your clan that they would fear most of all. Now I have protected you. You are my own wife, landless and clanless as I am, no threat to them now."

"You have made me landless and clanless?"

"I am Fianna. You are as I am. But were you not always so?"

Again she shook her head, feeling that she needed to clear some fog.

"No, there is more here, some truth that I do not know. Knowing all that you have told me, I would have chosen for you still. What passed between our families does not pass between us. There is more! I feel it! I have felt it poised above me since the day of Mac Bran's death. What of my mother? Tell me of my mother, Mac Aidan."

"Now you are wise, priestess." The thin nasal voice came from just inside the door. Banbh moved into the light of the fire and Aislinn saw the flames draw a blue gleam from the crow's feathers on his mantle. Aislinn felt fear congeal hard beneath her throat.

Mac Aidan stood, lifted his sword against the chest of the druid. Banbh waved his hand at him, the way one would wave away gnats in the heat of summer.

"Foolish Fenian. Did you think you could feed her the truth in honey-drops? Do you think you can stop the tide of it now? Oh, yes, there is more, priestess. Has your Mac Aidan not told you that it was he who tore you from your mother, he who let her go to her death by your father's side?" He smiled, his teeth gleaming in the light.

Mac Aidan dropped his head, the sword tilting uselessly against the cold floor.

Aislinn came quickly to his defense.

"This Aodhfin has told me. Eoghan was a boy of seventeen. He brought me to my teacher."

Eoghan looked up at her, his face filled with hope.

"Ah, but there is more, priestess. You do not need him to tell you," Banbh said, dismissing the silent Eoghan. "You have your own powers! Has there not always been an unfinished vision? Let me help you to remember what is true." From inside the black robe he withdrew something that looked like a ball of cobwebs. Gently, he lifted away a strand, wafted it into the air. It settled into Aislinn's hair.

She closed her eyes, felt the web gather around the shifting memories of her childhood. Again she heard her own screaming, heard the harsh racking sound of her mother's weeping, felt the arms of iron around her midsection. This was the vision that had begun that long-ago day with Eoghan, the day he had touched her hand against the neck of the horse! The vision solidified, became real. Aislinn was a child again, five years old, her arms outstretched to her mother.

"No," she was sobbing. "No. Please don't take me from my máthair. Oh, please, not now with my athair gone."

In the vision, Aislinn twisted her five-year-old body in the arms of the man who was holding her, turned toward his face. She knew even before she faced him fully. For holding her with a grip she could not break was Eoghan Mac Aidan.

She cried aloud, willed herself to leave the vision. It was only as she began to pull up out of the vision that she heard her mother begin to speak, faint and far away. She did not stay to listen to her words.

Aislinn came out of the vision seated on the floor, sobbing.

"I remember you taking me away from my mother.

Eoghan, I remember how hard you held me."

"What you do to her is cruel, druid! She was a child being torn from her mother!" He lifted the sword against the dark shape, slashed down through the air. The blade seemed to cut through the shining cloak; there was a whisper of feathers, a frantic beating sound. Banbh stood whole and untouched on the opposite side of the room.

"There is more, priestess," said Banbh, moistening his lips. "He has not told you, this lover of yours, this husband," he spat the word, "that your mother was entombed alive with the body of your father."

He watched her face greedily.

"Alive? My mother was entombed? My mother died in the dark of the tomb? You left her in the tomb? Alone?" She looked pleadingly at Eoghan.

"Do not let him do this to you! Aislinn, see his truth for what it is! Your mother performed the death-fast for your father. She did this to protect you."

Eoghan lifted his sword, ran at Banbh.

"Enough! Leave her now or you will die, druii or no."

Banbh waved his hand and Eoghan let out a cry. His sword clattered to the floor. Where his palm had been closed around the hilt, red blisters rose. His hand smelled sickly of burning flesh.

"Nay, I cannot leave her yet. You have not told her why her father died. Your father was a masterful fighter, priestess. He should have won at combat with Aengus Mac Gabuideach. Your mother and he should be ruling the Deisi today, with you, their beloved daughter, by their side. No, your lover has not told you that the wine your father drank was drugged. Nor that he, your beloved Eoghan, served the wine."

She saw Mac Aidan's head snap up, saw him turn toward Banbh, a look like astonishment on his face. She felt her anger rise hot and clean behind her eyes.

"You drugged my father, sent my mother to her entombment, tore me from them. What further cruelty is this that you have married me? Are you composed all of lies, poet? Was each thing you said a lie? And I, poor fool, marrying you, believing that you had saved me from certain death. Why did you not kill me too, a stripling child, unable to protect herself? What game do you play in marrying me to this family of shame?"

She found her dagger and threw herself against Mac Aidan, slashing at his arms and shoulders and face, watching the blood begin to ooze from his skin, all the while sobbing, her naked body pressed against his. He made no move to stop her, caressed her hair, whispered only that he was sorry, so sorry.

Banbh watched avidly, still, his arms hidden beneath the shining black cloak. When at last she collapsed sobbing to the floor, Banbh whispered softly.

"Ah, poor Aodhfin. How distraught he will be when he knows the treachery that has trapped his beloved foster-child."

Aislinn's head snapped up. She ceased weeping.

"My father. I must speak to my father."

In a flurry, she lifted her dress and cloak over her head, ran for the door.

"Wait," Eoghan cried. "Let me tell you . . ."

"No more!" She held her hand up, palm out. "All of this you should have told me long ago. I will believe no more of your half-truths and lies. Yours is a family of shame. May it sit upon you forever."

Outside, Banbh had tethered a horse beside the lodge. Aislinn unhitched the animal, threw herself over its back. Banbh, watching from the doorway, made no objection, turned his head in a small, satisfied smile.

Aislinn rode away, alone and directionless into the windy, rainy night, finally turning toward the hill of Tara and Aodhfin.

But they took her at the ford of the river Boann.

15

There were two of them, dressed in the colors of the tribes of the Deisi. They were elaborately polite, careful not to touch her. They held the bridle, spoke in ritual sentences.

"Honored priestess. She who is wife of our chieftain would like to speak to you."

"No." She reached down for the reins, misunderstanding the situation.

"You are a priestess and therefore inviolable. We will not harm you. But Macha would like you to know that it would be tragic if the horse of a woman with child were to bolt, tragic if that woman were to fall, if her babe were to die." He shifted the reins slightly, lifting the horse's head so that the horse nickered and laid back his ears.

Aislinn felt prickles of fear creep along her arms. How did the woman know that she was with child? Only Aodhfin knew. She had not even yet told . . . A sob broke from her at the thought of Mac Aidan, of the life she had imagined. Her hand crept down and rested against her abdomen. Why was she riding like this, so ungently, with the babes? Had she forgotten the twin spirits she cradled? She shook her head, felt some clarity returning.

"Very well." She nodded. "I will speak with this woman. Nothing she can say can harm me now."

She laughed, a harsh, rasping sound. She tipped her head back toward the starless sky, stretched her arms out to her sides.

"O you gods!" she cried, her arms outstretched. But she could think of nothing further to say. She waited there for a moment, listening, and when no answer came she let her body do what it most wanted to do. She cried out, a high, horrible sound, part wolf, part mourning woman, part child. She let the wail carry across the river and around her for so long a time that she saw the men around her making the sign against the evil.

She laughed again, dropping her arms.

"Let us go, then."

The men were silent for the entire ride.

They did not go back to the hill of Tara, nor did they ride toward the tuath of the Deisi. Instead they forded the river and headed north and then west more than three hours into the forest until they came to a small, thatched, and circular hut. The gleam of light from the cracks indicated, even from a distance, that the occupant waited there.

Inside, a small fire burned on a central hearth and tea was brewing. The woman was there, elaborately garbed in the colors of chieftainship and heavily ornamented with jewelry, from bracelets of silver and gold to a wrought crown of silver and bronze. Her face was flushed with pleasure. She actually clapped her hands when the soldiers ushered Aislinn into the tiny room.

"Ah, priestess. I am so pleased that you have come. This will be a most civil conversation, I promise you. Will you take tea?"

Aislinn nodded wearily, sitting on one of the small crescent-shaped stools near the fire.

The woman walked behind her, lifted a hank of Aislinn's hair, and let it run through her hands.

"It is so lovely," she said. "Your mother had lovely

hair, though it was the color of bronze. I remember how it used to shine in the firelight, how your father used to lift it sometimes, just as I am doing now. Ah, but I discuss things past, do I not?"

Aislinn nodded dully. Things past. All things past.

"Well then. We will have our tea."

She poured the steaming tea into the heavy cups, handed one to Aislinn, sat opposite her on the camp stool.

Aislinn held the cup in her hands, felt the warmth pressing against her palms. She lifted the cup against her forehead, let the heat have a clearing effect. She sighed.

"Why have you brought me here, Macha?" She felt no fear, only an all-absorbing weariness.

Macha smiled. "We should discuss things past. After all, we are family now."

Aislinn's head snapped up. "All of my family are dead."

The woman smiled, looked sympathetic. "I understand your anger. He didn't tell you, did he, my noble stepson? Well, drink your tea."

Aislinn lifted the cup to her lips, took a deep sip, felt the warm liquid sear its way down her throat. She looked up to see the woman veiling a look of pure triumph.

Suddenly, Aislinn felt the beginnings of panic. She looked down into the cup, inhaled deeply.

"What have you done?"

The woman smiled, licked her lips.

"Relieved you of a problem."

Aislinn felt the cramps begin then, deep in her belly.

She clutched her abdomen, walked shakily to the small sleeping shelf in the corner of the hut, and lay down.

"Not my babes. Not my babes."

The woman Macha raised her eyebrows.

"More than one? He will be surprised to learn of this." She laughed easily. "So he is not infallible after all. Well." She gathered her things, wrapped her cloak around her, and pinned her brooch carefully.

"I must return to the festivities at Tara. I would not wish to be missed."

She stepped into the darkness, spoke to the guards.

"I cannot tarry longer. The wife of a chieftain will be missed. One of you will escort me back to the feis, the other will remain with her. She is not to be allowed to leave here." She gestured to the guard who would remain. "You are to watch for blood and summon me when it comes."

Outside, Aislinn heard the guard make a sound of protest.

"Nay, be obedient and do not let your superstitious fears overcome you. She is a mere slip of a girl for all that she is a druidess. There will be plenty of gold and plenty of sport for both of you in this night's work."

"What sport do we speak of, Macha?"

"Of the type that the three of us have enjoyed before."

Aislinn heard the guards' rough laughter and Macha's high-pitched breathless excitement, then the sound of a slap.

"Not now. I must remain clear of this night's work. There will be plenty of time in the weeks to come."

The sound of hoofbeats retreated into the distance. The door of the hut flew open and Aislinn glimpsed the red-faced visage of the guard. She sat up, staring at him, absolutely silent.

He made the sign against the evil, slammed the door shut as he retreated to the forest.

Aislinn forced her breathing to be even and regular. She lay back down, pressed her hands across her abdomen. She thought about the tea, reasoned that she had drunk but less than half the mug. Still, the cramps grew more severe, moving lower into her belly, rippling across her stomach in great waves. She felt the panic rise up in her throat. She knew what herbs to take to counteract this poison, knew what would stop the cramping, hold the blood within. But how could she find what she needed?

She could not move. Another spasm of pain shot across her abdomen. She began to weep.

"Brighid, you who are goddess of mothers and children, you who bring fertility, hear me now, save my babes."

Then, with absolute clarity, she knew what she must do. She glanced around the hut, searching for a sharp object. Her eyes lighted on her brooch, still clinging to her cloak. Slowly, she rose and inched across the little hut. The cramps increased their intensity. She gathered the entire cloak, returned to the narrow bed, and lay down, allowing the cramps to subside. When they had calmed somewhat, she unpinned her brooch, raised her gown above her waist. Taking the pin from her brooch, she made two deep long cuts along the hidden inside folds of her legs. When the blood began to flow, she lowered her gown, pressing it down into the blood, allowing the red color to flood both the front and the back of the gown, squeezing against her legs to increase the flow until the gown was soaked.

For a few moments, she lay back exhausted, her hands trembling, the sweat at the inside of her legs making the cuts burn. Then, she slowly and painstakingly licked her brooch pin and each of her bloody fingers clean. With shaking fingers, she repinned her brooch to her cloak, then threw the cloak the little distance toward the wall where she had found it. It collapsed in a heap on the floor, looking simply as though it had fallen from the peg.

Now Aislinn lay still against the sleeping platform. She closed her eyes, willed her breathing to slow, to still. She called upon all of her druii training, whispered over and over in her mind.

"I retreat to the center of myself. I retreat to the center of myself."

She felt her heartbeat go stiller, softer, felt it become almost nothing. Her mind retreated from the front of her forehead, from behind her eyes, moving down to a spot deep within herself.

She felt the color drain from her face, knew that her

hands and feet felt icy, cold, but by now she had retreated so far that she could not come back to warm them. At the center of herself, she whispered to the spirits of the babes.

"Sleep, sleep, my tiny ones. We must remain together."

When the guard stepped in to check on her an hour later, he let out a strangled gasp.

"By the gods. She cannot die, Macha will have my head."

A few moments later Aislinn heard the faint sounds of hoofbeats retreating in the distance.

It was the voice of Banbh she heard first when the hut door opened and she felt a tiny flicker of fear at the core of herself. He would know that it was a druii trick, this stillness of the body.

But it was the blood and the male fear of things female that saved her.

He lifted the gown, let it drop.

"Macha! You have given her too much of the herb."

She heard the sound of a hard slap.

"Nay, I gave her one cup, and even then she did not drink it all."

"She has lost the babes, but I think she is nearly gone too. We must give her alkemelych. I thank the gods that the guard had the sense to tell us about the blood. We must stanch the flow, return her courses. I told you that I did not wish her to die. My goddess wishes her; I will not lose her to your stupidity."

From deep inside herself, Aislinn smelled the potent herb as Banbh removed it from his pack, set up a tea to brew. She pictured the eight-pronged scalloped leaves, the tiny green and yellow clusters of flowers. She willed her heart to beat slowly, her breathing to remain convincingly shallow.

When they poured the warm brew down her throat she rejoiced with the spirits of the small ones.

"Hush, my little ones. Let it work. Stay still. Let it keep us together."

Two hours later the cramps ceased entirely and Aislinn let her breathing become just a little deeper, allowed the blood to return to her face.

She felt Banbh's hands against the pulse at her wrist and in her neck, felt the shadow of him lower against her face.

"Good, she will live. Now I must go before she awakes, Macha, and realizes that I was here."

Again she heard the sound of a slap.

"Did I not tell you that I was not to be involved? Foolish woman."

"When my guard said that she was dying, I was afraid. I knew that you wanted her for your own purposes. So I came for you."

"We will deal with your failure later. For now, I will go. You must bring someone here to nurse her, Macha. She must not leave here until she has gained in strength, yet neither Aodhfin nor Eoghan must know where she has gone."

There was a wind and he was gone. Aislinn felt the woman Macha bend over her, felt her hands begin to lift the gown. She willed herself up behind her eyes, willed the eyes to snap open. The woman jumped back. Aislinn raised up a little, stared at the blood on the gown. Her shoulders began to shake and she allowed herself to weep, dropping back onto the sleeping platform and letting the tears run sideways down her face and into her hair.

The woman smiled a small smile and returned to her seat by the fire.

Only Aislinn knew that she wept with relief at the steady beating of the two hearts deep within her.

Aine arrived two days after the bloody night of Banbh and Macha. Macha brought her to the isolated hut to serve as a nurse for Aislinn, but Aislinn suspected that Aine's disabilities were the real reason for Macha's choice.

Aine was deaf and dumb.

She was also toothless and wizened, with a silent laugh that shook her entire body. She was fond of dancing to some internal music, whirling about the tiny hut, her skirts coming far too close to the fire, smiling and nodding as if at some strange interior conversation. Aine was mad.

She was not, Aislinn discovered soon after her arrival, slow or unkind. She knew every herb of the forest, knew them even better than Aislinn with her druii training. Daily, Aine strengthened Aislinn with teas and tisanes designed to regulate the courses and strengthen the womb and the uterus. Aislinn suspected that Aine knew that she was still carrying the babies, but when Aine surprised Aislinn at her surreptitious daily sponge bath and saw her swabbing at the ugly red streak at the top of her thigh, she was certain. Aine's face lit up with delight then. She pointed to the scar, nodded in swift approval, tapped the side of her head to show Aislinn how wise she thought her, then placed her finger firmly on her lips to show that she would not tell Macha, even if she could.

From that day on, Aine made warm poultices and laid them against Aislinn's inner thighs. She redoubled her efforts with the strengthening herbs and cooked meals far too large for the two of them, insisting that Aislinn eat more than half, all the while bobbing her head and pointing at Aislinn's belly, then cradling her arms to indicate that the babes must grow strong.

Aine was Aislinn's comfort through the long winter weeks for as soon as Aislinn grew strong enough the guards began a system of moving her from dwelling to dwelling—two days in a cave here, a week in a remote hut in some forest, a night or two in a cold bothy by a nearly frozen stream, always looking over their shoulders as if they feared some pursuer.

The guards remained loyal only to Macha. They always built their bothy outside whatever dwelling Aislinn and Aine occupied, though Aislinn heard them complaining daily about the lonely duty and the cold winter woods. Aislinn lived in fear that one of them might notice her thickening waist and report the change to Macha, but they seldom entered the hut. Aislinn suspected that they were afraid of her. Daily, she thanked the goddess Brighid that they were men who rarely noticed the changes in a woman.

Most terrifying were the visits from Macha. Aislinn would hear the thundering hooves of her horse long before she swept into the clearing and burst into the hut. On her first visit, her cheek was blackened and heavy rope burns circled her wrists. She was angry with Aislinn.

"Do you see what you have done, priestess?" She held out her wrists, lifted her gown to display bruises that ran all the way up her legs and across her buttocks. "I like pain with my pleasure, but because of you he denies me the pleasure and metes out the pain. Bah!" She spit at Aislinn, lashed out, and hit her hard across the cheek.

By the next visit Macha was heavily adorned with jewelry, dressed in her finest cloak and gown, but she seemed agitated and angry, strung tight as a harp string. She scrutinized Aislinn, lifted her face into the light.

"You are not like your mother," she pronounced. "She was much more beautiful; her color was higher. You are too pinched and pale. But you have your father's eyes."

She pinned Aislinn against the wall, smiled as fear and disgust rose up in Aislinn's eyes. She placed her hands under Aislinn's breasts and lifted them just a little. Aislinn feared that she might expose them, might notice that they had become heavier, but Macha returned her hands to her own breasts, lifted and fondled them.

"Yours do not match the weight of mine. Perhaps he will be disappointed by the smallness of their size." She shrugged. "But I think that he will have you."

She shook her head in anger. "He will not let me give you to the guards. Do you see? I think he saves that pleasure for himself."

Aislinn spoke softly, "You speak of Banbh?"

Macha looked momentarily surprised, made no reply. Aislinn spoke directly to her.

"He will not have me. None will have me again."

Macha seemed encouraged at Aislinn's resistance, nodded as if they had decided some important thing together.

"Well, we need not worry it now. Your courses will not return to normal until the third month."

She turned on Aine then, pushing the old woman against the wall of the hut.

"Does she eat?" she cried in a loud voice, making a spooning motion with her hands.

Aine shook her head, made a sign with her fingers for a meager portion. Behind her back, Aislinn almost laughed aloud.

"Have her courses returned to normal?" Again she screamed, pointing between Aislinn's legs.

Again, Aine shook her head, scrabbled in her hearthside basket for a bloody piece of cloth she had used for last night's rabbit, held it aloft proudly. Aislinn felt tears start behind her eyes at the old woman's fierce determination to protect her. Eoghan had been that way. And Aodhfin. But there could be no remembering them now.

Macha was talking again, agitated.

"Still bleeding. Well, I will tell him that." She smiled at Aislinn, baring her teeth. "Three months. That is what I told him it would take." She left the hut in a flurry of whirling cloak and clanking jewelry. Aislinn hurried to hold Aine to her heart.

With each visit, she and Aine endured Macha's trysts with the guards. They were tied in the cold bothy while the guards accompanied Macha into whatever hut or cave served as shelter. Macha took great pleasure in tying Aislinn to the bothy, pulling her arms up hard behind her, braiding Aislinn's hair into the pine boughs so that she could not move her head. All the while Macha talked to the guards about the pleasures that would reward them for their services. Soon the sounds of their rough play and lewd comments would drift out from the warm fireside to where Aislinn and Aine were tied. At least, thought Aislinn, Aine was spared the sounds, though certainly she knew what was happening, for she watched the girl with pity throughout each night.

Aislinn lived daily with the fear of the three-month deadline, stared each day at her belly to see if the babes had begun to show. She missed Corra ni Brith, wondered if the child would remember her, would forgive her for her abandonment. The last month of fall turned to the first months of winter. The shortest night of the year passed and winter began its slow crawl toward spring. Aislinn began the second month of her pregnancy.

Banbh never came to any of the huts or dwellings and Macha never mentioned him by name, but Aislinn knew that he was the one who waited for her at the end of her captivity. She lived in fear of it. Nightly in her dreams she relived her childhood memories of him, of his sour breath and grasping hands, of the huge blackness of his crow-feather cloak. What was it that had made him want to hurt her even then?

Daily she relived that last night with Eoghan Mac Aidan. She saw the sorrow in his eyes as Banbh told her the tale of her mother's death, saw the astonishment when Banbh said that her father had been drugged.

Eoghan had not known!

Aislinn was sure of it, replayed again and again the look on his face. Astonishment, disgust. He had not known!

She should have known that Banbh would trick her, would trick them both. He was all lies, all trickery. And she, a one-day wife, had laid more shame upon Eoghan who had kept himself from his father's trickery, who had put himself in danger, a stripling boy, just to save her life.

Slowly, her heart began to heal itself of the way of her parents' deaths.

At last, in a dark night of dreaming, she entered again her vision of herself as a five-year-old child. Again she saw herself screaming and stretching her hands to her mother, again saw the face of Eoghan, felt his strong arms around her childish frame. But this time she heard what her mother had said to Eoghan in the vision.

"May the gods bless you, Eoghan Mac Gabuideach, for this great kindness to my child."

When she awoke in the morning, Aislinn was ready to escape.

16

Eoghan entered the lodge in a whirl of robes and snow, shaking himself in the same way Sheary shook before the fire.

Aodhfin stood from the fireside, ladled him a cup of warm mulled wine, spoke gently.

"Still no sign of her?"

"Signs! There are signs aplenty, old one. An abandoned hut deep in the northern forest, littered with bloody rags." He held up his hand to forestall the old man's question. "The blood of rabbits according to Fionn, but there was the scent of her in the air. I smelled it myself. And the bothy, long abandoned, the fire stones cold, with the long strands of her hair twined into the pine boughs. Who has her, Aodhfin? Where is she? She is shielded by some powerful dark magic when even Fionn of the forests cannot find her."

He drank the wine at a single gulp, threw the cup against the fire stones.

"It is Banbh, the evil one. I know this, Aodhfin. And she is not his willing guest, but his captive. I can wait no longer despite your counseling me to caution. His darkness is powerful; should she succumb to it! I will ride him down and find him whether he be in Eire or departed from it. And if he will not tell me where he keeps her, I will kill him." He turned for the door, called Sheary to his side, turned back to Aodhfin.

"Wait, Eoghan!" Aodhfin called to his retreating form. "It is not Banbh who shields her from us. It is Aislinn herself."

Eoghan turned back, stared at the old man.

"What do you know?"

"It is more what I sense. I have listened for her throughout these dark months, have waited to feel her presence within me, even as I felt the link for those long two years that she was a wanderer. The link that helped me to know that she was alive, though lonely. But I have felt nothing of her, no presence, such emptiness that I feared she might be dead."

"This is my fault, father, mine all for not telling her—or you—of the shame of my family name. And yet I swear that I knew nothing of the poisoning."

Aodhfin waved him away, almost impatiently.

"I have told you that I believe you well. When Aislinn listens to her heart, she will also believe in you and know that such treachery could not live in you. Hear me now! In this last fortnight that you have been gone again searching for her, my sense of her has changed. I feel her again, the faint warmth of her presence. Until now she was not ready for us to find her, so deep was her feeling of betrayal. But now her mind has accepted what her heart always knew. She is ready to come back to us, Eoghan. I sense it. You must remain here with me. We must be ready when she calls for our aid."

Eoghan strode across the length of the lodge, gripped the old man by the upper arms.

"You are sure of this, father? You are sure that she is well."

"As sure as I can be with these gifts I have been given."

Eoghan stared hard at the old man for a long moment, then dropped to a place beside the hearth and buried his head in his arms, his shoulders shaking like those of a small child.

The last night of the cold month came and Aislinn began the third month of her pregnancy. Tomorrow was the feast of Imbolc, feast of the goddess Brighid, the day Aislinn intended to return to Tara.

With walking fingers and a series of pointing gestures, she conveyed to Aine that together they would make their escape. Aine nodded enthusiastically and clutched at Aislinn's hands, pressing them to her lips.

Sitting by the fire, Aislinn fashioned the straw sun-symbol of Brighid. Aine made nodding motions, as if she understood what Aislinn intended. Carefully, Aislinn laid ready the torch for the morning. Outside she heard the thrashing and calling of the wild fowl she had asked the guards to fetch for the traditional sacrifice. She had been delighted with their superstitious compliance.

Aine laid ready their two cloaks and set out the cloths she would use to wrap their shoes against the thin dusting of snow. Then she fed them a huge meal in case they had to go without food for a time. Aine wrapped her arms around Aislinn, stroking her hair, then she kissed her forehead as though she were her mother. She started one of her strange dances around the firelight and she did not seem surprised when Aislinn took her hands and joined in, whirling silently in the light from the fire. Then, as flames died to embers, they slept.

Aislinn awoke in the middle of the night. The room was filled with light and Aislinn stared about, unable to remember where she was. The woman was standing at the foot of the bed. She was as Aislinn had remembered her on the hill at Tara, luminous, pale, the light that came from within her giving the whole room its translucent glow.

The woman had stepped in the ashes of the fire and her small footprints were visible on the rough floor of the hut.

"You are Brighid, goddess of fertility, protector of the lamb, mother of mothers, giver of poetry."

The woman smiled gently.

"So I am called. So I shall be called again."

"Why have you walked in the ashes of my hearth? How am I to be favored?"

Again the woman smiled. "I will be with you tomorrow, though at first it may not seem so. I have been with you and with your babes at all times. Your heart has also come to believe in those who love you, has it not?"

Aislinn hung her head. "I have been foolish, mother. I have believed in the whisperings of evil."

"Not foolish, child, human. Though sometimes they are the same."

Aislinn looked up to see gentle humor on the face of the woman.

"You must go to Aodhfin, daughter."

Aislinn nodded. "I will go to him tomorrow, mother."

The woman shook her head. "You must go to him now, that he may help you on the morrow."

"How may this be done?"

The woman gestured toward Aine's cloak with its bold plaid of the Deisi.

"Wear the cloak of the old one."

Aislinn donned the cloak obediently.

"Now you must carry my symbol in your hand. In this way, Aodhfin will know that what will occur will occur tomorrow among the Deisi."

"But it will not. It will occur here."

"Trust me, daughter," the woman said softly. "Now take my hand."

Aislinn reached out her hand and placed it in that of the woman. She saw her own hand grow transparent, felt herself rush up out of her body in a sweep of wind. Suddenly, she was in the chamber of Aodhfin and the woman of the Other was nowhere near her. She stood before his table, saw his head bent over his papers, saw the weight of sorrow that bore him down. She wanted to speak to him, to reach out and stroke his hair, to say that she knew that she had caused the sorrow, but she found that she could neither move nor speak. She stood still, swathed in the cloak of the Deisi, holding the sun-sign of Brighid before her, willing him to lift his head.

When he did, he snapped his eyes up, as if he had heard someone call his name. He saw her instantly.

"Oh, my little one. You are well. You are alive. You have lifted an old man from his sorrow."

He was about to embrace her, then seemed to realize that he could not. Aislinn wanted to ask him of Eoghan, to warn him of Banbh and the woman Macha. Still she was unable to speak or move. Aodhfin looked at her for a long time. At last, a smile played across his features.

"Ah, now I understand. It is she who has sent you here, Brighid of the Others. This is her sign. And you in the cloak of the Deisi."

He seemed to ponder for a moment, then stood and headed for the door of his hut, shouting at her as he opened the door into darkness.

"We will be there tomorrow, child."

Aislinn was seated on her sleeping shelf in the small hut, her hand just above the hand of the woman, the plaid of the cloak entwined about her and the sun-sign in her hand. She stared at the woman confused.

"Was I there, with my tutor?"

"That part of you which continues was there. That part of you which we call Aislinn ni Sorar was here."

An awareness came over Aislinn and she looked at the woman in wonder.

"As you are, so shall I be?"

Now the woman smiled in full radiance and Aislinn wanted to put her hand inside hers again and stay within that radiance forever. She put out her hand, but the woman shook her head.

"I am the protector of the lamb," she said. "One day your name will be called by the new God. His name is forgiveness. His name is love. Will you answer, Aislinn ni Sorar?"

Aislinn felt a flowering in her heart.

"Those who forgive may love."

The woman smiled. "You must forgive Eoghan Mac Aidan. You must give him time to forgive you. You must go to the child Corra ni Brith. You must be ready when forgiveness calls your name. Can you do all of that, child?"

"I can try, lady."

And then the woman was gone.

When the light came full against the wall of the hut, Aislinn lit a torch from the fire and opened the door onto Imbolc morning.

She began the walk around the hut, following the direction of the sun, holding the torch aloft.

"Brighid, of the triune goddess, this is your day," she cried aloud. She heard the guards stir in their bothy and rise. Except for their nocturnal migrations and for the times when Macha visited, Aislinn had not been permitted to leave her prison dwellings in all the two months that she had been a prisoner. She felt the fear clench at her heart as the guards moved toward her. Would they believe that her druii duties on the sacred feast of Imbolc called her forth? Yet, she had asked for the fowl and they had captured one willingly enough.

Her feet crunched against the frost-covered ground, her breath came out in white puffs. She found just the right angle of light and lifted the sun-sign of Brighid into the shaft. The shadow of the sun-wheel was cast upon the ground.

"Oh, you, the goddess of the ewes, protector of the lambs, bring back the light to the people of the Gaels. We ask you for an early spring, for a fertile ground, for flocks and fields of plenty, O Mother of the Earth and its creatures."

The guards stood near her, watching with awestruck, suspicious looks as the shadow of the sun-sign enlarged upon the ground. She turned to them, spoke in her most commanding druid voice.

"Bring me the fowl which you have captured for our sacrifice."

They complied immediately, hurrying to bring her the thrashing bird.

"You will carry the sacrifice," she commanded, pointing at the younger of the guards. His hands trembled, but he held fast, afraid of her wrath if he let the creature go, awed by the change in her, by the power in her voice and her stance.

"Lead me to a place where three waters join. There we will make sacrifice to Brighid of the triune goddess."

As they walked, Aislinn began to chant the lays of Brighid, the druii poems in praise of the goddess. She kept up her recitation all the way to the side of a rushing stream. The guards turned and followed the stream northward to a place where the gentle brook joined a deeper rushing pool of water. At the fork created by the two waters, a stream bubbled forward near a statue of the water goddess.

Aislinn closed her eyes for a moment, memorizing the route by which they had come, calming herself for what she must do. She could feel the guards watching her with superstitious awe. She opened her eyes and nodded.

"You have provided well. At the joining of three waters, we will make our sacrifice. Each of you hold the bird by one wing. Face the water."

They did so, holding the flapping, quivering bird between them, its wings spread wide.

"You have taken my dagger," Aislinn spoke softly behind them. "One of you must give me yours."

The younger guard turned with his dagger in the palm of his hand but the older of the guards drew his and pointed it in her direction. Aislinn ignored the pointed dagger.

"Brighid," she intoned, "we make sacrifice at the joining of three waters. May it be pleasing to you."

She stepped forward and slit the throat of the bird, so that the blood gushed forward, then handed the bloody dagger back to the guard. The guards relaxed, shifted their stance, trusted her by her action.

"Quickly," she said. "Step forward so that the blood is given to the water."

The guards stepped closer to the bank, held the bird with its now limp neck over the rushing stream. Aislinn watched as the blood made contact with the water, listened as the warm blood hissed in contact with the near-frozen stream.

She closed her eyes, took a deep breath, nodded at Aine. Quickly and silently, they each stepped behind a guard and pushed.

They were running, hand in hand, back along the way they had come, even before the first scream filled the air. Aislinn turned back only once, to see the bobbing red head of the younger guard as the frigid rushing water carried him downstream. They would survive, but they would first endure a cold ride to the nearest bank. They would remember this as the coldest Imbolc of their lives. Aislinn laughed aloud.

"To their horses," she cried to Aine, who ran beside her as though she had indeed heard.

They reached the bothy, threw themselves bareback upon the horses' backs. Far behind her in the woods she could hear the thrashing and cursing of the frigid soldiers as they attempted to follow her. She turned the horse's head south.

"To Tara!" she cried. To Eoghan, she thought. To the arms of my beloved.

She rode like the wind, shouting aloud in the exhilaration of her freedom. Behind her Aine kept pace with the terrified look of one who is not a horsewoman. For three hours they rode, heedless of direction until at last Aislinn knew her surroundings. They turned south and kept their pace to the ford of the river Boann.

Macha and four of her soldiers were waiting.

"He said that you would try something today. He said that you would feel the full thrust of your powers on the day of the goddess." Macha smiled. One of the guards took the reins, wound them around his hand.

Macha nodded in the direction of Aine. "Kill the old one. She is not loyal to me."

"No," Aislinn screamed. "No. You must not harm her. I forced her to come. She knows nothing. I will do whatever you ask but you must not harm her."

She threw herself from her horse, ran to stand beside Aine, pushed against the horse of the guard who sidled near, his dagger drawn. Aine, high in the saddle above Aislinn, looked around her in confusion.

"Can't you see? She knows nothing. You cannot do this, Macha! You must not!"

"Now!" Macha commanded.

Aislinn felt a hand descend upon her hair, looked up to see Aine's face smiling at her. Gently, Aine lifted the sun-sign of Brighid up where it rested against Aislinn's cloak, holding it so the light fell against it. When the guard's dagger pierced her heart, she gasped once, then smiled still, as her blood flowed down across Aislinn's face and hair, as it entwined in the sign of Brighid.

"No! No!" Aislinn reached up as Aine's body toppled against her and bore them both to the ground. She sobbed wildly, clinging to Aine's arms and cloak as the guards dragged the body from her and carried it to the river.

When the body disappeared beneath the river's surface, Aislinn ceased weeping, raised her arms into the light.

"May the goddess Boann cradle you, may Brighid the mother of women, the protector of the lamb, bring you into her arms. The part of you that continues and the part of me which will continue will meet again in the place of Tir Nan Og."

She turned, her arms still raised, and saw the guards and Macha shudder. The blood was entangled in her hair, splashed on her face and cloak, interwoven in the sun-sign.

She smiled almost pleasantly.

"Where do you propose that we go, Macha?"

She saw Macha shudder back, understood for the first time that Macha feared her. Macha looked desperately around at her guards, none of whom would look at her or at Aislinn. At last she answered.

"We will go south. He waits for you there."

Aislinn continued to smile.

Eventually Macha looked away.

"Guards," she said. "We will stop among the people of the Deisi. I must be adorned in all my jewelry when I go to meet him."

They turned west, toward the tuath of the Deisi. None of them saw Aislinn turn back and raise her hands toward the points of light that sparkled from the surface of the river.

17

They arrived at the tuath of the Deisi at midday. Macha stopped before the hut of the chief, oblivious to the stares of the people.

The tribe would have heard, surely, that the druidess, wife of the son of their chieftain, had disappeared on her marriage night. Now here she was, bloodied and bowed, in the tow of Macha's guards. Would they not ask questions? Macha read Aislinn's thoughts.

"It does not matter. By the time they deliver the news to your Eoghan, we will be gone to the south. I need suffer these fools no longer."

She lifted one of the blood-encrusted strands of Aislinn's hair.

"I had thought that I might have you cleaned, but the longer I look at you, the more I think that you will go to him this way. Let him see you this way. Perhaps then he will see you truly."

She pushed Aislinn before her into the small hut. Aengus Mac Gabuideach was seated at the far side of the hut. He was already in his cups, staring morosely into the fire, a silver goblet lying on its side beside him. But he stood quickly when Aislinn came through the door.

He lifted her chin, stared at her bloodstained face.

"By the gods!" He turned to the woman Macha.

"What have you done to her, wife? My son and all at Tara believe her dead. Now she comes with you and looking like this. What have you done?"

Macha waved her hand at him.

"Leave me alone, fool. What I do or do not do has never been business of yours."

Aengus looked at Aislinn, his face a mask of sorrow. He placed his huge hand gently against the side of her cheek.

"What has she done to you, child?"

Aislinn said nothing.

Mac Gabuideach turned angrily to the woman.

"Have you deprived her of her reason, Macha? This is the woman my son loves. As I am chief of the Deisi, I tell you that if you have harmed her you will die."

His hand went menacingly toward his dagger. For a moment, Aislinn saw a flicker of fear in Macha's eyes. She stepped to the door of the hut, motioned her guards inside with her. When they flanked her on either side, she spoke.

"Should I fear you? Chief of the Deisi. You would be chief of nothing had it not been for me."

"I won the chieftainship in fair combat."

"You won nothing. You could not have beaten Sorar in combat. Search your memory, straw man. I need suffer you no longer. It is time you learned the truth."

"What are you saying?"

"It was I who wanted the chieftainship, I who wanted the woman's jewels, her position. It was I who goaded you to challenge the child's father."

"What of this? It was I who took it for you."

"Do you think I wanted you? I wanted him. I wanted Sorar, her father. I offered myself to him but he would have none of me. So I settled on you because your size was large and because you had a reputation as a strong warrior." She laughed.

"There was the problem of your first wife, mother of Eoghan, of course."

"What did you do?" Aengus Mac Gabuideach was staring at her now in openmouthed horror. His voice came out strangled.

"I poisoned her."

She moved around the room adorning herself, layering on heavy bracelets, a golden torque, a circlet of gold for her hair. Her guards stayed poised on Mac Gabuideach, their daggers drawn. "It was easy. I gave her just a little in her tea or her wine, day after day. She sickened gradually and her death seemed so natural. You suspected nothing, did you? And you were so grateful for the comfort of my warm breasts and body."

She smiled up at him. Mac Gabuideach sat down heavily.

"Still I knew that you could not defeat Sorar, so I drugged him. It was your son who served the wine all unaware. Do you not remember? He was so proud, just returned from fosterhood, serving the wine and quaffing at the feast. They would have suspected me, but not the honorable Eoghan." She laughed, waved her hand in the air.

"He wanted no part of me either, so I felt it fitting that he play some part in the dishonor. Can you tell me that you have not suspected all these years? You knew that you were not the warrior Sorar was."

Aislinn watched Mac Gabuideach's face take on the growing awareness that what Macha said was true.

"You killed my wife. You dishonored my son and drove him from me. You have dishonored me. I am not the true chief of the Deisi."

"You are not," she said bluntly. "Though I have enjoyed my reign as their queen." She shrugged. "Still, I take the spoils with me."

She gestured at Aislinn. "My only downfall was the woman, Eibhlain. Your mother. She knew that I wanted her dead, and you as well. I believe she even suspected that I had another lover. We women are always better at these intuitions, are we not, priestess? On the night of Sorar's death, she searched out Eoghan. She told him of her suspicions, told him that she knew that I would kill her and her child. It was Eoghan who went to the druii, who found Aodhfin, who took you to him so that he would take you under his protection."

She shrugged.

"Once you were safely spirited away, Eibhlain stayed with your father, announced that she would be entombed alive with him. She knew that if she died and you were in Aodhfin's protection no harm could come to you." Macha shook her head.

"Your foolish mother began the war among the Deisi. She brought the sympathy of the Deisi to your family with her death-fast. It was her entombment that caused the forces of O'Domnhnaill to unite against you, Mac Gabuideach, that drove your son to the Fianna."

She smiled at Aislinn.

"And then so recently you came back to haunt us. Well, it does not matter now. Once we are with him in the south, you will no longer be a threat. He will see to that." She clasped on the last spiraling snake bracelet, looked at Mac Gabuideach.

"I am finished here." She called out the door. "Guards, bring the priestess. Good-bye, Mac Gabuideach." The guards each clasped one of Aislinn's arms.

The dagger appeared suddenly in Mac Gabuideach's hand as his big bearlike body stumbled drunkenly toward Macha. She dashed behind her guards, leaping to her horse in the yard outside the dwelling. They dropped Aislinn's arms but Mac Gabuideach pushed the guards aside, ran at Macha, raised his dagger. He clutched drunkenly at her ankle where it rested against the withers of her horse. She yanked the foot free, kicked hard at him, striking him between the eyes. He fell to the ground, grunting heavily.

"Bring her!" Macha yelled to the soldiers.

Again the guards clasped Aislinn by the arms dragging her toward the waiting horse. She felt dazed, but certain of the truth of the revelations. Her father drugged, her mother protecting her by going to her own death, her beloved Eoghan playing only the part of a pawn in the scheme.

The soldiers were dragging her into the saddle and Mac Gabuideach had begun to stagger drunkenly to his feet when Aislinn heard hoofbeats in the distance.

They swept into the tuath like an army, horsemen and chariots, the plaids of the tribesmen and the greens of the Fianna. She saw Cairbry and Cellach, the sons of Cormac. Her old Aodhfin was riding tall and angry in the back of the chariot of Cairbry. For a moment, she glimpsed Eoghan, driving his own chariot. His look of love and relief turned to horror as he regarded her bloodstained form. Then he swept past her, dragging the woman Macha from her horse and pulling her into the chariot beside him.

It was Cellach, the son of Cormac, who pulled Aislinn into his chariot. She clung to him as though he were her own kin. She looked around for Aengus Mac Gabuideach, saw him standing tall and angry beside Aodhfin in the chariot of Cairbry Mac Cormac. Cellach turned to her then.

"It will be well, priestess. My father will convene the brehons. We will hear the truth."

Aislinn felt his kindness and concern wash over her and she leaned against his back, wrapped her arms around his waist, and wept as the procession thundered toward Tara.

18

"N ay! Silence!"

Cormac Mac Art held his hands aloft to quell the wild melee in the hall of Tara. Beside him, Eoghan held Macha by her arms while Aislinn sat clinging to the hands of old Aodhfin. Fenian soldiers shouted. Aengus Mac Gabuideach strained at the arms of the two men of the Fianna who held him. Macha screamed a stream of invective at her husband. Aislinn glanced wildy around the room, as if searching for someone.

"Silence!" Cormac called again. "We will know what has transpired here."

He searched around the room, looking for someone who could tell the tale unembellished. Embellishment was highly prized among his soldiers and songsters, but Cormac suspected that this crisis required direct telling. His gaze fell upon Aodhfin, seated quietly beside Aislinn.

"Aodhfin, the Wise. I call upon you who are known for truth. What has befallen?"

Aodhfin stood with dignity, still holding Aislinn's hand.

"My foster-daughter, the priestess Aislinn, whom we all feared dead, is alive. This must be a case for the brehons to hear, for it would seem that the woman Macha has been holding her prisoner for these two months."

He raised Aislinn to her feet, turned her toward the sight of the king. The pell-mell journey in the chariot of Cellach Mac Cormac had covered the hem of Aislinn's white gown with mud and slush. Aine's blood still stained Aislinn's hair and face, the front of her gown and the sun-sign of Brighid.

"Beyond what you see, there is more. It seems that the woman Macha tried to kill . . ."

Aislinn whirled back to face Aodhfin, her eyes pleading for the safety of her babes. Aodhfin stopped speaking, stared at her eyes for one moment, resumed.

"Tried to kill my foster-daughter. This must be a case for the brehons to hear."

"Can you speak, priestess?" Cormac regarded her gently, stepped down from the dais to lift her bloody hands in his. Aislinn nodded.

"Macha, stepmother of my husband, Eoghan Mac Aidan, wife of Aengus Mac Gabuideach, took me as I rode near the river Boann on the night of my marriage."

She said nothing of why she was riding near the river, nothing of what had transpired between she and Eoghan, who had not yet spoken to her at all.

"She has held me as her prisoner for these past two months. This morning, on the feast of Imbolc, I tried to escape, but she found me. She killed the nurse, whom she had brought to care for me, because that good woman was helping me to escape."

She said nothing of her babes, nothing of Banbh. She knew that he had been Macha's accomplice, knew too that there was still too much danger in letting either of them know that the babes lived. And she dare not speak against a druid without the full proof that the brehons would require. She watched Macha's face, saw that her omissions brought a smile of triumph to the woman's lips.

"Why?" The roar came from Aengus Mac Gabuideach, still pinioned by the soldiers of the Fianna. "Why, Macha?

Why have you done this thing to the wife of my son? Are you so jealous of her?"

Macha swung her head, shifted her masses of hair, made no move to struggle against the hurtful hold of Eoghan Mac Aidan's arms.

"Foolish man!" she called across the room. "Did you think that our design to take the chieftainship of the Deisi was the only design? There were larger and grander designs, made by wiser men than you."

She smiled, bared her teeth, grew reckless with her words.

"I killed your mewling wife, mother of this boy, Eoghan, just as I caused the mother of the priestess to be entombed alive. What does it matter if I kill this one or any brats of hers?" Behind Macha, Aislinn heard Eoghan make a strangled sound. Macha laughed in triumph. "Yes, that is what I did, I did not kill her, I killed the babes she carried!"

Aislinn turned toward Eoghan. He was staring at her with a look of such remorse and sorrow that it was all she could do not to shout the truth.

"Do you think you can harm me?" Macha continued. "Any of you? His power will protect me. The power of the dark goddess will protect me."

With a mighty roar, Aengus Mac Gabuideach hurled himself free of the arms of the Fenians holding him. He snatched a Fenian spear, ran at Macha.

"You will die!"

"Nay!"

Cellach, the son of Cormac, detached himself from his father's side and raised his hands. Aislinn felt a wash of gratitude for him, for young Cellach who had bravely brought her back to Tara in his chariot.

"This is a matter for the brehons! You have heard my father speak. This matter must be decided in a Celtic court of law."

Hands grasped at Mac Gabuideach but he pressed forward, tearing free, the spear raised above his head. Eoghan released Macha from his grasp, started toward his father, palms upraised, but it was too late. Aengus hurled the spear at Macha with all the strength in his arm.

Macha moved swiftly. In one single sideways step, she moved behind Cellach, son of Cormac. The spear, with all the weight of Aengus Mac Gabuideach behind it, thrust deep into the young breast of Cellach Mac Cormac.

"By the gods, what have I done?" Aengus Mac Gabuideach screamed in anguish. "Woman, what have you done?"

Cellach cupped his hands beneath the outrush of his heart's blood as if his hands alone could stop the flow. Aislinn rushed toward Cellach, cradled him in her arms. She lowered them both to the ground.

Cormac leaped from the dais, pushed through the crowd toward Cellach's side.

Above them Mac Gabuideach whirled in anguish, drew his dagger from his belt.

"She must die!" Mac Gabuideach bellowed drunkenly. With a single flick of his wrist, he sent the dagger spinning. It found its mark—in the eye of Cormac Mac Art, High King of Ireland.

Cormac howled aloud, yanked the dagger from his eye, dropped to his knees beside his dying son. The eye dangled, bloodied, from its socket, bumping against his cheek as he lowered himself to the side of Cellach.

"Cellach!" he cried aloud. "Oh, my son!"

"The prophecy!" people began to scream. "The prophecy! It is the eye of the king and his son dead!"

Mac Gabuideach sank to his knees, sobbing. Standing silent now, Macha remained unscathed. Mac Aidan dropped to his knees beside his father.

Cormac seemed not to notice the wild melee, the dangling eye. Gently, he gathered the body of his dying son from Aislinn, gently cradled him in his arms. Aislinn knelt back to rise, but Cormac reached out and clutched her hand. Aislinn put her arms around him as he began to shake with sobs. The new blood of the king of Ireland and his son added itself to the blood of Aine on Aislinn's cloak and gown.

The pandemonium in the room quieted, stilled. The huge hall grew absolutely silent.

Cairbry, the second son of Cormac, stepped forward as if to address the assemblage, but another voice spoke first. Aislinn remembered it, raised her head. The voice was neither male nor female, higher than wind, sweeter than song. It said nothing at all, or perhaps it spoke the name of Cormac Mac Art. Aislinn could not tell.

In an instant, it was gone. A sudden stream of light cascaded from the ceiling of the great hall, illuminating the bloody threesome. Aislinn held her hand out in the light, felt it lie warm against her skin in colors of blue and gold, in the translucence of mother of pearl.

A ripple of awe spread across the room and then the silence of absolute terror.

Only Cormac Mac Art seemed unafraid. He stood in the shaft of light, bearing the body of his son up with him, tipping his head back. And then, in a moment that each of the company would remember forever, he smiled, a smile childlike and wondrous, devoid of any sorrow.

Then the light was gone.

Cairbry held his hand up then.

"Fenians!" he called to the warriors of the Fianna. "Bear away to imprisonment this woman named Macha and the man Aengus Mac Gabuideach."

Aengus and Macha were led through the crowd that began to disperse, some crying aloud, some weeping openly.

"What will become of Eire?" a single voice cried over and over again.

Eoghan and Aodhfin came and gently drew Aislinn away from the king with his terrible burden.

At the center of the room the one-eyed king bearing his dead son remained, smiling gently, the strangest testament of all to the events of the day.

19

Y̶ou must tell him."

"How can I tell him, father? He has not spoken to me, has not come to me since I returned, bringing all these sorrows with me. I cannot even say that he is glad that I am alive."

Old Aodhfin shook his head.

"Don't you understand? It is his shame and the dishonor of his family that keeps him from you. Look at what they have done to you. Your father, your mother, and now he believes that your babes, his babes, children of whom he knew nothing are also gone. You must tell him, daughter, or the shame and sorrow will destroy him."

Aislinn sighed.

"Yes, I understand. And you are right. To tell him will give him heart's ease. But no others, Aodhfin. I must also protect my babes with my silence. Macha lives. And Banbh is nowhere to be seen."

"She will not live long if I judge the outcome of today's proceedings aright."

"Then I will tell him when these proceedings are over."

The waiting crowd shifted against the predawn darkness, formed two columns. Through the line came Cormac

Mac Art, surrounded by his wolf pack, followed closely by his brehons and druids. To all appearances, he seemed the same man that he had always been—strong, proud, his head held high. Until Aislinn looked at his eye.

The socketless and bloody hole was exposed for all to see, for Cormac scorned bandages or carefully placed scarves and plasters. He seemed unafraid of his disfigurement.

Aislinn felt wonderment for him swell in her breast, for all of the Celts knew what the socketless eye proclaimed. Cormac could no longer be king. A king must be strong, brave, truthful, and possessed of all his parts and limbs. Sometimes, when a king was damaged, he was put to death. Yet Cormac went forward fearlessly, almost joyfully to this day of reckoning.

Aislin shook her head. What had he seen in the light? She had felt it bathing her, had felt its calm and serenity. But she had seen and heard nothing after the voice. She looked again at Cormac, at the way he clapped his Fenians on the back, at the gentle way he lifted the hand of his wife, at the strength of love he gave in the embrace to his remaining son Cairbry. The man was bursting with joy. Aislinn wished to stand next to him, to ease some of her sorrow at the part she had played in his disfigurement. The fear of the day's proceedings closed her throat.

"Father, I cannot do this."

Aodhfin pulled her arm through his.

"You must, daughter. We have no choice now, for Fate is carrying all of us like a wind into this day."

All of Eire, it seemed, filled the hall for the trial of Aengus Mac Gabuideach and his wife Macha, so great was the scandal that the chief of the Deisi, who might not have played fair for the crown, had drawn the blood of the king. Ailsinn saw Eoghan standing behind his father, as his name and lineage required. Their eyes met briefly and then he turned away. Aislinn clutched hard at Aodhfin's arm.

"My justice has cost our king his eye, has seen his son

Cellach gone too young to ground. Now I will take the last of Eoghan's honor from him. Oh, Aodhfin, this victory feels hollow!"

Aodhfin shook his head sadly.

Flahari, chief brehon of King Cormac Mac Art, stepped forward and addressed the crowd.

"Today is the day of judgments. Here is our king who has been maimed, his son taken from him. Here is a priestess who has been wronged. We the brehons must decide today who should bear the burden for these deeds. Who will speak first?"

"I will speak."

Aislinn's head snapped up as Eoghan rose from his seat.

"I am Eoghan Mac Aidan, once Eoghan Mac Gabuideach, son of Aengus, husband to the priestess Aislinn ni Sorar. I am also poet and master, ollamh, to the Ard-Ri King Cormac Mac Art. As such I claim the right of glam dicen!"

Gasps and screams spread across the hall. Soldiers moved quickly to contain the crowd. Macha stood, holding to the railing of her compartment, and began to scream imprecations and denials. Aislinn stared in horror.

Glam dicen was the most powerful weapon in the arsenal of Eire's wordsmiths. It was the great satire, the satire from the hilltops, in which the poet orally flayed and flogged anyone he wished, from a king to a warrior. It bore so much weight that it had been known to bring about the death of the subject or to cause him to become afflicted with disfiguring scars and blemishes. It always brought about the total dishonor of its subject.

Flahari raised his hands and the room grew silent. "As poet, it is your right to elect glam dicen, Eoghan Mac Aidan." He stressed the Mac Aidan of the name. "Come forward."

Eoghan swept forward, the blue and green of his cloak swishing loudly in the expectant and terrified silence. He stood before the assemblage.

"I, Eoghan of the tribe of the Deisi, of the clan of Gabuideach, come before you today to speak of honor." So,
Eoghan began the poem of power.

"What name shall we honor among the Deisi—
Mac Gabuideach, bearer of shame?
He who challenged the noble Sorar
Knew well that he was not fit to rule.
When the wine of combat has been drugged,
Chieftainship by combat honors none.
How should this Mac Gabuideach be called?
The Divider of the Deisi, Shameful One.

Shall we honor the woman Macha
Who wears another woman's gold?
Who dishonors the name of the Deisi
Who made of me a motherless son,
Of the priestess a motherless child,
And so again a childless mother.
Shall we be ruled by cunning and deceit?
Cleanse our tribe and let us choose another.

Who among the Deisi so dishonorable
As to hold a druid captive?
To defile the person of a holy one?
To kill the babes who might achieve the crown?
What honor breathes among the Deisi
Who let themselves be chieftained so?
If honor rests among the Deisi,
Let it speak that we may know.

What shall we speak of Eoghan,
Son of Aengus but called Mac Aidan?
I, poet of the Ard-Ri, Fenian
Who did not speak or bear the shame
Of the name Mac Gabuideach
Even to my beloved

She who was trapped in the web
Of our dishonor and deceit.

We are the tribe of the Deisi, loyal to the Ard-Ri
Cormac the Wise, high king of Eire.
See what our shame has wrought
Upon our king, upon his son,
That we by our compliance and our silence
Lose the sight of our gentle king
Lose for him his beloved son,
Lose for Eire, everything."

Here, Eoghan paused, waited for a response. Mac Gabuideach hung his head, weeping openly, his shoulders shaking. The hall remained in absolute silence. Eoghan finished with the ritual plea for justice.

"We are the Gaels, known for our honor.
We fight fearless, but always true.
We do no dishonor to women or children.
We abide by the justice of our laws.
Among the Deisi, deceit has raised its head;
Among the Deisi, dishonor has ruled in stead.
Purge our tribe to truth and honor.
Brehons, rule exile or death!"

Eoghan stopped speaking.

A wild chanting broke out among the assembled clans of the Deisi.

"Death, death, death. Death to Mac Gabuideach. Death to the woman Macha. We among the Deisi cry for death!"

Aislinn wanted to leap to her feet, to shout that her babes were still alive, that Macha had not triumphed, but she saw the woman watching her, calculating, and she knew that somehow Banbh was watching as well.

Now she understood why Eoghan had not told her of her past, of the sorrow of her parents' deaths. Was she not now protecting her own babes with her silence? What would become of them now, of Eoghan's people? She felt no pity for Macha. Her choices were all for darkness. But pity rose in her for the betrayed and lost Aengus Mac Gabuideach, for Eoghan, his fatherless son, so trapped by his family's dishonor.

Flahari rose.

"The brehons have heard and decided. We will rule upon the lives of Aengus Mac Gabuideach and Macha, his wife. For the woman and her crimes, we rule death. Yesterday, among us here at Tara Hill, she defiled the sacred feast of Imbolc. She has kidnapped the priestess Aislinn, murdered the nurse Aine. By her treachery she has brought to ruin the tribe of the Deisi. At her incitement, she has cost Eire much. Therefore, the manner of her death is prescribed. Macha will be sewn into a sack, weighted with rocks, and condemned to a death by drowning in the river Boann."

Macha smiled, managed a small, conspiratorial silence. She looked to the rafters above her, where a crow lifted its wings, flew out the fire hole, and circled away to the south.

The bag was brought immediately, weighted with stones from the fire. Aislinn imagined the hissing sound they would make if they were still warm when they made contact with the cold water of the river. For a moment she remembered her sacrifice of the bird on Imbolc morning and the hiss of its blood on the water. She shivered. Macha was brought forward, forced to step into the bag atop the warm stones, stripped of all her golden jewelry. Still, she smiled.

"You will not succeed at this," she called aloud to the assembled crowd. "Even now a great power is gathering to overcome you and set me free."

Aislinn felt anger at Macha wash over her, drew close to the woman, spoke softly.

"Don't you see, Macha? He will not come for you, will not rescue you. You are the only one who can give him away. With you gone, who can speak and have proof against him? I have only whispers and suspicions. He will welcome your going."

She saw the woman's eyes go wide with suspicion, then certainty. Macha let out a bloodcurdling scream then, which muffled when the bag was sewn closed over her head, grew thinner and more distant as the guard of the Fianna carried her to the waiting chariot, thundered off toward the river that had swallowed Aine only three days ago.

"Now to the matter of Aengus Mac Gabuideach, chief of the Deisi," Flahari intoned.

"Wait!" Aislinn stood, raised her hand to the company. "Eoghan Mac Aidan has spoken, but there are things he does not know. Macha herself admitted to killing the mother of Eoghan, to forcing my own mother to die"— she paused for a moment—"to feeding me the herbs which would kill my babes. You know too that the wine which weakened my father Sorar was drugged. But what Eoghan does not know is that his father knew of none of this. If Aengus has a sin, it is the sin of foolishness; he believed that he won the chieftainship in combat and knew nothing of my captivity."

She felt Eoghan turn to her, regard her with astonishment.

"Why would you do this?" he asked. "My family has cost you everything."

Aislinn answered him with a gentle smile.

"That is all well, honored priestess," cried Flahari, "but we cannot excuse the man the heinous crimes committed here. For he has killed Cellach Mac Cormac, son of our king, and he has deprived our ruler of his eye. For that he must die."

Cormac Mac Art, High King of Ireland, stood and raised his hand to the brehons.

"I require mercy for this man!"

A gasp of astonishment ran through the crowd.

"Hear me, o my brehons. It is true that I have lost and

for those losses I will sorrow. But has not this man lost also? For he has lost his true first wife, the love of his son, the honor of his family name, and his chieftainship. Are not his losses sufficient punishment? For I tell you that a new king stands before you. And I tell you that we must learn a new word. Vengeance must give way to forgiveness."

He smiled directly at Aislinn.

Aengus Mac Gabuideach sat with his head hung low, a beaten man. The brehons gathered. At last Flahari again addressed the company.

"The brehons have tempered justice with mercy. We rule that the clan Mac Gabuideach with all of their offspring and relations be henceforward and forever exiled from Meath. No longer are they welcome in the province of the High King of Ireland."

"I abide by the judgment of the brehons, and am grateful to the mercy of my king," shouted Aengus Mac Gabuideach. "I will sojourn among my kin in Munster." He stood and strode from the hall.

Eoghan sat with his head lowered, lost in thought.

Suddenly, he stood again, faced the dais. "My king, may I make a request?"

Cormac nodded, held out his hand. Eoghan spoke.

"I too am of the clan Mac Gabuideach and I know that under our law this exile applies also to me."

Aislinn's head snapped up. She had not realized, had not thought, that she and her babes would once again be exiles. She stood, ready to walk toward Eoghan, but he continued.

"I do not wish to accompany . . ." he stumbled against the word father, "Aengus Mac Gabuideach to Munster. I have in the past served Eire as a soldier of the Fianna and as the king knows, the fortress of the Fianna is at Almhuin in Kildare to the south. If it is well with my Fenian brothers and acceptable to the brehons, I will soldier with the Fianna at Almhuin."

"Always a Fenian, brother," came the shout from the assembled men of the Fianna. "You are welcome and one of us."

Cormac conferred for a moment with the brehons, then Flahari rendered judgment.

"It is well, Eoghan Mac Aidan, and our king wishes this company to hear that he does not hold against you for the weight of his sorrows."

Eoghan nodded.

"Then I must state one thing more. It is the custom among our people that we may divorce by returning the unwanted spouse to her family. I no longer want Aislinn ni Sorar. I return her to her foster-father Aodhfin the Wise."

"No," cried Aislinn. "Oh, Eoghan, no."

But he was striding from the hall, and the sound of his retreating hoofbeats echoed across the hill of Tara before Aislinn could reach the door.

20

Aislinn let the hot tears fall from her eyes, felt them turn cold against her cheeks. The winter wind moaned and screeched around the crest of the hill. Aislinn rested her arms on the top of the wooden walls. From her place on the watch platform, she could see the ice-blue ribbon of the river Boann far below her, gleaming in the naked light of the cold moon. She shut her eyes and rested her head against her folded arms. She felt a presence behind her, a rustle like wings, a silence. Hope leaped up in her heart and she turned with a glad cry.

"Eoghan!"

Fionn Mac Cumhail stood beside her on the platform. He was dressed strangely, all in white, like a druid. For a moment, Aislinn thought that his cloak was feathered. She leaned in and peered more closely, saw only white wool. Yet, it was said that Fionn could shape-shift into the bodies of animals. Aislinn searched the sky above her head. Fionn laughed aloud.

Aislinn looked back at him, dashed the tears from her cheeks, bowed her head.

"I give you good evening, honored Fenian."

"It is long past evening, priestess. In a short time, it

will be dawn again. Why do you keep alone at the walls of Tara on so cold a night as this?"

"Where did you come from, Fenian?"

Fionn laughed again. He lifted his thumb to his mouth, rubbed its surface against the front of his teeth. Briefly, he bit into the soft flesh. His eyes grew round and he nodded.

"I see now. It is love that holds you here in darkness. I am sorry that my presence disappointed you, Aislinn ni Sorar."

Aislinn looked down at the ground.

"Do you understand why he set you aside, priestess?"

"He does not wish me anymore, for all the sorrows I have brought upon his family and upon our king."

"Do not be foolish!" Fionn snapped out the words. "I have been foolish over the meanings of love. Such foolishness causes more tragedy. Your Eoghan left you because he did not wish to harm you any further. He did not want you to be cast into exile because of what his family had done. He left you for love of you."

"He has done us no favor with this abandonment."

"You are angry because you carry his babes."

Aislinn gasped.

"How do you know of this? Have you spoken to Aodhfin?"

"Nay, priestess. I . . . know. That is all."

"You must not tell Eoghan of this. I do not wish him to know that I carry his children."

"It is not my place to tell him. It was yours and you did not. You cannot be angry with him now for what he did not know."

Aislinn sighed. "I was protecting them with my silence. She tried to kill them. And the other one, the Dark One."

"So you did what any wise and loving mother would do. Who is to blame here, priestess?"

Aislinn reached out blindly.

"Oh, Fionn, you are wise. They say you see what other men cannot. Tell me the end of my story. Tell me that I will keep my children safe, that I will see my Eoghan again. Eire is so wide and so long. I fear that we will never meet again!"

Fionn clasped her hands in his, held them tight. He smiled sadly.

"I cannot tell you how your story will end, priestess. Where humans are concerned, no one can predict the ending. We are the most unpredictable of all of the creatures of the gods. Even my own tale has never been clear to me. But I can show you one thing that will comfort you. I can show you that Eire is very small. Come."

Fionn turned Aislinn around so that her back was to him. He lifted the folds of his white robe around them both, closed his arms tight around her chest and arms.

"Lean in against me, priestess. Do not be afraid."

Aislinn leaned backward into Fionn, rested her head against his shoulder. Inside the cloak it was incredibly warm. She could feel Fionn's heart beating against the wing of her shoulder. Her heart took up the same rhythm.

"Close your eyes, priestess."

Aislinn complied.

Suddenly she was flying over the river Boann, her body skimming just above the silvered water, her arms outstretched like the wings of an owl. Northward, she turned, arching over the green mountains of Mourne, curving along the sea to the rugged, rocky causeway the giants had built between Eire and Alba. She heard a piercing cry just above her, turned in the arms of that cry, winging down the west sea coast of Eire, lifting in the wind currents above the high cliffs that towered seven hundred feet out of the sea. Together, they swept around the south coast of Eire. Aislinn cried aloud exultantly as the sun rose pale and golden out of the east, lighting as frosted emeralds the green fields that swept to the rocky shores of the sea.

In a matter of moments, she felt her feet again on the platform of Tara's walls. She opened her eyes to morning light. She was alone on the platform, a feeling of exhilaration tingling across the surface of her skin, her hair a wind-tangled web. In the light dusting of snow that covered the ground around the platform, only her own footprints were visible.

Moylann, chief of the druids, led the white mare into the circle in the open air on the hill of Tara. Behind the mare, Cairbry Mac Cormac, naked and shivering in the February cold, followed. When he reached the center of the circle, he knelt on all fours beside the mare, his pale naked body mimicking her white beauty, then stood and mounted her, sitting astride.

Aislinn had never seen a coronation—Cormac Mac Art had been king for the entire duration of her life—but she knew the symbolism. The mare was the purity of the land of Eire, and the naked Cairbry knelt beside her to show that he too was an animal and thus linked inextricably to Eire.

Now he sat astride so that his people could see that he was in full manhood and without blemish. Aislinn watched his proud upright pose and felt only pity for him, exposed to the cold, so young to have so much thrust upon him.

The people had selected Cairbry Mac Cormac as their king, hoping that he would continue the wisdom of his father's reign.

Aislinn watched him suppress a shiver. Cairbry dismounted and his father Cormac wrapped him in a warm red robe lined with the fur of seals.

Moylann and the druids circled the mare three times, rapping on their golden bowls with the hilts of their daggers. Moylann intoned the ancient ritual.

"We are the people of Eire, the people of the ancient land of Eire. We are the blood of her blood, the bone of her bone. Wisely, in harmony with the land itself, must our king rule."

In a single motion, Moylann slit the throat of the mare, catching the first blood in his own golden bowl. Behind him the druids followed, filling one bowl after another with blood. The mare whinnied in terror, sank to her knees. The honor guard of the Fianna stepped forward and lowered her to a pallet on the ground. She would be borne away, butchered and boiled. Cairbry would bathe in the broth made of her juices and drink of it as well. All of the people would taste of the flesh that symbolized their land.

Moylann and the druids stood in a circle facing the people, holding the bowls of the blood. Cairbry walked into the center of the circle. The druids turned to face him and Moylann called out.

"Cairbry Mac Cormac, will you accept the burden of the land of Eire?"

"I will," Cairbry called aloud. Moylann handed him the bowl and Cairbry drank of the blood of the mare.

"I am Eire," he cried now, raising his hands to the people, visible traces of the blood still staining his lips. "I am the ancient land of Eire. Hear me, O you gods! Wisely may I rule. Wisely may I guide her people."

Cormac stepped into the circle and lifted the golden circlet from his own head, handing it to Moylann. Aislinn watched the quick look of anguish pass over Cairbry's face, watched the gentle smile on the face of Cormac, the reassuring touch he gave to his son's arm.

At a signal from Moylann, a circle of brehons formed behind the druids, then a circle of the soldiers of the Fianna. Flahari stepped forward from the ranks of the brehons and Fionn Mac Cumhail, leader of the Fianna, entered the circle. He wore the blue and green plaid of the Fianna, seemed well rested. He did not look in Aislinn's direction. Aislinn wondered if her meeting with Fionn had been real, or a product of her teeming and confused spirit. She watched as together, the threesome lifted the crown of Cormac and placed it on Cairbry's head.

"Thus do you see before you the choice of the people, the high king, the Ard-Ri of Eire!" they cried together.

A wild cheer arose from the crowd, subsiding when

Cormac Mac Art stepped beside his son. The bruise around the eye was black and purple now, the socket itself still a pulpy mass. Cormac was crownless, his golden hair haloing in the bare February light. He smiled at the crowd.

"People of Eire. You have chosen as your king my beloved son Cairbry. Now your will must decide my fate, for I am blemished, no longer fit to rule. If it is your will, I will submit to the ritual death ceremony of the druids." He paused, as if waiting.

Aislinn closed her eyes and prayed to the woman of light, "Brighid, let no further sorrow come from my own."

Murmurs of dissent rose from the crowd, cries of "Cormac must live!"

Cormac continued.

"If you do not wish my death, I would make a request of you. I will no longer remain at Tara." A strange murmur went through the crowd. "If you give me permission, I will build a hut on the banks of the river Boann. There I will study and serve as an adviser to my son Cairbry. What is your choice?"

Flahari stepped forward.

"You have been a wise ruler, Cormac Mac Art. Your wisdom as an adviser would serve both your son and the people of Eire."

It was the warriors of the Fianna who began the chant "Cormac, Cairbry, Cormac, Cairbry" until the entire crowd had taken up the rhythm linking father and son together. Flahari held up his hands.

"Thus, it is decided by the will of the people. Cormac Mac Art will retire to the banks of the Boann."

Wild shouting went up from the crowd. Aislinn felt the relief wash through her like clean water. She watched as Cormac and Cairbry conferred for a moment. Cairbry stepped forward and raised his arms.

"My father has asked for permission to address the assembly at Tara one last time. Heed my father, Cormac Mac Art."

Cormac stepped forward, smiled gently, held his hands out in a supplicating posture.

"People of Eire," he said, speaking so softly that the crowd became absolutely silent, leaned forward to hear. "I will speak to you of the Light."

There was an audible gasp, followed by wild babbling and noise. Cormac waited quietly until the crowd silenced, until there was no sound on Tara Hill but the wind. Aislinn strained to hear Cormac. Behind her eyes, she could still see the smiling Cormac standing in the light, the dead Cellach in his arms. She could still hear the voice, feel the warmth of the light as its reflection bathed down upon her. She felt some of the people in the crowd stepping away from her, remembering also. Cormac spoke.

"I tell you that there is a new god, a triune god as those that we have known, but not the same. For this is not a god of war or a god of the fertile earth, but a god above the gods, the god who is the maker of all things. It is this god who has spoken to me. And the god calls himself an Foinse, the Source. And he calls himself an Firinne, the Truth. Between the Source and the Truth is the light that you have seen. And they call what is between them an Solas, the Light. I have felt the light and there is more joy within it than I have ever known.

"This is what the God has said to me: 'The time is coming when this land will be my land, when my truth will inform even the rocks and the trees of Eire, when the wisest scholars will carry my name from Eire into the world. You, Cormac Mac Art, are the third person in Eire to hear my Name. You must speak it to the people. Some will hear it and some will not, but I ask you to speak it to all. You may tell them that they need no druii to speak to me, that they can speak to me and I will hear. You may tell the people that my name is not vengeance, that my name is not war, that my name is not darkness. You may tell them that my name is Love.' "

Cormac stopped. "So I have done. Now I tell you that

I will go to the Boann to study and to write down the history of Eire. Those who wish to speak of the God may come to me and I will speak. From among our learned men, I will request a scribe."

For a moment, the reaction of the entire assemblage was absolute silence. Then a sound among the people swelled into a crescendo. Some cried out against the light, others screamed that they believed. Some shouted aloud at Cormac's strange request for a scribe. Moylann stepped forward.

"Silence! Silence. I call for silence." Slowly the crowd subsided.

"Our respected king has lost his son. He has lost his kingship. Such sorrows lead a man to visions which may not be true. You know our gods, know that we druii speak to them directly. You know too that it is the way of the druids to consider all matters of the universe. We will consider what Cormac has said. Be calm in our consideration and await our ruling."

The crowd silenced, reassured somewhat by Moylann's calm manner.

Moylann turned to Cormac.

"My king and my friend. You know that we cannot give you a scribe, for it is druid law that the great truths may not be written, that they must be preserved in the memory, passed among the learned on the tongue."

Cormac shook his head.

"This must change. I will write the history of Eire, the laws of Eire, the wisdom that I have gained by being king. The time of the people of Eire is coming. Soon the knowledge must be open to the people."

Moylann threw up his arms.

"Cormac Mac Art will need an escort to the Boann," he said, as if deciding to ignore Cormac's speech as the ravings of a madman. "Who will serve?"

It was old Aodhfin who stepped forward from the ranks of the druids. He stood beside Cormac.

"I will serve as escort and companion. If my king wishes, I will also be his scribe."

Aislinn gasped. Her own teacher would break the taboo against writing.

Cormac shook his head. "You are a good old man, and a brave one, Aodhfin, but you are druii. I will have near me no druii who cannot accept the truth of the new God."

"I do accept."

Astonishment rose from the crowd, from the druii.

"Hear me, people of Eire! Have not we druii always known that there was another god, a god whose name no man knew, a god who existed above all other gods? You all know that I spent time as a slave among the Romans who rule across the water. There, I have heard much of this god and of his son, who was a brave and gentle warrior. Now this god has spoken to us, to the people of Eire, to our king."

Aodhfin turned to Moylann and the circle of druids who surrounded him.

"Should we be surprised that he has spoken his name to our king and not to one among the druii? Cannot the gods choose whom they please? The God of the Light has spoken to Cormac Mac Art. I believe."

In the pandemonium that followed, Aislinn stood still, closed her eyes, listened within herself, willing the woman Brighid to come to her, to tell her what was true. For a long time she felt nothing, then at last, the stirrings of some presence at the edge of her consciousness. But where was the Light that accompanied the woman? Where was the feeling of giddy warmth? This presence felt cold and dark. Her eyes flew open.

He was staring at her from the edge of the crowd. The black feathered cloak gleamed almost blue in the winter light. The steam from his breath curled eerily around his sharp-featured face. Banbh had returned.

21

Aislinn shook her head vehemently.

"Nay, father, I cannot stay."

Hurriedly, she threw her few belongings into her leather traveling pack.

It seemed a lifetime ago she had come to the hill of Tara. She closed her eyes, remembered the feel of Eoghan's body against hers, felt the small swell of the babes in her belly. She opened her eyes to cast away the longing that threatened to overwhelm her.

Aislinn sighed. "Banbh has returned."

"I know this, but you cannot run from evil forever. You must confront it or it will follow you like a shadow."

"It is more than just Banbh. I came back with such hope. I wanted to learn of my ancestry, of the lives of my parents. I thought that the knowledge would set me free, but look what has happened. Oh, yes, I know now who they were and how they died. My honor has been restored. But am I any less an outcast? And the sorrow I have caused!" She put her hands against the side of her head, pressed hard against her temples.

"Had I not come here, Macha would not have held me

captive. Aine would live, Aengus Mac Gabuideach would not be exiled, Cellach would live still, and the blinded Cormac would still be our king. See what my history has caused." Aislinn stopped, turned away, caressing the soft rounding of her belly.

"And these babes, who will never know their father. When their time comes, what will they think of the mother who drove him and all of his clan into exile? I should rightly be exiled from Tara; I have cost us our beloved king!"

Aodhfin clasped both of her hands in his.

"Do you think that your tale has ended, daughter? Can you not feel the threads that remain unwoven?"

"No!" Aislinn pushed his hands from her, slung the leather traveling bag over her shoulder. "I followed the quest you gave me. I found the child, and I abandoned her. I found the man and I exiled him. You will say that here at this place forms the doorway between the dark and the light. Do you really want me as the still point between them, father? It could very well be that my presence would descend us all into darkness."

"Do you not see? The turning has already taken place. It occurred when Cellach rescued you from the Deisi, when he was killed protecting his father, when our Cormac lost his eye. In those moments the new god showed his presence to us. You fulfilled the destiny you were given."

"Then I fulfilled it as a pawn. I ran from it and I would run from it again. I will run from it now. I can bear no more. I must leave this place to protect my babes."

"Is it the new god?" Aodhfin was asking her. "For if it is, I know that Cormac will give you time to listen and learn. Do you fear the new god for the pain its coming has brought you?"

Aislinn shook her head impatiently.

"Nay, father, it is not the new god. I do not know what Cormac saw, but I know that he saw something. I have spoken with Brighid of the Other. She has told me of changes to come. You yourself taught me always to be open to the workings of all the gods."

Aodhfin nodded.

"All of those years that I spent among the Romans as their slave. How I loathed those years. Yet now I see that the god was working on me, for it was there that I learned the skill of writing which Cormac now requires." He stopped, looked at Aislinn.

"He is working on you too, this god, or he would not have sent the woman of the Other. Stay with me. Let him work. There is more to come, more that will unfold. Hear me, daughter."

"Nay. It must unfold without me."

Aodhfin lowered his head resigned.

"Where will you go?"

"To the crannog of O'Domnhnaill and Gobinet. I have there a daughter whom I have not seen for three changings of the moon. Surely she believes that I have abandoned her."

"Your welcome there may not match the first one you received. Eoghan Mac Aidan is the foster-son of O'Domnhnaill and Gobinet and much beloved of them. They may blame you for his exile."

"Then I will take Corra ni Brith and go."

"Go where? Will you return to the life you had before—a wanderer, afraid and alone, but heavier now with children and sorrow than before? You know that you are entitled to the chieftainship of the Deisi. It is your birthright. Claim it, daughter, if you cannot remain with me. Let it be your safety."

Suddenly, Aislinn's head lifted. She threw her arms around Aodhfin and kissed him gently on the forehead.

"The chieftainship of the Deisi. Yes, father. I know how I will insure my welcome at the crannog and secure the protection I need for my children. I will confer upon O'Domnhnaill the chieftainship of the Deisi, for did he not fight long ago on the side of my own father?"

Aodhfin looked at her in surprise, then nodded slowly. "This is wise, daughter. But the ceremony must be performed with all the pomp that a druidess and chieftain's daughter is entitled to. You must not skulk into the camp in the frightened and secretive way you went before. Your protection from Banbh must be in all of the Deisi knowing and respecting your choice and your power. Come. I will make the arrangements."

The retinue specified by the law arrived at the bruidhean in the late afternoon of the third day. Aislinn felt stifled by the sheer force of the numbers accompanying her—soldiers of the Fianna, members of the bardic class, female attendants for her clothing and her hair—twenty-four attendants in all. Even old Aodhfin had decided to accompany her at the last moment to see her safely to O'Domhnaill. She remembered her trip to Tara with longing, the still evenings when she and Eoghan had first explored the beginnings of their love. She felt tears gather behind her eyes and willed them back. Where was he now? How did he bear his exile believing his children to be dead, believing himself to be the cause? She feared for him, whispered a prayer that the gods would watch over him body and spirit.

Now she sat astride her horse, waiting while her soldiers announced her to the bruighaid, the keeper of the public house.

Her hair moved and shifted in the cold February wind. Aislinn drew her cloak closer. She was unaccustomed to the cloak of the Deisi with its rich blues and greens or to the feeling of the soft wool gown beneath the cloak. The heavy gold brooch with its ruby and emerald inlays that held the cloak in place had been her mother's, as was the braided torque that lay so cold against her neck. The jewels were those Macha had confiscated, yet Aislinn longed for the simple white cloak and gown of her druii days. She thought of the white cloak of Fionn, of the wild ex-

hilarating flight around the coastline of Eire. How could
she have believed that to be real? Like so many other
things in her life, it had been a dream. Only a dream. She
sighed. She felt so tired, so sad. She had not felt that way
traveling with Eoghan toward Tara. At least she had to
admit that she had felt safer on this trip than before, surrounded by so many people and by the bristling weaponry
of the Fianna. Not once had she felt the dark presence of
the crow man.

The bruighaid and his wife entered the yard followed
by their own retinue of family members and serving people. "We are honored by your visit, priestess, and will
provide well for you and for those who accompany you,"
he called, sweeping his hand toward the door of his bruidhean.

Two of the Fenians helped Aislinn to dismount. She
entered the public house with her retinue trailing behind
her. The bruidhean was warm and spotlessly clean. Immediately, the bruighaid began serving mugs of warm ale
and mulled wine and the fresh whole loaves of bread with
pots of honey that would precede the meal. Aislinn
glimpsed the bloodied apron of one of the cooks who was
already slaughtering pigs for the evening meal. She called
the innkeeper to her, thanked him elaborately, praising his
hospitality, then drew him aside.

"I am fatigued and would rest before the evening meal.
Is there a quiet spot where this may be possible?"

"I shall see to it that your rest is not disturbed, priestess," the innkeeper fairly bubbled at her. He led her across
the small yard with its tidy ornamental garden to the
sleeping house. The long, rectangular building was partitioned off into sleeping chambers, each with its own
sleeping platforms and warm pelts. A central fire blazed
at the center of the hall and the bruighaid hurried to send
servants for warm stones wrapped in cloth that would heat
Aislinn's sleeping platform and warm her body. He took
her to the center of the hall, to the warmest of the chambers. She settled gratefully on the warm layer of pelts and

drew the coverlets over her. She was asleep before the servants had left the room.

When she awoke the chamber was shadowed. Aislinn experienced a moment of confusion, thinking herself asleep in the druii lodge at Tara and her hand reached out for Eoghan.

"You are alone," said a voice from somewhere in the chamber beside her.

Aislinn sat up, frightened. Was this yet another of the messengers of Banbh? A tall, angular woman stood near her feet. Her hair had once been red, but now it was laced with gray. It stood out wild and untamed around her face. She had gray eyes, prominent cheekbones, a jutting chin. She did not smile, but regarded Aislinn with utter seriousness.

She stepped forward and placed her hand on Aislinn's belly.

"There are two of them."

Aislinn scrabbled backward under the coverlet, drew her arms across her belly.

"That is difficult. More difficult."

"Your difficulty will be with me if the Dark One has sent you." She drew her dagger from its scabbard, held it forward. "I will not hesitate to kill you to protect these babes."

The woman's eyes widened. She laughed aloud.

"A tough one then, a fighter. Good, good. That bodes well." She held her hands up, palms out. "I am not here to harm your children. I am Maille, the physician. She sent me to you, the woman of the Other. She says it will be a difficult birth. She does not wish a birth by the knife."

"By the knife?"

But Maille was already bending above Aislinn's stomach. "May I?"

She gestured at Aislinn's bulging belly. Aislinn nodded, held the dagger aside, but did not relinquish its grip.

Maille disregarded the knife entirely, placed both

hands on Aislinn's belly, moved them slowly in a circle. "They are small still, but they are not placed well. They lie to the sides. I can feel this already. But it is too soon to turn them. Too soon. If I turn them now, they will return to this position. We will have trouble with them when the time comes to move through the birth river."

"You are wrong. For how else should they come?"

"We will need to assist them with my instruments, my knife."

"No! You frighten me. I have heard of these births by the knife. Too many die. Almost all die."

"You must send for me close upon their time, one moon before the birthing. I will need to turn them, to try to turn them."

"And if you cannot turn them?"

"Then we will take them by the knife."

"And I will die?" Aislinn's voice rose in high-pitched terror now.

Maille regarded her unflinchingly.

"Most die. But I am skilled. My instruments are clean, my linens boiled. One of the women whose child I took in this fashion did live."

"One? Of how many, physician?"

Again, the hard, unflinching look.

"Of more than a dozen."

The woman turned and left the chamber. Aislinn stumbled to her feet, headed blindly for the door. Terrified she made her way across the yard and into the public house. Aodhfin looked up at her entrance, cried aloud.

"What is it, daughter?"

"There was a woman in my chamber. Maille she called herself. She frightened me."

"How?"

Aislinn looked around her, afraid to speak of the babes in so large a crowd, afraid of the news reaching Banbh. The bruighaid hurried forward.

"My humble apologies, priestess. There is no reason

that she should have bothered you. She is the local physician, the midwife. We call her Maille of the knife, for she is known for her skill with births by the knife. She lives over there." He pointed to a small hut that straddled a rushing stream.

Aislinn shuddered. She had heard of births by the knife, knew that the physicians of Eire were trained in these births, but she also knew how many died in such births, a few babes surviving but their mothers perishing, almost all, of the wound. She felt terror clench at her heart. All the pleading and apologies of the bruighaid could not induce her to eat the feast that he set before her. Nor could she sleep that night. Through the long darkness, she stood at the open doorway to the sleeping chamber, staring across the moonlit winter field at the hut of Maille the midwife, wondering who would care for her motherless children, praying in the hollows of her heart until the rising sun called the company to the final day of their journey.

Aislinn saw movement beyond the causeway, watched as O'Domnhnaill came forward, saw the look of dread on his features. She eased her horse forward so that she was at the head of the company. Behind O'Domnhnaill and his contingent of warriors she could see Gobinet, her hand firmly grasping the wrist of Corra ni Brith. She felt her heart swell. My child. At last my child.

A soldier of the Fianna stepped in front of her horse, crossed his shield over his chest, and raised his spear. He cleared his throat and began his announcement.

"O'Domnhnaill of the Deisi, I bring before you Aislinn ní Sorar, priestess of the druii and claimant to the chieftainship of the Deisi by birthright and by the brehon courts of law. It is she who requests your presence."

O'Domnhnaill nodded curtly, compressed his lips.

What was he thinking? Aislinn wondered. Did he fear

that she would exile him and all of his people the way she had exiled his foster-son? She took a deep breath, began her recitation.

"O'Domhnaill of the Deisi, you were friend to my father, Sorar, companion and warrior, defender in battle. His loss and death exiled you here to this crannog. I now make honor payment for that exile. With the approval of the clan of the Deisi, I would like to confer upon you the chieftainship of the Deisi for the remainder of your life."

Absolute silence fell over the crowd for a moment, then wild cheering went up among O'Domhnaill's warriors and spread to all the people of the crannog.

O'Domhnaill looked stunned.

"I accept the offer of Aislinn ni Sorar," he shouted above the crowd.

It was Gobinet who pushed forward, who took her husband's arm, who spoke in her blunt, clear way.

"What have I told you, husband? This woman is not the cause of suffering; she is the victim. Does she not seek now to heal the wounds of the Deisi? We will honor her. What do you wish in return, Aislinn ni Sorar, from the people of the Deisi?"

O'Domhnaill stared at his wife, then nodded in sudden agreement.

"Ask Aislinn ni Sorar, daughter of my friend."

Aislinn smiled.

"I ask to live among the Deisi as one of you. I ask to serve as your priestess. I ask for your acceptance and for your protection for myself and for all who belong to me."

"Done!" cried O'Domhnaill and Gobinet rushed forward to help Aislinn dismount.

"I ask for one more thing, mother," Aislinn said softly as she placed her hands in Gobinet's. "I ask to see my child, whom my heart has missed so sorely."

A strange look crossed Gobinet's face, but she cried aloud. "Bring forward the child Corra ni Brith."

Two women of the tribe stepped forward, holding Corra ni Brith's arms between them. Aislinn gave a glad cry.

"Oh, my child, my little girl." She stretched forward her arms to embrace the child but Corra ni Brith pulled free of the grasp of the women and ran to stand beside Gobinet.

"You are not my mother," Corra cried aloud, "for you broke your vow to me as a mother would not have done. You said that you would return in a fortnight, but many moons have passed. I will not have you as my mother any longer!"

Aislinn's heart thudded loud in her chest; she could hear it even above the crowd. She looked at Corra's face, saw the rage and anger. She reached her hand forward; the child slapped it away. Inside her chest, Aislinn felt her heart beat faster. It galloped now, like a horse spurred by fear. In a moment, it would carry her away, speed her away. It raced like the wind and she followed it toward the west, toward Tir Nan Og, toward the isle of the dead.

Corra huddled low beneath the wolf skins, listened as Aodhfin and Gobinet discussed Aislinn.

"We must find a way to make her eat," said Gobinet. "The babes take all their nourishment from her. Soon all three will die."

"There is no one in that body to eat or drink," said Aodhfin, shaking his head sorrowfully. "She is gone. She has decided to go and to take her babes with her. Why would she not? Her husband has abandoned her, she considers herself responsible for the death of Cellach and the blinding of Cormac. And there is Banbh, the Dark One. He believes her children dead, tried to have them aborted by one of his minions. She looks for him over her shoulder and in the face of each new encounter. Now Corra blames her for abandonment. Aislinn's heart could bear no more."

"Poor Corra," said Gobinet. "She hides and looks wild. She fears that she has done this thing to Aislinn."

Aodhfin shook his head again. "When I think of what

Aislinn told me of her captivity. How she fought for the babes and kept their existence secret and how each day she wondered and worried if Corra ni Brith would understand. She nearly died there. Instead she will die here among those who love her."

There was a flurry of motion. Corra rose from her hiding place beneath the wolf skins.

"She is dying?" She turned toward Aodhfin, a panicked note in her voice. "The priestess Aislinn is dying?"

"Nay," said Gobinet. "Hush now, child."

But Aodhfin held up his hand.

"We must tell the child the truth. I protected Aislinn too well from the truth of her own childhood. Now see the weight of the accumulated sorrow."

Aodhfin bent toward Corra, took her hands in his.

"She is dying, child. She is dying because those she loves have turned from her and because the weight of her sorrow is too great. She has gone inside herself and cannot come forward."

"Have I done this thing to her?"

He stroked the child's hair gently. "No, child. An evil woman has done all of this. She kept Aislinn a prisoner in a place far away. That is why she could not come to you."

"Where is that woman?"

"She is dead. But her power continues for she keeps Aislinn from us."

"Do you think that I could bring my máthair back?"

Aodhfin smiled gently. "You could try, child, but I do not know."

Corra started toward the little hut where Aislinn had been lying for three days. Gobinet made to follow her, but Aodhfin held her back.

"Let her go alone to her máthair. Aislinn loves the child greatly. Perhaps Corra will indeed be the one who brings her back to us."

*   *   *

From deep in the darkness, Aislinn waited patiently for the last of the light to extinguish. Something moved above her. Her eyes remained closed, but felt as though they had opened. She looked up from far beneath the surface of a dark, cold lake.

He was bending above her, his yellow eyes boring into hers, his wide black wings outspread over her. She smiled tiredly.

"So, Banbh. You come for me yet again. I knew that you would find me here."

"Ah, poor priestess. They have all abandoned you, have they not?"

"They have. My máthair, my athair, my husband, and now my foster-child." She knew that she should cry, but could not produce tears, here, so far below the water. Banbh smiled.

"I would not abandon you, priestess."

"You would not?"

"I would keep you with me always. We would do the bidding of my dark goddess and the doing of it would make you happy. You would sit beside me at all of the ceremonies at Tara and I would weave for you a robe of darkness. Is not my darkness warm to you now?"

"It is warm, Dark One. It is good to be comforted when I have been alone for so long."

"Of course it is. That is what I have been trying to tell you since you were a child. My darkness will keep you warm. I will never abandon you."

"Never?"

"Never. I promise it. I would keep you with me until death and even after it. I would be your teacher. My dark goddess would invest you with great power."

"I wish no power, but I grow tired of being alone."

"Of course you do."

"I have wearied of being strong, Dark One."

"Look at how wide my wingspan is. My goddess and I will carry you."

Aislinn stared up from below the water at the wide dark wings spread over her. She sighed.

"Do you see how I will enfold you?"

"I do."

"You wish for me to keep you warm, pretty priestess. Only give me two things and I will keep you warm."

"What two things, Dark One?"

"You will give me your body, Aislinn."

"I cannot give you that, Dark One. It belongs to Eoghan Mac Aidan."

Nasal and thin the voice came then. "He who has divorced you? Abandoned you?"

Beneath the water Aislinn felt the first stirrings of panic. This was a voice she knew. She moaned aloud, thought of the babes in her womb.

"No, Banbh. I cannot give you that. Not now."

He calmed her, fanning the dark wings above her, softening his voice.

"Then my desire will wait, pretty priestess. But give me now your most precious jewel. It is yours to give now. When you have given me that jewel, I will comfort you from your sorrow. I will fold you into the dark warmth of my wings."

"I have no jewels, Dark One. None but those which belonged to my mother. What jewel would you have from me?" Aislinn relaxed back into the warmth, the dark blanket.

"You are druii trained, priestess, as am I. I will answer your question with a question."

"I will answer."

Banbh laughed softly. "What is the seat of the soul?"

"The head. My soul lies behind my eyes, down here where I am."

"Very good. That is the jewel you will give me. You will give me your soul. You will open your mouth and I will reach my beak into your mouth. I will pluck your soul into mine."

The dark form of Banbh moved down close over Aislinn. She could feel the cold tip of his beak at her lips, see the yellow of his eyes so close to hers. Aislinn felt no anger or fear, only a calm, floating sensation.

"I do not think that I can give you my spirit, Dark One."

"Ah, but you can. Others have done."

"I do not think it is mine to give."

"To whom does it belong?"

"To the Light."

"What light is that?"

"The Light that remains in here with me."

The form of Banbh moved in closer. The wings pinned Aislinn's arms to her sides.

Corra screamed and screamed again.

Gobinet came running into the hut, followed by Aodhfin.

A crow, its black wings spread wide, sat atop Aislinn's lifeless body. Gobinet ran at it, her hands waving wildly.

"Begone, carrion bird. She is not dead yet!"

The bird hopped to the side, but did not fly the platform. It cocked its head, turned its yellow eyes in Corra's direction. It let out a single harsh caw, began to flap its wings as if it would fly at Corra.

"Down, Corra!" Aodhfin screamed. "Gobinet, enfold her and cover her eyes. And close your own."

The black bird lifted from Aislinn's sleeping platform and flew lazily in their direction.

Gobinet cried out in terror. She ran to Corra and wrapped her arms around her, burying the child's head against her skirts. She lowered the child to the floor, covering her with her own body. Then she closed her own eyes.

A wind moved in the room. The crow cawed triumphantly. Suddenly there was a thunder of wings, as if thousands of birds moved in the air of the tiny hut. Raucous cries split the silence. Above their heads, Corra and

Gobinet could feel the beating wings of the birds. Corra screamed again and again.

"Get ye gone!" The voice of Aodhfin echoed from the rafters, filled the room, the voice not of an old man, but of the wind, the sea. Then Aodhfin cried out in pain.

Silence fell.

Gobinet opened her eyes. Aodhfin lay on the floor, his arm at a twisted angle, jutting away from his side. The crow was nowhere to be seen. Gobinet ran to Aodhfin, dropped to her knees beside him.

He raised himself to a half-seated position on his good arm, winced at the pain, but smiled tiredly at Gobinet.

"It is well. We broke the arm in our struggle with the crow."

"We?"

"Those who helped me. I carry into the physical world the injury we bore in the other."

Corra rose from the floor and ran to the sleeping platform where Aislinn lay still and white as death, her eyes open. She lifted the lifeless hand and stroked it. Gently, she repeated the words Aislinn had once spoken to her.

"Do not be afraid, máthair. I will not let them hurt you anymore."

Aislinn's pale form did not stir.

Corra stroked Aislinn's hair, rained tiny kisses on her hands and cheeks, hummed a wordless little tune. The form on the bed remained motionless, openmouthed and staring.

Corra climbed onto the bed, wrapped her arms around Aislinn, her care-taking lost in the panic that she would lose her, that nothing could be done. She began to sob.

"Oh, please do not leave me. Máthair, I need you. I love you so."

There was a shudder from the silent figure on the bed, a sound like a sob and then Aislinn's pale slender hand moved gently and began to stroke the copper length of Corra's hair.

22

The Beltaine fires blazed brightly on the meadow outside the crannog. The people of O'Domnhnaill lined the fields in the May sunshine, their cattle beside them, waiting for the ritual purification.

In the space at the head of the two fires Aislinn lifted her rowan wand and called aloud.

"We purify the cattle of Eire. May they give abundantly of milk and meat. May they multiply and fill the fields."

She brought the stick down with a swooshing sound that was the signal to begin. The cattle of O'Domnhnaill came first with the chief himself driving them between the fires of purification. Aislinn tapped each animal with her rowan stick and tried to settle her body for the long ritual. She planted her feet more firmly apart, moved her hand up the small of her back.

Her six-month belly protruded before her. She hoped that she would not be too tired by the end of the ritual. O'Domnhaill and Gobinet had provided well for her. Nearby, a table laden with fresh fruit and clear water waited beside a low stool that would ease her should she need to sit for a time. The cattle of O'Domnhnaill's tribe numbered in the hundreds, and each one must be driven

individually through the purifying Beltaine fires on the
first day of May.

Already Aislinn's face was flushed from the heat of the
twin fires and her back ached.

Even so, she would miss the people of O'Domnhnaill.
For tomorrow, when the Beltaine rituals had been completed, O'Domnhnaill and most of the members of his
tribe would depart for the larger tuath where once her
father and mother had ruled. Only Aislinn, Gobinet,
Corra, and a small contingent of Deisi soldiers would remain here on the crannog, for Aislinn had requested that
her birthing take place here where she felt safe and protected from the spies of Banbh. After the birth, they would
join the others of the Deisi.

Aodhfin, his broken arm healed, had long since departed for Clete Acaill, Cormac's new community on the
Boann, where he would serve as Cormac's scribe.

Aislinn pressed her free hand against her stomach and
shook her head. It was more than the prying eyes of
Banbh that kept her here. She felt once more for the heads
of the babes, felt them lying crosswise in her belly. It was
the woman, Maille. She had not seen or heard from her
again, but her warning remained in Aislinn's mind as
fresh and terrifying as it had been in the February cold.
The babes were turned to the side. She could see the
pressing bulbs of their heads, each at one side, feel their
little feet hammering two-sided on the drum of her belly.
And soon there would be no room within her for them to
shift their little bodies. Here, on the crannog, she was
within one hour's ride of the strange midwife. And she
was afraid to be farther.

She tapped the heaving flanks of yet another cow and
stared out toward the line of the woods. A horseman rode
into view from the tree line, the green of his Fenian cloak
visible to Aislinn. She gasped, her hand flying to her hair,
her face. She strained to see his visage. Had Eoghan returned to her at last, come back to claim her, learned
somehow of their little ones? She watched, holding her

breath, until the brown of the rider's hair, the tilt of his head, became clear in her view. She bent her head in disappointment, swallowing the hot tears. The rider was not Eoghan.

She had expected him throughout the long winter, had greeted every rider to the crannog, had swallowed her bitter disappointment when Eoghan did not come, when none of the riders were sent by him.

Now she looked at the approaching Fenian again and recognized him. Darragh. Eoghan's Fenian brother from the hill of Tara. He rode closer. Aislinn positioned her swelling belly behind the back of a cow, rested her hands on the back of the animal. The procession of cattle stopped.

Darragh dismounted.

"I greet you, priestess of the Deisi. We have heard now at Almhuin that you reside among the Deisi. I am sent to inquire of your health and happiness."

"Who has sent you on this mission, Fenian?"

"He who is the foster-son to the chief of the Deisi." This he shouted aloud to the assembled crowd.

O'Domnhnaill and Gobinet approached. Darragh spoke to them.

"He who is your foster-son sends his greetings and his love. He wishes you to know that he is well among the Fianna."

Immediately Gobinet began asking questions of Darragh. Did Eoghan eat well? Was he healthy? How fared his state of mind? Aislinn stood still and silent behind the cow, bitterly disappointed that no greetings of love had been sent to her.

Darragh turned again in her direction.

"How fare you, priestess?"

"I am well and healthy, surrounded by the love and concern of the people of the Deisi."

Gobinet watched Aislinn quietly. She had kept her promise to the druidess, had not sent a messenger to Eoghan to tell him of Aislinn's pregnancy, for Aislinn had pleaded that if Eoghan did not want her, he did not want the babes who grew within her. But daily Gobinet doubted the wisdom of her decision, as she watched Aislinn's loneliness and disappointment grow. Something had to be done to bring the two together. Now, with Aislinn's belly hidden by the cow, Darragh would return with a tale of her health and happiness. Eoghan would believe he had freed her of obligation. Gobinet shook her head.

Slightly, subtly, she motioned to Corra, who stood among the gathering of young people of the tribe. Corra moved forward, her eyes questioning Gobinet. She looked at Darragh, at Aislinn, at the concealing animal. Suddenly, she understood. Her face lit with laughter. Stepping behind the next cow in line, she cracked the animal sharply on the rump with the flat of her hand. The cow gave a startled bellow and moved forward against Aislinn's bulwark cow. Aislinn stepped back quickly, started to move for the concealing cover of the next animal, but it was too late.

Darragh of the Fenians was staring in astonishment at the rounded mound of Aislinn's six-month belly.

Aislinn raised her hands to the warm June sun and sang a snatch of an old lullaby aloud. Her voice echoed crazily back to her across the water of the lake and around the empty circle of the crannog.

The sound of the crannog was almost eerie now that O'Domnhnaill and most of the people of the Deisi had departed for the hilltop stronghold formerly occupied by Aengus and Macha.

Gobinet and Corra remained with Aislinn until the lying in. Together the three worked on clothes for the coming children, baked bread, and sang in the warm light of oncoming summer. Of course there were the soldiers who guarded the crannog, the causeway, the woods beyond, but as with most men, they remained far from the things of women and did not intrude on Aislinn's solitude.

She ran her hands across the huge mound of her seven-month belly and smiled. One of the babes had shifted its position. Aislinn knew this now with certainty, felt the round head at the top of her belly. He was feet first at the birth canal, but babes came through the canal that way often. Did they not? One little moon would tell the tale. One little moon and she would send for Maille, who would try to turn the other. And perhaps that one would also turn. Aislinn's heart felt light.

She was happy here. The babes grew stronger every day, moving within her and kicking. The circle of love that moved among Aislinn, Corra, and Gobinet made Aislinn feel strong. Her only sorrow was the absence of Eoghan.

She wondered where he was now. From May through September the Fianna lived off the land, wandering, hunting, building rude bothies in the forests of Eire. She remembered the bothy that she and Eoghan had shared on the way to Tara, remembered the gentle way he had stroked her face, the strong, rhythmic sound of the poetry he had recited.

Had Darragh of the Fenians taken him the news about the babes? Aislinn stroked her belly again as one of the twins kicked out exuberantly, smiling at the whirling feeling within her.

She sat quietly on her favorite bench by the water-gate, the spot she had once shared with Eoghan. She closed her eyes, tipped her head back in the sunshine, dreamed of Eoghan combing out the tangles in her hair. When the voice spoke, it sounded so much like Eoghan's that Aislinn snapped her eyes open, surprised that her reverie could sound so real.

"Why did you not tell me?"

He was standing above her, the shadow of his plaid cloak casting an arc around him on the ground, the sun behind him so that his face remained in shadow.

Aislinn stood, moved to an angle where she could see him.

"Eoghan? Oh, Eoghan, you have come for me, for us."

She ran to him, lifting her arms around his neck, but he pried them down and lowered them once again to her sides. She saw that he had grown thinner, more sinewy. His hair was long and braided, his face unshaven and shadowy. His mouth was a hard, thin line. He held her arms stiff against her sides.

"I have come because I was told that you are heavy with child. Why did you not tell me?"

"I tried. I knew on that first night that they were conceived. I tried to tell you then and again on our marriage night, but Banbh was always there. And then, on that last day when I wanted to tell you, you left me at Tara Hill."

"I believed that they were dead. You let me believe that Macha killed them."

She clenched her fists, lifted her head, defiantly.

"I protected them from Banbh with my silence. Still he does not know. And would it have made a difference if you had known? Would you have kept me with you for the sake of your babes?"

Eoghan's head shot up.

"Babes?"

"There are two, a boy and a girl."

Eoghan made a strangled sound and turned away, staring out over the water.

"Nay, it would not have made a difference. I would have set you away from me still." He hung his head. "You lived too many years in exile and the life of the forests is a good life for a man alone, but not for a woman and children." He sighed.

"Forgive me then, for not telling you of them. I have protected them so long with my silence." She stepped before him, lowered her head in supplication.

"Forgive you?" His laughter was bitter. "I am the one who requires forgiveness. It was my name that dishonored yours, my family who made you motherless, a wanderer. I tricked you into marrying me. I should have told you the truth—or at least what I knew of the truth. I am ashamed that a Fenian should be so dishonest. Now I have left you with child—children—and alone. I wanted only to love and protect you. Look what I have done. Before we met, you were a wanderer, alone and afraid. I thought that I could protect you, could take from you your fear and loneliness, but look what I and mine have done. What are you now but still a wanderer, a mother of children with no father to defend and provide?"

He released her arms and turned away. It was not until Aislinn saw the shaking of his shoulders that she realized he was weeping.

She faced him, lifted her hands against his cheeks. She pressed his tears to her own lips.

"Hear me now, Fenian, I who am your true wife. I too have felt in need of forgiveness, for was it not my history, my family, my rescue that cost our great king his eye, his son? And yet, where is the blame for this on me? On you? In history? In lineage? We are the accidents of their past, Eoghan. There is nothing to forgive. I know what part you have played in my sorrow and it was the part of honor. You saved my life. The wine you served, you served all unaware. My mother's blessing lies upon you for all time. There is nothing to forgive unless it is the mischievous god who brought us together at the start. I understand all that you have done, Eoghan. I will always love you. Now it is time to forgive yourself.'

Eoghan dropped to his knees, circled his arms around her full stomach, rained kisses upon it, stroking gently with his hands. He stood and lifted Aislinn's face between his hands, regarded her seriously.

"Mo ghra, my beloved one. Your forgiveness sets me free to love you, you and the babes we have made." He folded her against him, placed his right hand on her belly. "Our children, the sweet reunion of old enemies."

Aislinn laughed aloud. "Perhaps Aodhfin was right; perhaps the gods have written for us. For will not all of our sorrows at last bring reunion to our divided tribes? Come, we must tell Gobinet and Corra. We must pack to go with you."

Eoghan released her suddenly. He stood, looked out over the water, shook his head.

"It would be unwise for you to go with me. You are far along; the rough travel of my life could endanger the babes. You must remain here where you are guarded, where Gobinet can care for you properly. Nor can I linger long in Meath. I am still an exile here. Even this brief visit brings danger. If I am seen here, Cairbry Mac Cormac must act against me. I cannot force him into such a trial."

Aislinn thought again of the woman Maille and her strange warning.

"You are right. We must be wise for the sake of our small ones." She blinked back the tears that threatened to belie her words. "Oh, I cannot bear for us to be parted again."

"The love that has been spoken between us at last will keep us together, even while we are apart."

"Will you come for us after the babes are born?" she whispered.

Eoghan wrapped his arms around her, rested his chin against the top of her head.

"Perhaps I can do better for you, love. I will send one of the Fenian brothers here. When your time is near, he can send for me. If the gods are on our side, I can be with you when the babes are born."

Aislinn laughed aloud.

"Then we can return to Almhuin together. The birth will be easy. Why not, when their life within me has been such joy? Corra will help me on the journey. Perhaps we can prepare a wagon. Oh, Eoghan, we can all be together!"

"And you will not regret the life of an exile?"

"What exile if we are together?"

Eoghan nodded suddenly, convinced.

"Perhaps the gods will be with us, at last. Perhaps it can be so. I will believe it, love, all the while that we are parted."

23

23

Aislinn squatted down low beside the birthing table and pressed her palms flat against the rough stone. She let out a low moan as the watery ripple of the pain washed across her belly and moved low into her back.

The pains had been like this—uneven, deep, and irregular for almost nine hours now, throughout the long night. She crouched when they washed over her or knelt against them like a field animal. Between the pains, she walked, drank Gobinet's watery distillation of sweet wine and gentle relaxing herbs. Gobinet had immediately, hours ago, posted the Fenian soldier south toward Almhuin when the rippling warning pains began, but Aislinn feared that Eoghan could not arrive in time. The babes were early. She had only just finished her eighth month, had not yet sent for Maille. One of the babes was still turned sideways!

Now Gobinet lifted her to the table while Corra prepared more watered wine.

"Let me look again, child. I am worried that no water has come."

She pushed back the loose birthing tunic and opened Aislinn's legs wide, searching with her fingers for any sign of water or of the relaxation of the birth door. She shook her head and stood.

"No, you are not ready yet. The birthing door is tightly closed and there is no water."

"Does the babe still lie sideways in the womb?"

"One does, but your pains are not yet strong enough to make them turn; that may begin soon."

Aislinn grimaced as another wave of pain collected in her abdomen. She clutched at one of the lodge poles and sank down against the pain, panting as it rolled over her.

"I am not sure now that his arrival is a blessing, mother. I would be just as satisfied if he came to find the babes washed and healthy and me well rid of this thunderous pain."

Gobinet laughed easily.

"My pain was more than I expected each time. It is the same for all women. This last pain was a good sign, though. Your body is speeding up. Soon there will be little space between the pains."

Aislinn laughed, then gasped as another wave of pain began.

"Should this wisdom make me glad, mother?"

Gobinet smiled, gave her a sip of the herbed wine. Corra ni Brith dipped a cloth in cool water and gently rubbed Aislinn's wrists and temples. The heat of the last month of summer had been intense, pressing down against all of them. No breeze stirred across the lake to cool the crannog and in the final weeks Aislinn's wrists, fingers, and ankles had begun to swell as her abdomen grew huge.

Gobinet walked to the doorway and stared out at the empty crannog with its sparse population of guardian Deisi warriors. She shook her head with worry. All men. No midwife. And the babes not yet turning. She thought of the midwife—Maille. But the birth by the knife was far too dangerous. Best to let nature do its work, if it could.

The long day stretched toward nightfall. Now Aislinn's pains were monstrous, cresting waves, with almost no time between them. She was exhausted, her face drawn of all color, her hair soaked to her forehead and scalp. In the few seconds between each pain, she slept, seeming almost drugged. Still no water came and the birth door did not open.

Worriedly, Gobinet felt for the heads of the babes, found one pressed against the side of Aislinn's abdomen.

Gobinet made a decision. She moved to the door of the hut and called into the darkness.

"Conor!"

In seconds, the huge bristling captain of the Deisi guard stood before her.

"I must ask you to perform a service."

"No, mother," Aislinn moaned from behind Gobinet. "Do not send for her. I should not have told you of her and her wild tale."

"It is well that you told me, daughter. It is time." She turned back to Conor.

"There is a physician, one Maille, who lives near the bruidhean at the Tara road crossroads. It is one hour's hard ride. Go and bring her here with haste. And tell her she may have a birth by the knife."

Conor sucked in his breath.

"My horse!" he called to his aide. "Bring him quickly and saddled."

Maille stood from her examination, washed her hands in the laving bowl Gobinet provided. She stretched her long frame upward, turned her back to Aislinn so that her red hair haloed in the light.

"You were wise to call me," she said softly to Gobinet. "Do you see how swollen her hands and ankles are? Her own fluids have poisoned her system. More than that, her birthing door will not open. One of the babes is turned head down to the birthing door; the other lies sideways. I will try first to turn that one, but if there is too little space we must take the children by the knife."

Aislinn moaned softly.

"Corra," she whispered. The little girl brought her face close to Aislinn. "If I die by the knife . . ." Corra pressed her fist to her mouth, made a small, whimpering sound. "No, my strong daughter. Hear me now. If I die by the knife, you must go with Eoghan. You must help him raise these, your brother and sister. Can you do that for me? For them?"

From some wellspring, the child drew herself up, squared her shoulders.

"Máthair," she said, "I will make myself strong for you."

Maille took both of her hands.

"I will speak the truth to you, priestess, as I did when we met before. The danger is less to the babes, more to you, but yours will not be the first babes my knife has brought into the world. I am trained. I will use all the good practices of my training and we will petition the gods."

Aislinn gasped as another wave of pain washed over her.

Maille turned to Gobinet.

"Open the door and uncover all the windows. Let clean air sweep through the room. Heat water that I may cleanse my instruments and again another cauldron that I may wash. We will also need fresh water for after the birthing and water for an herbal drink."

Corra and Gobinet set about the preparations as Maille drew a vial of dried herbs from her bag, mixing the herbs with the warm drinking water.

"You must drink this, child," Maille said as she lifted Aislinn's head. "It will help you to go beneath the pain."

Next, she took out a sharp iron needle with a curved hook and a large pair of tongs. These she put into the boiling water, cooling them on clean linen towels when she had removed them from the water. She laved her arms from the fingers to the elbows, dried them on clean linen, inserted her left arm gently into Aislinn's womb. Aislinn screamed aloud. When Maille had found the tiny head of the child she reached for the tongs, inserting them beside her arm. Aislinn screamed once in an agony of pain, then passed out into darkness.

"Good," said Maille. "Now her abdomen will loosen against my ministrations. I stand a better chance of turning the child." Gently, gently, she manipulated with her arm and the tongs. Suddenly, she removed the instrument, stood smiling in triumph. "It is done. Now we must speed them through the birth door."

There was a sudden flurry of horse's hooves, a movement of wind, and the swirling figure of Eoghan swept into the hut. He took one look at Aislinn's still form, at Maille, and blenched. He grasped Gobinet's hand.

"What is it, máthair? What has befallen Aislinn?"

Before she could answer, Aislinn moaned low, her hand clutched in Corra's, as trying to raise her back against the sweeping pain she returned to consciousness. Eoghan took in her pale wet face, the terrified look on the face of Corra ni Brith. Gently he laid his arm beneath Aislinn's back, gently lifted her into the contraction, holding her tight as the pain washed across her, then lowering her to the pallet. She fluttered a pale, water-swollen hand against his cheek.

"You have come, love," she whispered, her voice no louder than a whispering leaf. "I knew that you would come."

Another great wave of pain rolled over her. She twined her fists in Eoghan's tunic, moaning low until the pain stopped, then permitted Maille to lift the goblet to her lips. Maille nodded to Eoghan.

"Give her the potion in little sips until she has drunk it all, for now we must break her water and widen the birth door."

Eoghan lifted the glass once again to her lips.

"Wait," Aislinn cried out. "Eoghan, if I die . . ."

"Nay, hush, love, you will not die."

She held up her hand. "If I die, take Corra and the babes to O'Domhnaill. Let them be raised among the Deisi. Do not let them be wanderers as we have been."

Eoghan nodded his head, his face sad.

"It will be as you have asked, love."

Maille washed in near-boiling water, held her hands aloft to dry. She positioned herself at Aislinn's legs, gently inserted her hand into the birthing door, probing with the little hook. Aislinn screamed out against the pain, but at that moment water gushed from her, soaking the birthing tunic and the table on which she lay. Maille nodded her head, felt around at the cervical opening.

"You are as wide as you will go, priestess. There is not enough room. I must widen the birth door."

Aislinn moaned in pain, but Maille regarded her solemnly. "This is a great victory, priestess, for we have turned the child and both will come through the birth door. We will need no birth by the knife, only this widening to permit them through. Drink the rest of the herbal."

Again Maille washed. She laid out thread and a needle of bone, then took a thin iron scalpel from the boiling water. When the instruments were ready, Maille held her scalpel by the hilt and raised it in the firelight.

"O you Dian Cecht, god of the physicians, yourself a healer, hear me. As this knife is my instrument so am I the instrument of your power. Make steady my arm, make true my cut. May your power bring new life into the world. May your power preserve the life of this mother. Before the power of your healing I am humble." Maille brought the scalpel toward the place where she would create the episiotomy incision.

Aislinn nodded, the drowsy warmth of the herbal potion overtaking her.

"Brighid, goddess of mothers," she whispered, but she could not remember the incantations. Instead, in a room behind her eyes she heard the voice of the woman of light.

"I am with you, child. Come away, now. Come away."

She felt a whirling sensation as of a tunnel, but it was not the tunnel of her visions. She felt her body lift, move through the darkness. Suddenly she was standing on a hill.

Eoghan was beside her and they were holding hands, smiling gently at each other. Below her she could see the sparkling waters of the river Boann. She laughed aloud to know that they were together, there so near to Tara and then a curtain fell and there was darkness.

She awoke, to find him there beside her, tears streaming down his face, a babe in each arm.

"Look, love." He raised his arms so that she could see his twin burdens. "Look what our love has brought into the world."

Tiny and dark-haired, the babes curled silently in their father's arms. Aislinn laughed, lifted her head up.

"Draw in the air of life," Maille said, lifting Aislinn into an upright position.

Aislinn did so, then gasped and began to cough, clenching her hands tight against the sewn episiotomy. She moaned and lay back against the clean linens Gobinet and Corra had laid for her while she slept.

Gently Eoghan placed a tiny daughter in Aislinn's arm, cradling his body against her weakness while Gobinet braced a small son against her other side. Then Eoghan sat behind Aislinn, bracing her upright as one by one she nursed her newborn babes.

The physician nodded, pleased.

"Good, the drug has worn off and now her body must begin to heal." She lifted Aislinn's tunic, looked at her stitchwork.

"Clean and tidy." She pressed a hot linen cloth filled with herbs against the wound. Aislinn screamed aloud. Maille ignored the scream, gently pressed the poultice into the stitches. "The wound must be cleaned and laid with these hot poultices twice each day. No sickness must be allowed to enter the wound; these contain agrimony and other healers." She patted Aislinn's hand. "They will hurt less each day." Maille looked at Gobinet, continued.

"The priestess must lift nothing for one full turn of the moon, nor may she ride astride or in a chariot. We will lift and hold her when she nurses the babes and she must begin to walk a little around the hut, but only once each day." She looked directly at Aislinn.

"There are still dangers, priestess."

Aislinn turned toward the sleeping babies. Maille shook her head.

"Not to them, to you. There is danger of tearing. There is danger of sickness entering the wound. You must drink an infusion of these herbs twice each day as well." Maille removed a packet of herbs from her bag.

"Alkemelych," said Aislinn. She smiled a little sadly, remembering Aine and her silent ministrations of the potion that would save her babes.

Maille nodded. "It will strengthen you."

Eoghan smiled at Corra ni Brith across the room. "The little daughter you have taken to your heart will help to care for you and for these two that we have brought into the world. And my beloved mother." He smiled at Gobinet. From his bag he withdrew a beautiful gold torque, tightly braided and fronted with running horses.

"Physician, this is a gift from Fionn and the Fenians and from me, a soldier and Fenian brother. I thank you for giving Aislinn a long life with us."

Maille faced Eoghan.

"I accept your gift with thanks, Fenian. I will remain with your beloved until the next moonrise. But now you had best be away. Each moment that you remain here also endangers the woman and the babes."

"No!" Aislinn sat bolt upright, gritting her teeth against the pain. "Make me ready to go with him, physician, for we must be together."

Maille made an explosive sound, then laughed aloud.

"You are a stubborn one. Even with all my years as a healer, priestess, I could not make you ready to go. All that holds you within yourself are the fragile threads of my stitching, layers upon layers of them like the seams of some frail garment. Until your birth door closes and is itself again, you remain in danger of the very air. You can go nowhere, daughter."

Eoghan drew his arms around Aislinn, leaning her back against his chest, stroking her hair softly.

"Nay, then, love. I will stay with you and the babes until you are well enough to go."

Maille held up her hands.

"I am an old woman and one who has seen many things. I recognize the poet, ollamh of the Ard-Ri. You know that my profession requires my silence, but silence is the last quality of the men of the bruidhean. How many of them will whisper that one of the Deisi came to fetch me? That the wife of Eoghan Mac Aidan, exile, is heavy with child? That such a one would move the wind to reach her at her time? How many even now are riding hard toward Tara, hoping to be the first to fetch the fugitive's fee? If you stay here with your wife and child, you will surely forfeit your life."

Gobinet stepped up to Eoghan, laid her hand on his arm.

"The physician speaks well, my son. You must go. Corra and I will care for Aislinn and the babes. When she is well, we will go to live among the Deisi, under the protection of O'Domhnaill."

Aislinn stroked Eoghan's arms where they crossed her chest, then lifted them to her lips and kissed them.

"You must go, love. I spoke only from my fear and this new pain. We will be well here, and you must be safe. Go to the babes and then leave us."

Eoghan lowered Aislinn gently to the sleeping couch. He kissed her lips softly, holding her face between his hands. Then he strode to the sleeping babes in their box by the fire. Gently, he knelt above them, gently placed his finger on the forehead of each sleeping child.

"Remember me, your athair, whose heart remains with you though we are parted."

When he stood, his eyes shone wet. He returned to Aislinn, gathered her into his arms, burying his face in her hair.

"Oh, love, will it ever be thus, the two of us so far apart and longing?"

Aislinn drew her head back, placed her cheek against his hand so that he looked directly into her eyes.

"Nay, husband, it will not, for I have seen. In the moment before the knife, I saw us together, hand in hand, laughing near the waters of the Boann. You must believe in this vision."

Eoghan kissed her forehead, lowered her to the sleeping table.

"I will hold to your vision with all my heart."

He turned, enfolded Gobinet in a hug, then stooped and touched the face of Corra.

"Take care of them, little one," he whispered. He clasped Maille by the shoulders, soldier fashion.

"Physician, you have the gratitude of the poet of the Ard-Ri."

"Do not thank me yet, Fenian. Thank me when no infection has come. Now go."

He strode toward the door.

Aislinn struggled to her elbows again.

"Eoghan," she called to his retreating form. "Believe!"

He did not turn back. For a moment he stood silhouetted in the light from the doorway, then he raised his right hand, clenched it as a fist, and brought it forward across his heart. As his hoofbeats retreated across the causeway, he could not hear Aislinn whispering to herself over and over.

"Believe."

24

Aislinn awoke with a start. Someone was in the dwelling! Had Banbh discovered the babes? She slipped her hand beneath her wolf pelts until it closed around her dagger. Turning quietly, she faced the direction of her sleeping babes. She winced at the slight tugging on the eight-week-old scar, arose silently despite the pain.

He was bent above the cradles, the firelight reflecting off the blue and green plaid of his cloak. For a moment Aislinn almost gave a glad cry, thinking the figure to be Eoghan, but then the light of the fire played against his long red braid. Aislinn stepped behind him quickly.

She placed the dagger at the spot below his ear where his life blood would pour forth most easily.

He started, but said nothing. Quietly he spread his arms wide. His own dagger was clutched in his right hand and he laid it on the floor, still wordless. He began to stand.

"Nay," Aislinn commanded. "Sit."

He did so. With her foot, Aislinn pushed his dagger so that it was beyond his reach. Her words had awakened Gobinet and Corra. Gobinet rushed forward, her own dagger grasped firmly in hand.

"Who is he?" she asked. "And how has he gotten past our guards?"

"I know not yet, but he was near the babes. Hold him, mother, while I see if they are well."

Gobinet stepped into Aislinn's spot. Aislinn knelt beside the crib, placed her hand on each tiny chest. The twins slept, oblivious to their danger. Corra moved from her sleeping platform to the twins' cradles and began gently rocking. Aislinn sighed with relief, turned back to Red Braid.

"Speak. How came you here and why?"

"I am Fenian. I am sent here by your husband Eoghan Mac Aidan."

Aislinn shook her head, disbelieving.

"How came you past our guards? Why were you not announced? Why were you here, bent above my children like a thief in darkness?"

"I swam to the crannog and scaled the wall."

Gobinet bent and felt his cloak, closed her hand around his braid.

"This much is true, daughter. His cloak and hair are wet and cold."

"Why?" Aislinn impaled him with her glance.

He looked around uncomfortably.

"May I take off my cloak and sit by your fire?"

"You may not. You have only two choices—to speak or die."

He turned his face full into the light cast from the fire. Aislinn gasped.

"I know you. You are a Fenian! I watched you at the hill of Tara when you passed the tests of Fianna—almost a year ago now. I remember Fionn saluting you when you passed the test of spears."

For a moment, the warrior stared at the floor. When he lifted his head, he did not meet Aislinn's eyes and his speech seemed sad, almost resigned.

"I am indeed Fenian, priestess. I am called Tomaltagh,

friend and Fenian companion to your husband Eoghan
Mac Aidan. It was he who sent me to see if you are well,
you and his children, but I was to tell no one, see no one.
I was to see you in your sleep and depart."

"Why is this? This makes no sense. Why would he not
send me messages, post me as to his health and welfare,
and take back messages of the same? He has done so once
before in the last turning of the moon."

Tomaltagh looked uncomfortable, glanced toward the
fire, shifted his position.

"Why, Red Braid? Speak."

"He did not wish to endanger any of you by his presence in Meath."

"He is not in Meath."

"He is not; that is why he has sent me."

The soldiers of the king had come only a day after
Eoghan's departure and the birth of the twins, searching
for him halfheartedly, hoping not to find him, even as
Cairbry Mac Cormac hoped that he would not be found.
Aislinn understood their need to be true to the law. They
were deferential to her, rained blessings on her children,
wished her a full recovery from her wound, departed
quickly under the wrathful eye of Maille who had ex-
ploded at them for carrying soldier dirt to the crannog.
Their presence had effectively insured that Eoghan could
not return to Meath. And afterward Maille had forced Aislinn to take a near-boiling bath, then applied compress
after boiling compress to her raw wound.

Aislinn knelt and placed her dagger flat against the hollow of the Fenian's throat. "Speak truth, Fenian, or I
swear you will die. You endangered my children and I
will not hesitate to kill you."

Red Braid shrugged his shoulders, resigned.

"I would not have harmed your babes." For the first
time he looked up, directly at her eyes. "Believe me,
priestess. I would not."

Aislinn nodded. The Fenian looked down again.

"I sought only knowledge of them and of you to bring

to Eoghan. He did not wish you to know that I was here because he knew that you would have questions."

"What questions? Is something wrong with Eoghan?"

"Eoghan was injured in a fall from a horse."

"A fall? From Becan?" Aislinn shook her head, remembering the symmetry of Eoghan and Becan, remembering Eoghan astride the chariot at the samhain festival. "Nay!"

Red Braid shook his head. "The horse was not Becan. Eoghan was training one of our young men, letting him ride Becan, teaching him the ways of mounting and dismounting when the horse is in full gallop. The young man fell and Eoghan rode his own mount toward him, but his mount stepped in a hole and threw your husband."

Aislinn spread her hands.

"But these things will happen. All horsemen expect to fall. Why does Eoghan not wish me to know this?"

"His leg was broken in the fall, priestess. Broken in many places. And it has not healed well. Indeed it has become infected. Eoghan burns with fever. There are some who say he will lose the leg, some who say he will lose his life. He wished only to know that you were well, but he did not wish you to know of his wound. He feared that you would wish to ride to him." Red Braid hung his head. "In that I have failed him."

The story had the ring of absolute truth. Aislinn was already gathering her cloak, stuffing packets of healing herbs into her leather traveling bag.

"Indeed you have, Fenian, for I will ride to him."

She turned to Gobinet.

"Mother, you must find a wet nurse for the twins."

Gobinet shook her head.

"Daughter, this is not wise. Your own scar is only eight weeks old. It has healed well, but what if it should tear? Or become poisoned? Then what will become of your babes? And your milk will come even without them. Your breasts may swell and become infected. You have not ridden since they were born. It is all too much."

Aislinn stopped her preparations, looked at Gobinet.

"Maille has left me with reassurances of my health and healing. She has encouraged me to walk, mother." Still Gobinet shook her head. Aislinn tried again.

"What would you do if the news were of O'Domnhnaill?"

Gobinet nodded resignedly. "I would ride to the tuath of the Deisi. If you must go, at least let me send some of O'Domnhnaill's soldiers to accompany you."

Aislinn nodded but Red Braid stood, shaking his head.

"Nay, priestess, if you must go, it is better to go in the Fenian way, silent and unobtrusive in the forest. You too have enemies."

Aislinn thought of Banbh again. She nodded at Tomaltagh's wisdom, drew Corra to her, whispered in her ear.

"I abandon you again, little one." But Corra shook her head.

"Nay, máthair." She lifted her head, made a brave face. "I will care for my brother and sister."

Aislinn kissed her forehead.

"Then my heart is lightened."

It was only after she had mounted behind the Fenian and they had crossed the causeway and faded into the darkness of the forest that Aislinn began to question her own wisdom. Five miles beyond the crannog, near a hastily constructed bothy, the Fenian had tethered another horse. Aislinn mounted it in silence, rode behind him saying nothing. No Fenian brought a second horse without anticipation of a rider. He had planned to tell her of Eoghan all along, planned for her to accompany him. Aislinn believed his story: Eoghan was in deadly mortal danger. But so was she. What she did not yet know was why.

Toward late morning, Red Braid stopped.

"It is better if we sleep during the day, priestess," he offered. "We can travel under cover of darkness and in daylight our fire will be less likely to be noticed."

She wondered who or what they were hiding from, or if Red Braid was still relying on the fact that Aislinn feared enemies of her own.

"You are most cautious. Do you fear my enemies or yours?"

"I am told that you have powerful enemies."

"That is so, Fenian. But I also have powerful friends."

She watched him in his preparations. He was Fenian in training and habits, of that much she was certain. He built the bothy of saplings and pine boughs, made a nearly smokeless fire, expertly skewered and cooked rabbit for their meal. Aislinn watched and was silent, knowing that she must wait for the truth before deciding what to do.

Her breasts ached with the unsuckled milk and the stain of their leaking had spread through both her gown and cloak. She could feel the stretching of the episiotomy scar and the weary muscles of her hips and legs that were unaccustomed to horseback. When Red Braid lay down to sleep, she did the same, grateful for the chance to let the weariness seep from her body into the earth.

She awoke in the cool October dusk. From the far side of the fire, Red Braid was seated on his haunches, watching her. She smiled, nodded, removed her cloak. When she lowered the shoulders of her gown, he turned away. So he was Fenian in his respectful treatment of women as well. Aislinn squeezed as much milk from her breasts as her own hands could manage, wincing at the uncomfortably full and tender feeling. She dressed and joined him at the fire.

"Your year with the Fianna has taught you much, Tomaltagh. You have learned the woodcrafts well."

A pained look crossed his face.

For a moment it seemed that he would speak, but then he stood and began to disassemble the camp, to clear away the traces that they had been there. She watched him at his work. He was younger than she, perhaps eighteen or nineteen in his years, close upon the age when Eoghan had become a Fenian. His movements were youthful and strong, but something in his face was old or perhaps weighted.

"What is your guilt or sorrow, Fenian?"

He swung to face her, the question taking him by surprise.

"Priestess," he stammered, his stare beseeching. But then he set his jaw and turned back to his preparations.

By dark, they were mounted and riding south again toward Almhuin.

The moment that Aislinn had been expecting came toward morning. The shift in direction was subtle, worthy of a Fenian, but a shift nonetheless. They were no longer traveling south, but were arcing steadily toward the west.

Begging the need to relieve herself, Aislinn dismounted, walked toward a copse of trees, shed her cloak, and dropped the shoulders of her gown so that Red Braid would not approach. She turned her back to him, faced west, closed her eyes. She waited quietly. Slowly in her vision, the westward direction became a road, the road led to a small hut. She willed her mind to open the door of the hut, willed herself to look inside. He was bent above the fire, but the black of his cloak, the tilt of his head, were recognizable instantly. Banbh.

Aislinn began the process of retreat, of pulling back into her own body, but at that moment Banbh turned, looked directly at her, smiled his thin, evil smile. At that same moment, she felt the huge hands of the Fenian close hard around her bare shoulders.

Red Braid tied her hands to the saddle, winding the rope around and around until the threads cut into her wrists. Aislinn winced. Immediately, he loosened the bonds, his face registering guilt.

"He knows you well, this one who has sent for you. He said that you would suspect him when we turned in his direction. He said that I should watch you carefully then."

"Too well," she answered. "He seems always to know too much, too well."

She regarded the Fenian curiously. His treatment of her had been courteous, respectful, according to the Fenian laws. Even when he had come behind her in the forest, he had allowed her to dress facing away from him, had helped her to mount, had loosened these wrist bonds. Why would such a man be taking her to Banbh?

She ventured a question.

"The story about my husband. It is not true, then?"

"It is true. I think perhaps the druid caused your husband's fall, he seemed so sure of the way of it." Tomaltagh looked at her and spread his hands wide.

"Would you not have seen through an untruth, priestess?"

Aislinn shook her head. "We cannot always see clearly what is closest to our heart."

An expression of anguish crossed his face.

"This is true, priestess."

"Tomaltagh, you must let me go to Eoghan. I love him; I have the training. Perhaps I can heal him."

Red Braid regarded her for a long moment, then turned his face westward.

"I cannot," he said. "I am no longer Fenian."

"What do you mean? I read people well—Fenian. I see in you the Fenian training and the Fenian code. I also read your sorrow. Speak to me of that sorrow. Perhaps I can help you."

But Tomaltagh kept his face turned away from Aislinn, answered stubbornly. "I am no longer Fenian."

When it was still a few hours from dawn Aislinn made her decision. She could go no closer to Banbh. Every mile westward was a mile farther from Eoghan. No matter what, she must put an end to this journey.

Aislinn kicked her horse into a gallop, let her body go slack, let it fall sideways from the saddle. Her wrists twisted sharply and then she was dangling head down, her long hair catching beneath the horse's hooves. She cried out in pain and terror. The horse panicked at the sound, at the feel of his rider dragging beside him. He ran harder.

Aislinn's head slapped hard against the saddle twice. The horse shifted position, kept up his panicked pace. Aislinn felt her shoulder lodge against a tree, heard the tearing of her garment. She screamed in pain as something in her shoulder gave way with a cracking sound.

She awoke in a freshly made bothy. Her hands were untied and she tried to roll to her side and stand but cried out at the pain in her shoulder. Immediately Red Braid was at her side.

"Is it broken?" she asked him.

"Nay, but it is pulled from the cradle which holds it. This I can repair, priestess, but the pain will be great."

Aislinn bit her lip.

"Go ahead."

Tomaltagh lifted the arm from the elbow, maneuvering it gently, concentrating his attention, one huge hand cupping the small bones of her shoulder. He searched gently with his thumb and forefinger raising the arm up and down. Aislinn bit down hard at the motion. When he had found the alignment he sought, he gave the arm a sharp inward push from the elbow. The shoulder dropped back into its socket with a kind of popping sigh.

Aislinn cried out. Blood ran from her lip where she had bitten down too hard. Gently, he lifted his cloak to her lip, gently swabbed away the blood.

"We must bind the arm or it will come free again."

With her right hand, Aislinn held forth her tunic, but Red Braid shook his head, tearing at his own cloak with his dagger, forming a firm sling that eased the pain. Aislinn pointed to her leather bag.

"I thank you, Fenian, but there is still much pain. I have herbs. Will you brew me a tea if I tell you what to do?"

He drew the gourdlike cups from his saddlebag, used a bark bowl to bring the water from the stream and heat it, poured the steaming liquid over his own strong tea. Aislinn felt almost regretful for what she must do. When the cups were full to steaming and he had watched her fill her own with herbs to make her sleep, she did the simplest thing she could think to do. She waited until he walked into the forest to relieve himself and switched the cups.

By the time he returned from his ministrations, she was lying on her back, her face a mask of drowsy contentment.

"I am better now, thank you," she told him. "But I must sleep."

She closed her eyes, breathed deeply and regularly, listened for the sound of him sipping his tea, for the sound as he rolled himself into his cloak, for the deep and even breathing of his drugged sleep. Then she rose quickly, went to her own saddle, and removed the ropes he had used to tie her hands. Her shoulder protested at the tugging motions, but she tied the Fenian's feet, looping the ropes through the bridle of his horse. Now if he moved too fast when he awoke, the startled horse would drag him across the forest floor.

Next she undid her own sling. Working fast, Aislinn bound his hands with the sling, then tied the loose ends of the sling to the bothy. Again, if he pulled hard, the entire lean-to with its branches and boughs would cascade down on him. With Tomaltagh stretched between the horse and the bothy like a deer on a spit, Aislinn dressed herself and made ready, then sat down beside the Fenian, her dagger pressed to his throat.

He awoke shortly after dawn. His first stretch caused the horse to nicker and back off in alarm, raising the Fenian's feet above the ground. Tomaltagh opened his eyes and took in his situation, then nodded in Aislinn's direction.

"You are a worthy opponent, priestess. You drugged the tea."

Aislinn did not answer. She lowered the cold blade of the dagger against the Fenian's throat.

"Tell me everything."

"Most of what I have told you was true. I was Fenian. I knew your husband. That much is true. But I am no longer Fenian. Just after Beltaine of last year, my Fian decided on a cattle raid. You know that is the best time for stealing cattle, because they have already been blessed in the Beltaine fires. They produce better milk or meat or offspring."

Aislinn nodded at the common knowledge.

"In the raid, the bo-aire, the cattleman, was killed."

Aislinn nodded again. "Such raids are common as are the deaths of the cattlemen. It was just so that my first daughter came to be the property of the chief I took her from. What of this?"

She gestured for the Fenian to continue.

"The bo-aire had a wife," he said. "She was beautiful, the mother of two small children." He stopped, looked shamefaced, then turned his head away.

Aislinn knew the Fenian code for women. They must always be treated with dignity and respect. The bo-aire's wife and her children would have been taken back to Almhuin with the Fenians. She and her children would have been cared and provided for. Suddenly she felt a cold spot form around her heart. She pressed her dagger tighter against his throat.

"Did you rape her?"

"By the gods!" A look of horror crossed Red Braid's face. Aislinn felt relief wash over her. The Fenian code did not allow for the rape of women in war.

"Nay," he said. "Nay. I did not rape her, but my crime is worse, priestess. I caused her death. I entered the hut and found her there sheltering the small ones. I thought that she was terrified, but when I went to lift her to her feet, her hand came forward with a dagger. She slashed me again and again. Here, tear forward my tunic. See the truth of my words."

Aislinn slit his tunic, saw the unhealed welts and slashes. He continued.

"At last I could bear no more of the knife thrusts and I pushed her from me. But she ran at me again, tripped on her own cloak, fell forward, and struck her head on the fire stones. She was dead before I reached her."

"You defended yourself; you did not cause her death.

This does not violate Fenian code, though I can feel your sorrow in it. You have more violated the code with me than you have in this."

He hung his head. "It was the children, priestess. One was a girl, perhaps seven, the other a small boy of three or four. They rushed to her, threw their bodies on her, sobbing, staring at me with those accusing eyes. I left them like that, priestess. I told no one and I did nothing, so great is my shame. I left my Fian that day. I have not been Fenian since, nor can I be again.

"That is when I became a soldier for hire. In the long way of things, your Banbh found me. He said that I was perfect for his purposes. He offered me Roman gold. Roman gold to allow me to leave Eire and my shame behind. He told me that you had been his student, that you had turned against him and were using his ways against him. Then he gave me the story of Eoghan with which to draw you away from the crannog, and the way of telling it that would convince you of its truth. I see now, of course, that you were never his student."

Aislinn shook her head.

"And that is why you were kneeling over my babes with your dagger. He told you to kill them."

"He did, priestess. When I gazed upon them, I knew that I could not do that part of his bidding."

Aislinn wondered how he had learned of them. Had some traveler from the bruidhean of Maille the physician told the tale too often, of the priestess and the exiled Fenian, or the birth of their children on an empty crannog? No matter, now he knew. The children were in mortal danger again; the only grace was that the one Banbh had sent to endanger them lay on the forest floor at the point of her knife.

Aislinn stood, stepped outside the bothy.

"Your failure is your success, Red Braid. I will tell you what I have learned in my little time in this body. I have learned that we cannot run from our shame. No matter how far your Roman gold would have taken you, you would have carried your shame with you. Shame must be faced with the truth. I have also learned that journeys which begin with children are journeys of great change. Yours is a journey of children. You must find those children whose mother you murdered."

He regarded her quietly for a moment.

"And when I do?"

"You must give them back all that you have taken away. You must be their father and their mother. You must make them safe. Then you will no longer be ashamed. Then you will be worthy of being called a Fenian."

He remained silent for a moment, then looked directly up at her.

"Your words are true, priestess. They move in me clear, like water."

He began to get up, his horse nickering back in fear, the bothy shaking above him. For the first time in the two days that she had known him, Red Braid laughed, his body shaking in its bonds.

"I see that I must wait a bit to begin my journey."

"So you must," answered Aislinn. She mounted her horse, moaning out when she had to use the bad left shoulder to brace herself, when the childbirth scar protested at the slinging of her leg over the saddle. In the trees above her, a black crow lifted and winged north. But when Aislinn turned the horse's head, she did not turn it north toward the crannog, but south toward Almhuin, the stronghold of Fionn Mac Cumhail. South toward Eoghan Mac Aidan.

25

Aislinn reached Almhuin at nightfall. For the last two hours, she let her beaten body lay forward across the saddle of the mount Red Braid had brought her, trusted that the horse knew the way. She had been right, for now she saw the light of the smoky torches above the high wooden palisades of the fortress.

The gates were already closed against darkness and the possibility of invaders. Aislinn drew herself up in the saddle, rode around the outside wall crying in her loudest voice.

"Open up for the priestess Aislinn, wife of Eoghan Mac Aidan!"

At last she saw the wide doors creak open, saw light spill onto the causeway. She rode into the huge enclosure of Almhuin, stronghold of Fionn Mac Cumhail and the Fianna. She nearly tumbled from her horse into the arms of one of the Fenian warriors.

"Take me to Fionn!"

He bent to lift her, but Aislinn shook her head.

"I will walk, if you will lend me your support."

The warrior braced his arm firmly around her, led her toward the great hall of the Fianna.

The Fenians rose as one when Aislinn entered the great hall, following the Fenian code of behavior to women. The wavering blues and greens of their cloaks seemed to Aislinn like an interior forest. She feared that she might topple among these trees, might let her pain and exhaustion carry her to the floor. She shook off the Fenian who supported her, raised her chin. She winced as she straightened her shoulders, but headed swiftly for the raised dais at the center of the hall.

She scanned the faces of the warriors she passed, hoping for the face of Eoghan. But the faces of the Fenians seemed perplexed, seemed not to know why she was here.

Never mind. Fionn would know. He had eaten of the salmon of knowledge. Aislinn remembered her wild flight with Fionn around the coast of Eire, thought of the warmth of the white wings. She prayed that the journey had not been a dream. At that moment Fionn Mac Cumhail swam into view above her as he stood in her honor.

"We meet again, priestess. I am honored by the presence of the druidess Aislinn. How may we of the Fenians serve you?"

"I am told that my husband is dying. I am here that I may try to heal him."

A wash of sound flooded the room as the Fenians all began to speak at once. Fionn raised his hand for silence.

"Dying?" he said, an undisguised look of surprise on his features. "Eoghan Mac Aidan is not even here among us."

Aislinn's hands reached out beside her for something to cling to but there was nothing. She felt her knees begin to give beneath her. Immediately, Fionn stepped from the dais, placing his strong hand beneath her elbow. He signaled to the captain of one of his Fians.

"I take the priestess Aislinn to my chambers. Heat water for bathing and bring meats and warm wine." Firmly, the leader of the Fianna guided Aislinn out the door of the great hall and into the darkness.

He insisted that she bathe and eat, leaving her to the

warm light of his own dwelling. It was an unusual dwelling. Fionn's hounds, Bran and Sceolan, lay quietly before the fire. Couched on a warm bed of straw in the corner, a fawn regarded Aislinn warily before going back to licking its fur. On the floor beside the bed two rabbits cavorted and chased each other in an impromptu game of tag. But the room was warm, filled with wolf pelts and soft furs. Aislinn felt revived by the warm water and savored the meal of venison and bread with honey.

When she had finished and dressed, Fionn came through the door with a young woman holding her babe in her arms. Gently, he lifted the child into his own arms, brought him to Aislinn while the young woman stood smiling behind him.

"This is my grandson," he said proudly. "You would do us honor to give him suckle."

Tears of gratitude came into Aislinn's eyes.

"Thank you for sensing my discomfort." She lowered her gown and put the child to her breast, sighing in relief as her pent-up milk gave way to the tugging of the tiny mouth.

Fionn sat down across from her, his knees touching hers. The little fawn tottered up and leaned against him and he stroked its side.

"Tell me of Eoghan," he commanded gently.

"A Fenian came to me, one Tomaltagh. He said that Eoghan had been injured in a fall from a horse. According to his story, the leg has become infected and will not heal."

Aislinn shifted the infant to her other breast and leaned back.

"But this Fenian was sent to me by an evil one, a druid named Banbh. Now I do not know what parts of the story are true and which are lies, though the Fenian swears that Eoghan is injured. I came to you because I thought he might be with you. Or if he was not, I knew that you could find him."

She looked at Fionn directly.

"Eoghan has not been with us for many weeks. He returned after the birth of your children, his heart torn at being separated from you. He asked permission to ride south to the coast where we have been training young men for the Fianna. He left before the last turning of the moon."

Fionn placed his hands gently on either side of her face.

"Look at me, priestess." Aislinn looked deeply into his eyes and experienced a shock. They were a strange aquamarine, not so much eyes but a sea. She was close enough to see the wisps of gray hair that threaded through his braid and the crow's-feet that formed the corners of his eyes. She felt the leathery hide of his hands against her skin.

"It is true what they say of you, isn't it? They say that you are older than any man of the Fianna, but that you run and shoot as a young man. They say that you can transform yourself into the shapes of the hounds and the hinds when you don your cloak of magic. I did not imagine our flight, did I?"

Fionn lifted the sleeping babe from her arms and returned him to his mother who departed. He stood and walked to a peg on the wall. He lifted down a cloak of blue and green, different from the cloaks of the other Fenians only in that it was hooded, the hood so deep that it formed a cowl. This he placed over his shoulders, lifting the hood up over his head until his face disappeared into obscurity. Again he sat down opposite Aislinn.

From deep within the hood she heard his voice.

"All transformations are matters of the mind, priestess. This you know from your training. It is not that I live in the bodies of the creatures but that I live in their minds and they in mine. So do I become like the deer of the forests or the fish of the sea or even the wide, white wings of the owl."

He drew Aislinn toward him, moved his head forward until his forehead touched hers and they were both within the cowl. She smelled the rich peat smell of the cloak, the blending of smoke and fire, the pine-pitch smell of the Fenian forest bed. She drew the smell in as though it were medicine.

"Tell me what you wish of me," she said to Fionn, "for I must continue my search for Eoghan."

She felt rather than saw his smile.

"It is your search that I desire, priestess. I sense your body. It is weary and unhealed; it cries out for your babes. You are not well enough to continue this journey."

As if to prove his words he placed his hand against her injured shoulder. She winced. Immediately a warm feeling coursed from his hand into the shoulder and the pain receded, disappeared. He continued.

"Eoghan Mac Aidan is one of us, a Fenian, but you know him as none of us do. Let me dwell within you as I do with the forest creatures. Let me know your Eoghan. I will continue your search and you will return to your babes."

Aislinn felt the warmth of his breath, the sweetness of his voice. She felt a great weight lift from her, felt the fear leave her body for the first time since Tomaltagh had knelt beside the babes.

"I entrust you with my journey."

"Good." Fionn placed his hands beside her head, pressed his forehead more tightly into hers. She felt a strange sensation of drifting with him into a river of light.

"One thing more," she whispered drowsily.

"Name the thing."

"The moment you know that he lives, you will bring me word."

"Done," he answered.

Aislinn slept and dreamed deeply of Eoghan. In the dream they were standing again on the hill overlooking the river Boann. Below them was a little village. Near them, the twins gamboled in the sweet meadow grasses. She felt Eoghan's hands move gently against the side of

her face, sighed deeply, pictured for a moment the face
of Fionn Mac Cumhail. Then she drifted into dreamless
slumber.

At last Fionn drew back from her, lifted her in his arms
and carried her to his own sleeping platform, gently covered her with warm wolf pelts. He moved to the door of
his chamber, signaled to the two Fians waiting without.
The twelve men entered the room in silence, made a circle
around Fionn who stood near the fire. He spoke to them
softly.

"Eoghan Mac Aidan is our brother, a Fenian, beloved
of this priestess Aislinn. She believes that harm has come
to him. We will find him and restore him to health if we
can."

The twelve lifted their daggers into the firelight and
swore the Fenian oath.

"Truth dwell in our hearts, strength in our arms, ful-
fillment in our tongues. For the Fianna and for Eire."

Silently they left the chamber for their horses and the
waiting darkness. But Fionn remained behind for a while,
standing beside the sleeping Aislinn, listening to her
dreams. Softly, he whispered to her sleeping form.

"I am old now, priestess, but I too have loved and lost.
The pain remains with me still."

At last he turned to the door. When he reached it, he
turned back toward the sleeping Aislinn and raised his
dagger.

"For love," was the oath he whispered.

The wagon ride back to the crannog took three days, but
for Aislinn it was a ride of such comfort that the time
passed quickly. She was accompanied by eighteen Fenian
warriors—three full Fian bands. She rode on wolf skins
and pillows, drank the finest wines, and ate smoked meats,
salmon, and sweet autumn fruits. She was almost embarrassed by the treatment Fionn had insisted she be given.

The huge company clattered across the causeway to the

crannog in the early afternoon of the third day. Immediately Aislinn knew that something was wrong. No soldiers were posted on the causeway and none in the tower. From the enclosure, she could hear no sounds of the blacksmith's hammer, no nickering of the soldiers' horses. The crannog was completely deserted. She leaped from the wagon, terrified.

"Corra!" she cried. "Gobinet! Where are you?"

She ran from dwelling to dwelling. She had nearly completed the full circle of the dwellings when Conor, captain of O'Domnhnaill's guard, stepped from a doorway into the light.

"Priestess," he cried out in relief. "It is indeed you. I have remained here for three days, hoping and waiting."

Immediately, the Fenians stepped forward with their daggers, but Aislinn stopped them with a gesture. She ran to Conor, clasping her hands against his shoulders.

"Where are they? Gobinet and Corra and my babies?"

"They are well. We have taken them to the tuath of the Deisi. When you did not return, we feared for your safety. Then the traveler came."

"What traveler?"

"He was a strange man, dark and small and wizened. Our warriors stopped him, would not give him access across the causeway. He said that you rode toward death and that Eoghan had met that same fate. Gobinet was called to the causeway to hear him, but she was rocking the babes and sent Corra to us. Corra became hysterical. She kept calling him the 'yellow-eyed crow,' begged us not to allow him passage. We did not. After his departure, Gobinet said that we could no longer remain here, that his presence had tainted the place with darkness. I sent them, that very night, to O'Domnhnaill."

"Bless my little Corra for her wisdom," said Aislinn. "For surely that voyager was Banbh, enemy to my life and to my children."

Conor sheathed his sword and dagger.

"Come," he said. "I will take you to them."

The leader of one of the Fian bands stepped forward.
"We will accompany you, priestess."

"That is not necessary. Conor will guard me."

But the Fenian shook his head impatiently.

"You do not understand. We must accompany you. It is the order of Fionn."

On the late afternoon of the second day's trip toward the Deisi, the fifth day since they had left Almhuin of the Fenians, they made camp in a small grove of pines, a fidnemed or forest shrine.

At the little statue of the goddess that graced the place, Aislinn lit fragrant herbs and gave thanks. They would reach the Deisi in the morning; Aislinn was grateful that she had been brought this close to a reunion with Corra and the babes.

Around her the Fenians were busy laying out their beds of pine boughs, preparing the fire, hunting the game. When the meal was nearly prepared, an aged crone with graying hair came shuffling into the fidnemed. She moved among the Fianna, keeping her eyes to the ground, bowing humbly to one of the Fian captains.

"Good captain," she called in a wavering voice, "an old woman of the forest begs hospitality. May I sup with you?"

The captain answered graciously.

"First among the Fenians is our duty to hospitality. Tonight you will eat to surfeit, woman."

Aislinn watched the woman curiously. She sat apart, eating her dinner with her head bowed, but eating full and heartily, filling her bowl again and again as though she had not eaten for days. Aislinn felt strangely drawn to the old woman. She went to sit beside her but the woman would not raise her eyes or look in Aislinn's direction.

"I see by your gown that you are a priestess," she said, still staring at the pine-covered forest floor.

"I am," Aislinn acknowledged.

"Will you cast a blessing upon a woman of the fringes?"

"It will be my honor."

Aislinn knelt before the woman, lifted the woman's huge hands into her own, felt their strange, warm, leathery quality.

"May the gods grant you three things, old one. May your dwelling be always warm and dry. May the embers of your fire burn always until the next morning. May you never be hungry."

"This is a wise blessing, priestess," the old woman said. She lifted her head and looked directly into Aislinn's eyes. Aislinn gasped in recognition. The eyes were aquamarine, not so much eyes as a sea.

"Eoghan lives," said Fionn Mac Cumhail. Before Aislinn could ask any questions or cry out his name, he rose to his feet and loped away into the forest like a young deer.

26

Aislinn stirred the porridge, asked the messenger to repeat the message.

"You swear that he is well?"

"Priestess, I have seen him with these eyes. He lives; there is no fever. All that was poisonous in the wound is gone. But what Fionn has sent as his message to you is also true; the leg heals slowly. One of Fionn's physicians broke it yet again."

Aislinn winced, twined her fingers together to stop pain she felt on Eoghan's behalf. The Fenian messenger shrugged.

"Better that the bones heal straight. Eoghan must be able to ride again, to fight again. Even so, the physician says that he will always walk with a limp. But now the leg is bound between sturdy poles. What can heal, heals straight and true. And Eoghan sends you his great love. He asks me to tell you that his heart yearns toward you and his children. He says that as soon as he is able to walk, he will come for you."

Aislinn sighed in relief, then felt a growing anger rise in her.

"But three months! Why has it taken them so long to

send word? His children could be walking and speaking for all Mac Aidan knows of them."

"Part of that blame must be laid on me, priestess. I was about Fionn's business. There were other tuaths to visit, other messages to deliver. I have been more than a fortnight in coming to you."

Aislinn held out a placating hand.

"Nay, Fenian, I hold no anger for the messenger. I myself have been a messenger and not of such good news as yours. Only you must understand that the business of women is to worry and fear for those they love. Will you take back messages from me?"

The Fenian grinned.

"I do not think Mac Aidan would allow my return to Almhuin if I did not."

"You must tell him the names of his children. I have called his daughter Eibhlain; it was the name of my mother. Say to him that her name is Eibhlain Mac Eoghan, for that will give him joy. His son I have named Aidan, the 'little fire.' Aidan Mac Eoghan."

"This will indeed give him joy, for he asked of his twins and said that I must see them for him. He asked also of Corra ni Brith, the child of your fosterage."

"You shall see them all, then."

"There is one more thing, priestess. Eoghan wished me to say it in his words."

The Fenian had drawn himself up, had spoken so oratorically, as if he imitated the poetic voice of the man he spoke for. She repeated the memorized words to herself as she had done every day for the last five months.

"Wife, I dream for both of us; remember your vision of the Boann. Beloved, continue to believe."

It had been five months since that message, five long months since she had had any word from Eoghan.

Aislinn stirred the warm mash brewing above the hearth, then stood and ran the back of her hand over her forehead. The damp warmth of early June combined with the fire made the dwelling humid and uncomfortable, but the small ones would need their porridge for the growing strength of their nine-month-old bodies.

She wondered if Eoghan had received the message. The Fianna lived from the forests in the warm months. Had the messenger returned to Almhuin? If not, Eoghan might not hear his children's names until autumn.

She and the children were well and safe among the Deisi, her name honored, her gifts prized, but none of that filled the well of Aislinn's loneliness. She longed for Eoghan. Too, she missed old Aodhfin, her foster-father. How did he fare at Clete Acaill, working as scribe for Cormac, breaking the druid geis against writing? She might never know for Banbh was at Tara and Aislinn feared to take her children near him. She sighed at the weight of protecting them alone.

She stood and walked to the door of the little dwelling, grateful for the cool hardness of the dirt beneath her bare summer feet. Before the door of the lodge in the sunlight her two black-haired infants slept peacefully. From beneath the shady boughs of the oak, Corra glanced up and smiled.

"They are well, maither," she said softly.

A strange sense of repeated time washed over Aislinn and she stood still, closing her eyes. Where had this happened before? She searched her memory.

"The night they were conceived," she said aloud.

Corra looked up startled and the beginnings of a blush colored her hairline. She had just come into her twelfth year, had begun to giggle effusively when little Aidan accidently sent his water squirting into the air, had begun to look with wonder at her own tiny budding breasts.

Aislinn waved her hand in the air.

"It is nothing, daughter. Merely a memory."

Corra returned to pulling the veins of the oak leaves. Aislinn moved into the darkness of the hut and leaned against the wall.

The night they were conceived. It was this vision that had come to her then, the small ones sleeping, Corra minding them in the sunlight, Eoghan nowhere in the vision at all.

"Almost two years ago," Aislinn whispered. "If I had known. So much loneliness and sorrow. I fear we will never be together again."

She slid down along the wall, sat on the ground, the soles of her feet still pressed against the cool dirt. She allowed her head to drop to her knees.

"Believe," she whispered. "Believe."

But what was there to believe? She would never see Eoghan again. She would live out her days here among the Deisi, honored priestess and mother, surrounded by their respect and love, burning with desire for Eoghan. Perhaps next winter when the Fianna wintered in Almhuin. Perhaps then she could join Eoghan in the south. She would find a way to reach him even if he couldn't come to her.

"Believe," she whispered again. "How will I do when I can no longer believe?"

The woman was standing before her when she opened her eyes, the unearthly blue of the light bathing the entire room. Her bare feet were covered with the ashes of the fire and the tiny footprints were visible on the dirt floor of the hut. Beside her was the lamb Aislinn remembered from the hill of Tara.

Aislinn scrambled to her feet, ashamed, as if she had been caught napping at her lessons, but the woman merely smiled.

"For the third time, and the last, I come to speak with you, Aislinn ni Sorar."

Aislinn hung her head, the long hair falling forward like a curtain.

"I am no longer worthy," she whispered.

"Not worthy?" The woman made a gentle, caressing motion. "Because you have suffered? Because you have doubted? Because your hardships have made you bitter toward god?"

Aislinn's head snapped up. The woman smiled again.

"Daughter, you are more worthy in your weakness than you were when you believed you could call the gods at will. Now you understand the sufferings of others. Belief is difficult; it requires fearsome strength. You who are human do not have that strength at every moment."

"Do you?"

"I do not need belief, daughter, for I have knowledge. How much worthier you are who struggle and still make the leap of faith."

From outside, the thin wail of a baby drew Aislinn's attention. The front of her gown stained with her breast milk.

"My babes," she said, gesturing helplessly toward the door.

The woman lifted the lamb, caressed it, bringing it close to her heart. Tears gathered in her eyes and she smiled through them.

"May you have joy of them," she said. "May they walk with their hands in the hand of the god." She looked directly at Aislinn.

"Soon the new god will call your name. Will you answer, Aislinn ni Sorar?"

Aislinn made a small helpless gesture.

"He does not speak within me. I have not stood within the Light. How shall I believe?"

"It is not necessary for you to know the name of the god, for he knows your name. It is not necessary to believe in the god, for he believes in you. Answer, Aislinn ni Sorar. The moment will come when you will know that you are standing in the Light."

Aislinn held out her hands.

"For what I know of you, woman of the Other, I will answer."

A look of pure joy passed across the face of the woman.

"Keep my love with you always, Aislinn ni Sorar, for

it is with you at every moment of your waking and sleeping."

When Corra ni Brith brought the dusty messenger to the door, they found Aislinn, the front of her gown stained with breast milk, her feet filthy with ashes, her face radiant with joy.

"I can tell you no more, priestess, only this which I have committed to my tongue. Aodhfin the Wise sends greetings to his foster-daughter and requests that she come at once to the place on the Boann known as Clete Acaill."

Aislinn shook her head stubbornly, shifting Eibhlain from her breast to Corra's arm and moving Aidan to her other breast.

"This he would not do. He knows that there is danger for me near Tara." She eyed the messenger suspiciously. "Describe to me the man who sent you with this message."

"He is old, with a whitened fringe of hair. His pate is bald. He serves as the scribe to King Cormac Mac Art." The messenger made an exasperated sound. "Everyone knows Aodhfin the Wise, the only druid who had the courage to serve our king."

Aislinn smiled. So they still thought of Cormac as king. She wondered if Cairbry was wise enough to not be jealous. She wondered if he allied himself with Cormac and allowed the love of the people to extend to him. She sighed, shifted the baby on her arm.

"I do not fault the messenger, nor his memory of my tutor. I fault the message, which seems to me strange from what I know." She locked her eyes with the boy's, stared at him directly.

He looked down at the floor, out the door toward the sunlight.

"There is more here!" she cried triumphantly. "Now you must tell me, or I will call down upon you the soldiers of O'Domnhaill and they will have the truth from you."

The boy set his chin stubbornly, remained standing where he was.

"Very well," said Aislinn. She stood and handed Aidan to Corra. Bare-breasted and barefoot, she raised her arms and began the druii chant.

"Anger of fire . . ."

The boy's face grew terrified.

"Nay," he said, holding up his hands. "Do not call the gods down upon me. I will tell you what you wish to know, though I fear old Aodhfin will be angry with me for the telling."

"Tell me, then," Aislinn demanded.

The boy shifted his feet, looked longingly toward the doorway.

"Understand that Aodhfin the Wise did not say this to me. I am telling you what I know, not what he told me to say."

"Understood," Aislinn said impatiently.

"It is known among us at Clete Acaill. Even if we did not whisper it among ourselves, we would see the truth in his face." The boy looked at her with anguish.

"Aodhfin the Wise is dying."

27

Aislinn threw herself from the wagon before the wheels had stopped turning, then stared, amazed by what she saw. The place called Clete Acaill was a community on the Boann, not the single hut Cormac had envisioned. There were bakehouses and storage bins, and a busy smithy judging by the sound of the hammer. She had been gone for more than a year. Were these Cormac's retainers? Followers of the new god?

She shook her head impatiently. She had to find Aodhfin. She pointed at two of the soldiers of O'Domnhaill who had accompanied her on the journey, gestured at Corra and the twins.

"Stay with my children. Do not leave them, even for a moment."

The soldiers saluted, closed around Corra, who held both twins.

Aislinn chose what seemed to be the largest dwelling and ran toward it.

She burst through the doorway of the hut unceremoniously. Surely this was the dwelling of Cormac. Warm wolf pelts covered the sleeping platforms and heavily wrought chests inlaid with jewels and decorated with gold spirals boasted of the wealth of the owner. No fire burned on this warm June day, but even in the semidark Aislinn could sense that no one was within. She picked her way to the other door of the dwelling.

Beyond was a small garden adorned with flowers, facing the river Boann. There, on a wooden bench in the sun, was Aodhfin. He appeared to be dozing. Aislinn approached quietly, her heart torn by what she saw. Was this tiny wizened man her Aodhfin? His skin had taken on the texture and color of parchment and it seemed to be stretched across the bones. Each blue vein in his knobby hands stood out in relief against the nearly transparent skin.

Aislinn stood above him, swallowing hard. Even as she watched, a slow smile spread across the features of her tutor. His eyes flickered open.

"I welcome you home, daughter, but you needn't have run. We still have some time."

Aislinn dropped to her knees, winding her arms around the old man's waist. He closed his arms around her, stroked her hair softly.

"I see that you are not well."

"The body fails me, but the spirit is healthy and full of joy."

"I am glad that you called for me. I have brought the twins and Corra ni Brith. They will be joyful to see you."

"I am glad of that as well, but I called you for other purposes. Someone must take over my work. I must teach you the skills of writing, for you must be scribe to Cormac Mac Art."

"I? I am a woman alone, with small children. Have you forgotten that there is danger here for me, father? And for my children. Banbh is too close by."

"We do not see or hear of the Dark One here, but no, I have not forgotten. I have spoken to Cormac of this, daughter; you and your children will be guarded well."

"But I do not possess this skill of writing, and I fear it, athair, for it breaks our old druid laws."

"Daughter, this work is important; Cormac's work will make Eire a place of learning and light. Many among the druids and the brehons have already come to believe this; they ask for pieces of Cormac's wisdom to be read to them at assembly. Those who fear the written word fear it because it dilutes power. Do you see? If nothing is written, then only those who contain the knowledge have power. But if it is written, and if anyone can learn to read that writing, then all who read or write can have equal power. This frightens some of the druii, some of the brehons. That is all, but fear is powerful."

Aodhfin stroked her hair, cupped his hand beneath her chin. "Once again I ask much of you, daughter. Years ago, I sent you questing after your child, your lifemate. It was a journey that brought you much suffering, I know."

Aislinn smiled. "But also much joy."

Aodhfin nodded. "Now, again, I ask you to serve as the still point between darkness and light. For Cormac's words are a doorway to the light. I am as certain of this as I am of anything in my life."

Aislinn thought of the woman of light. *For what I know of you I will answer.* So she had said. So this was how she was to be called. The new god was calling her through her beloved Aodhfin. She must answer. Somehow she would answer.

"I will do it, athair," she said. "All that you need me to do, I will do."

"I knew that you would answer so." He smiled, patting her hand. "And I promise you that you will not be alone. Not only will our king guard your children, but Cormac in his wisdom has provided another who will also be his scribe. You will learn and work together. See there he comes now."

Aislinn turned. Limping across the garden toward her, a look of radiant joy on his face, was Eoghan Mac Aidan.

*　　*　　*

They were seated in the garden, Aidan cradled in Eoghan's arm while the other arm held Aislinn tight at his side, as if she might disappear if he were to let go. Aodhfin fussed over Eibhlain. Corra stretched before them on the warm grass.

Aislinn lifted her arms out over her head to the warm sunlight and turned to Aodhfin.

"How has this been done, father?"

Aodhfin smiled gently, his attention absorbed by Eibhlain who was sucking at his finger.

"Cormac petitioned the brehons. He mustered an army of arguments. He said that he required his own poet, that none other can master his words and deeds. He argued that because Eoghan bore the name of his mother, he was not of the clan Mac Gabuideach, argued that now that you had borne his children, he was linked to your family and thus to the family that had been wronged at first. He argued that Eoghan was first a Fenian and thus clanless and landless, subject to no family exile. He argued that no punishment should be meted to the father of the wronged children." Aodhfin shook his head and laughed.

"Never have I heard so much weight of legal argument."

Laughter boomed from the far side of the garden.

"Let us face it, friend. These brehons are captivated by the idea of seeing their laws written down. They believe my books will pass on their wisdom. They allowed Eoghan Mac Aidan to return so that we could continue to make them look wise."

Cormac Mac Art strode into the circle of the garden, his four wolf dogs frolicking like puppies at his heels, then breaking up to sniff at the newcomers and lick at the faces of Corra and the babies. Cormac looked strong and happy, the eyeless socket covered by a red silken square of cloth.

Eoghan handed over the squirming Aidan. His wounded leg dragging, he made his way across the garden to Cormac. Cormac laughed aloud, pointed at his covered eye.

"It would seem, friend, that life has battered at these two old warriors."

"I am for all time in your debt for this reunion, my great king."

"No longer a king, but always your true friend."

The two clasped arms at the elbows, then clutched each other at the shoulders, the wolves frolicking all the while between them.

"It is well that I left my Sheary at Almhuin, for how would he fare with these four or they with him?" asked Eoghan. He laughingly pushed at one of the wolves who clambered on him.

"Nay, friend, send for your Sheary at once, for the four-legged beasts settle their differences much better than the two-legged kind. But tell us what has befallen you. News of your wife we have had, but I heard from my Fenians only that you had been injured."

Eoghan moved stiffly back to Aislinn, wrapped his arms around her.

"I was nearly taken from these that I love. I was thrown from a horse, the leg broken. I was training a boy who claimed he wished to be Fianna, but he disappeared after my injury. None of us has seen him again. And the hole my horse plunged into was deep and wide, carefully camouflaged with field grasses. Not the hole of an animal."

"Who did this thing?" Cormac asked.

"Banbh." Aislinn spat the word. "He sent a Fenian to capture me and take me to him, but he misread the boy's soul, mistaking guilt for evil." She turned to Eoghan. "But, love, when I heard nothing, how I feared for you."

"For days I was alone. I bled the wound, but it festered. I raged with fever. Then Fionn and two of his Fian bands found me. They returned me to Almhuin, cleaned my wounds and bound my leg, but by then, I had been many days alone. The leg heals poorly."

He lifted Aislinn's face between his hands and spoke softly.

"Most strange, love. Sometimes when Fionn tended me, I thought that he was you."

Aislinn smiled at him. "It was me, for Fionn carries us within him now as he carries the creatures of the forest. I rode to him for help when you were injured. He dwells here where my spirit dwells." She pressed her hand across her forehead.

Eoghan scooped Aidan from Aislinn's arms, bent and gathered Eibhlain from old Aodhfin. He turned in a game-legged circle, a twin on each arm. The little ones laughed aloud at the spinning sky. Corra jumped to her feet to reach for them; Eoghan laughingly planted a kiss on her forehead.

"And you, little golden rose. Look at this copper hair! You have become a great beauty to the eye of this poet, who remembers you as a skinny bird."

Corra giggled and blushed.

"I can no longer be skinny for how much my máthair feeds me. And she brushes my hair for hours each night by the fire."

"Hours!" Aislinn laughed. "How you go on, silly one!"

They smiled warmly at each other.

Eoghan spread his arms wide.

"One bad leg is a small price to pay for so much happiness!" Eoghan declared.

"Just so, I feel about this eye," said Cormac. "For its loss has reaped me great joy." He turned to Aodhfin. "Our work will go on well here, Wise One."

Aodhfin nodded.

"The god weaves slowly, but the pattern is always in his mind."

From far away came the sound of a drum, steady and ominous on the afternoon summer air. Cormac glanced away, then turned to smile at Eoghan.

"What is it?" Corra stood, frightened, moved to sit on the bench beside Aislinn.

"It is a most ominous sound," Aislinn agreed.

"It is Moylann and some of the druii. And yes, Banbh is among them." Aodhfin answered her unasked question. "They carry out this ritual three times each day, at all of the stone circles and dromlechs. They fear the loss of the old ways, the coming of the new god. They petition the gods to bring death to Cormac. And to me."

Aislinn gasped, running to kneel on the grass before him.

"Then have they succeeded, father, for surely your life wanes within you."

"Nay," said Aodhfin, "do you not see how the god has provided for us? He has given me the gift of a slow death so that I could bring your family together again, so that I can teach you the writing. He has allowed us to continue what we have begun."

He stroked the side of her face with his thinning hand.

"But we must begin the learning today."

"That is well," muttered Cormac, "for if those fools have their way, we will be given precious little more time."

Aislinn lay still against Eoghan's shoulder, sighing contentedly. Near them a slow summer fire burned at the center of the dwelling and outside in the darkness she could hear the rushing music of the Boann as it wound past the little village.

She did not know how many times they had loved each other through this long night of their reunion, but the tears that had fallen from her eyes against Eoghan's chest at their first coupling had given way now to soft laughter and contented sighs.

"Husband," she whispered so as not to wake the sleeping twins and Corra ni Brith. "Tell me that it will always be thus now, that we will never be parted again."

Eoghan drew his arm around her, stroked her hair, and kissed her forehead gently.

"Even if we were to be parted again, would it not be always thus between us? What is between us remains within us and even in the air around us."

Aislinn laughed, raising herself on one elbow.

"You speak as a poet would."

Eoghan reached both arms up and drew her hair as a curtain around their faces. Aislinn lowered her lips to his.

"How else should I speak of this?" Eoghan looked bemused for a moment, then laughed aloud, softly.

"This god in whom Cormac and Aodhfin believe—I think perhaps that he laughs."

"That is a strange thought, even for a poet."

"Look at us, the son and the daughter of two great enemies. Now our love and the children that love has produced have bound those enemies together in their clans for all time. Yet just when we are together again, when at last we could live among our own and be accepted, we have chosen to exile ourselves from druii and poets alike by becoming scribes for this deposed king—a king the druii believe to be possessed or crazy."

"Do you believe him possessed or crazy?"

"I have known our king for much of my life. He has always been just, always a warrior, always a wise ruler. But I have never seen in him as much contentment as I have seen today. If it is true, as Cormac believes, that this new god arranges when it suits him, he arranges with his laughter hidden behind his hand."

Eoghan brushed his hand gently along the curve of Aislinn's cheek.

"And if it is Cormac's god who has arranged to reunite us, then I give him the salute of all my joy."

He kissed her lips gently and stroked the small of her back. She buried her head beneath his chin and kissed the hollow of his throat where his heart beat, then curled down into Eoghan's shoulder, brushing her hands softly across his chest. He moaned, shifted beneath her touch, turning on his side to allow her breasts to press against his chest. He drew her to him suddenly, pressing the length of her against him with his muscular arm, holding her as though his body could absorb hers.

"I love you!" he cried. "Before Cormac's god himself, I swear that I love you."

"I tell you what I believe, love," Aislinn whispered softly against his ear. "If indeed this new god of Cormac laughs, tonight it is the kindest and most gentle laughter ever heard among the gods."

28

Cormac and Eoghan and their assorted wolves and hounds had departed an hour earlier for a morning of hunting, so there had been little of Cormac's dictation to copy this morning. Aislinn was glad. Let Eoghan copy the bulk of the day's work when they returned from the hunt; today she was worried about women's matters.

Aislinn stood from her writing and stretched the fingers of her right hand in her left. She stared down for a moment at the printed page, amazed as always that the words of Cormac had appeared there. It was their own language they composed, Aodhfin told them, not the language of the Britons or of the Roman descendants who remained there. Their own language, the speech of the Gaels. She stared at it again, amazed at old Aodhfin for having pulled the words from the air, for having taught her how to render them to skins.

She covered the precious pages against wind and damp, walked to the fire at the center of the hut. She banked it with the iron, then added two more logs. Now the hut would be warm when the men returned.

She clutched her cloak about her and lifted the door pelts aside to step out into the autumn cold. With a long hurried stride she made her way across the short stretch of space to her own hut. The fall had been damp. The twins suffered with coughing and Aislinn feared that Aodhfin could not last much longer. Two omnipresent guards stood stolidly at either side of the door; Aislinn nodded her thanks and they saluted, briefly. She lifted aside the pelts of her own doorway and stepped within. The twins were awake, holding to sleeping shelves and lodge posts as they tested their new skills of walking. The fire burned bright and warm and Corra stirred a fragrant mash on the cauldron above the fire.

In the far corner, the slender shape that was Aodhfin slept under a pile of wolf pelts.

Aislinn moved over to Corra ni Brith, kissed the top of her head gently.

"A chailin bhig. My little girl. So much a woman and a mother have you become."

Corra drew herself up with pride at the compliment.

"The little ones are much improved, máthair. I gave them your herb for coughing in a sweetened tea."

Aislinn bent, gathered the two small ones to her, listened to the even, smooth sounds of their breathing.

"You have done well, little mother," said Aislinn, smiling at her. She began spooning up a bowl of the hot sweet cereal for the twins. "Now you must be a child again. Go, find your friends, and have a game of seek and find."

Corra laughed. She reached for her cloak, pulling the hood up over the shimmering masses of copper hair so that the long strands came forward over her shoulders.

"How beautiful you are, daughter," said Aislinn as first Eibhlain and then Aidan tottered to her and leaned on her lap. She spooned them their porridge, smiling at Corra ni Brith. "Soon the young men will begin to clamor at the door of our dwelling."

Corra blushed, just enough interested at her twelve years to hope that they would, just enough embarrassed to hope that they would not. She made for the door, then turned about. A look of poignant sadness crossed her face.

She gestured toward Aodhfin in the corner.

"Máthair, the seanathair, the grandfather." She gestured toward the corner, then let her hand drop, watching Aislinn.

"Nay, child, I know. There is nothing our ministrations can do. Go now, and let me worry for a while."

Corra left the hut and Aislinn moved quietly to the corner and knelt beside the sleeping platform.

Aodhfin opened his eyes and smiled gently, moving his hand so that a little of Aislinn's hair cascaded softly across it.

Aodhfin had gone all to bone now. His legs and arms were skeletal. When he moved, he looked like the wooden dolls that children clamored for at feis times. His skin was stretched across his cheekbones and jaw so that the skeleton beneath was clearly visible. Aislinn remembered the druii belief that the skull was the seat of the soul.

"So small a dwelling for so great a spirit," she whispered, smiling at Aodhfin. She helped him to shift his position so that his body would not develop sores, then brought him a bowl of warm porridge and a steaming cup of sweet herbal tea.

He took one spoonful of the sweet mash and drank a little of the tea. Aislinn knew that he did this for her, to ease her need to minister to him. He leaned back on the wolf pelts now, exhausted with the effort.

"How long is it until samhain, daughter?"

He had been asking this question for days now but she answered patiently.

"Three days now."

He stared at the fire for a long moment, then looked at Aislinn directly, beckoning her to come and sit beside him.

"I cannot die on samhain, daughter. Moylann and the druii would think they had triumphed, that their foolish magic had brought my death to pass."

"Then you shall not," Aislinn said firmly, standing to return for more porridge, but Aodhfin made an impatient gesture and motioned her to remain beside him. She did so, sitting still on the edge of the platform.

"I am past the point where food and drink will heal me, past the point where even the gods will intervene." Aodhfin smiled. "I am content to go if you are content to let me go."

"Today?" Aislinn's cry of alarm brought the twins toddling to her side. She rocked them gently, first one and then the other until they sighed and slept. She returned them to their sleeping corner, removed the porridge from its place above the flames to set it on a warm stone at the edge of the fire circle. All the while, Aodhfin waited patiently, lying motionless, staring at the ceiling. At last she made herself return to him, forced herself to sit still on his sleeping shelf, to take the thin hand between hers.

"I will tell you a story, daughter," he whispered, licking his dry cracking lips. "Long ago when I was a man close upon the age that your Eoghan is now, I was given a child to raise. I do not know why Eoghan chose me of all the druii teachers at Tara Hill. He said that when he knew what Macha planned for you and your mother, my name alone filled his mind and he rode from among the Deisi thinking only my name."

He patted her hand gently.

"I must speak the truth to you, daughter. I did not want to take you. I was a man alone with no woman and you were a girl child. I took you as a duty to your lady mother, thinking that I would find a nurse, someone who could raise you apart from me and send you at age seven into the proper fosterage." He smiled again.

"Oh, I was a man so full of myself then. For had I not crossed the waters? Had I not been at the side of Cormac Mac Art when he ruled in Alba? Had I not traveled among the Britons and learned the Roman way of writing? I thought myself the wisest and most learned among the druii.

"I brought you back to Tara and found a woman to care for you and began to ask among the families for fosterage.

One day I came home from my teaching in the Forradh. You were seated in the sunlight, playing with a little doll that I had brought for you. I saw that you were well, asked the nurse about your progress, then turned to go. You were five years old then. I reached the door and you called after me: 'Where do you go, athair?' Even now I can hear the tone in your voice, the pleading.

" 'I go to my studies,' I answered. You jumped up then and ran to me and gave me the little doll. 'Take her with you,' you cried. 'For then you can think of me all day as I think of you. And if she is with you, we will not both be so lonely.' At that moment I knew that I had never been wise at all. From that day until the day that Banbh drove you from Tara, I kept you beside me always—in the Forradh, at the druii ceremonies. Through you I learned to be wise. I learned to value what is real. I believe that it is because of you that I could understand the new god at the moment when he called Cormac's name."

He stopped, exhausted. Aislinn fetched him warm sweet tea, lifted his head into the crook of her arm and let him sip, lowering him again to a resting position. When she spoke, it was barely above a whisper.

"And now I must learn to be wise, for I must let you go. Is that the way of it?"

"That is the way," he answered gently.

She held his hand between hers.

"Go then. I promise that I will take care of things here."

He closed his eyes momentarily, then opened them wide.

"Banbh. You have been protected while you were with all of us, but after I am gone he will come for you somehow. He will think that my death has made you vulnerable."

She nodded.

"Then I will confront him first. Is not our Cormac always saying that a position of attack is stronger than one of retreat?"

Aodhfin smiled.

"This is wise, daughter. I will be with you when you go. This I promise. You will know that I am with you."

Suddenly he looked over her shoulder and his face seemed to light from within.

"Look who has come, Aislinn. Look."

Aislinn turned, looked at where he was staring, saw no one, felt no one. She turned back to him.

"Who is it, athair?"

"It is your lady mother, the beautiful Eibhlain, so honored am I."

Aislinn turned again.

"Máthair?" she whispered to the empty corner. "Take him with my love."

When she turned back, Aodhfin was looking directly into her eyes.

"A chailin bhig," he whispered. "My little girl."

When Cormac and Eoghan returned flushed and in high spirits from the hunt, they found her cradling the body of an Aodhfin long since gone.

Between two tall burning torches on a long wooden trestle, Aodhfin lay dressed in his finest druii gown and his white robe of office. From time to time, gusts of wind that moved through the hall stirred the swan feathers on his robe and Aodhfin seemed almost to move. Aislinn smoothed the moving feathers then, resting her hand against Aodhfin's chest as if she still comforted him in illness.

She stood behind the bier dressed in her finest white gown with its gold embroidery and her white cloak. She had not spoken since Aodhfin died, followed the motions of Cormac's direction of the ceremonies with a simple, nodding silence. Her attitude was not one of grief, but of waiting.

Cormac had decreed that Aodhfin would be given the funeral ceremonies and burial of an ollamh, a master.

"He was the first among us to stand by my side, the

first to acknowledge that I have indeed heard the voice of the new god," he said, when he gathered the community together to announce Aodhfin's death. "It was his courage alone that brought our books into writing. He has paid dearly for his choice to stand beside me. He shall be honored as no druii before him."

Now Cormac in all the finery he had once worn as king stood at the head of the bier; Eoghan in the six colors of a poet stood at the foot. Aislinn, still and silent, stood behind the bier.

The people of Clete Acaill had gathered in their finest raiment to pay respect to Aodhfin. Women wore gowns of green and blue and elaborate cloaks of plaids in green, blue, purple, red. Their arms shimmered with golden bracelets; fine torques graced their necks. Many had braided their hair with ceremonial balls of silver, gold, and bronze and they made a clicking, almost bell-like sound as they moved about the room.

The men wore plaid leggings, wide leather belts, plaid cloaks with elaborate golden brooches at the shoulder and gleaming golden daggers at the waist. Some had limed their hair so that it stood up like a forest of trees, an ancient warlike gesture in honor of Aodhfin, a man of courage.

A huge feast had been prepared in Aodhfin's honor. Loaves of steaming fragrant bread and pots of honey crowded the table along with butter and cheeses of every variety. Venison steaks, delicately prepared rabbit seasoned with the finest of herbs, and fish, steamed and stuffed with rare ocean grasses, were arranged around a precious bowl of salt.

Bearers entered the room, carrying a wild boar that had been roasted for the last two days in a steaming, stone-lined pit. Behind them came the drink bearers with flagon after flagon of the finest wines, of mead and ale, for great drinking and eating was necessary to honor the spirit of the deceased.

Cormac raised his own wine goblet. It shimmered in

the torchlight, gleaming gold, the stem and handles en-
crusted with rubies and emeralds.

"This is my decree for my departed friend. He will have
the hero's portion of the boar, the thigh, the part that is
reserved for the king."

A murmur of appreciation ran through the crowd; one
of the bearers hurried to cut the thigh portion and place
it on a silver platter that Cormac himself placed at Aodhfin's head with a ritual praising.

"In this company are you honored, and shall be forever."

Cormac dipped his fingers into the wineglass and
pressed a tiny drop against Aodhfin's still lips. Then he
drank from the glass himself.

"I drink to you, friend, in the place of the other, in the
place of Tir Nan Og, as do all of us here in the Tir inna
m Beo, the land of the living."

He handed his goblet to Eoghan who drank and then
to Aislinn who drank without seeming to be aware of
what she did.

Cormac raised his cup into the light again.

"Friends of Clete Acaill. We are a community here. As
Aodhfin was family among us, so does he remain even
apart from us. Drink from the goblet of kinship to the
continued life of our beloved priest."

The crowd gasped. It was common for everyone in a
king's circle to drink from a common cup at a feast but
Cormac wanted them all, the highest and the most lowly,
to drink from the cup. As the golden goblet made its
rounds of the room the spirit became one of joyful sharing. Still Aislinn stared ahead of her, one hand resting on
Aodhfin's chest, seemingly unaware of her surroundings.

Eoghan stepped forward.

The crowd grew silent, for they knew that the poet
would have prepared a rosc, a chant in honor of Aodhfin.
Somewhere in the room, one of Cormac's musicians beat
on a bodhran, a skin drum. When the deep, heavy thrumming ceased, the finest harper of Clete Acaill stepped up

beside Eoghan and began to pluck the strings so that the
haunting music filled the hall. Eoghan stepped forward
and began the ritual praise of Aodhfin.

> *"What praise is more glorious than this*
> *That so many among us call him teacher.*
> *From his lips came words of wisdom,*
> *From his life came deeds of courage,*
> *Deeds of learning, deeds of love.*
> *Each among us owes him blessing,*
> *The priestess for her fosterhood,*
> *For love as strong as that of blood.*
> *Cormac, once our king, will praise him*
> *Who renders his words and deeds to life,*
> *Who preserves for Cormac the laws of Eire,*
> *Who teaches we who follow to do the same.*
> *And I among men praise him most highly*
> *For through him I have been given my life,*
> *The wife of my heart, she who was his daughter,*
> *The children of my loins and fosterhood,*
> *The place that we of Clete Acaill have made*
> *Together, in the light of the new day.*
> *Each of us here is his child,*
> *Each of us here his pupil.*
> *What better praise on the life of a man*
> *That so many have called him teacher."*

A moment of silence followed the rosc, then Cormac
raised his arms.

"Let the celebration of Aodhfin's life begin!"

The bodhran began beating from the back of the dwelling and was soon joined by the rapid thready sound of
the whistles as the tunes for jigs and reels took the place
of the delicate harp music. The feast table became
crowded and circles of dancers filled the floor. Some of
the couples began to move away two by two for the lovemaking, which was the greatest tribute to the life of the
departed one and a powerful shield against the presence

of death. Aislinn stood still and silent behind Aodhfin, listening, waiting, for what she did not know.

The door burst open and a gust of wind fluttered the torches and moved the swan's wings on the cloak of Aodhfin. Cairbry Mac Cormac stood framed in the torchlight, Fenian soldiers at either shoulder. He raised his hand to Cormac.

"My father, people of Clete Acaill, I give you greeting. May we who also loved the good old man pay our respects at his feis?"

Cormac threw his arms out in a welcoming gesture.

"Welcome, Ard-Ri of Eire and all who are in your company. The honor is mine and that of my friend, Aodhfin."

Cairbry and his Fenians filed in followed by Flahari and the brehons and some of the noble families of Tara. Behind them a small contingent of druii entered last in their white ceremonial robes. The music seemed to thread down, the drum giving out a last few ominous beats. The dancers stopped and the room grew silent.

"What is this?" Cormac asked, looking directly at Cairbry, but it was one of the younger druii who answered.

"We petitioned your son to be allowed to pay our respects to this good old man. Not all among us believe as Moylann does. For some of us, Aodhfin was our teacher as well. We are wise enough to know that there is room in this universe for many gods and that the gods may speak to whom they will."

Aislinn's head lifted from her contemplation of Aodhfin's cloak and she spoke without consulting Cormac.

"Then may you come in and be welcome here, for Aodhfin would have wanted nothing better than that these wounds be healed."

Cormac regarded her for a moment, then walked to a chest at the foot of the bier and opened the lid. He rose with a white garment in his hand.

"Truly the foster-daughter of Aodhfin is wise in his teachings. Druids, you are welcome here among us and may you be the first among the druii to see that Aodhfin confers upon his daughter the mantle of his wisdom."

He stepped to Aislinn and loosened the brooch that held her cloak, handing it to Eoghan who had stepped to her side. The cloak he draped around her shoulders was of the softest lamb's wool, woven to the finest and most delicate warmth. It was so white and clean that it seemed to shimmer in the torchlight. Where Aodhfin's white deer-hide cloak had been covered with the white wings of swans this cloak was covered with the wings of doves and then, more strangely, with the scales of fish, so iridescent that the garment seemed to give off rainbows in the fire-light.

Suddenly Aislinn remembered the words of the woman at Tara Hill on the long ago samhain eve.

"You will wear a new robe," she had said, *"a robe that no druii has worn before you. Your robe will be the soft wool of the lamb and the blood of the lamb. Your robe will be the wings of the dove. Your robe will be the scales of the fish who moves like light in the deepest ocean."*

Aislinn turned to Cormac, her face a mask of wonder.

"How did he know this thing?"

"I know not what he knew, honored priestess, only that he declared that this cloak should be made for you in this fashion and so it has been done."

Aislinn stroked Aodhfin's chest, ran her hands down the soft downy swan feathers.

"Athair," she whispered. "How did you know this?"

She felt the torches make a circle of their light then, saw the rainbow of her cloak arc through that circle, knew that everyone else saw the light as well by the awestruck silence of the room. Only Cormac seemed to smile at her as if it were all expected.

The voice, when it came, seemed to hover in the air above Aodhfin's head. It was a voice neither male nor female, higher than wind, sweeter than song.

"Daughter, your Aodhfin is with me."

"I know you," she cried aloud. "You have spoken to me before."

"You have always known," said the voice and then it laughed. And the laughter was the sound of children rolling in a new spring meadow and the laughter of their mother who watches them and thinks that her heart will burst with the joy of them and the laughter of the husband and father who looks at them all and cannot believe that such treasure has been given to him.

And there in the rainbow circle of light above and around the body of Aodhfin, Aislinn ni Sorar threw back her head and laughed aloud.

"Husband!" she cried, reaching out one hand to Eoghan, one to Cormac Mac Art who stood at her side. "Husband, you were right after all. The god of Cormac Mac Art laughs. The new god laughs!"

29

The druii grove was blanketed in darkness, for the huge twining overhead branches of the oaks shut out the remaining light. Aislinn walked along the corridor of the parallel oak trees toward the altar at the far end, where the oaks formed a curving semicircle. She felt strangely calm in her mission.

She had dressed carefully in the empty hut at Clete Acaill, certain of what she must do and how it must be done. She had braided her hair with trembling fingers, attached the golden ceremonial balls, donned the cloak of power that Aodhfin had left her, and fastened it at the last moment with her mother's brooch.

She had told neither Eoghan nor Cormac for they would have tried to dissuade her. Tonight, at the time between the times, at the turning of the year, they would celebrate samhain at Clete Acaill with fires and prayers, with awareness of the presence of the Others. She would be needed for the sticks of prophecy. But first, she must confront the powers of her own darkness, the forces of Banbh.

She must at last put his darkness away, away from herself, from her children, from her family.

Aislinn had slipped quietly from her empty dwelling in

the late afternoon when the autumn dusk was settling over the community. The Boann looked smoky, blue and gray in the half-light, steam rising from its surface as she hurried beside it. She had stopped only once, glancing back at the little village with a visceral feeling of longing. How she wanted to turn back, to run to Eoghan, to clasp her babes to her or sit teaching Corra to read the words of Cormac by the firelight. But this thing must be done. She must lift the darkness that had brooded above her for so long and she must do it now, on samhain, with Aodhfin only three days gone.

She took a deep breath. He would come. Of that she was certain. She had neither seen him nor heard from him in the six turnings of the moon that she had been at Clete Acaill, but his presence was always just outside her line of sight, in the thundering of the druii drums or the gleaming black wings of a crow lifting from the trees. Aislinn shivered. Whatever it required, she must put that presence out of her life forever.

From the twining, dark branches of the trees on either side of her, lighted skulls stared down at her. They had been filled with candles for samhain and their toothless grins and eyeless sockets glowed yellow and orange from within. The samhain wind made them sway back and forth almost as though the heads were dancing. Here and there a candle had been blown out by the gusts.

Aislinn raised her hands to them in silent greeting, remembering when their candles had ignited for her and Eoghan so long ago. She did not fear the ancestors, nor the dwellings that had held their holy spirits. She feared little now, she knew. Her journey had been difficult and lonely at times; it had brought physical pain, separation, loss. It had made her strong. The love she felt for her children, for Eoghan, for Aodhfin, for Cormac, was like a buckler; inside it she was stronger. And there was the Light, the Presence she had met, a sudden wind of joy that could arise unexpectedly from the smallest tasks of the day. Aislinn had become strong.

Now she feared only this human darkness that lived and breathed and had form.

Human darkness. Aislinn realized with a start that she no longer thought of Banbh as superhuman, a darkness above all others. He was small and mean and terrified, but he was human. And in that realization, Aislinn knew that she had already defeated her enemy.

She stood quietly, waiting, her hands calm on the altar stone. He did not disappoint her, but his arrival behind her was so quiet that she did not hear or see him until the black of his raven-feathered cloak billowed around her in the wind.

She turned to face him. The crow that had been sitting impassively on his shoulder cawed once and lifted away into the trees above them.

For the first time, Aislinn realized that she stood eye to eye with Banbh. By the standards of men of the Gaels, he was short. She wondered if her fear had made him tall. He smiled, his thin lips stretching across the yellow teeth.

"So, priestess. Your Aodhfin three days dead and already you have come to me. I am flattered by your haste."

"You mistake, Banbh, for I come not to you but for you. It is time to put my fear of you to rest."

"Is it?" He smiled again, glanced idly up at the bird above their heads as if they shared some grand humor. "And how will you do that?"

"With the truth. It seems to frighten you more than it frightens me."

Banbh stared at her, a look of surprise framing his features. Aislinn smiled.

"You see that I am not the green girl you frightened away from Tara so long ago, Dark One. I am a wife now and a mother. Those who are encircled by my love I protect with all the fierceness I possess. You will not harm them."

He shook his head impatiently.

"Nay, foolish girl, you never did understand, did you?"

"I am listening. Tell me what can be understood."

He glanced again at the crow, looked down the long lane of oaks with their grinning skulls, made a strange, almost helpless gesture with his hands. He spoke.

"Long ago, when I was younger still than you are now, the goddess that I serve sent me a vision, a vision of the changes that were to come. In that vision I saw you with your mother and father and I came to believe that somehow you were to be the vortex of those changes. It was then that I found the woman Macha, turned her to my purposes, began to plan with her to destroy you and your family. But that foolish boy who is now your husband intervened." He spat on the ground.

"You survived when the others died because of Eoghan Mac Aidan. They did not matter; your death was crucial."

"Why?"

"Do you not see what has happened with this vision, this new god? We druii of the darkness lose our power. The old ways are going. I thought that if I could stop you, I could prevent this loss. I watched you under Aodhfin's tutelage at Tara. To destroy you while you were under his protection would have been impossible, but I thought that if I could suborn you to the dark ways of my goddess, all would be well. When I succeeded in frightening you from Tara, I thought my purpose served as well. I thought that what was to happen could not happen in your absence. But you returned, didn't you?" He stepped closer to her, threatening.

"You returned with your poet and the babes in your belly and even then I failed to stop what came. I thought that if I could kill the babes, sever the connection between you and Eoghan Mac Aidan, the enmity of your clans would have continued to serve the darkness. But you survived, your babes survived, your Eoghan survived." He shook his head, almost perplexed. Aislinn spoke.

"Change will come, druid; it is life's only certainty. Have you not thought that there were other gods working against your purpose?"

Banbh shook his head impatiently.

"Not so; it was my vision that was flawed. I did not see that it would be Cormac to whom the new god would speak. You were the catalyst, but Cormac was the vessel." He threw his arms into the air.

"So you come to me now and tell me to leave you alone. What do I need with you now? Have you seen me in all these months at Clete Acaill? Of course I knew you were there. But you are of no use to me now."

Aislinn felt surprise at the revelation. A giddy sense of freedom washed through her, followed by caution, by suspicion.

"You have tried more than once to kill Eoghan, to kill my babes!"

"You have robbed me of my power, priestess; I would have robbed you of that which means the most to you. But now I see that such vengeance is futile. Killing you or yours will stop nothing now. That time is past. Why do you think you have seen or heard nothing from me in all these months since you have returned to Clete Acaill? Killing you or yours will stop nothing. It is Cormac we must destroy now, before his foolish tale of this light spreads any farther."

Aislinn laughed.

"It is your time that is past, Dark One. Can you not see that? The time is going when you can hold the people with the power of their fear. Your power will be lost to you. There is nothing you can do." She turned to go.

Banbh's face contorted with rage. The dagger seemed to appear in his hand from the air. He yanked hard on Aislinn's cloak so that she was jerked backward against the stone altar. He held the knife flat beneath her chin. With his other hand, he undid the brooch that held her cloak. It fell back against the altar. The wind lifted at the braids of her untrapped hair. They stretched out behind her and the golden balls made a sharp clicking sound in the air. Banbh smiled.

"You speak of power, priestess. You think to dismiss

mine. Mine and that of my goddess. Now we see how fast power can change hands, do we not?"

Aislinn slapped at the wrist that held the dagger. "If your power rests in this weapon, then it is little enough. The meanest soldier can wield this much power, priest." She twisted to reach for her discarded cloak.

His hand caught at the neck of her gown; he used the dagger to slice through it so that it fell away useless at her feet. He laid the cold blade flat against her back, below her heart.

Aislinn's heart began to beat wildly, but she stood tall and still, her chin held high. The pulse at her neck throbbed and jumped like a pinioned bird. Banbh turned her to face him, placed his finger at the pulse.

"I will enjoy this. Even if it is too late, I will enjoy this. I have thought about it for most of my life." He licked his lips. "A little pleasure. A little vengeance for my deposed goddess. A little pain for those who love you so."

He laughed aloud, a wild, desperate sound. Reaching his hand around behind Aislinn, he bunched her cloak up and threw it at the head of the altar where it lay in a discarded heap. He pressed against her, the black feathers of his cloak swirling around them both, encircling them.

"Sit," he ordered, pressing the knife beneath her breast. She felt the blade crease her skin, gasped. Banbh pulled it away and looked at the trickle of blood. He shrugged.

"There will be more of that, priestess. Not yet, though, so I must be more careful.

"I said sit, priestess."

Aislinn placed her arms against the sides of the stone altar and boosted herself to a sitting position. The stone felt cold and unyielding beneath her naked buttocks.

Banbh opened her hand, pressed the blade of his knife against her open palm, made a clean, thin slice. Blood welled up in her palm.

Releasing the bleeding hand, Banbh pulled hard on one

of the braids with its ornamental gold ball. He sliced cleanly through the bottom of the braid, discarded the ball into the dirt. He held the remaining curl of hair aloft in his hands. Aislinn forced herself to speak disdainfully.

"I know what ceremony you perform here, druid. Do you think you will control me with this foolishness? I am no superstitious peasant to be awed by locks of hair and blood. I have had the same schooling you have had. And I have seen what you have not."

Banbh laughed. He took the lock of hair and held it in the blood on her palm until it was saturated. Then he took the lock of hair into his mouth, eating, swallowing, seeming to savor the taste. The bloodstains remained on his lips and chin.

"You see the ceremony I have performed. I control that which is without you and that which is within you. I control your life forces."

Aislinn gathered the bile that rose in her throat, spit it hard at the druid. The wind carried most of it away, but a few drops of spit sprinkled on his face, glittered in the darkness.

"You control nothing, least of all the spirit that moves in me. There is no real power in knives or blood. You lean on the power of fear. You are an old fool and I pity you."

At these words, Banbh became enraged. He slapped hard at her face, knocking her backward, over the edge of the stone. Aislinn fell to the cold ground, but he grabbed her by a fistful of her black braids with their gold and silver ceremonial balls. He dragged her back to a sitting position on the altar.

"I will cut out your heart. Imagine the powers I would control if I should decide to eat your heart, priestess."

He stepped forward, holding his knife blade flat beneath Aislinn's left breast.

Aislinn refused to look at him, looked high into the trees above her. She thought of Aodhfin and his promise to be with her when she confronted Banbh.

Banbh nodded.

"So, you think of the old one. You feel abandoned here. Good. Now we will be able to speak more honestly of fear."

"No, Dark One, they have not abandoned me. None of them I love have abandoned me. They are with me like the lighted faces of these ancestors." She gestured toward the candlelit skulls in the trees. "That is what I know now that I did not know before. I am never alone; not for one breath am I alone. You can cut out my heart, Banbh, but that will not give you my life. What I have you can never take from me. But here is my pity; I give it freely. Your time is gone." She held her hand out to him, almost gently.

He slapped at it like a petulant child, pushed his hand against her forehead.

"Lay down. Tonight, you will be the sacrifice on this altar."

He pressed the blade of the knife against her belly and pressed his forearm beneath her neck until she laid down on the cold altar stone. Above her head she could feel the stirring of the wind in her white cloak.

Banbh laughed as he hoisted himself up on the stone, kneeling between her legs, his dark cloak riding the wind above them like a huge black bird. Aislinn rolled backward, drew her legs together, made a battering ram from them. She pulled them hard up under her chin, kicked out at Banbh's stomach. He tumbled backward from the altar stone, but he caught himself, landed on his feet. Aislinn swung sideways, tried to come to her feet. He caught at her, throwing his body across hers, grinding her right hip hard into the stone.

"Let us talk of real power, priestess." Banbh lowered the blade into the hollow of her throat and ran it down the entire length of her body, stopping just below her navel.

"You believe that there is no power in the darkness. You are wrong. There is always power in the place where the dark spirits dwell. Admit it, priestess. Admit that you have seen my power and that you respect it and fear it." He twirled the blade delicately inside her navel.

The voice came into Aislinn's head unbidden and she recognized it instantly as the voice of Brighid, the woman of light.

"Do not give him your fear, daughter. It is what he desires. It feeds him. The darkness always grows on the fear of the innocents."

Aislinn gathered her courage, looked directly into Banbh's eyes.

"Do you call this power, Dark One?"

He laughed.

"I do. For I will have you as I desire and when I am finished I can cut out your heart and eat it if I wish. I can destroy the happiness of the family you so prize. And no vengeance of your Eoghan or even of Cormac Mac Art himself can negate the power that I will have wielded over you."

Aislinn rolled to her back beneath him, forced her legs to go slack on the cold stone, forced her hands to lie open at her sides.

"You will do what you will, then, Banbh, for the darkness always moves as far as it can away from the light. You can destroy this body, but when you are finished, you will still have no power. For she who continues will continue in the light. You have no power over me. You have no power over the forces of this world or the other. You cannot control them any more than you can control this wild samhain wind."

Banbh made a strangled angry sound and raised the dagger above his head. Aislinn looked up at the upraised arms, the twisted, bloodstained face, the cloak snapping wildly out in the wind. She closed her eyes and dropped her arms wide out beside her. She thought of Eoghan and Corra and the little twins, of Aodhfin and her mother and father.

"I love you!" she cried aloud.

Suddenly the wind that had been howling around them ceased. Aislinn opened her eyes. The skulls hung still in the limbs of the trees, their candles burning steadily. Banbh lowered the knife, scrambled from the altar. He stood sniffing at the air around him as though he sensed the presence of others. In the tree far above him, the crow that was his companion lifted into the darkness and flew away, cawing.

Aislinn felt them then, knew their presence surrounding her. She felt a wild surge of joy. She scrambled to her feet, standing atop the altar.

"Máthair," she cried. "Athair, Aodhfin. And you, Brighid of the Other. I have told this Dark One that you are with me here on this samhain night. You are with me always."

Banbh ceased his wild staring, looked directly at her. He curled his lip in disdain.

"Do you seek to trick a druid with a druii trick, priestess?"

There was a sudden sound as of wind, but the skulls stayed still; the trees did not move. Behind her head Aislinn felt something move and she watched as the expression on Banbh's face turned to terror. He lifted his hands before him, dropped the dagger into the dirt. Aislinn turned toward where he stared. From the rough stone of the altar, her discarded cloak had lifted into the shape of a great white bird. All of the wind in the grove was concentrated into the wild beating of the wings. Iridescent rainbows glanced from the scales of the cloak into the candlelight of the still and silent grove.

Aislinn raised her arms above her head, silent tears streaming down her face. When the cloak ceased its motion, she gathered it gently around her battered body, then leaped to the ground. She picked up her mother's brooch from the dirt at her feet and fastened it at her shoulder. Quietly, she walked away.

When she was nearly free of the druii grove, Banbh began to call after her.

"Do not think that this will stop us, priestess. We will destroy Cormac Mac Art. We will prevail."

His voice grew hoarse, louder, and more frenzied as she walked, but Aislinn did not turn back.

She heard their hooves thundering toward her as she walked along the Boann. Eoghan leaped from his horse, crying out to her.

"Where have you been? We searched everywhere."

Cormac followed him to the ground, his tone chastising.

" 'Tis samhain eve, priestess. You, better than others, know what forces are abroad on this of all nights."

Aislinn laughed aloud.

Eoghan closed his arms around her, then pushed back, staring at her nakedness beneath the cloak, at the bloodstains on her body.

"Who has done this? I will put him to my blade. Who has harmed you?"

"The evil Banbh, who has done this, has seen the force of an avenger much greater than we." She smiled at them. "I will tell all, but let us go home now to our own samhain ceremonies. This you should know, my husband and my king. Even on the darkest of nights, even when we do not know or see, the light surrounds us in the darkness."

She motioned to Eoghan to mount, then took his arm and came up behind him. As they rode home toward Clete Acaill, her cloak arched out behind her in the moonlight like the wings of a giant bird.

30

"Máthair!" Corra ni Brith stepped through the doorway. From outside came the sound of hollow drumming.

Aislinn glanced up quizzically from the writing, pressing her left hand automatically against the cramped fingers of the right. She regarded her foster-daughter.

"They are at the ceremonies again? The dark druids?"

"They are, máthair, but that is not why I interrupt you."

In the two years since Aodhfin had died, Corra had become a beauty. She was tall, her skin pale and luminous, her face dappled with freckles across the bridge of the nose. Her woman's body was firm-breasted and strong. Already, several young men of the community had begun to seek her out at the dances, to request her company at the feis.

Aislinn smiled at her now. Together, they were like sisters, Corra tending the small ones while Aislinn worked at Cormac's books and Aislinn teaching Corra the skills of writing when the small ones slept, the two of them giggling behind their hands at some remark of Eoghan's or some gossip of the village.

Eoghan treated Corra as his own daughter, even teaching her some of the Fenian woodcrafts and taking her with him and Cormac on some of their riding and hunting expeditions.

They would all return together, their faces flushed with the outdoors, laughing.

"Look!" Corra would cry in delight. "Look what athair has taught me today."

Aislinn would meet Eoghan's eyes above the copper swirls of Corra's hair and her heart would so overflow with love that her eyes would threaten to fill. Then she would jokingly address Eoghan.

"Do you think to make her worthy for some Fenian, athair?"

She would emphasize the "athair" and the three of them would share a conspiratorial, joyful smile. Eoghan would shake his head, playfully serious then.

"No Fenian could be worthy of my little girl," he would say and Corra would push at him, protesting with laughter that she did not even know a Fenian of her age.

"Máthair!"

Aislinn looked up at her again.

"I am sorry, daughter. The writing sometimes makes my mind wander. Why have you interrupted me?"

"There is a man here. A Fenian with two children. He says that he must speak to you."

"Now?"

It was well known among all the residents of Clete Acaill that the time Cormac's scribes spent with his books was sacrosanct, not to be interrupted.

"He is not of our village. He says that you will know him and will wish to speak with him. Indeed, he does seem familiar, but I find his manner offensive, mother."

"How?"

"He is much too demanding for one who should be aware of your position."

Aislinn smiled at her daughter.

"You are my own Fenian, daughter. But I tire of the writing. My hand cramps. I welcome this distraction. Where have you kept this demanding Fenian?"

"I sent him to sit in the garden by the river."

They walked together into the warm spring sunshine. The sound of the blacksmith's hammer rang out on the air of the village. Near the stables Aislinn could hear the sound of children's laughter. Her own three-year-old twins would be there, listening to the tales of the seanchai. She smiled, wrapped her arm around Corra in a hug of happiness. How she loved their life in the little village. Aside from the thrumming of the druids over the crest of the hill, nothing had disturbed their happiness for two idyllic years. And even they, now, seemed more like a minor irritation, a foolishness to be tolerated, perhaps to be pitied. She reached down for Corra's hand.

The man was seated on a bench facing the river, watching the antics of two children, a girl of about seven and a boy of perhaps five years. He did not hear her approach over the rushing of the spring water across the stones. Aislinn stopped for a moment before she reached him. There was something familiar about the tilt of his head, about the tightly woven red braid. She cried aloud.

"Tomaltagh! Red Braid of the Fenians! How have you come here among us?"

He turned to face her, dropped to one knee, lowered his face to the ground.

"Priestess. I have made this journey to ask your forgiveness and to request a place here for myself and for my children."

Aislinn smiled mischievously, stepped forward, and drew him to his feet.

"Your children?"

"My foster-children, priestess. Cailin and Dhiarmuid."

"So you found them, then."

He nodded, red-faced. "I did, though the journey was long and hard and they did not want me when I did find them. But I have persevered with them."

The little boy ran up to him then, his grubby fist clenching a little bundle of wildflowers.

"May I give them to the beautiful lady, athair?"

Tomaltagh nodded, reached for the bouquet to hand it to Aislinn, but the little boy shook his head stubbornly.

"Nay, athair. This beautiful lady." He stuck his little arm out toward Corra ni Brith. She crouched to her knees, drew the little fellow in with her arm.

"They are beautiful," she whispered to him. "I will cherish a gift from so fine a suitor."

Aislinn watched in surprise as Tomaltagh stared at Corra, as his face turned a warm shade of red. Corra looked up, her own face coloring to match his.

"I will go and put these in water, máthair," she said, turning away from the little group.

Tomaltagh found his voice. "Your daughter, priestess?"

"My foster-daughter, Red Braid."

"She is comely." He watched Corra's retreating back, turned and looked at his own two children. Aislinn spoke briskly.

"What is your point in coming here, Red Braid?"

"I am again Fianna, priestess, reinstated by Fionn Mac Cumhail himself. It was he who told me to come here, to bring my small ones with me. He said that I would find a place here where they could grow surrounded by love and caring. He said too that you would forgive me, so sure he seemed in his knowledge of you."

Aislinn smiled, thought of the sea-green eyes of Fionn Mac Cumhail.

"He has reason to be sure of me, Fenian. You are welcome here among us, but it is not my saying alone that can keep you here. You must first gain the trust of Cormac Mac Art, and of my husband Eoghan Mac Aidan. And they will know who you are and what our past has been."

Tomaltagh looked flustered.

"I fear their acceptance, priestess, for it is not just my past that they may hold against me. I am also a messenger. I have been to Munster, priestess. I have seen Aengus Mac Gabuideach, the father of Eoghan Mac Aidan. He sends messages to his son."

* * *

He sat to Aislinn's right at the table, next to Corra ni Brith. Cormac accepted him at once, declaring that the past was just that and that Tomaltagh and his foster-children were welcome as members of the community of Clete Acaill. Eoghan was less kind.

He watched the Fenian throughout the meal, responded to his comments with gruff, grunting sounds. When Tomaltagh addressed some remark to Corra ni Brith that caused her to color, Eoghan spoke sharply.

"What is it that you have said to my foster-daughter, Red Braid?"

"I have told her that my son was wise in choosing a bouquet of flowers to match her beauty," Tomaltagh stammered, his own color going a furious red.

"You dare to speak of beauty, you who kidnapped my wife not eight weeks from her childbed, and would have delivered her into the foul grasp of the druid Banbh!"

Tomaltagh stared down at the tabletop, his face red, his throat working.

"I have begged her forgiveness for that, poet, as I beg yours for any part I may have had in your suffering."

"Wait, Eoghan." Cormac placed his hand on his friend's arm. "Do you not see how the god was working on this Fenian even then, when he brought him together with your wife? See how he has redeemed himself, has made these children his own."

Cormac looked at the drooping head of the Fenian, at the tilt of Corra ni Brith's head as she watched Red Braid. He felt a sudden certainty grow within him.

"Bid forgiveness within you, Eoghan. Give the god time to work."

"I will hold my forgiveness as my own, so it please you."

Eoghan stood, would have strode from the table.

"Husband, wait." Aislinn placed her hand on his.

Eoghan stopped then, his love for her mingling with his anger. "Tomaltagh brings you news of your athair."

Eoghan regarded Red Braid.

"Of what interest can this be to me? I have no athair."

Red Braid stood then and squared his shoulders. He faced Eoghan directly.

"It was Fionn who sent me to him, who said that I should see Aengus before I came to you here."

"Fionn meddles where he should not."

"Fionn sees what we do not. I know only what your wife has taught me—that we must make amends for any sorrow we have caused. Your father is exiled in Munster and cannot make amends. That anguish has taken its toll on him, Mac Aidan. Where once there was a bear of a man, there is now a shrunken shell, a man much lost to himself. He speaks of you and of your wife. He much regrets what was done to both of you, speaks constantly of his foolishness over the woman Macha. He is fierce in defense of your wife, calls her the most merciful of women. He says that he is heartsore for speech with you. He asked me to send you his greetings and his love."

"Love! What does that man know of love?"

Eoghan slammed his cup on the tabletop and strode from the room.

It was not Aislinn but Corra ni Brith who comforted Tomaltagh then.

"Give my athair time, Red Braid. He and my máthair have suffered much. My father nurses his suffering in anger." She placed a gentle hand on Tomaltagh's arm.

He looked down at the small hand, looked up into her eyes.

"I only regret any part I may have played in their suffering," he said softly. His eyes did not leave her face.

Aislinn found him sitting by the river. She drew up behind him, wrapped her arms around his neck.

"Husband, I have told you of this Tomaltagh. Even when I was his captive, I knew him to be a man who struggled within himself that the good might win."

Eoghan ran his hands along her arms.

"Perhaps in time I can come to accept him. For now he is a reminder of our suffering, of what we have been through. He calls up in me fears that we may suffer again."

"We have been so happy here at Clete Acaill. Sometimes I too fear to trust this idyll."

Eoghan drew her down into his lap, kissed her long and gently.

"My cet-muintir, my beautiful wife. It is this happiness I fear to lose, for I could not bear for us to be separated again. Yet daily the druids cast their spells against Cormac. One day they will move against him, and what will happen to us then, who have been so close to him? And there is Banbh."

"I have dealt with him. He will not bother us further."

"Do not believe it, wife. He lies in wait, silent, as evil always does. But one day he will strike again."

Aislinn stroked the side of his face.

"I think that this news of your father troubles you more than you will say. Perhaps you should go to him, Eoghan."

"Nay, I cannot. His exile is of his own making and I will not be parted from you and the children. I must be where I can protect you always!" He spoke vehemently, drawing his arms tightly around her.

For answer, she stood, loosed her shift, stood before him. She cradled his head between her breasts, then leaned back.

Gently, she loosed him of his tunic, gently sat astride him there on the bench by the river, pressing her warm breasts and body against his, covering his face and throat with warm kisses, rocking gently back and forth with him until his arms drew tight around her and he cried aloud with the joy of her. She lifted her arms around his shoulders then, pressed herself into him.

"Come, husband," she whispered when they were calmer, when they stroked each other's back lovingly and gently. "What can we not forgive or endure when we have had such love together?"

31

The drums began again. Aislinn dropped her delicate embroidery into the basket beside her and stepped out from beneath the shading boughs of the tree into the warm midsummer sunshine.

She shielded her eyes from the sun and looked in the direction of the beating sound, then stretched and began walking toward the little hill that formed the western border of the village. Immediately the twins, now five years old, came running up beside her.

"Máthair, where do you go? May we come too? Please."

She laughed and held out a hand for each one. Together they climbed the little hill and looked down on the scene below them. Moylann, Banbh, and a few druii were chanting before a circle of standing stones, drumming and circling around and around a small altar on which she could see a wishing stone covered in the blood of some sacrificial animal. Their audience consisted of a few stragglers, standing in a clump at the outside edge of the circle.

Eibhlain and Aidan stared for a few moments at the distant scene, then Eibhlain made a snorting sound.

"It's just those silly old men again." Both children

looked at Aislinn impatiently. She dropped their hands, laughing.

"You may go then. Return to the village and your games."

Hand in hand, the two of them skirled away toward their playmates. Aislinn looked back down at the scene below. Foolish old men, Eibhlain had said. And she was right. Aislinn wondered if the child would even believe her if she told her that once these had been dangerous and evil men or if she would find it too funny to contemplate. She wondered if Moylann and Banbh realized their own status.

Corra and Tomaltagh approached, hand in hand.

"Red Braid! I thought that you had gone hunting with my husband and Cormac."

"I wished instead to spend time with your daughter."

Tomaltagh blushed in the way that had now made him famous among the residents of Clete Acaill, his face coloring up to match his hair. Aislinn thought of the first day that she had come upon Corra and Tomaltagh kissing on the bench beside the river, Tomaltagh's red hair entwined with Corra's copper. They had both colored so deeply at her approach that the color of their hair mated with the color of their skin. On that day, Aislinn had known that they would marry. In fact, she suspected that they would take their vows in three days at the Feis Leabhar, the Feast of the Books.

Tomaltagh stood at the rise of the hill and looked down at the druid ritual.

"What is it that they say, priestess? Though I have heard their drums for this past year, I do not know their words."

After all these years, Aislinn knew their ritual by heart, though she could not hear it from her place on the hill.

"The golden image is the god they petition today. They have used up all of the gods of Eire and not one has come to their purpose. Still, they will circle the altar and turn over the wishing stone and then chant their curses against

Cormac in the hope that this god will hasten him to doom." She shook her head.

From the hollow below them, the chanting sounded like meaningless rhythms.

Aislinn repeated the words for Tomaltagh.

> *"Cormac, we curse you in flesh and bone,*
> *You who deny the old gods a home,*
> *You who change the sacred ways,*
> *May the gods of power number your days.*
> *Cormac, we curse you asleep and awake.*
> *We petition your death for the old gods' sake.*
> *The true druii priesthood demands your death,*
> *May the gods in their vengeance choke your*
>   *breath."*

She smiled at Red Braid.

"At first their ceremonies and incantations drew hundreds from the hill of Tara, anxious to see whose power would win, which of the gods could wield the most influence so that they could turn all of their fear and their offerings toward that god. But now, as you can see, no one watches, no one listens when Moylann rants in the hall of Tara that the new god must be destroyed. The people shrug and go about their business. Most give their prayers and allegiance to whatever god seems appropriate at the time."

Aislinn turned back to look for the matching heads of her twins at their play. Below her, the little community on the Boann had become a true rath.

Cormac had established a school of learning where those who had been trained as aes dana, the intellectual class, could add the skills of writing to their repertoire. Daily, more young men and women came to add the once forbidden knowledge to their store. There, Eoghan, Aislinn, Cormac, and a trained body of teachers spent much of their time.

Corra watched her mother shield her eyes. She spoke up.

"They are with Cailin and Dhiarmuid, maither. I have sent them all to the seanchai for stories."

Aislinn laughed aloud.

"So you are still reading my mind, little seanmhaithair?"

Tomaltagh came and knelt behind Corra, wrapped his arms around her.

"Then she is the most beautiful little grandmother in all of Eire."

Corra leaned back against his chest and laughed. "You would not love me so much if your children had not taken to me so."

"What child could help but take to you, love?"

He kissed the top of her head, bent for her lips. Corra swatted at his arms, ducked away. She looked in Aislinn's direction. Aislinn looked deliberately away in the direction of the village. Corra pecked at Tomaltagh's lips, then jumped back.

"Go away now. Máthair and I have preparations to make for the feis."

"So I should have gone hunting after all." Tomaltagh stood and looked toward the forest. "Perhaps I can catch them." He loped away toward the stables.

Aislinn and Corra sat for a moment in comfortable silence. Aislinn leaned over and took her foster-daughter's hand.

"He is right, you know. About the children. Your gentleness with them is like that with your brother and sister. I am glad you have agreed to Cormac's request to teach the children in his Forradh. They all love you."

"But first we must celebrate the feis."

"Yes. At last, the three books of Cormac are complete."

"Will you be sorry to lose your duties as scribe, máthair?"

"Not sorry, but so proud of what we have done."

Aislinn mused on her four years with Cormac's books. The Teagasc an Riogh, Instructions of a King, had been the most difficult to compose. It contained Cormac's instructions to a ruler, but both Aislinn and Eoghan knew that it was intended for Cairbry. It had cost Cormac much introspection and worry. He had talked it over with them endlessly.

"How shall I propose to tell this young man, my son, how to be wise, when I myself have been such a fool? Look at the mistakes I have made! The battles I should not have fought, the taxes I should never have levied."

Eoghan had responded patiently.

"Have we not all been fools, old friend? Let him profit by what you have done well and by what you would do differently. Write him a book that separates the foolish from the wise."

So from their hours of discussion came a book that captured the true way of thought—a system of questions from Cairbry to his father:

> "My father, Cormac the Wise, grandson of Conn of the Hundred Battles, tell me what is the wisest course for a king?"
>
> "This I will answer," Cormac would respond. "A king must honor his poets"—here Eoghan and Cormac would laugh heartily—"worship the great God, speak only truth, remember the ancient truth and tales, care for the sick, protect the weak, foster education . . ."

These lists would take hours and often Eoghan would rewrite them for days as rhythmic chants that could be committed to memory for later generations. Aislinn recited some of it now for Corra.

> "O Cairbry, son of Cormac, hear the ways of wisdom:
> Do not discard the poor, though you be rich.
> Do not ignore the blind, though you be sighted,
> For what is heard can often not be seen.
> Take gentle care of the sick for you are strong.

Speak in the hall of kings when speech is needed.
Be silent in the forest, beneath the stars."

"How I love the poetry of it. What Cormac created and we refined and wrote is a book of beauty, the finest poetry our language can achieve."

Corra smiled.

"But The Book of Acaill is the one you complained of most."

"It was so tedious. It contains all of the principles of brehon law, written for the first time. We had to encode laws for recovering a debt, for owning cattle, for sailing the seas, for paying taxes and tributes, for dealing with criminals and every type of crime. They were detailed and intricate, each law with subclauses and special circumstances. We named it The Book of Acaill for our little village, because life went on around us and without us even as we wrote."

Aislinn laughed aloud.

"But it is the Psaltair of Tara that holds my spirit, daughter. Never forget. You must tell your brothers and sisters and Red Braid's children these tales. And later, you must tell these tales to the children you and Tomaltagh will make together."

Corra blushed again, but Aislinn just laughed. She continued earnestly.

"The Psaltair contains the genealogy of all the great clans of Ireland. In this book, Cormac's grandfather, Conn of the Hundred Battles, fights again. The great Ulster hero Cu Culainn defends his people from harm. Fionn and his Fenian warriors protect all of Eire. The warrior queen Medb comes back to life. These are the tales which make us proud of who we are.

"More than that, daughter, the genealogies of the families of Eire are chronicled. In the Psaltair of Tara, my family plays out our tragedy as does the family of Aengus Mac Gabuideach. Then our families are forever reunited in the union between Eoghan and me, in the birth of our children. You and I are linked for all time in the Psaltair, Corra, and soon your Tomaltagh will be added to our book as well. Promise me that you will pass these stories down, even when I am gone."

"I promise, máthair, for how would my love for you let me do otherwise?"

Aislinn smiled. The Psaltair of Tara had at last made her feel cleansed and complete, as though a circle had closed. She was proud of her families' small stories in the huge book.

Corra frowned slightly.

"I saw the books this morning. Your speaking of them makes me think of Aengus Mac Gabuideach. Tomaltagh still speaks of him. He says that he has great pity for his sorrow. I wish that athair would send him a message."

"As do I. But forgiveness must come in its own time. I have learned that well. We must give Eoghan time. But you said that you saw the books this morning."

"I did. The artwork that Cormac commissioned has been inserted. It is more beautiful than you hoped, máthair. All the creatures of Eire leap from the pages like a rainbow. And the casks that will house them! One gold, one silver, and one bronze, each with the most intricate chasework and inlaid jewels."

Aislinn nodded.

"Stands of delicate iron have been wrought to display them, not only for the feast, but in the hall of learning after the feis is over." She gasped suddenly.

"Speaking of the feast, we must check on the food! I feed the mind here and forget all of the bodies we must fill at Clete Acaill."

She stood and dusted herself off. Together, they hurried to check on progress.

Late in the afternoon, Aislinn found Eoghan and Cormac bent over a game of fidchell under the rustling leaves of an oak near the river. She slipped quietly up beside them.

"So? Men of leisure now that our books are finished?"
They laughed and Eoghan drew her to his lap.

"Who is the master of fidchell on this beautiful day?"
Cormac made a wry face.

"Who is always the master of fidchell? If the kingship
of Eire were determined by the pieces on this board, your
husband surely would rule at Tara."

Aislinn laughed and nuzzled at Eoghan's ear. Cormac
made an exasperated sound.

"Is my game to be cut short again?"

"Nay, my king," said Eoghan, finishing the game with
a winning move. "The game is over."

Cormac sighed exaggeratedly and began gathering the
pieces into their leather bag. He waved his hands at
Eoghan and Aislinn.

"Go then, go. I will find some other way to amuse
myself for the afternoon hours."

Laughing, the two walked hand in hand along the bank
of the river. When they were out of sight of the little
village, they slipped from their clothes and slid into the
cold waters of the Boann, their arms about each other,
Aislinn's long hair trailing behind them in the rush of the
stream.

"Our daughter will declare her marriage intentions at
the feis."

"The Red Braid is a good man."

"You did not always think so."

Eoghan laughed.

"Do I sense some lesson here, wife?"

"I think only of your father. How lonely he must be."

Eoghan said nothing. Aislinn kissed him gently on both
cheeks.

"Such happiness," she whispered against her husband's
throat. "Such perfect happiness we have found here."

Eoghan nodded, kissing her deeply, then lifting her chin
in his hands.

"May it last forever," he whispered.

*   *   *

Aislinn felt warm in the glow from the torches. She fanned herself and was glad of the momentary summer breeze that wafted in through the open doors of the banqueting hall.

In front of their dais on the raised iron pedestals stood the three books of Cormac Mac Art, the reason for the joy of this feast. The hall was crowded, not only with the people of their own village but with visitors from the hill of Tara.

Aislinn sat between Cormac and Eoghan, her hand resting lightly on her husband's arm. To Cormac's right sat his son Cairbry dressed in all his ceremonial finery. Flahari of the brehons sat to the right of Eoghan.

Aislinn was dressed in the full ceremonial finery of the Deisi. Her light green gown was covered by a pale blue woven tunic. She wore her mother's torque and brooch, her arms braceleted in the golden finery that had belonged to Eoghan's mother. She felt flushed, successful, gloriously happy.

From across the room she watched Corra rise, watched her lift her wine goblet. She pressed Eoghan's arm gently. He lifted her hand to his lips.

"So this is to be the moment."

"I feel old and young at the same time. Oh, husband, she is so beautiful!"

It was the custom among the women of the Gaels to choose their mates by this ceremonial pouring of the wine. Aislinn watched as Corra lifted a pitcher of wine and walked to the table where Tomaltagh was seated with the other Fenians of Clete Acaill. She watched as her beautiful daughter leaned over him, as she poured wine into his goblet.

She felt her eyes tear at the blush that stained Tomaltagh's cheeks when he looked up at Corra, at the way he could not take his eyes from her as they stood and drank their wine together.

When they had finished, Corra turned toward the high dais and lifted her goblet. The room grew silent.

"Máthair, athair, I have chosen this man for my bridal bed, and we have sealed our bond in the pouring and the drinking of this wine. May we ask of you your celebration of this union."

Aislinn felt that she was moving underwater. She rose slowly, feeling overtaken by some surprise. How had her little girl grown this fast? Was she leaving her so soon? The tears shimmered in her eyes and she rested her hand on Eoghan's arm.

Together they raised their goblets and all four of them drank. The entire rest of the hall rose after them, lifting their goblets, drinking and crying out blessings to health and love and children. In the melee Corra made her way to the front of the room, Tomaltagh in tow behind her.

Aislinn stepped from the dais and walked forward to embrace her.

"My beautiful daughter," she whispered. "Child of my heart. May you have the happiness that I have had with Eoghan."

Corra held tight to her, the tears now streaming down her own cheeks.

"Máthair," she whispered, "máthair. Your love has saved my life and shaped it and made it what it has become. I will love you always as if I were the daughter of your womb."

They clung to each other until Cormac stepped forward from the dais and stood behind the three books and raised his hands. The crowd silenced.

"This is our Feis Leabhar," he cried. "The Feast of the Books. But it is more a feast of our love. For here at Clete Acaill we have created not only these books, but this community. Here for the past five years we have labored on our words and our wisdom. We have worked hard and the new god has shed his light upon us. I will ask now his blessing upon these books and upon all of us who have labored here at Clete Acaill."

He raised his goblet into the torchlight.

"Bail O Dhia ar an obair!" he called. "Bless, O God, the work!"

As one the company rose and lifted their goblets into the light, even Cairbry and Flahari standing at the dais their cups raised.

"Bail O Dhia ar an obair!"

32

"Nay!" Aislinn slapped her open palm down upon the tabletop. "I do not like it, my king. I do not trust them and neither should you."

Cormac laughed gently.

"Your friend and not your king. For how many years shall I say it to both of you?"

"For all of our lives together," said Aislinn. "And I say again that you should not trust them. My king." She stressed the last words with two emphatic nods of her head.

"I did not say that I trusted them, priestess. I said that I would accept their invitation."

Aislinn shook her head again.

"You do not know Banbh as I know him. He has no intentions but evil ones. And as for Moylann, have not his daily curses and incantations for these five years given you some idea of his intentions?"

Cormac continued to smile. Aislinn whirled about and threw up her arms in exasperation, then made a pleading gesture toward Eoghan.

"Speak to him, husband. Counsel him toward wisdom."

Moylann and his druids had sent their messenger with the invitation only that morning. They wished to reconcile. They saw now that the gods could live in harmony. They regretted their actions of the last five years. They wished to speak with Cormac, to learn from him of the new god. To that end they would hold a feast in his honor at the druii hall in three days' time. Cairbry Mac Cormac had been asked and had assented to attend the feast in his father's honor as had the brehons. Would Cormac and his retainers and advisers be kind enough to attend?

Aislinn had said no from the moment the messenger left the room. Cormac had insisted that he would go. Eoghan, thus far, had maintained a watchful silence.

"Do you not see, Cormac? It is a trick, a druii trick. They will lure you there and drug you or harm you. They may try to kill you. Please, for the sake of all here at Clete Acaill, do not do this thing."

Eoghan spoke for the first time.

"He has no choice."

"What does this mean? He has a choice. He can say no. All would understand after their actions of the past five years."

"No." Cormac shook his head. "Your husband understands the politics of the thing, priestess. I know that you argue for my safety, but do I not teach of a god of forgiveness? How then could I not go? Is not my son the Ard-Ri of Eire? And should not his father seek to reconcile all of the political forces of Eire? I must go, for the sake of my son and our country. I am bound to try to reconcile it all. The druii know this."

Eoghan sighed, stood, walked around the room.

"How is it that these druii have at last become wise? They could have realized years ago that they could catch you sooner with politics than with curses and incantations. What has decided them on this course now?"

Cormac stood and walked to the doorway looking out over the sun-drenched late summer landscape.

"How beautiful it has been this summer," he said softly. "So little rain." He sounded like a man gone far from home. He turned toward them again.

"It was all of us who forced them to this choice. Do you see? We finished the books and held a great feast in their honor. We let all of Tara and soon enough all of Eire know that we had written the laws and history of Eire. We created the school that draws the aes dana here away from the druii. We even enlisted the participation and support of not only the brehons but the Ard-Ri of all Eire." He stopped, smiled.

"We bruited our triumphs. We have made them small and desperate. Had we simply gone silently away to write our books in some forgotten haven, they would have left us be, like some curiosity, a fireside tale. But here we have created a school of reading, writing, and learning. We have caught the imagination of the people of Eire. Look how many druids are here among us, themselves students of the word. We have forced the Dark Ones to cunning, like animals trapped."

Eoghan nodded slowly.

"They can reach us best in the place where we are both strongest and weakest. Our principles. Our love of country. As long as they were chanting their foolish incantations we could ignore them. Put us to the political sword and we must capitulate."

Cormac sighed, ran his hands through the golden hair now gone almost totally gray. He pressed his hand to his eyeless socket in a way that Aislinn had not seen him do in years.

"Friends," he said softly. "The time has come to discuss my death."

"No!" Aislinn cried, whirling on him.

"A wise man prepares for death as a contingency, just as he prepares for battle. Is this not so?"

Aislinn shook her head.

"I care not for politics. I care for you, for my husband

and children, for the life that we have all created here at Clete Acaill."

"As do I, priestess. That is why we must prepare for its continuation if something should happen to me." He turned to Eoghan.

"Send for Fionn now, but tell no one. Fionn Mac Cumhail must be here. If something happens to me you must leave Clete Acaill. You must take your family and the books and go elsewhere. Most of the community can stay. They will be under the protection of Cairbry and will pose no threat to Moylann and Banbh and their followers. But you will be a great threat for the two of you have been my voice and my ears. You must save the books and yourselves. I know Moylann and he will use any victory to turn the tide back to the old ways."

Aislinn nodded, sitting down at the table with the two of them.

"As will Banbh. What else do you wish, my king? We will see that your wishes are carried out." She laid her hand gently across the hand of her aging friend. Cormac smiled, laying his hand over hers and closing his free hand over Eoghan's.

"How happy and peaceful the years of my old age have been," he said. He looked again at the square of summer light in the doorway.

"I do not wish to be buried at Brugh na Boann with the ancient kings of Eire. Bury me instead at Ross na Riogh, facing east toward the rising of the light. Will you see that it is done?"

"We will," answered Eoghan and Aislinn as one.

Cormac stood and walked to the doorway. He spoke over his shoulder.

"It may not come to that, but if it does, I will like to think of the light spreading over me at the start of each day."

* * *

Even Aislinn had to admit that the druids had outdone themselves. The hall was polished and lit with dozens of torches and the finest tables and tableware gleamed in the light. Cormac was seated to the right of his son, Aislinn and Eoghan to his left.

Moylann, Banbh, and the others of their group had abased themselves, sitting at a ground-level table placed at right angles to the main table.

Wine and mead flowed freely and the feast was a masterpiece of hospitality.

The huge roasted pig that formed the centerpiece of the feasting table was only a small portion of the lavish meal. Loaves of bread with honey, oat, barley, and rye cakes vied for attention with steamed cabbage and leeks, and parsnips and carrots in delicate herbs and butter. Wild fowl stuffed with ocean grasses of dulse and laver surrounded the pig as did several varieties of steamed and boiled fish, including delicately poached salmon dressed with watercress.

One entire table was covered with a bounty of fruits. Sloes, the rich summer plums of Eire, were heaped on a tray surrounded by strawberries, whortleberries, and rowanberries in sweet cream. Apples and hazelnuts overflowed a silver bowl.

Still, Aislinn could eat nothing, declining even water, saying only that she was keeping priestly vigil for Cormac. She noticed Banbh's eyes on her with each item she declined, glittering with malice, hiding some secret laughter.

"Do you not eat, priestess?" he asked.

"I do vigil for Cormac Mac Art," Aislinn responded quietly.

"Ah, but look how Cormac enjoys our feast. You dishonor us with your abstention."

Aislinn leaned over the table, hissed softly at Banbh.

"The word honor should burn your tongue, Dark One."

Banbh only laughed in response.

It was true that Cormac was indeed in high spirits. He

drank to the health of the druii and the brehons, to the wise rulership of his son, to Eoghan and Aislinn. He feasted on the sweet fruits, laughing as the juice of a plum ran down his chin. At one point, he stood and made toast.

"To the rich land of Eire," he cried, "which has been so bountiful to me."

More than any of the other foods, Cormac delighted in the delicate taste of the salmon, eating filet after filet, complimenting the druii and their cooks on its delicacy. At the right angled table, Moylann and his company nodded and smiled, toasting the once king and his health, toasting their renewed friendship.

Suddenly Cormac stood. For a moment, Aislinn thought that he would propose yet another toast and she readied her hand for her cup. Instead his face grew red and his breathing became labored. He clutched at his throat, his remaining good eye bulging from its socket. Eoghan stood beside him.

"What is it?" he cried. Gasping now, his face turning purple, Cormac pointed at the salmon on his plate.

Aislinn leaped to her feet.

"He chokes, husband! It is a fish bone. He chokes!"

Eoghan began to clap him on the back, then to pound against his back like thunder, but the bone did not dislodge. Cairbry launched himself to his father's back while Aislinn ran before him, forcing Cormac's mouth open with her knuckles, inserting her fingers, probing for the offending bone.

All the while the druii sat still and silent at their table, not speaking, not moving. Only when Cormac's eye rolled back into his head and he sank devoid of breath, blue and dead to the floor beneath him, did they begin their solicitations, running to his side, hurrying to comfort Cairbry, lamenting loudly the accidental tragedy that had befallen their late king and now, when they were at last to be reconciled.

Only Aislinn remembered the words of their daily chant:

Cormac, we curse you in flesh and bone,
You who deny the old gods a home . . .
The true druii priesthood demands your death,
May the gods in their vengeance choke your
    breath.

33

"It was his request that he be buried at Ross na Riogh!"
Aislinn repeated what she had already said before,
though she had the doomed feeling that no one was heeding her words. The great hall at Tara was full with brehons
and druii, Fenians and noble families. Cairbry sat in the
high chair of kingship. He looked lost and very young.
She wished that she could speak to him quietly, wished
that she could say that she understood, that she too had
felt just as alone and confused. Instead she was trapped
in this role—pleading Cormac's wish for burial before the
combined legal and religious bodies of Eire.

Moylann stood, smiling unctiously at Cairbry, then
turning toward the brehons.

"We cannot know what great Cormac requested. We
can know only what honor and tradition tell us. Are not
all of the great kings of Eire buried at Brugh na Boann?
Shall we dishonor the wise Cormac Mac Art with such a
hugger-mugger burial as this? The cairns at Brugh na
Boann are sacred. They have been used by generations of
kings, blessed by the sacred ceremonies of generations of
druii. Shall we do less for great Cormac?"

Young Cairbry raised his head and nodded a little at Moylann's argument.

Aislinn felt Eoghan at her elbow, smelled the moist outside smell of his cloak. He had just come in from the rain. He stood beside her as Moylann droned on before the company.

"He argues well, that one," Eoghan whispered in her ear.

"Too well I am afraid. Has he come?"

He nodded.

"Where do we meet him?"

"In the forest beyond Clete Acaill."

"And the books?"

"They are safely hidden for now. Corra and Tomaltagh guard the children in the village. But as soon as these arguments are finished we must flee as Cormac warned us."

Aislinn nodded. At their table the brehons began their discussion of the merits of the two arguments. Finally, at the front of the company Flahari rose.

"People of Eire. We have heard the plea of the priestess Aislinn that Cormac Mac Art be buried at Ross na Riogh. We have heard the arguments of Moylann that only burial at Brugh na Boann will do him honor. We of the brehons rule that Moylann is correct.

"Tonight we will hold our great feast with Cormac Mac Art. Tomorrow he will be buried at Brugh na Boann. May he be remembered with honor by all of us."

Aislinn felt Eoghan's hand at her elbow.

"Come," he whispered. "We have much preparation before the feast."

Corra pulled the hood deep over her face and hair. She lifted Tomaltagh's little Dhiarmuid into her arms. Aislinn cradled Eibhlain while Eoghan and Tomaltagh held Cailin and Aidan.

"You must make no sound," Aislinn whispered to the children at the door of the hut. "No sound at all."

"Is it a kind of game, maither?" Eibhlain asked.

"Yes, love. A very important game. Do you all understand? You can make no sound." She watched as Aidan nodded, his eyes round, his face serious. He understood; the fear was clear in his face. She turned toward Eoghan in anguish.

"Did I look just so when you took me from my máthair? This anguish?"

"Just so." Eoghan's face looked as though it might fold in on itself. "Come. Haste is our best ally now, as it was then."

They moved single file on foot along the Boann, the children cradled in their arms, the darkness shielding them from view. Aislinn remembered her flight with Corra ni Brith, Eoghan's flight with her when she was a child. She wanted to cry out in anguish. In the sheltering darkness of the forest, they moved gingerly, glancing around them, searching. A soft nicker of a horse came from their left. Eoghan made a low, screeching sound, like the call of a hunting owl. Another call returned from the darkness.

Fionn stepped forward into a little clearing, his horse behind him. He looked at the foursome with their terrified burdens, made another low call. Fenians moved softly from the forest around him, extra horses tethered behind their own.

Eoghan set Aidan on the ground, stepped forward to Fionn. They clasped their upper arms in silence. Eoghan whispered the question.

"Cormac's books?"

"Where you had hidden them. You were right that they would not cross the threshold of his tomb so close upon his burial. We have them with us now."

"Where will you hide them?"

"We will scatter them across Eire. Only Cormac's wolf brothers will know where they are hidden."

"This would please him well, that the wolves of the forest guard his words."

"It would." Fionn turned to Aislinn. "How fare you, priestess?"

In the kindness of his look, her terror overtook her. She clutched Eibhlain to her chest.

"I cannot do this, Fionn. I cannot send my children into the forests of Eire without me."

"You must, priestess. If you flee with your children, the followers of Moylann will follow."

Fionn stepped to her and lifted Eibhlain from her arms. He handed her gently to a Fenian, who lifted her atop his own horse, holding her in front of him. Aidan was settled before another warrior. Saddled horses were brought forward for Tomaltagh and Corra. Red Braid swung up and Eoghan lifted Cailin into his arms. He took Dhiarmuid from Corra. She turned toward her horse, turned back toward Aislinn.

"Máthair."

She wrapped her arms around Aislinn, leaned back, and wiped at the tears streaking down Aislinn's cheeks.

"I will keep them safe until you come for them. I will protect them as you have protected me. Cormac would say that this was why the god has given us to each other. Is it not so?"

Aislinn nodded, unable to speak or to stanch the flow of tears from her eyes.

Eoghan helped Corra to the saddle, settled Dhiarmuid before her.

Aislinn looked up toward the dark sky.

"Máthair! Now I know. Now I understand. The terrible weight of your sorrow!"

Suddenly, Fionn stepped toward Aislinn. He placed both hands on either side of her face, drew his hood deep over both of them. He pressed his forehead to hers. For a moment Aislinn's shoulders continued to shake, then they grew still. From deep within the hood, she sighed softly.

"Yes, you are wise. It is well."

Fionn released her and she stepped back. Eoghan raised his arm.

"May the god ride with you, Fionn Mac Cumhail."

Fionn mounted and raised his arm in salute. The little party turned and disappeared silently into the forests of Eire. Aislinn watched until no shadow or movement remained. Then she dropped to the forest floor, curled silently against the leaves. Eoghan lifted her, cradled her in his arms, carried her all the way back to Clete Acaill.

Aislinn endured the feast for the sake of Cormac but felt it go by her as if in a dream. The swirl of royal colors, the smoking torches, the gleam of the great bronze panel behind Cairbry's throne all seemed to her part of some other life, no longer hers.

She drank the ritual toasts with Eoghan, listened to his rosc in praise of his friend, held young Cairbry's hand when the moment came for him to toast his father's passage to Tir Nan Og. Once she placed her hand over the cold hand of Cormac, stroked the silk of his royal tunic, and brushed her hand against the gray of his hair.

"Good friend," she whispered, "we have failed you in our final promise."

Once or twice through the haze of swirling dancers and smoky torchlight she caught the face of Banbh watching her, feral, calculating the depth of her pain, but he did not approach or speak. She judged that his own remembered terror kept him from her. She wondered how long that terror could hold back the wall of retribution if they stayed at Clete Acaill.

Toward morning, when the first thin threads of dawn were spreading on the eastern sky, the druii circled the body of Cormac and began to intone the ritual burial chants. Slowly they lifted Cormac's bier to their shoulders, bearing it for the walk to the ford of the Boann where they would cross to the valley of the kings. Aislinn shuddered when she saw that Moylann and Banbh were among those who shouldered the royal burden.

"Look at them, husband. So far have they come already in insinuating themselves into the graces of the people. They have convinced everyone that Cormac's death was an accident while at the same time hinting with their smiles and significant nods that it was their powers, their chants and incantations that brought his death."

"More danger for us, as well. Be glad that our children are safely gone."

Aislinn nodded.

By the time the funeral procession reached the ford of the Boann, the rain was coming down in a steady gray drizzle. Cormac's fine garmets were wet. They clung to his arms and legs, made him look shrunken and smaller.

At the river's edge, the bearers set the body down. More chants, more incantations, petitions to all of the gods to bring the spirit of Cormac to Tir Nan Og. No mention of Cormac's god. As if, now that he was dead, the light and its wondrous joy could be forgotten.

Aislinn let her head drop, let the carefully hoarded tears drop on the front of her gown, mingle with the rain.

At the edge of the river, Moylann, Banbh, and the other druii bearers hoisted the bier to their shoulders and stepped into the water. Aislinn lifted her head and watched them, thought idly that the river was low, remembered Cormac's comment of so few days earlier that the summer had seen so little rain. She shook her head. These last days had made up for that. When had she last seen the sun?

"Aislinn."

Aislinn looked at Eoghan, but he stood silent, with his head bowed. She glanced about, saw no one.

"Daughter Aislinn."

The voice was familiar. She found herself wishing to hear it again. It was warm, gentle, a voice like that of old . . .

Aislinn's head snapped up. She looked about her frantically. Cairbry's head was bent with weeping. Beside her, Eoghan held his hand before his eyes. The last of the bearers entered the water.

It was then that Aislinn saw Aodhfin. He was standing at the far side of the river, his robe of white swans' wings billowing gently around him. He lifted his hand to her.

Aislinn laughed aloud.

A few people in the crowd turned to stare at her.

"Athair!" she called.

Still more turned in her direction. Murmurs of concern and fear moved through the crowd. Eoghan moved closer to her side.

"Ask, daughter," Aodhfin said, still smiling. "Ask."

Slowly, as if with a will of their own, Aislinn's arms raised above her head.

"I ask!" she cried aloud.

Her fingers stretched out and the rain ran in rivulets along her arms and into her sleeves. She laughed aloud again. Now all of the company turned from watching the progress of Cormac's bier across the river. They stared at her. In the middle of the river, Moylann stopped, twisted his head over his shoulder, and sneered, but Aislinn saw the quick look of fear that passed over Banbh's features.

She closed her eyes, said nothing, standing still with her arms upraised. Suddenly she knew, as clearly as if the words had been spoken aloud.

"O you, the god in whom Cormac believed, I ask that you choose. Great Cormac wished to be buried at Ross na Riogh, yet none will heed his wish. What do you wish for him, God of the Light?"

Nothing happened. Aislinn stood still, arms upraised while all around her the assemblage whispered, then began to call.

"She is crazy!"

"Surely there is no other god."

"Go forward to Brugh na Boann!"

Smiling triumphantly, Moylann began again across the river.

A little wind came up, spun the long grasses beside the edge of the river, bent them low.

Again the bearers with the bier stopped, looked around them.

The sound began from far away, a moaning, then a deep thrumming, a sound like a bodhran, like a hundred bodhrans, thunder arising from the stretched skins, filling the sky, the grasses, the river. Then, it was a roar, all of the winds and the mad rush of the sea combined. From around a bend in the river came a wall of water, green and yellow, frothed with white, bearing in its center whole uprooted trees, mad, whirling branches. It rushed toward the funeral bier, overran the banks of the Boann.

The people screamed in terror, scrambled away from the banks of the river.

Two of the druids bearing Cormac's bier let loose their hold and were swept away.

From the middle of the river, Banbh turned and looked directly at Aislinn. His face registered surprise. He continued to stare at her as the water rushed over him. Then he was swept upside down in the wall of green. Behind him, the seven tumbling colors of Cormac's royal garments disappeared in the froth of a wave. Suddenly Banbh appeared again, trapped upright in the water, frozen, as if behind ice. His hands seemed to press against the wall of water. He stared at Aislinn from behind the seething green wall, his teeth bared, his face filled with fear and awareness. Then the water curled over him, he turned upside down, was swallowed up in the dark crow feathers of his own cloak, disappeared forever.

The wall of water swept past, leaving the water undulating behind its wake.

The rain ceased; sunlight shimmered off the surface of the river, poured down on Aislinn's upraised arms. Everyone but Eoghan moved away from Aislinn. Even Cairbry Mac Cormac stepped away, his look a mingling of fear and anger.

In the river, the bier of Cormac, Cormac himself, and all of the druids who had borne him were gone.

Dozens searched for Cormac all through the night, walking by the light of smoky torches through the woods and fields on both sides of the Boann. Two bo-aires from Clete Acaill found him at last, bearing his body quietly, secretly, to Eoghan and Aislinn just before dawn, their cattle lowing and nuzzling around them, their bells clanging in the predawn silence.

The cattlemen helped Aislinn and Eoghan to dig the little grave at Ross na Riogh, facing east toward the strands of light in the sky. They helped them to cover the cairn with stones, but they left the little grave unmarked, graced by no sign of the king who rested within.

"We have heard the tale of the rising of the river," they whispered. "We will tell the others of Clete Acaill that Cormac is buried at Ross na Riogh as he wished, as the god wished for him. But we will tell no one where."

When they had gone, Aislinn and Eoghan stood silently, waiting for the light of dawn to move across the plain and reach them, their horses with their traveling packs tethered nearby. Eoghan gathered her into his cloak, whispered against her hair.

"When the light has reached him, we must go. We will not be welcome here again for some time."

Aislinn said nothing, watched as the sun crept along the foot of the stones of Cormac's little cairn.

Eoghan mistook her silence for sorrow.

"It need not be forever, love. Not now that Moylann and Banbh are gone. We will see that the books are safe, go to Almhuin and gather our family back around us. Once events have calmed here, we can return."

Aislinn said nothing.

Dawn light washed like a wave across the plain, reached the foot of Cormac's cairn, and stroked the stones, warming them.

"We must go to Almhuin," Eoghan said softly.

"Nay," Aislinn said. "For Fionn has not gone to Almhuin."

"Where has he gone? Where are the children?"

"He has taken them to Munster."

Eoghan looked puzzled for a moment, then a slow comprehension gathered in his face.

"To Munster. To Aengus Mac Gabuideach, my father! Is this his wisdom?"

"It is, for he says that your father will protect his grandchildren with all of the fierceness that remains to him, and with all of the loyalty he can offer to the son he loves and lost."

"When was this decided?"

"He told me in the forest, when he pressed his forehead to mine."

"And you agreed to this?"

"I did. My children will be safe with your father. I believe that."

"Then you believe more in the power of forgiveness than I do."

"Nay, husband, I believe in the power of love."

He turned to her then, gathered her close within his arms, and kissed her gently.

The sun, which had been resting full and warm against the stones of Cormac's cairn, bathed them in golden radiance. It passed over them and continued its journey to the far horizon. For a moment, they stood still in each other's arms. Then they mounted their horses, and followed in the path of the light.

HISTORICAL BACKGROUND

This is a novel that interweaves real personages and real history, with myth, legend, and pure invention. It is not easy to separate myth from history; in ancient Ireland the line between the real and the unreal was not so much a line as a river or a curling ribbon. The worlds of myth, spirit, and invention were not looked upon as separate from (or incompatible with) the worlds of science or history. In fact, they were seen as inextricably and necessarily entwined (perhaps a wiser view than ours). Having so said, I will attempt to separate them in these notes.

Cormac Mac Art was evidently a real historical person. Most historical accounts agree that he had a long reign of some forty years, marked, if the legends can be trusted, by wisdom and plenty, a reign in which no one had to bolt the door, guard the flock, or want for food or clothing. He rebuilt the great hill fortress of Tara, including a sun house for women, the first watermill ever built in Ireland, a house for the Fianna, Cormac's standing army, and a banqueting hall 750 feet long. Where all of that once stood, there are now earthen rings, empty green grass, and blue sky.

Cormac was forced to abdicate his throne when his eye was put out. Irish law elected its kings from a roster of worthy candidates, but kings had to possess physical, intellectual, and moral perfection. According to history and legend, Cormac lost his eye when Cellach, the son of Cormac, kidnapped a woman of the Deisi, the daughter of Sorar and granddaughter of Art Corb. Aengus, chief of the Deisi, followed hard upon the heels of the kidnapper, killing Cellach in the presence of his father and putting out Cormac's eye. Aengus and his clan were then exiled from Meath. For the purposes of this story, that woman became Aislinn, daughter of Sorar.

After his eye was put out, Cormac retired to a little community on the Boyne called Clete Acaill where he wrote three books, in violation of the taboo (or geis) against writing. (The druids did actually have a form of writing, called ogham, but it was available to druidic initiates only.)

Cormac's first book, the Teagasc an Riogh or Instructions of a King, may have been his instructions to his son Cairbry as the book consists of the precepts of wise rulership, in the question and answer format indicated in the story.

The Book of Acaill contains the written principles of Irish law, known as the brehon law for the lawyers (brehons) who memorized and administered it. Brehon law was highly detailed and was passed down orally and through memorization for centuries. This may explain the Irish-American predilection for the law in all its forms, even in the present day.

Cormac's third book, the Psaltair of Tara, is the history and genealogy of Ireland. None of the three books survived extant, or at least they have not yet been found. Somewhere in Ireland they may still be buried in the finely ornamented "book coffins" that Cormac designed for them, waiting for us to find them, to hear his voice again, to find our own ancestors in them.

The legends also tell us that Cormac became a Christian seven years before his death, refusing afterward to worship stones or trees and claiming that there was a creator of all things who had power over all elements. This did not endear him to some of the druids, who cursed him daily and called the vengeance of their gods down upon him.

Cormac was, according to the chroniclers, the third person to believe in the new god in all of Ireland. Indeed, Christianity must have had a firm foothold in Ireland before Saint Patrick arrived, for when Pope Celestine sent the first bishop, Palladius, to Ireland in 431, it was to an established Christian community.

Cormac died in 267 A.D. His death and the subsequent strange events that accompanied it are drawn directly from the legends.

Surely this is one of the most fascinating periods in Irish history; from it have arisen the stories of the Fenian cycle, my personal favorite of the cycles of ancient Irish storytelling. Fionn Mac Cumhail and his Fianna seem to have been real historical personages. The Fianna, the standing army of Ireland, is referred to not only in Irish histories but in the references of foreign historians. However, the legends have Fionn and his son and grandson living each for hundreds of years and crossing often back and forth between this world and the world of the Others. On the other hand, we also have rich, historical-sounding detail of the rites of entrance to the warrior band, of women who passed these rites, of the numbers of warriors in peacetime and in wartime, details of horses and dwellings and food, and even of the Fenian code of honor by which these warriors lived. The Fenians did indeed declare themselves landless and clanless in order that any wars or battles they might fight in would not result in protracted and costly court cases against their families or home villages (obviously a society as litigious as ours!).

Two of the regular practices in the novel—the practice of fosterage and the practice of medicine—are true to these historical times as well. Fosterage was practiced regularly for hundreds of years in ancient Ireland. Children were fostered out at the age of seven, sometimes to family relatives, sometimes to close family friends in other villages. Foster-children were raised as if they were the blood children of the foster family and were taught the necessary skills for functioning in the adult world. Girls were returned to their birth families at about the age of fourteen, boys at the age of seventeen. This practice allowed young people to meet and marry outside of their own clans; it also bonded various villages and groups of a tribe.

Medicine in ancient Ireland was most interesting. Both men and women could practice medicine and the Celts had a good grasp of advanced concepts like sterile procedure. In fact, physicians built their own huts over or near running streams with four open doors or windows for good ventilation. (The Celts in general had a very good grasp of the concept of personal cleanliness, with daily and weekly bathing being required.) Physicians did indeed sterilize instruments and knew to wash thoroughly before surgery. They also used a wide array of herbal remedies for pain and other bodily ills. The instruments described in the novel—the forceps, hook, and scalpel— really were in common medical use. While cesarean sections were performed, Aislinn was most fortunate in not requiring that surgery, as most mothers simply did not survive the procedure.

And what of Aislinn ni Sorar herself? Strong, learned women were typical among the ancient Irish. Women enjoyed many privileges and prerogatives under ancient Celtic law. They could hold property. Property that was theirs on coming into a marriage remained theirs if the marriage terminated. Celtic women also had an equal say in their choice of a marriage partner. Druid priestesses were common and there are numerous accounts of women warriors, queens, brehons, and physicians.

As for Aislinn? I can only say that she came to me one rainy Hudson River morning in November, standing near a rain-washed wall behind my eyes. I recognized her instantly as a woman of body, mind, and spirit, and knew that I must tell her story. I hope that I have done her justice.

Juilene Osborne-McKnight

Bail O Dhia ar an obair.
Bless, O God, the work.

SELECTED BIBLIOGRAPHY

Bamford, Christopher and William Parker Marsh. *Celtic Christianity: Ecology and Holiness*. Lindisfarne Press, 1987.

Chadwick, Nora. *The Celts*. New York: Penguin Books, 1971.

Cunliffe, Barry. *The Celtic World*. New York: McGraw-Hill, 1979.

Delaney, Frank. *The Celts*. London: BBC Publications and Hodder & Stoughton Ltd., 1986.

Dillon, Myles, ed. *Irish Sagas*. Edition 4. Dublin: Mercier Press, 1985.

Forde-Johnston, J. *Prehistoric Britain and Ireland*. New York: W. W. Norton & Co., 1976.

Gantz, Jeffrey, trans. *Early Irish Myths and Sagas*. New York: Dorset Press, 1985.

Glassie, Henry, ed. *Irish Folk Tales*. New York: Pantheon Books, 1985.

MacManus, Seumas. *The Story of the Irish Race*. Old Greenwich, Connecticut: The Devin-Adair Company, 1921.

Markale, Jean. *Women of the Celts*. Rochester, Vermont: Inner Traditions International, 1986.

Matthews, John. *Fionn Mac Cumhail: Champion of Ireland*. Illus. by James Field. Dorset: Firebird Books, 1988.

McCaffrey, Kevin. *The Adventures of Fionn and the Fianna*. Dublin: Fitzwilliam Publishing Co., 1989.

McMahon, Agnes, ed. *The Celtic Way of Life*. Dublin: O'Brien Educational, 1988.

Neill, Kenneth. *An Illustrated History of The Irish People*. Dublin: Gill and Macmillan, 1979.

Norton-Taylor, Duncan. *The Celts*. New York: Time-Life Books, 1974.

O'Faolain, Eileen. *Irish Sagas and Folktales*. New York: Avenel Books, 1982.

O'Kelly, Michael J. *Early Ireland*. Cambridge: Cambridge University Press, 1989.

Piggott, Stuart. *The Druids*. London: Thames and Hudson, 1985.

Powell, T. G. E. *The Celts*. London: Thames and Hudson, 1980.

Ranleigh, John. *Ireland: an Illustrated History*. New York: Oxford University Press, 1981.

Rolleston, T. W. *The High Deeds of Finn*. New York: Lemma Publishers, 1973.

Rolleston, T. W. *The Adventures of Finn Mac Cumhail*. Dublin: Mercier Press, 1979.

Roy, James Charles. *The Road Wet, The Wind Close: Celtic Ireland*. Dublin: Gill and Macmillan, 1986.

Scherman, Katharine. *The Flowering of Ireland: Saints, Scholars and Kings*. Boston: Little Brown, 1981.

Sharkey, John. *Celtic Mysteries: The Ancient Religion*. London: Thames and Hudson, 1975.

Sjoestedt, Marie-Louise. *Gods and Heroes of the Celts*. Trans. by Myles Dillon. Berkeley, California: Turtle Island Foundation, 1982.

Smyth, Daragh. *A Guide to Irish Mythology*. Dublin: Irish Academic Press, 1988.

Yeats, W. B., ed. *A Treasury of Irish Myth, Legend and Folklore*. New York: Crown Publishers, 1986.

GLOSSARY OF TERMS AND PRONUNCIATIONS

Terms used in the novel are a mix of old and modern Irish and are included to give the flavor and sound of the speech. In most cases, except where an actual historical term required it, I have opted for the modernized Irish spelling of words, to reduce the number of consonants and the resulting difficulty with spelling and pronunciation.

a chailin bhig *(e calleen vig)* My little girl.

aes dana *(es da ne)* The intellectual class of Ireland, they comprised the poets, druids, physicians, and lawyers. They were allowed the freedom of Ireland's roads and could travel between tribes and counties freely. Many of these professions required twelve or more years of intensive study. Memorization was especially important since no written texts were permitted in Celtic Ireland and all knowledge was transmitted orally.

Almhuin *(all oon)* Fionn Mac Cumhail's stronghold in Kildare. In legend, it was a fortress with gleaming white walls.

amaireach *(a mar och)* Tomorrow.

athair *(a her)* Father.

Badb *(Bive)* Badb was crow goddess, patroness of war.

Beltaine *(Bal tawn ye)* May 1 festival. Cattle were driven through fires of purification on this feast. Most pre-Christian civilizations had some May 1 ritual that has now been translated into the May Day festivities of many countries.

Boann *(Boyne)* The river Boyne, once considered the sacred province of the goddess Boann.

bodhran *(baur an)* A skin drum that is held in the hand and played with a small two-headed stick.

bothy *(baw hee)* A small forest hut of boughs and branches, similar to a lean-to.

braichs *(brakes)* Loose, baggy pants of plaid that taper in at the ankles and are held up by a wide leather belt.

brehon *(bre hun)* The lawyers of ancient Ireland. Irish law was extremely complex and specified every detail of ancient life. For example, there were laws specifying the degree of recompense owed to a person who is injured on his face as opposed to being injured in a bodily part that does not show. One famous law deals with the honor price owed to a harpist should his plucking finger be damaged.

bruidhean *(breen)* A public house or tavern. Often they existed at the crossroads in ancient Ireland. There were very specific laws regarding the amount of food, ale, and beds an innkeeper must have on hand.

bruighaid *(brewy)* An innkeeper.

Brugh na Boann *(brew na Boyne)* A place on the Boyne river east of Newgrange that was the traditional burial site for the ancient Celtic kings.

cailleach *(kal ach)* A local goddess or wise woman.

Celts *(kelts)* Pronunciation derives from the Greek *keltoi* and is not pronounced like the basketball team.

cet muintir *(kayd win tir)* Chief or first wife. Celtic law permitted a man to have more than one wife although the law was also very specific that the chief wife had first rights to the household and even had specific rights to jealous revenge during the first three days that the new woman was in the house!

Clete Acaill *(klete awkel)* The community founded by Cormac Mac Art on the Boyne river. According to the histories, he retired here to write his books after his retirement from rule.

cumal *(koo el)* A slave.

Deisi *(desh e)* The tribe to which Aislinn, Eoghan, and many of the other characters in this book belonged.

Diancecht *(dien xext)* The god of physicians.

dithir *(dee heer)* Landless. Fenian warriors must give up their rights to land ownership when they joined the Fianna.

ecland *(ek cland)* Clanless. Again Fenians must give up their clans and their clans must swear that they will not take revenge in the event that a Fenian is slain.

feis *(fesh)* A festival or celebration.

fidchell *(fid kell)* A game much like chess played with pieces on a board.

fidnemed *(fee ne ve)* A sacred woodland shrine. Remnants of these shrines can be found throughout Ireland.

fili *(fil ee)* A term of respect for the highest and best of the poets of ancient Ireland.

Forradh *(for a)* Cormac's school at Tara.

geantraighe *(gan tra ee)* The laughing music. Originally attributed to the harp of the Dagda, chief of the gods, who played crying, laughing, and sleeping music for his wife Boann while she gave birth.

glam dicen *(glav dee gen)* Considered the most powerful weapon of a poet, this was a satirical poem. Words possessed such power for the Celts that a person subjected to glam dicen would be exiled for shame, might break out in boils and rashes or even die.

Gobniu *(gob an)* God of blacksmiths.

grianan *(gree nawn)* The sun house, built at ceremonial locations for the women of the tribe.

Imbolc *(im bolek)* February 1. In ancient times this was a festival of ewes and of lambing as well as being a festival of Brighid, goddess of women, poetry, fertility, and ewes. It is now St. Brighid's day.

leabhar *(laur)* Book

Lia Fail *(lee e fall)* The ancient Irish installation stone of kingship, it stood on the hill of Tara between the house of Cormac and the banqueting hall.

Lugh *(Loo)* Lugh is the sun god, god of light and genius. He was reputed to be good at everything and is the divine father of the ancient Irish hero Cu Chulainn.

máthair *(ma her)* Mother

ogham *(om)* The ancient language of sticks still found on many tombs and ancient rock formations. To form the language, strokes in combinations of up to five branch off from a central stem. The language is associated with druids and magic.

ollamh *(ol ev)* A master at his discipline. A poet who was an ollamh was considered equal in stature to a king.

rosc *(rosk)* A poem of high praise composed by an ollamh.

samhain *(sau win)* October 30. To the Celts, this date was the turning into the dark half of the year and was fraught with danger. They believed that the people of the sidhe came out from their hiding places and worked mischief on humans on this night. Today we celebrate this festival as Halloween.

seanchai *(shan ach ee)* Storyteller.

seanathair *(shan a her)* Grandfather.

seotho a thoil *(sho ho a hoyl)* Hush, darling. From an old Irish poem.

sidhe *(shee)* The banished people of the ancient race known as the tuatha de danaan. These folk now live beneath the mounds, under the water, and in the secret places of the earth.

suantraighe *(soo en tra ee)* The sleeping music played by Dagda for his wife after she gave birth.

Tea-Mur *(ta wur)* Tara, ancient seat of the high kings of Ireland.

Teach Mi Cuarta *(chalk vik art)* The banqueting hall of Cormac Mac Art on the hill of Tara, it was reputed to have been 700 feet long.

Teagasc an Riogh *(ta gask en ree)* Instructions of a King. One of Cormac Mac Art's three books, this one delineating a wise rule.

Tir inna m Beo *(teer ne mo)* The land of the living.

Tir Nan Og *(teer ne nog)* The place after death. Sometimes visualized as an island in the western sea, this afterlife was a place where all the inhabitants remained youthful and beautiful and where singing, feasting, love, and laughter were the primary pastimes.

tuath *(too e)* A tribe.